A Goodreads *"Best Contemporary Women's Fiction"* Listopia Book
A Goodreads *"Favorite Chick-Lit/Women's Fiction Books"* Listopia Book

First Edition Praise of
WAITING FOR PAINT TO DRY

"Lia Mack writes a beautifully eloquent painting of a life...
reminding us that we paint the picture of our lives and even if it
starts dark, we can frame it with a happy ending."

– Angela Shelton,
Award-Winning Director & Survivor Advocate

"This isn't a book only about ugliness and trauma... Uplifting...
full of heart and hope and featuring an appealing heroine and
trauma survivor."

– Kirkus Review

"Lia Mack has written a raw and wrenching novel about rape...
and the soul-crushing aftermath of such trauma. Watching Matty
Bell move from shut-down victim to triumphant survivor is a
stirring experience... An inspiring and powerful tale."

– Yona Zeldis McDonough,
Author of *The House on Primrose Pond*

"This blistering psychological powerhouse of a love story will
make you get up and cheer the glory of self-reinvention."

– Mindela Ruby,
Author of *Mosh It Up*

WAITING FOR PAINT TO DRY

a novel

LIA MACK

Blissfully Beguiling Books

BLISSFULLY BEGUILING books

Second Edition Published by Blissfully Beguiling Books.
First Edition Published by Pen-L Publishing.

ISBN 9798985550191
eBook ISBN 9798985550184

Dedication

To those who have survived sexual assault.
May you find your road to healing.

And in memory of those who lost their
battle before finding theirs.

TRIGGER WARNING

Please be forewarned.

This book contains elements that may bring about trigger episodes in those who have experienced sexual assault.

However, this is not a book that focuses on the horrible and the ugly.

On the contrary, this book focuses on the healing aspects one must go through to find peace and light at the end of the trauma-healing tunnel.

Proceed at your own pace. 

Thank you for your purchase, as all proceeds of this book benefit RAINN's sexual assault hotline.

1.800.656.HOPE

RAINN.org

CHAPTER ONE

Memories

summertime , 1995

Not a day goes by that I don't see the ocean or run alongside its gray blue expanse. It's the only place I feel free. Pounding the sand with every step I take, I envision my stride taking me farther and farther away.

I only wish I could run on water.

The Pacific Ocean nips at my heels, and I feel the July sun working its way through the fog to warm my skin. My father is ahead of me, but we're not racing today. Enjoying the feel of the sand as it pushes back against every step, we're just running to clear our minds and feel the chilled morning breeze brush against the sweat on our skin.

I see him look back and smile, waving me on. We've passed the pier twice already and are now headed south, where we'll make a U-turn at the lagoon and head back up toward home: our typical morning run along the beach.

It's nice to be doing it together again. I've missed my dad.

I smile in greeting as I pass the only other runner I've seen who's braved this zero dark hundred hour. Then I jog up to where my father is stretching, waiting for me, and we catch our breath as we peer into the deep, hazel waters of the lagoon, side by side.

We're both mesmerized by water. Nothing needs to be said when the sounds of the surf are kneading your skin and the watery arms of the tide are pulling you under.

I smile up at my dad just as he hitches his head homeward.

"Come on, Tilly Bell," he says in his lingering Southern drawl. "I'll race you home. Got a surprise waiting for ya."

Before I can catch up to his sprint, he's already gone up the beach, as though he's the one turning nineteen tomorrow and not me.

Head down, arms pumping, I maintain my form and swing my arms through the air just as he's trained me to do. The wind smacks against my face as I press on, and I dare it to slow me down. I dig deep and find the second wind I have yet to use, feeling the sand kick up against the back of my legs as I effortlessly glide down the beach.

My father slows and I gain until I pass him altogether. Not looking back, I hear his joyous laughter as I speed on. The Oceanside Pier is ahead of me, and I widen my stride, pulling my arms through the air and the oxygen deep into my lungs. I feel the burn in my legs and love it.

Jogging to a halt, I walk it off until I feel my heart simmer to a slower pace. I reach up and undo the hairband that's holding back my long, blonde hair, letting its sweat-laden heaviness encapsulate my face as I bend over and stretch. I pin my body flat against one outstretched leg and then the other before I flip my head up and refit it all into a ponytail.

My dad approaches as I do.

"Didn't go all out today, huh?" I ask of his lagging behind.

"Just enjoying the run," he says with a far-off look in his green eyes.

Something in that look makes my heart do a nervous sputter, and I turn away.

"So what's the surprise?" I ask, trying to sound nonchalant.

"Oh, so you heard me?" he smiles and pats me on the back as we start home.

We make our way up toward The Strand and cross over, where he lets me go first. We walk between beachfront homes and jog up the skinny path and then the stairs that lead up to where South Pacific and Ash Street meet.

Home.

It's the house my parents bought when I was younger on my dad's first tour in Southern California. For someone who lived their whole childhood all over the map like me—Japan, Italy, Hawaii, Mississippi, and now back to California—it's unusual that you ever get to come back to the place you call home. But there is a perk: I can pick whatever hometown is befitting to me.

I'm a military brat. I'm from everywhere and nowhere.

I look both ways, jog across the street to our grassy lawn, and strip my feet of sandy shoes and sweaty socks. The short, green grass feels good between my toes, and I can't help but sit down and lean back onto it.

I close my eyes. Take in a deep, satisfying breath. When I open them, I see my dad with his arm stretched out and I take his offered hand to get up.

"So what's the surprise?" I ask again as I wipe damp grass from my shorts.

He doesn't say anything though while I follow him around the back of our two-story bungalow or when I knock my running shoes together to get rid of the sand and place them on top of our weathered picnic table next to his.

"I'll show ya in a bit. Shower up, and I'll see you in fifteen," he finally says with a wink and dashes off into the house.

"Dad . . ." I whine, but with a smile.

Knowing I won't coerce the secret from him, I make my way through the dim kitchen, passing the table that's covered in my sister's wedding-day preparation debris. I flick at one of the flowers lying there and send it flying off the table and onto the floor.

I tiptoe up the wooden stairs so as not to wake her or my mother, and take a quick Navy shower: five minutes to get wet, lather up, and rinse. The cold water hits me, and I have a quick flash of what my nineteenth birthday will look like tomorrow: swallowed whole by my sister's big day.

I towel-dry my long hair on the way to my room, welcoming the emerging sunlight that streams in through my east-facing windows. Yet I can't help but be annoyed.

To deal with that, I walk over to my art desk and decide to work off my frustration. So what that she purposefully chose her wedding day to be the very same day I wanted all to myself? She's been taking things from me all my life.

I find charcoal bits that match the colors I picked up on my morning run and quickly sketch what's in my head. It pours out of me and onto the new art notepad: blues, whites, and beiges, all in a gray hue. I fill the page and the next, my hand pulling the scene up and out of me. And it does the trick, as always.

It soothes me.

As I sketch, I hear someone pull up outside but don't care to look out my window to see who it is. Deep in my artistic flow, I usually forget to eat, sleep, and shower until I'm totally satiated. Only this time, with time short, I force myself to be done so I can get back to my dad.

Dressing in cutoff jean shorts and a red, white, and green Italian flag T-shirt I got while we were stationed in Naples, I recall the clear, turquoise water of the Mediterranean Sea. Then I quietly head back downstairs, careful to avoid all the creaks that could wake my mother, grab my flip-flops by the back door and head outside.

My dad's standing at rest in front of the picnic table, arms crossed and wearing a big grin. I look down at my watch and see I'm one minute ahead of schedule.

"Not bad, Matilda Bell. Not bad." He beams at me, his green eyes, like mine, sparkling.

I watch as a slight breeze kicks up his whitening blond hair that's always cut to just above his ears.

"As you know, your sister's all tied up in knots, trying to impress this family she's marrying into," he says, taking in a deep breath and letting it go. "And your mother? Well, she's having a time with it, too."

I ignore the look in his eyes and pretend to be concerned with wiping the colors of the day from my hands onto my shorts. With my sister's wedding stress piling up—plus the constant worrying of when my father's next tour of duty will be and how long he'll be gone this time—I already knew my mother had started drinking again.

"Well, I was thinking," he says. "They have their plates full. So why don't the two of us celebrate your birthday today and forget all this wedding nonsense?"

"Sounds like a good plan," I say with a smile.

I watch as he turns around to pick something up off the picnic table.

"Happy Birthday, sweetie," he says and hands me an envelope.

I rip it open to reveal a birthday card with a picture of some brunette chick whose hair is blowing in the wind, wrapping around her face in whimsical form as she's driving down a tree-lined country road. The sun setting far off in the distance. Inside is a cute saying about me— the birthday girl—going places, along with my dad's loopy handwriting saying, "*Love, Dad and Mom.*"

"Thanks, Dad."

"And there's a little something else, too." He reaches into his back pocket for something that jingles, and I watch as he hands me a set of keys. "For you, Matilda Bell. To help get you to those places."

"A car?" I ask, stunned at what's in my hands.

"Well, not a car exactly," he teases. "Here, take a look."

With that, he guides me over to the other side of our one-car garage, and my heart leaps out of my chest. There, parked in the gravel drive, is a light-blue Ford Bronco truck with a thick, white stripe down each of its sides.

"She's used and a little beat up," he says. "But she runs like a champ. Plus, I know how you like doing things a little different than everybody else, so I didn't want to get you something like your sister's little red sports car. Thought this was perfect."

"It is perfect!" I exclaim and jump into his hug.

Within another few seconds, I'm inside the truck's cab, touching the steering wheel and feeling toasty warm from the sun that's already risen enough to heat up the insides. I jump down again to the pavement and run around to look at the back hatch. Run my hand over the back spare tire. Walk around to the other side. Admire the big tires. Pop open the hood and check out the engine.

The body is a little rusty here and there, and she might need an oil change soon by the looks of the dipstick. But she's beautiful. And not what you'd expect. Just like me.

Happy tears sting my eyes as my dad walks up beside me.

"I thought you needed your own ride to get to the Art Institute down in San Diego. So when I saw her, I knew you had to have her," he says with a proud smile.

I step back, look up at him.

"I, uh . . . thank you, Daddy," I stammer, realizing I hadn't told him I wasn't going to accept the scholarship. Not yet, anyway. I'm still hoping to hear from other art colleges farther away, San Francisco being my top choice.

"I'm very proud of you, Matilda."

"Thanks, Dad." I lean into his hug, feeling him encircle me in his strong arms and letting go of all thought to just hold on tight.

So much of my life has been spent letting go of my father that I'm still getting used to him being home this time. Too soon, tears creep out, and I'm crying, wetting the front of his gray polo shirt.

"Oh, Tilly Bell," he says, his drawl coming out thick in a way that confirms my fear. His heavy Southern accent only comes out when he feels it's all he needs to do to make things better.

"You're shipping off soon, aren't you?" I say into his shirt. It's more of a statement than a question.

"You know how it is."

I harden at the sound of his softened words. Then, out of learned habit, I retreat from my state of disappointment. He has his duties, and I have mine.

"It's okay, Dad. I understand," I say, taking a step back. "When?"

"We ship out two days after Eleanor's wedding. Be gone until just after Christmas."

I swallow hard.

He just came back last month, and now he'll be gone for the next six, leaving me to take care of the mess.

"It's okay. I understand," I lie and fake smile up at him.

"*Howard!*" my mother calls out in demand, and we both flinch.

My dad chuckles it off though and gives my shoulder a quick squeeze. "Looks like the admiral's up," he jokes and gives me a wink before jogging back into the house.

Now that my mother is up, I know he won't be able to do anything other than what she wants. So much for our *just the two of us* birthday celebration.

I stand at the edge of our yard like a hardened statue and then shut the hood of my new truck. Staring at the morning sun's reflection in the metallic, pale-blue paint, I run my hand along the hot metal, waiting for the burn to hurt before removing my fingers.

I look up at the steering wheel, the rearview mirror, the road out through the back window. And my heart pounds with a thought.

Maybe, one day, I'll get in behind that wheel and never come back.

"*No!*" I scream out into the pitch-black of my room, the vibration of my voice forcing its way out of my body.

I bolt up in bed and grab onto my just-prickly bare legs, whispering to myself, "It was just a dream. It was just a dream," like a mantra with no end.

Then, sick to my stomach, I stumble out of bed, tangled in sheets that hold me back. I fight with them, falling once. Run out into the hallway into the bathroom just in time to vomit.

My hands clench onto the cold porcelain as my body rids the scenes of the nightmare from my mind. I lean down, pressing my forehead against the cool bowl.

"It was just a dream," I whisper to myself, twisting my head back and forth. Tears burn hot streaks down my face, and I wipe at them with shaky hands. "It was just a dream," I say again and cry, begging myself, "Please, Matty, please. It was just a dream."

In the eventual silence, my mind finally quiets. I sit back against the wall opposite the toilet and stare into nothingness.

She said you'd do it, I hear him say.

My abuser.

I swat at the air above me, but no one's there.

She said you'd do it, I hear him say again, and I see him smile before my eyes, as though he's standing right in front of me, the bathroom suddenly drenched in a golden-hued light.

She said you'd do it.

Sex.

I squeeze my eyes shut and pound the sides of my head with white-knuckled fists until the images and sounds stop.

Shaking, I swallow hard and wince against the pain of my raw throat. Feeling around in the darkness, I find the fuzzy bathmat lying on the floor next to me. Lower myself onto it.

"It was just a dream," I tell myself as I close my eyes.

Only I know better. It was no dream. It was a repressed memory come back to haunt me.

～

"Get out of the bathroom, Matty! I need it."

The sound of my sister banging on the bathroom door wakes me up. My face is caked to the bathmat with a mixture of drool and sweat.

I pull myself up to my feet and flush the toilet.

"Hurry up in there!" Eleanor beats on the bathroom door.

My body resistant to movement, I slowly wash my face. Rinse my mouth and spit. Lift my heavy head and look up at my reflection.

My eyes are red-rimmed and puffy, my hair a snarled mess. And then an image of him jumps in front of my eyes again, leaving me grabbing hold of the countertop for balance.

More banging on the door. "Matty, what the hell are you doing in there that's so important? I'm the bride. Get out!" Then, "Mom!"

She said you'd do it.

In an instant, I'm at the door, ready to claw my way through until I break out the other side and sink fangs into her face. But I stifle the instinct since today is her wedding day, and I'm her little sister.

I unlock and open the door with forced nonchalance, but my blood burns the moment I see her. Fortunately or unfortunately, she barges in past me and slams the door in my face before I can do or say anything.

"My stars. What's all the fuss?" my mother drawls as she sways her way toward the commotion of the morning. Dressed in a cherry-pink silk Japanese robe, with her hair done up in curlers, my mother's elegant form would be reminiscent of Southern days gone by if it weren't for her slight slur and the cocktail in her hand, ice clinking against glass.

"Really, Mom?" I say of her drink and purposely bump into her as I move past toward my room.

"Goodness gracious, Matilda Bell. What? I'm not allowed a glass of water in the morning?" she asks, accusatory, as if no one knows it's just plain vodka.

I slam my door shut, lean my back against it, and slide down to my butt. In the solitude of my room, I smile for the first time today. It felt good to lash out at my mother—helped me ignore all the images in my head. Only, in that very instant I think I've won, everything comes rushing back and I hear him say *she said you'd do it* in my head over and over again until I have to smack the sides of my head with hardened fists to make it stop.

Stubborn to win, I get up and walk over to my art desk. Grab a sketch pad and unzip my little canvas bag that holds all my favorite tools. I dig around and find my drawing pencil. Stand with it in hand and wait.

By now, I should have a half-crazed drawing, with whatever's on my mind blowing out of me like a wind on fire. But I can't make my hand move. Can't get myself to draw.

I turn around, grab up the fallen sheets from my three a.m. fight or flight, and make my bed until I feel normalcy start to creep in. Walk back over to my art desk. Stand and wait for either inspiration or frustration to spur imagination.

But my mind is void.

Annoyed, I go back to fluff and straighten the blue satin-edged pillows propped up against my headboard. Only I let my hand linger a bit too long along the intricate swirls of the brass headboard.

A moment too still.

It's the same headboard I had back in Italy, the one I got from a friend who had just moved back to the States. It wasn't attached to my bed frame yet, just leaning up against the wall at the head of my bed.

A few weeks past my sixteenth birthday, I was on my way to a sleepover at Claire's house. And I couldn't wait. Because of my boyfriend, Jett, I hadn't seen her or any of my friends in a while.

My parents had just left the house for someone's going-away party at the Officer's Club. But when I went into the bathroom to grab my toothbrush, Jett was hiding in the shower and jumped out at me, as though I enjoyed his surprises.

Heart pounding, I told him to leave. To get out. That he shouldn't be there.

He just laughed me off and pushed me toward my room. Got me on all fours on the bed.

All I could see were my tears dripping down and onto the sheets below me. Unable to make him stop, I begged God to help. *Please!*

That's when the headboard fell away from the wall and slammed into his head. Jett fell off me and onto the floor. I curled into the fetal position as I listened to him run from the house, cursing at me for being a bitch somehow. Only I didn't get up. Didn't follow him in apology like I had done so many times before.

Instead, I stayed on my bed, whispering, "Thank you, thank you, thank you," over and over as I cried grateful tears. I rocked and cried, curled up on my bed, until the blackness swallowed me whole.

~

Somehow, some way, I didn't have memory of Jett raping me.

She said you'd do it.
Not the first time on my sixteenth birthday.

She said you'd do it.
Not until the nightmare brought it all back to me.

I told him no.
She said you'd do it.

I told him I didn't want to.
She said you'd do it.

I told him it hurt.
She said you'd do it.

She said I'd do it.

She.

My sister.

~

"*Why?*" I scream at myself in a demanding fit, pushing angry hands into my hair, hard against my skull. When I can't answer— I'm a stupid blonde, after all—I fling pillows off my bed and watch as they slam into some painted canvases I have leaning up against the wall.

A few lamely topple over.

Needing more satisfaction, I rip the quilt and sheets off my bed with a growl and throw them to the floor. And when that doesn't feel cathartic enough, I push the damned mattress up off its railings until it smashes into my art desk and heave it up onto its side until it's towering over the mess I've made.

Then I grit my teeth and punch the mattress until my hands hurt, chastising myself for not remembering something so awful, so traumatizing as being raped, that I punch, punch, punch until it doubles over and onto me, knocking me down.

Unable to move against all that's drowning me, I lie spent underneath it and weep.

I hear my mother walk in and make myself move out from under the mattress. My head is hung low but I look up through drenched lashes. She's halfway ready for the day and wide-eyed, staring into my room.

"My word! Matilda Bell, this is no time for rearranging your room. Get a move on!" she yells in exasperation. "Hairdresser's gonna be here in half an hour."

I glare at her through hot tears and debate running— somewhere, anywhere—when I hear the doorbell ring and she turns to rush downstairs.

Within seconds, the house is a beehive of wedding-day activity: hairdressers, makeup artists, bridesmaids. I hear my dad directing traffic downstairs and feel for him when my mother interjects her two cents and drowns out his organizational efforts. I watch as my sister, Eleanor, darts past my door, wrapped in a towel, and listen as she storms her way down the stairs to contain the mess to her own liking.

Home not being a place he has command of, I know my father will retreat upstairs soon.

I pick up the mattress. Wipe my face with the fallen sheet.

"Knock, knock."

My dad raps his knuckles against my open door just as I'm pulling the last corner of the fitted sheet over my put-back together bed. I do a quick look in the mirror before turning around, only looking half-crazed now.

"Hey, Dad." I lean in sideways, head low so he doesn't see me full on.

"Happy Birthday, sweetie," he says and gives me a sideways hug. "Sorry about yesterday. Weddings are a team effort."

I'm glad I'm not facing him so he doesn't see my eyeroll.

"Maybe you and I can drive behind the limo on the way to Del Mar for your truck's maiden voyage… You know, just the two of us."

I cringe internally. How many times have I heard those words—*just the two of us*—and never seen it happen? I slink away from his touch.

"Sure, Dad. That would be fun," I say as I face the other way, pretending to care about the yellow bridesmaid dress hanging on the outside of my closet door.

I listen as he retreats from my room.

After a quick shower, I sit quietly downstairs in my robe as some hairdresser does my hair, backcombing and curling my locks until I've got a heap of curls atop my head and cascading down my back.

"Just like Julia Roberts in Steel Magnolias," the hairdresser says with a toothy grin.

"Thank you," I say numbly, though I'm really not in the mood.

Besides the flashbacks replaying on and on in my mind while having to watch the degrading interaction between my parents through the eyes of a house full of strangers, there is my sister, sitting right in front of me, in my direct line of fire. I watch as she's doted on by what seems to be every wedding guru this side of L.A. I roll my eyes as I hear the photographer snap candid photos of the whole performance every so often.

My sister looks my way for a second, and my adrenaline spikes. I have to hold myself back from getting up and slapping her in the face.

"Go get dressed, Matty," Eleanor orders without looking at me, speaking through pursed lips as more gloss is applied.

"As you wish," I growl.

"Excuse me?" She swings around in her bathrobe, batting the makeup artist out of the way to look at me straight on. "You've been giving me dagger eyes all morning. This is supposed to be my special day, Matty. What the fuck?"

I open my mouth to scream at her. I want to shake her until her head snaps off her neck, but I can't move.

"Well?"

With everyone looking at me, wondering what's next, I decide not to further embarrass my family and turn to leave. But then Jett jeers, *"She said you'd do it,"* in my head. And I spin around on her.

"Why did you…?" I demand, my heart pounding so fast my mind goes blank. "Why did you …?"

"Why did I what?"

"Why did you… have Eve as your maid of honor and not me?" I ask as though this is the monumental thought that's been eating me alive all morning.

I'm such a coward. Unlike El, who bounces up and gracefully darts over to me.

"Don't you dare embarrass me, Matty," she whispers softly yet forcefully into my face. "Just because you're my sister doesn't automatically make you more important than everyone else. Eve is

Mark's sister, soon to be my sister-in-law. You know how his family is. I need to make sure everything is perfect."

She backs off and puts on a fake smile, looks around the room at everyone, laughing it off as if there's nothing to see.

Then she sends me a blazingly-sweet smile, with dramatic pause. "You'll always be my sweet little sister, Matty. Go on now. Get dressed, sweetie."

Dutiful me, I hike up to my room and close the door, not thinking twice about what just happened. I pull on and zip up my yellow, Southern belle-inspired bridesmaid gown.

Seeing myself in the mirror and having seen the flowers downstairs, this whole wedding is truly reminiscent of the flavor of Mississippi.

El and I were little girls when our family was stationed there. And while around that type of elegance and Southern charm, we often dreamed about how our big white wedding days would be. Now she's living her dream. So no matter that I'm finding it difficult to handle what's going on in my head, I can't let what's going on with me ruin her day.

Despite how I feel about her, I do love her.

I listen on as bits and pieces of what's going on downstairs float up to me. I fasten my painted toes into yellow, strappy heels and listen as my sister ever so elegantly barks her orders in her typical Miss Ringleader style.

She said you'd do it, I hear him say again.

"Shut up!" I yell at my head. Except he doesn't. In the quiet of my room, the images of what he did—of what she did—crash on me like an ocean with no end.

I hold my breath. Hold back the tears.

She said you'd do it, I hear his voice, husky above me. Nausea waves through me. My insides shake.

She said you'd do it.

I force my eyes shut. Hold them there until new images start to conjure in my mind. Images of choking my sister at the altar.

But I can't ruin her day.

I hold my breath. Try to envision something else. Me free from all this. I look in the mirror, my green eyes blankly staring back at me.

In a second, I know I can't do this alone. I need to talk to someone before this hell from the past swallows me whole. I run down the hall toward my dad.

"Dad?" my voice warbles out of my mouth and into my parent's room. I stop from going in though when I see my mother. She's seated at the foot of their bed, hair done, dressed and ready for the big day.

I watch, paralyzed, as she raises her glass to her lips. Takes a sip.

She looks up at me, and I can tell she doesn't want to be bothered. Not now. Not ever. And I don't want to talk to her either. She's never been the kind of mother I've wanted, needed.

"Where's Dad?" I swallow, holding back tears.

"He'll be back soon. I sent him on some last-minute errands."

Cemented in place, I start to shake from the pressure of all that's in me, demanding to be released. I try to move my legs, to walk away, to wait for my dad.

Only the need to purge is far too great, and before I can think of an alternative, I blurt out, "I need to talk about something," which hurriedly turns into, "It's bothering me so much, I don't know what to do." Only having to say what happened and who did it stops me from saying more.

I start to cry.

"My stars, what's gotcha now, honey?" my mother softly drawls.

It's her mellowed tone that opens the door to the tsunami inside me. And it springs forth, with all the weight and force three years of suppression can give it. Details aren't crucial to my relief. I can sense that the moment I begin to speak. I just need to get it out. Need the acknowledgement and understanding of someone who loves me. I need someone to know what happened to me. That I'm hurting.

That I need help.

"It's all because of El," I speed on. "I just can't stop hearing him say it over and over again that she said I'd do it. That I wanted to have sex. And when I said that I didn't want to, that I wanted to save myself, that I wanted him to stop, he… r—raped me," I say, forcing myself to say the *r* word.

Only it comes out so hushed that my mom has to lean in to hear it. The word tastes vile in my mouth, and it seems to hit her like the flashbacks have been hitting me all morning.

When she remains silent, her eyes locked on mine, I take it as an invitation to I enter the room and kneel down in front of her, a tearful mixture of agony and lightning. Although it will always be with me— the knowledge of what happened—I feel the burden of it all lift just by opening up. I can breathe again, and the anxiety of wondering if I can ever be normal again evaporates.

"He who?" my mother asks.

Nauseous just thinking about having to say his name, I instead answer in a whisper.

"You know. *Him*. From high school in Naples."

I hope she remembers who. I can't say his name. I know, if I do, I'll throw up.

I see her visibly relax, and I know she gets it. Everything's going to be okay. My mother knows now and, soon my father will too. And he'll help me deal with my sister. They'll help me work through this, together, as a family.

I won't have to face this alone.

"Honey," my mother speaks, and I lift my head to the sound I've waited for all my life: the sweet, maternal voice of unconditional love.

She takes my chin in her soft hand, and my heart aches from joy at her touch.

"Lord, girl." She shakes her head. "If it's bothering you this much, you obviously wanted it to happen: being a teenager an' all and wanting to experiment with sex."

"What?" I say, stunned. "No. I told him no. I told him to stop. That I didn't want to!"

"And now... seeing your sister is 'bout to wear white and truly be a virgin? Well." Her eyes turn to a shade of snide. "You've just changed your mind about what you did and want to cry rape."

At that, she lets go of my chin and leans back, downing the rest of her drink. "I know how it works, Matilda Bell. Girls cry rape all the time."

"What? No!" I stammer in disbelief. "That's not

"Matilda, please. I'm busy," she says and gets up.

"But—"

"And don't you dare bother your daddy with all this nonsense. It'd break his heart knowing you're trying to ruin your sister's day." She walks past, bumping into me as she head toward the door. With one last, disdainful look my way, she adds, "Get up. You're wrinklin' your dress."

The rest of the day is a blur. I vaguely remember attempting to confront my sister, only to be slapped in the face with her denial.

Then I'm in the limo.

Then, all of a sudden, I'm walking out onto the rooftop deck of the Del Mar Hotel, arm in arm with someone I don't know. I stand still in my place and close my eyes to hold in the tears.

I know El's saying her vows only three feet away, but all I can hear is my mother saying, *all girls cry rape*.

I try to breathe, but I can only fill my lungs halfway. My head pounds like a hammer, and soon I start to shake. I hear the ocean roar up behind me and I turn, opening my eyes to see it.

It beckons to me, as it always does.

Before I can stop myself, I dash off, knocking down the bridesmaid next to me.

Without stopping to apologize, I run at full speed until I find my way downstairs. I don't even feel my legs moving. I just run, never looking back.

Before I know it, I'm on the ground floor of the hotel and darting off toward the beach. I grab the front of the dress up into my hands. Sweet, billowy puffs of yellow taffeta dance around me as I run north along the Pacific Ocean, hoping the farther away I get, the more normal I will feel.

I should go back. Should find my dad. Tell him everything. But my mother's words peel away any thought that he'd believe me.

Mid-stride, I reach up with one hand and dismantle the wedding day up-do, freeing my hair. I feel it trail behind me, the weight of it rippling in the wind, tugging me in the opposite direction, urging me to go back.

And I should. Should wipe the sand off my legs. Wash the black-streaked tears from my face. Act as though nothing happened and paint a smile on my face, just as I always have.

But instead, I run until I reach the lagoon that claims the beach and stops the sand from continuing on in one unbroken northward stretch. The water here is calmer, hauntingly darkened by its depths.

Numb and wanting to feel something, I wade into its aquamarine pool. The water swirls around my body, and the dress' yellow cheerfulness puddles around me. Powerless, hopeless, I cry to the salty being, begging it to simply swallow me whole.

I float only long enough to realize it won't.

I don't know what time it is when I make it home, but I'm grateful no one's there to stop me. My long walk has helped clear my head enough to know what I need to do.

I strip out of the wet, sandy dress and drop it to the floor. I go up in the attic and pull out some old moving boxes that we always seem to have on hand. Empty my art desk into a couple of boxes. Cram all sorts of crap in others, not caring about organization.

I dress in what I had on yesterday and grab the keys off my nightstand, along with the letter I got from my friend Claire a few months ago. I hadn't spoken to her in almost a year when it showed up, and I remember laughing off the idea she proposed in the letter. But now it makes perfect sense.

I pack up my truck until I can't see out the back window and carefully tear off Claire's address. Tape it to the front door for my dad to see and write a quick note: *Ciao! I'm going to live with Claire.*

He'll read it and know where I am. He's always talking of plans and getting away. He'll understand.

Highways, gas stations, and quick stops to sleep. I drive nonstop as though the tsunami of doubt will catch up with me, but I win in the end. Three days later, when I finally park in front of Claire's brownstone in hot, humid Baltimore, I think I feel like myself again.

And, as I tell Claire all that's happened and why I decided to come, I finally feel miles away from it all.

After a good long shower, I lie down on Claire's brown couch, so exhausted that the itchy wool hardly bothers me. Tomorrow, I'll unpack my truck and figure out what to do. And it'll all make sense.

That I planned to do this all along. That this is what I want for myself.

Like I know what the hell I'm doing.

CHAPTER TWO

Not much to celebrate

I grip the handrailing and stand on tiptoe. From my rooftop deck, I can almost see it. Water. As the hot July sun sets behind me, just past buildings blocking my view, I see it: a sliver of water, glimmering off in the distance.

I sigh at the sight of it, yet feel no relief. Crowded and polluted, I don't feel the same yearning with Baltimore's Inner Harbor as I did with my Pacific Ocean back home.

Home.

Lowering myself, I stand flat. Lean into the wood railing with my body's weight and stare below at the backyard and concrete patio three flights down. Worn and weathered, the deck's railing could and should give any moment.

For that, maybe I'd be grateful.

I hear a ring from my back pocket and pull out my cell phone. Probably my boss asking why I've taken a personal day. Again. But it's not. It's a text from Claire.

Hey, Matty, on our way! Can't wait to celebrate! 30 years old!!!

My heart trips a beat, and I feel my skin break out into a cold sweat despite the heat. I totally forgot today was my birthday.

Pacing back and forth, my hands hold back the hair that's fallen from the haphazard bun on the crown of my head. I know I said I would do it this year. Try to do it. Forget my decade-long avoidance of my birthday and enjoy a little celebration in the name of me, Matty Bell, turning a new page.

But now that it's here, I don't know if I can.

Feeling a panic attack coming on, I sink down onto the splintered wood and sit with my back to the railing, trying to breathe past the constriction in my throat.

The railing gives just a little. *This is how it could happen*, I hear a voice in the back of my head. *No one would know you did it on purpose.*

I don't move right away, tempting the fear coiled in my belly to release so I can release myself.

Peace.

It's all I've ever wanted.

I feel a vibration under my butt from my cell phone. Grab it and see Claire's next text.

Dress down if you want, or wear what you wore to work. We'll be there in a few. Greg's out of town, so just me and the kids!

I text her back: *Sorry, Claire. I can't do it.*

I contemplate for a good excuse and type out a lie instead: *I forgot to tell you I'm working late again today. Can't do it. Have fun without me!*

I hit send, then remember. Hop up and run to the other side of the rooftop deck overlooking the street down below, where my truck is neatly parked out front.

I fling open the rooftop door to my apartment and run inside, tripping on clothes I've left strewn on the floor, and fly down the stairs so fast I barely feel the steps beneath my feet. Bursting out the front, I grab for the driver's side door and try to yank it open.

It's locked.

"Shit!" I yell at myself for forgetting my keys.

I dart back upstairs to my studio apartment and dig through my bag. Loose change. Hair bands. Hordes of paper from who knows where. I finally dump it all out and find the keys. By the time I make it back downstairs, I'm entirely out of breath.

So much for being a long-distance runner. My father would kill me if he knew how out of shape I've let myself become.

Well, not kill me. But give me one hell of a boot camp lesson if he knew.

I turn the key in the ignition. Nothing. I turn it again. Not even a sound of the engine turning over.

She said you'd do it, a voice says from the back of my mind, and I hit the side of my head with a closed fist to shut it up. Shake my head clear of the flashbacks the voice brings and turn the key.

The rumble of the engine soothes me, and I pull out into traffic with my big, rolling security blanket wrapped around me.

This is precisely why I've avoided my birthday for the past ten years. Why I've ignored all calls, cards, gifts, and reminders that the tenth of July bears any more significance than any of the other three hundred sixty-four days. I don't want to remember what happened that birthday long ago.

Born and dead on the same day.

Not much to celebrate.

Except, I'd be a liar if I said it only bothers me on my birthdays.

Spend enough mental energy running from something, soon it's all you ever think about.

I park my truck a few blocks away, and it dies out before I get a chance to turn it off. See the orange light glow from the dashboard: out of gas. I lean my head against the steering wheel and feel my heart drop.

"I'm sorry, Betsy," I say to my truck. "I'll take better care of you. I promise."

It's darker on the sidewalk here. Lonelier. And I feel too obvious in my shorts and tank top, showing too much skin. So I walk fast. But the humid heat makes the air thick, and I can't seem to take in a full breath of air.

I hear a noise in the alley as I pass by. Feel eyes on me as I cross the street. Hear footsteps following quick.

I look back. Check and check again. I can see that no one is behind me, but I hear footsteps nonetheless and my heart pounds.

Three more blocks.

Two blocks to go.

One.

I start to run until I reach my front stoop, out of breath and full of fear. And then someone says my name and I scream.

"Matty! It's just me." Claire rushes over to me, bringing me back to reality.

I sit on my stoop in the glow of the street light and put my head between my knees, sure I'm about to pass out from my self-induced anxiety attack.

"Breathe. Breathe," she says as I feel her squat down beside me and rub my back. "You okay?"

I sit up. "I'm fine," I smile weakly when I see the worry in her eyes. "You just startled me, is all."

Claire stands up in a breeze that has graciously arrived now that she's here, all grace and casual in her cork sandals, khaki capris, and flowy, sleeveless, peach blouse.

I gather myself up too, wishing I had dressed in something similar. She always seems so comfortable, so easy in her own skin. Only I don't own anything remotely close to her chic sense of style. Monochromatic and drab, my clothes suck.

"Where were you?" she asks. "I thought you said you were working late tonight, so we were just going to drop this off," she says of the gift-wrapped package in her hands.

"Oh, I was," I answer quick, not thinking straight. "But then I decided to go for a jog."

"In flip-flops?" she says, pointing to my shoes.

I look down at my feet and roll my eyes at myself. Unlike my sister, my lies have always been lame and completely transparent. "I mean . . . my truck . . . it died."

"Again? Matty," Claire says, switching over to her typical motherly tone. "When are you going to get a new car? You have a good job now, you know."

"Yes, I know," I say of the office job she helped me get. Made me get, rather.

"Well, it's got to pay more than being a dog walker or those random waitress jobs you've had."

"Yes, it does. Thank you."

"Because it's about time you start doing things right and taking care of yourself, Matty. I can't take care of you forever, you know."

"What is that supposed to mean?" I ask.

Instead of answering, she shoves the package into my hands. It's a big, heavy gift wrapped in crisp, white paper and a lovely, red silk bow.

My heart jumps into my throat. and I swallow hard. "What is it?"

"A birthday present from the kids and Greg and me," Claire chastises me, then softens. "Come on. I know it's hard, but Greg's out of town and the kids have been waiting all day. And I've kept it totally low-key, like you said. See?" She spins around. "No party. No tons of people making a big fuss. Just us."

"I know what I said," I interject, looking forlornly toward her minivan, feeling my throat tighten. "I just—"

"I mean, it's not every day your best friend hits The Big Three-O before you do," Claire adds, giving me a playful grin.

"Yes, I know," I say of her excitement and the promise I made last year, wishing now I hadn't thought I'd magically find the courage to instantly fix years of denial. "I'm sorry, Claire, but . . . I changed my mind," I say looking back at her, attempting to hand her back the gift. "I can't do it."

"Come on! The kids are so excited. I actually can't believe they've stayed in the car this long without whining," she adds, more to herself.

"Yes, I know. I'm sorry, but—"

"I mean, the AC is on and I left the movie going, but usually when they see you, all my mommy rules go out the window."

"Claire, you're not hearing me!" I yell, breaking off her monologue. "I don't want to!"

"Why?" Claire says in a condescending tone. "Because you might blow up if you do?" she adds, making fun of the way I've explained how accepting my birthday makes me feel: like it makes everything I've tried to ignore real again.

I open my mouth to lash back, but nothing comes out. Claire may not know everything that happened to me, but she knows enough. And she took me in years ago when I left home. Now her dismissal is like a slap in the face. My heart and head pound out my dismay.

"You weren't there," I say in a low, slow tone.

"Yeah, but it happened when you were sixteen, Matty," she says, exasperated. "Do you really like living as though you're dead? I mean, just throw that shit away already."

"Throw it away? Throw it away?"

I feel myself rise up out of my body and back up onto the rooftop deck. I should have done it. Should have pushed that railing hard and fallen. Then I wouldn't have to do this anymore. I'd finally have my peace.

"Dammit, Claire!" I yell, all feeling from my body gone. "Why can't you just leave me alone when you know I don't do birthdays!"

We stand in sudden silence, our words hanging fat in the humid air around us.

"I can't do this anymore, Matty," Claire says in defeat, hands raised. "You need help."

It's not the first time she's said it, but it hurts as though it's the first cut. I want to run. Lock myself up forever. Cower away from the voices and the flashbacks and the memories and die. But then I hear another voice speak up. A little voice.

"Aunty Matty?"

Claire and I both look down. Max, her almost-two-year-old, says my name again, peeking out from behind his mommy's legs.

Claire spins around and sees her other two climbing out of her always polished BMW minivan.

"No, no, no. Back inside. We're leaving," she says, picking Max up and directing the other two back to their car seats.

But it's no use, and I can see by the slump in Claire's shoulders that she knows it, too. Sure enough, her other two children maneuver around her to get to me.

Despite the tantrum I've just thrown, I don't hesitate. I open my arms wide to greet Molly and Marcus, her three- and five-year-olds. They both jump into my arms, and I give them a big squeeze hello. Unable to have children myself, I love Claire's kids like they're my own.

"Aunty Matty! Aunty Matty!"

I hug them tight, tears escaping my eyes at the calmness their presence brings. I wipe the tears away with the back of my hand. Feel little hands on my leg.

"Hey, Max-man," I coo down at him. I set Marcus and Molly down to scoop him up. Nuzzle his warm face, and all the tenseness in my body melts to heaven as he wraps his little arms around my neck.

"Mommy said we weren't supposed to get out of the car," Marcus informs me with a pouty lip. He climbs onto my back as I bend down to gather his sister Molly up in my arms.

"Well, you're out now," I whisper back to him with a wink.

Then I proceed to dance and bounce them all over to my front stoop and plop down in a puddle of giggles. There, Molly instantly moves to sit behind me and starts to undo the mess on top of my head, releasing my long hair into golden strands down my back. She loves the length. Anything that almost touches your butt is "mermaid hair" in her book.

I hand Max my keys and cell phone to play with. And, all the while, Marcus gives me his rendition of their latest adventure.

"… and then we saw the dolphins swimming underwater, and we didn't even get wet!"

"No way," I say, wide-eyed and full of fun.

"Yeah! And right after that, Molly got pooped on by a bird!"

"Oh, no," I say, looking back at her.

She nods her head, suddenly teary-eyed.

"Molly got pooped on! Molly got pooped on!" Marcus sings.

"Marcus," I take both his hands in mine. "That's not very nice. You're hurting Molly's feelings."

"But it's true," he pouts.

I want to smile at his earnest sincerity but know better, especially when I see Claire out of the corner of my eye, arms folded. So I situate everyone on my lap and await the lecture. Only her stern look turns slack, and suddenly my friend looks years older than she really is.

"It's late, kids. Say goodbye."

"But we want ice cream!" they all cry in unison.

"Aunt Matty can't go," she says matter-of-factly. "But we'll get some on the way home, okay?"

As they cheer and dance around the sidewalk, she scoops them up, one by one, and buckles them back into their car seats. When she's got them belted in and closed away behind the sliding door, she looks my way one last time and climbs in herself.

My stomach tightens in a knot. I want to call out, rush over and tell Claire I'm sorry, hop in the minivan with them and go wherever it is they wanted to go. Tell her I know she's excited I've hit The Big Three-O before she did and laugh off my craziness as that one-last-time I let the past gobble up my happiness.

But I'm stuck, left with the words trapped in my throat and my chest squeezed tight like a straitjacket.

I watch as Claire's taillights blend in with traffic and then disappear altogether down the street. At first, I stand in place, staring, waiting for them to come back. But when they don't, I look down at the gift on my stoop, its sweet bow staring back at me.

Once again, I feel the gravity of the day weighing me down.

I gather up my hair back into a loose bun, trying to forget the tiny fingers that just ran through it. I may have made a habit of pushing the past down so that I won't remember, but I never intended my running to hurt anyone.

Maybe Claire's right. Maybe I do need help.

I sigh and raise my eyes skyward. Illuminated by the city lights, it looks more rust-orange than midnight blue. Not a star shines through.

Another gift.

Stars only remind me of the time I wished for something so big, so out of this world, that I got it.

I wish I will meet a man who will change my life forever.

I had no idea what I was doing saying those words at the age of fourteen, but I wished for it anyway. Then learned the old adage well: Be careful what you wish for. I close my eyes and feel my mind start to vibrate with hurtful voices, demanding restitution.

See! they scream at me. *You did this to yourself! If you hadn't wished that, you wouldn't have been raped!*

I crush my head between my hands until the pain helps subside the guilt. But then I feel a sudden breeze and something touches my leg. I jump down off the stoop, ready to bolt, when I hear the meow of a cat.

A poof of burnt-orange, almost-red, fur frames its emerald-green eyes. The cat warmly glides its furry self along my leg, and I laugh at myself for losing it so easily. But my lighthearted mood ends quickly as I once again can hardly breathe past the constriction in my throat, my fight-or-flight response taking over.

Grabbing my things, I fish out my keys in an instant and unlock my door, my hands shaking. I slam the door and press my face against it.

"Stupid," I chastise myself. "How dumb do you have to be, Matty?"

In a quick succession of movements, I secure the bolt and padlocks, all the while reprimanding myself. "There are consequences to being alone in the dark. You're a girl. A stupid, stupid girl."

I flip on the three light switches next to me that illuminate the vacant first floor, which houses the living room and kitchen, as well as the bottom half of the stairwell. Fight back the tears as I climb the crooked, narrow steps, reminding myself that I don't deserve to feel scared.

It was my own dumb fault I sat out there in the dark, alone. I was lucky it was just a cat.

I run past the darkened second floor—the lone bedroom and bath that used to be Claire's—and rush up to the third floor. By the time I reach my sanctuary, my tears have dried and all's been forgotten, although never forgiven. Safely inside my studio apartment, my heart slows a little and I'm finally able to fill my lungs with a full breath of air.

I drop my bag on the floor. Kick off my shoes. Hold Claire's heavy gift to my chest.

Lock the door behind me.

My place—with its faded brown couch situated against a bare brick wall; a full-size mattress without a headboard pushed up against the other; a worn, faux-mahogany table used to separate the sleeping/ living area from the makeshift kitchenette, and several boxes I still haven't unpacked—would look just as it had when I first moved in ten years ago if it weren't for the mess I leave behind every day. I haven't always been a slob, but the fact that I am one now doesn't bother me much anymore.

I sit on Claire's itchy, old, brown couch and put her gift on my makeshift coffee table: three moving boxes lined up in a row, dressed up by one of Claire's old tablecloths she left behind when she got married and moved out.

I lean back and close my eyes, not wanting to think about anything but the here and now. So stuck in the past, it's something I've never been able to accomplish without a lot of strain. Yet I close my eyes and attempt to silence my mind anyway. Attempt to relax and feel something different. Maybe even something new.

Thirty years old, I think to myself. Finally.

Although on the outside I've worn my shield of indifference well, I know deep down I've been waiting for this moment. I'm thirty years old, entering a whole new decade. As such, something magical is about to happen. I just know it.

Excited, I wait for it, eyes closed, envisioning a sparkly mist descending upon me and my very own fairy godmother here to save me from myself. I tap my fingers on my thighs and hold my breath in braced anticipation. Tune out the hum of the window air conditioning unit as it blows cold gusts of air into the room. Ignore the sirens and honks from vehicles passing by on the street below.

I wait. And wait. But nothing happens.

No difference. No explosion of wisdom. No sense of security in myself.

Unable to believe it, I try two more times, sure I'm doing something wrong. I close my eyes and wait. Close my eyes and wait some more.

Nada, zilch, zero.

Nothing.

I'm just as uncomfortable in my own skin as I was before, unsure of my own thoughts and what I'm supposed to do with myself and my life. I still feel like a sixteen-year-old.

Frustrated, I get up to take a shower. Pulling off my top and unbuttoning my shorts, I leave a trail of clothing along the paint-splattered hardwood floor and into my bathroom. Then, standing naked and making sure to not look in the mirror, I pull out the hairband that's twisted into my long hair. Feel the weight of its length fall harshly against the pale tones of my skin.

I take a quick shower, finishing before my five-minute time limit, and twist up and secure my damp hair in the same hairband without bothering to brush it. Towel off without looking down at myself and put on the same pajamas I left lying on the back of the toilet this morning.

Digging around in my unmade bed and then under the couch, I find the remote control and sit myself down on the itchy, brown couch, my legs neatly curled under me, and heave a big sigh of relief in the familiar rhythms of solitude. Then I push aside piles of indiscriminate junk that are piled on the coffee table so I can stretch out and prop up my feet.

"It's time to unwind, Matty Bell-style," I say to myself and turn on the TV. The food channel comes to life. "Ooh! Iron Chef!" I cheer.

Having caught one of my favorite cooking shows midway through, I lean forward and watch intently to see if I can figure out the secret ingredient. From the looks of it, both chefs in *Kitchen Stadium* are using some sort of gigantic, reddish squid I've never seen before. Not exactly appetizing, but entertaining nonetheless.

After a while, my stomach starts to grumble and I glance at my cell phone. Ten o'clock. I haven't eaten anything since lunch, and that was just a bagel.

Tummy rumbling, I wait for a commercial break to dash into the kitchenette for a bite to eat. Opening my small freezer, I decide I have enough time to dish out what's left of the ice cream. It's not much, but it's my favorite—crazy-sweet, pink ice cream speckled with those fizzy pop rock candies that crackle and snap on your tongue.

I slip a spoonful of the ridiculously hot-pink, cotton-candy-flavored ice cream into my mouth and make it back to the couch just in time to see the last commercial drop out of focus.

"Twenty minutes to go," the announcer from Kitchen Stadium states.

"Now this is my kind of night," I say as I lounge back into the couch.

Although I'm no chef, I find watching others cook fascinating with their fast-flying chopping action and sautéing magic. I concentrate on the two varying methods of the competing chefs. The one from Japan—the legendary Morimoto—is stuffing his soon-to-be braised squid with a wasabi, seaweed, and candied ginger mixture.

"Go, Japan!" I cheer, feeling a kindred spirit as I was born there.

The guest chef challenging him turns his steamed squid and squash combo into a liquid. For some reason, this stomach-roiling yet oddly aesthetic combination wins the judges over.

With the show over, ice cream gone, and sleep still feeling miles away, I look again at my cell phone for the time. Eleven o'clock p.m. So I next watch some random movie that sounds interesting and ends up being a dud. Check my phone after it's over. One-thirty a.m. and therefore no longer my birthday.

I tap my fingers on my thighs for a moment, then pick up Claire's heavy gift.

I hold my breath as I pull the red ribbon with a gentle hand. Watch as it slowly unwinds itself from the package, then rip open the white paper. And breathe easy.

Just as I suspected. A book.

The Big Easy Cookbook.

"Ha!" I laugh, shaking my head. Perfect for the non-cook me. I flip through the pages, excited to learn its simple methods that will transform me into a capable chef. But instead, I find the book isn't as the title describes. The meals and recipes are nowhere close to easy. Intricate and culturally specific, it's a cookbook all about New

Orleans: *The Big Easy.*

"Oh, Claire." I shake my head with a smile, imagining my friend walking through a bookstore with her three little ones in tow. Her seeing the title of the book. Them seeing the size.

I pick up my phone to call them. Thank them. Laugh with them.

But it's too late, maybe in more ways than one.

I dismiss that last thought and open the cookbook again. It's filled with delectable photographs of scrumptious foods that make my mouth water and my stomach rumble.

Filled with a sudden thought, I walk over to the kitchenette and balance the open cookbook on the only available counter space between the sink and the stove, and start to rummage around for something I can make. Although it's been a long while since I've made anything outside of a microwavable meal, I'm feeling inspired tonight.

In the fridge, I see that I've got an egg, a few pieces of bread, some lunch meat, and some other odds and ends that I guess I can make a sandwich with.

I don't know. Doesn't sound exciting.

I open the cookbook a third time and flip through the pages. There are tons of dishes there I could attempt to make if only I owned any of the ingredients and had the know-how to not screw them up.

Defeated, I pull my cell phone out of the back pocket of my pajama bottoms to call for pizza. Turn the cookbook over in my hands while I wait for someone to pick up, and look at the back cover so I can glare at the chef responsible for this so-called easy cookbook and my maddening hungry stomach.

On the back is the photograph of a woman. Within a frame of sleek crimson hair, her green eyes exude such a strong sense of self, of confidence, that they hold my attention as though she were a real live person right here in my tiny kitchen.

I study her features and wonder how this woman got to be so strong. So sure of herself.

She looks like a woman who knows what she wants and how to get it. A timid thought dashes through my mind. *I want to be like that.*

I bite my lip and hang up the phone. Open the cookbook once more. See a recipe for Lake Charles Monte Cristo.

Although I've never seen anyone on a cooking show make anything like it before, the picture looks fantastic, and the directions, once I actually read them, seem easy enough to follow.

I scan the ingredients against what I have.

Bread? Check.

Eggs? Check.

Lunchmeat? Check.

Milk? None. But I do have yogurt.

"Maybe if I add a little water to the yogurt," I think out loud and begin to pull out the ingredients I have and the make-do substitutes for the ones I don't.

Try as I do, the eggshells crumble when I crack the eggs open, and I spend forever fishing out tiny shell pieces from the bowl. Unable to get them all and my hunger still growing, I leave a few in, deeming them tiny enough to be unnoticeable.

I add the "milk"—or yogurt watered down to the consistency of milk—and whisk it together with a fork. Smiling, I feel satisfied that my mixture resembles the picture in the cookbook so far.

I construct the sandwich—bread, lunch meat, bread—and place it face down in the egg-milk (yogurt) wash bowl. Anxious I'm missing a step, I reread the directions to make sure I'm doing it right. So far, so good. So I next search for a pan and put it on my hardly-ever-used, tiny stovetop on medium heat.

"Okay, now what?"

I have a hard time following directions, so I know to read and reread them for accuracy. That's how I realize too late that I didn't butter the sides of the bread before I put them in the egg-milk (yogurt) wash. Nor did I add some to the pan so the sandwich contraption doesn't stick.

A quick look in the fridge shows that I don't have any butter. But I deem that a minor setback, using the remaining yogurt as a substitute for the butter. I plop some into the heated pan and spread it around with my fingers, burning myself in the process.

With burnt fingers under running cold water, I refer back to the recipe directions, feeling the steps begin to jumble in my head. I read that I have to dip both sides of the sandwich into the egg wash for only a few seconds on each side and then add the sandwich quickly to the pan—not let it sit in the liquid concoction while talking to myself and rereading the directions a dozen times.

So I turn the sandwich over in the bowl to coat the other side, only to see soggy bits of bread fall away. And when I try to transfer it all to the heated pan, but the bread deteriorates even further, plopping back into the bowl. Not wanting to lose any of the ingredients, I pour everything into the pan, only too fast, allowing a small tidal wave of egg-milk (yogurt) and bread bits to splash out of the pan and onto the front of my pajamas.

Fortunately, the sizzle sounds about right from what I've seen on TV and almost resembles the picture in the cookbook. Almost. Somewhat satisfied, I put my finger back under the cold water while I towel off the egg wash from my clothes.

"I should be wearing an apron," I say to myself, charged with the excitement that I'm actually cooking and doing it right. I know I have an apron somewhere in my closet from one of the waitressing jobs I've had.

A hoarder, I don't throw much away.

I flip on the walk-in closet light and look around. Pushing aside piles of random stuff and fallen clothes, I search through what's on the floor and then look up at the shelf. There, on top of a moving box and under a pile of indiscriminate odds and ends, I see the stained strap of what I'm sure is my apron.

Steadying up on tippy-toes, I reach up over the moving box and sizzle my hand on the bare bulb that hangs too low. I yank my hand back to suck on the sting until it subsides, then reach up again and pull the strap. It won't budge.

Next, I resort to holding back all the junk with one hand while untangling the apron strap from some leftover dog leashes I still have from when I was a dog walker, all the while cursing my lack of organizational skills. I'm not done yet when I smell smoke, followed by the sound of the smoke detector screaming to life.

Frantic, I yank the apron with a quick, strong tug, only to realize too late that it was partially wedged under the moving box.

In slow motion—and for my entertainment only—an avalanche of junk comes crashing down: papers, books, dog leashes, forgotten clothes. Oh, and let us not forget the icing on the cake, the moving box—*bam!*—right into my face.

The box rips open, spilling its contents in a flood all over me and onto the floor.

Holding my crushed nose and my ears ringing from the fire alarm, I jump over the broken box and dart into the kitchenette to fan the smoke detector with a dish towel. Indignant, it roars on.

I grab the now too-hot-to-touch pan without a hot mitt—*I don't own a hot mitt!*—and throw it into the sink. Still fanning the damned fire alarm with a towel, I turn on the cold water to run over both my scalded hand and the pan below it while the smell of burnt food mixes with steam as it billows up into my face.

I survey the damage. My hand is okay, a little painful is all, but the sandwich couldn't be worse. Blackened and burnt to the bottom of the pan, Monte is crisp-o, for sure.

As for the smoke detector, I finally pull the batteries out, silencing it forever, and blow a puff of breath up at the wet hair that's fallen free in the chaos, clinging to my face.

Still hungry, eyes burning from the smoke, ears pounding in the new silence, finger burnt, nose hurt, hand scalded, I pout toward my bed. I'm stopped short of flopping down on the mattress, however, at the sight of the massive mess flowing out of my closet. Sprawled out on the floor like a drunken schoolgirl are my old art notebooks, dozens upon dozens of them, filled with the pages of my passion gone dry.

In disbelief, I pick one up and leaf through its color-spattered pages. Like magic, I feel the unforgettable tug in my heart. The excited sputtering I haven't felt in years.

In a rush to hold onto its sudden resurgence, I pick up as many art books as I can and hold them close, keep them safe like friends I haven't seen in a long time that might fly away too soon.

I open one. Then another. And another. I flip through their pages. Haphazard displays of artwork spill forth in a myriad of mediums— crisp acrylics, faded watercolors, smudged chalks, pencil drawings. It makes my heart leap for joy, and I feel my eyes fill with tears.

I haven't seen these notebooks since I left California.

I open another. And another, turning them over in my hands, flipping through their pages, running my fingers over the movements of life on every page.

Some pages are filled with playful practice strokes, others completed like mini masterpieces. I used to love the way colors swirled together, creating magical combinations of life.

The next one I open contains a simple pencil sketch of the beach near my parent's house in Oceanside, touched here and there with different colored smudges—clay cliffs a burnt sienna, the ocean a beckoning slate turquoise.

Picking up yet another, I find the one I dedicated to the portraits of any poor saps who would sit still long enough for me to try to capture their whole life in one single frame.

I look on with renewed ownership as I leaf through the pages, feeling my smile grow with deep satisfaction. Gratitude. There are no blank pages. As I remember, I was never without want to capture something, anything, on canvas. No matter where we went, I always had my little art bag in hand and an art notebook under my arm.

My mother never understood nor approved. My sister, the same. It embarrassed them.

But my father loved it. Said my talent came naturally as though born with me. And although I didn't always fit in with the in-crowd that way, it never mattered much to quirky, artsy me.

I pick up the last remaining notebook and see a crumpled piece of blue paper lying on the floor.

Leave it! a loud voice demands from the back of my mind, and I kick it away, my heart pounding. But then a different voice—a softer, more timid one than the first—whispers, *pick it up.*

Not used to hearing the softer voice inside, I hesitate before turning back and bending down. But I do pick it up, undoing its crumpled edges until it lies flat in my hands.

With no salutation at the beginning and no signature at the end, it's just a jumble of words on one lonely page of sadness and self-hate.

I don't recognize the handwriting and my heart goes out for whomever wrote it. Since it came from the moving box, it could be anybody. A friend from high school in California. Maybe even from someone I knew when we lived in Italy. Or any number of friends I've had to leave behind while moving around with my dad's assignments.

Although the note feels tortured, I'm intrigued to read more. To figure out who wrote it. Maybe in the words lies a clue. So I read on. Line after line, the tightness of the handwriting makes it illegible until one word halfway down the page seems to have been etched out with such force, it is literally sliced through the paper in three distinct letters.

WHY?

It's written, not as a question, but more as a demand. Somehow, I know this.

The words start to unravel and reveal themselves the more I read. I feel my throat tighten as I attempt to discern the meaning of the tearstained page.

Why, God? Why? it says.

After a snarl of words I can't make out, calm and clear writing emerges near the end of the page, and I read it with ease.

What's the point anymore? There's only pain.

I feel the hair on my arms rise when the next sentence reads itself to me, almost out loud, from somewhere in the back of my mind.

Only in death is there peace.

I don't have to look down at the paper to know what the next line says. I've read it before. I see it now. This is my handwriting. I wrote this.

You live and you die. And then finally, peace.

I clamp a hand over my mouth as tears sting my eyes.

I don't want to live like this anymore. I just want to—

"Die," I finish the sentence out loud.

Like a fist to the gut, the air is knocked out of me, remembering when I wrote all that one dreadful, lonely night after leaving home.

And now the same redundant questions start up again, just like they've been nagging me all day.

Why? Why me?

Why didn't anyone help me?

And why, please, God, do the aftereffects linger on and on like a heavy hand holding me down? I ran away from the pain and yet I'm still here, asking the same damned questions and getting no answers.

Why do I still feel I'm drowning in guilt? Why do I live in such unbelievable solitude?

To keep myself safe. That's always been my mantra.

"But have I really accomplished that?" I ask myself out loud.

All I wanted was to get away from it all, yet I've been set in stone and left to feel this way forever.

"If I die…" I repeat the thought that led me to write the note in the first place. "If I die, it all goes away."

It's the only answer I've ever come up with.

I pull a shaky breath past the constriction in my throat, not liking the sound of my own defeat. Feeling a heated tremor build up deep inside me, I scream out, pounding the floor with my fists.

"I hate this shit!"

I storm the few steps back into the kitchenette and turn on the stove. Lay the note over the heating element until it crinkles into smoldering ash, erasing it forever.

"Fuck him!" I say. "Fuck them all."

A waft of charred smoke puffs up over me like a calming hand. I close my eyes and breathe it in.

Feel a change. A pivot.

I round the corner and pause only for a second, noticing I never closed or locked up the door that leads out to my rooftop deck. I take a few cautious steps up until I'm standing outside, still in the night. The air is less moist up here, with a windy breeze and a serene view of city lights dancing in the night sky.

Sirens sound from the streets below, off in the distance.

I turn slowly and realize that, at this late hour, I can actually see the passing of boat lights in the harbor. Loose wisps of hair blow about my face as I walk over to the railing. Grab hold of that which protects me from the three-flight drop down.

Tears well up in my eyes, and I feel it all throughout my body and all of my existence. I still want peace.

Calm.

Tranquility.

Balance.

Only, as I gaze down at the pavement to where my truck should be, I know I won't get any of that from death. Not death in the real end-of-life sense.

No.

There has to be another way.

With a shallow breath, I walk back into my apartment. Close and lock up the rooftop door. Slide a tower of moving boxes back in front of it: the barricade I created long ago to keep me from walking out there in the first place. Back in my tiny kitchenette, I clean up the mess, slowly turning soapy circles in the burnt pan. That's when I hear the soft voice speak up in me again.

And it's right. What I want—need—is the kind of peace that doesn't come from death.

It comes from a new beginning.

CHAPTER THREE

Welcome to La La Land

Dynamite in the air.

The excitement level on race day is just that.

I stand crowded together with other American high school students whose families are also stationed in Italy, ready for the last race of cross-country season. A solid white line is drawn across an emptied street just outside Milan to separate our readied selves from the five-kilometer trek ahead.

One of the fastest females on our team, I've trained hard and aim to win it for Naples American High School. Yet, as I stretch, my mind is preoccupied, as usual.

I continue to warm up, stretching my legs, jogging in place, all the while mentally fixated on something so faintly brilliant, I can't get it out of my head. Standing there in the dimly lit church yesterday, I fell in love with a masterpiece.

L'Ultima Cena. *Da Vinci's* The Last Supper.

Painted across the inside of a domed ceiling, it had me entranced, imagining the difficulty Da Vinci had creating his vision to scale, hoping it would translate to those standing on the ground.

"Napoleon and his troops used the figures in the painting for target practice," our tour guide had stated with perfect English grammar, notwithstanding a heavy Italian accent.

I had felt my heart clench, imagining the since dearly departed da Vinci cursing the little giant from his grave. How could anyone have thought to hurt something so beautiful, much less carried out that intent?

Most of my teammates, not at all interested in either the historical significance or beauty of the barely visible artwork, had left the church as soon as they entered. I, on the other hand, stayed as long as my five American dollars and our tour guide allowed.

"On your marks!"

I hear the pop of the gun. Scramble up from my leg stretch and join twelve packed sets of high school women's and men's cross-country teams as we run down the side streets of Milan. Past harvested fields. Through trees. Along open streams.

The fall air is colder than usual, biting at my skin. Many runners have socks over their hands to keep them warm until the heat of the run catches up with them.

Fingers freezing, I wish I had been so smart.

The crunch of leaves underfoot is music to my ears, and I lose myself to the rhythm, thinking of the crimson reds and dulled golds. I pass the one-mile mark and forgo the water being handed out. Pass the two-mile marker and continue on the same.

I love to run. Always have. I can't think of anything else that makes me feel this free.

All of a sudden, I feel a sharp piercing pain low in my abdomen, causing me to double over.

"You okay?" someone asks as they run past.

I can't speak past the pain, can barely shake my head no. Then, just as fast as it came, it's gone and I can stand again. Breathe.

Relieved, I wave to my onlookers. Start running to catch up. Yet only a few moments later, the dagger of pain shoots through me again like a hot poker and I double over a second time.

The spasm spreads like hellfire throughout the lower half of my body, similar to menstrual cramps in location, only light years away from the typical pain. My lower back joins in. My hips. My thighs.

Everything hurts.

Then it disappears again, and I sprint to catch up. Pass runner after runner. Feel great with the cold wind on my heated skin.

But it happens again and again, each installment of sudden pain more taxing than the last. It takes everything in me to keep going, and I fall farther and farther behind. Have to walk some of the race.

No longer warmed by the excursion, my body chills, making me shiver. Making my muscles tense. Making the pain even worse.

I shuffle on in the slowest jog imaginable. Me, one of the fastest female runners for Naples American High School. I should be taking everyone by storm. But by the time I arrive at the finish line, the cheering crowd I'm accustomed to being welcomed by is replaced by only a couple of lingering people packing up, heading off to the showers.

My coach is nowhere to be found, and everyone from my team is gone. Everyone except my boyfriend, Jett.

I see the white finish line that's been spraypainted across the grass. I have only enough energy left to focus on it while I hold onto my middle. Shuffle my feet. Use up my last remnants of energy. Make it across the finish line.

And fall into his arms.

"*Matty!*" I hear my name yelled, followed by someone snapping fingers. "Miss Bell!"

I blink in quick succession, trying to remember where I am.

My therapist, Dr. Linda, with her long, multicolored gypsy skirt and equally long, gray braid, looks to be just as astonished as I am. So engrossed was I in my daydream of a flashback, I totally forgot I was sitting in her office.

"There you are," she says, crossing one leg over the other and smoothing out her skirt.

The late October sun streams in slats through the blinds covering her window. I study the resulting dots shining on my legs.

She looks at me, waiting for me to enlighten her with what just happened. And when I don't, she pointedly asks in her direct manner.

"Where did you go this time?"

"I'm sorry. You were saying?" I ask, searching my mind for what she was talking about before I veered off to La-La Land.

"I wasn't. You had just begun telling me about why you're unable to have children. And then, all of a sudden, you disappeared. Stopped talking. Where did you go?"

"I vanished?" I joke, another one of my stupid attempts at making light of the situation. This isn't the first time I've zoned out in her office.

"No, not physically. But mentally, yes," Dr. Linda says, now immune to my forced humor. She presses on, making notations on her red, leatherbound notepad. "In the past two months we've been meeting, you have—for lack of a better term—'left' on several occasions. You stop being here, in the present. Instead, you drift off somewhere mid-sentence, and I want to know where. What were you just thinking about?"

"I'm not sure I understand what you mean," I lie.

"Yes, you do," Dr. Linda says. "Remember, my office is a safe place. You came here with a goal in mind. An intention, remember? If you want to be free of the ropes that bind you, you need to release them. And talking about them is the first step."

Except that's the thing. I don't want to talk about them. It's too embarrassing to admit all that's bottled up inside my head. Plus, I've lost my initial bravery. At my first session, I had all the intention in the world of telling her everything. Total spillage. Full disclosure.

I even went to the effort of replicating the note I found so I'd have proof to show why I needed to see someone like her. Why I was so messed up that I needed a trauma speficic counselor to help put me back together.

But she wanted nothing of it at the time.

"Good therapy never starts with a detailed description of the abuse," is what she had said. "Believe it or not, we may never even talk about it in terms of what exactly happened. The details of the past aren't always important. What's important now is you in the here and now. We need to concentrate on you. To help you heal. To find out what is holding you back from reaching your full potential." I remember her words distinctly. "What's important isn't what happened or why it happened. What's important is where are you going now and then giving you the tools you need to get there."

Inside her dusky, warm-hued office, Dr. Linda has encouraged me to talk endlessly about where I am now. What I am doing now. How I feel now. She's afforded me tidbits of information about the past, and I've learned a lot. Like how I still yearn for the kind of bond I used to have with my family before things got bad.

But nothing more. Never more.

"That's all in the past," she keeps saying, "and we're not at all interested in going backwards, are we? What you want and need is to move forward."

That's one of her mottos: *forward motion only*. I'm supposed to repeat that to myself daily in my head and out loud. And I will, soon. This is all just so foreign to me right now.

Dr. Linda sits across the low, round, wooden table between us, waiting for me to speak. And I want to. But, like a broken record, I keep hearing this nervous voice in the back of my head saying, *Don't do it! Don't do it!* As though, if I do, a flood will come and we'll both be consumed.

Then again, I have no control over my mouth sometimes. "I was thinking about him," I blurt out.

"Who, him?" she asks, and I hold my breath, unable to physically answer.

"Him, him," I say, hoping the strain in my face explains who. I finger the cuff of my jeans and pull a stray thread.

Dr. Linda looks at me, determined to get the information out.

I feel my chest squeeze and I stare down at my crossed legs, fighting the tears that threaten to spill. "You know," I manage. "Him. It… The guy who, you know… raped me."

I whisper the monumental "r" word. Although it's all I've ever been able to think about, I haven't spoken about it out loud in years.

"Really?" I watch as she attempts to figure out how my tangent-filled thought process has connected this time.

Instead of waiting for her to formulate a picture from my dropped hints, I decide enough is enough and give in. I'll just say it.

"I was thinking back to when the endometriosis pain started back in ninth grade, and that's about the same time we started going out together. And how, for a while, he was great about it all."

The word "great" takes a lot of effort to say and doesn't taste all that wonderful either. "He wasn't all bad."

A well-worn statistic from one of the books Dr. Linda's had me read pops into my head, reminding me that before he was my abuser, he, too, was probably abused. *Over seventy-five percent of serial rapists report they were sexually abused as youngsters.* It's not an excuse for what he did, only the beginning to the story of why.

"Well, not everyone is all bad," she says, nodding.

"Everyone liked him." I hurry past her affirmation. "He was Mr. Popular. Star athlete. Soccer goalie on the varsity team."

Dr. Linda continues to nod, waiting for more.

"Mr. Perfect," I say again. "He had everyone fooled."

More nods from her. I want to hold her head still, as she's making me feel seasick.

"I never let him kiss me," I say, then tighten my lips, keeping in anything else that might spill.

I don't want to say anything more. It hurts too much to remember a time when I was the one in control of me. But Dr. Linda's unbiased expression helps me find a little confidence to proceed.

This is a safe place.

"We only held hands. It was totally innocent. I didn't want to do anything more." I sigh, remembering how different my innocence had been from some of the other girls on base. I may have hung out with some of the "fast girls," but I was never one of them. "He and I only went out for a few days in ninth grade. Then I broke up with him."

I stop breathing. This is where it starts to get sticky.

"And why did you break up with him?"

"He..." I dig as deep as I can to find the courage to speak. "He showed me his true colors, and I acted instinctually. Ran away from him as fast as I could. Proves I was smart at one point," I add, more to myself than to her. "Why I turned stupid later on, I don't know."

The puzzled look on Dr. Linda's face reminds me she can't read my mind and fill in the blanks to make sense of what I'm saying. I know this. I just wish she could. Even though I carry all the visuals inside, saying this stuff out loud, hearing myself say it— it's like it's happening all over again.

The pain.

The guilt.

The shame.

"Picture me in ninth grade, innocently holding hands with my new boyfriend, Mr. Popular. We're jumping over rain puddles one day, and he says to me, out of nowhere, 'I love you.'"

I shake my head at the silliness of it. "After only a few days of being boyfriend-girlfriend? I was only fourteen."

I shake my head again, thinking back. "I laughed, thinking he was joking. But then he stopped walking and said it again with this really weird look in his eyes. And when I stayed silent, he yanked me to him, insisting I say it back."

I feel my stomach tighten. My heart race. "When I didn't, he got really mad and said I'd better say it. 'When someone says they love you, you're supposed to say it back,' he told me."

I keep going. "I tried to be nice even though he was scaring me. I said that I liked him, but love? I couldn't lie. I was only fourteen years old, for crying out loud. What did he expect?

"But he didn't like my honesty. So I turned to walk away, and he held onto me so I couldn't go. Squeezed my hand so hard it hurt, and I screamed."

Seeing in my mind how his eyes darkened, feeling him tower over me, I shiver at the memory. "He scared the shit out of me. And when he finally let go, I ran home and didn't look at him or talk to him for a year. It's very hard to do when you're in such a small school, but I avoided him."

"Did you ever tell anyone?"

I pause, stupefied. "No," I say, plopping my head into my hands. All the questions I've ever asked myself always culminate into one answer: If I had only spoken up, I could have prevented everything.

"Okay," she says. "He scared you so much that you didn't talk to him again for an entire year. Yet you dated him again?"

"I know, I know," I mumble, tears falling. "I'm so stupid."

"No, no. Not stupid," Dr. Linda says and waits until I look up to continue. "How did you come to be his girlfriend again after what he did?"

"My sister, Eleanor," I grumble, remembering how she and her friends coerced me. "I don't know why she insisted I go back out with him. It's not like he was the one I was pining over."

"And who was that?" Dr. Linda asks, seeming genuinely interested.

I smile for the first time in months of counseling. "This skater boy, Gabe," I say. "He asked me out on a dare one day at the beginning of tenth grade; and well, I was already head over heels for him, so I said yes. Who cares that it wasn't a romantic moment."

I giggle. Bite my lip. "He was my high school sweetheart. My first kiss."

Dr. Linda smiles back with encouragement. Only I don't need it. I've never had trouble reliving the memories Gabe left behind.

"We went out for about six months during our sophomore year. We did a lot of things together," I say with a blush, thinking back. "A lot."

"But you didn't—"

"No," I say flat, interrupting her. "After fooling around at my pace for six months, he wanted to go all the way. I said I wanted to wait. He called me Mother Theresa. Broke up with me. And that was that."

I shake my head with a half-hearted smile. "We were only fifteen. Besides, I made a promise to myself that I wanted to wait. My sister and I had made a pact that we'd both wait and not have sex until we were married."

"That's a good pact."

"Yeah, it was," I say looking at my hands.

Dr. Linda jots something down in her red, leather-bound journal.

Typically, at the mention of my sister, I feel outraged enough to crush the world. But this time, my thoughts turn down a different avenue with a new thought.

"What if I had said yes?" I ask, a whole new alternate reality breaking open in my mind.

Reassessing my life with this new parameter, I see all sorts of variances that could have been. Should have been.

"I'd be a totally different person today if I'd said yes to Gabe. If I got to decide when I wanted to lose my virginity and who I wanted to be with. If it had been my choice…"

I've never thought along these lines before. "I wouldn't be here today if I'd said yes."

"But you didn't know you were going to be raped, Matty," Dr. Linda interrupts my history-rewriting daydream. She affords me a moment to dwell.

Dwelling. That's all I've done for years. And I'm rather bored of it. I'd rather go back in time and fix everything. Have sex with Gabe when he asked and be done with all this.

He was a great kisser, after all.

"So," my therapist says, reeling me back in from flying off into

La-La Land permanently. "Let's go back to this other guy who wasn't always a horrible person."

"What about him?" I ask, annoyed.

Dr. Linda eyes me. "Why don't you say his name?"

"Do I have to?"

"No." Dr. Linda shakes her head thoughtfully. "But it would make it easier for me to discuss this person if he had a name."

"What if he doesn't deserve one?" I say, my vengeance back. Dr. Linda nods slowly. "How about this then: We'll make up a name for him using his first initial. That way, I don't get confused, alright?"

I nod, thankful she's letting me avoid saying his shitty name out loud.

"What should this name we're going to use start with?"

My legs start to tremor, and I hold back, again physically unable to go further. I have to force it out. "J."

"Okay. J," Dr. Linda says and starts rattling off a list of names starting with such. "James. Jerome. Jeremy. Jonah. Jeremiah. Jacob. Joshua. Jack."

"Jackass," I say with a horrid smile.

"You like that one?" she says and jots something down. "Jackass it is. But we'll use Jay for short, okay?"

"Sounds perfect to me," I say, feeling as though I've won some sort of battle.

"So. Jay," Dr. Linda tries it on, and I give her the okay nod. She grins. "Jay wasn't always a bad person. Well, truth is, most people aren't."

"No." I shake my head at my weakness. "He showed me just who he was though. I knew just what he was from the start. I should have known to keep my distance."

"But he had changed, right? That's why you decided to date him again, correct?" Dr. Linda asks.

I pull my legs up and hug my knees, remembering the clues he dropped that he wasn't alright after all, hinting to his anger, his possessiveness. I shake my head, no longer willing to make excuses for him.

"You know," I say in a shaky voice. "After he reeled me in with his nice guy act, he did change. Changed back to the way he was before."

I pick at the seat cushion under my legs and then wipe the snot that threatens to drip from my nose with the back of my hand.

Dr. Linda holds out a tissue box, but I'm too deep in it. Too deep in my memory to take it.

"He left me in tears each and every night for the first three months, demanding I say 'I love you' back to him. When I'd tell him I wasn't ready, he'd change. Turn dark. Tell me I better do it soon."

I shake my head, humiliated. "I don't know why I continued to stay with him."

But then I remember his words. *I'll kill you if you leave me. I'll hurt your family.*

"He was so mean. Telling me I was ugly. That I should wear makeup. Then, when I'd wear it, he'd pull away from me, saying I stunk like makeup. So I'd go home, wash it off. Come back to find him laughing and pointing at me with his friends because I did what he told me to do. Like it was a joke.

"But I could see he was pleased. Three months of shit like that, and he wore me down. I finally told him I loved him so he'd just leave me alone. I said it through tears, with him glaring at me until I did."

"Oh, Matty. That's horrible."

"Worst part was, the moment I caved, it was like he won. I could see it in his eyes," I say, wiping tears from my face. "That 'I love you' was my white flag of surrender. Like he knew I was giving up control. Like I was telling him he had me now. That was the week of my sixteenth birthday."

At the mention of that birthday long ago, visions of that day start to pound through my head. I don't realize I'm hitting the sides of my head with my fists until I feel Dr. Linda's hand on mine, stopping me.

She hands me the tissue box again with the butterflies so sweet, and I take it this time. She nods, sits down, and takes a deep breath. "Matty, you do know you were way too young to understand the meaning behind his behavior, especially behavior you weren't accustomed to?"

"True..." I decide to accept what she says, although I've never before given myself that luxury.

"And like what we've been discussing over the past few months, it's easy to see where you learned to become an enabler."

I nod, recalling all the dissection and labeling of my family life. My sister and I were left to fend for ourselves with our unavailable, drunk mother when our father wasn't around. And we all pretended she never had a problem and that we were the perfect family when he was home.

"And what about your other boyfriend, Gabe, the skater boy?" she asks, looking down at her notes. "Was he abusive, too?"

I shake my head *no* and feel my breath come back to me at the thought of him. His tenderness.

Dr. Linda's face softens, and her eyes smile. "You loved him, didn't you?"

I laugh out loud, thankful for the change in mood. "I was a sophomore in high school. I was just a child."

"You seem to like to make concessions for your emotions," she says to me, like I'm supposed to respect myself and my feelings. "Just because you were a teenager doesn't mean you couldn't feel love."

I contemplate this and sigh, emotionally exhausted.

She jots something down on her notepad, and I lean back into my chair, spent. Up, down, pulled here, pulled there, feeling depressed, feeling euphoric, dredging up the past, learning things about myself that I wasn't exactly clueless about before but suppressed well enough to play the denial card. Self-denial, self realization.

It's all so exhausting.

Maybe the demons in my head are right. Maybe I don't need this. I don't need to examine the past. What good is it doing anyway? I come here, week after week, sometimes twice a week—and for what? To hear how stupid I was? Still am?

I already do a good enough job of telling myself that, thank you very much.

"There you go again," Dr. Linda says.

"Huh? What did you say?"

"You disappeared again. And you know what else?"

"No. What?" I ask, afraid she's about to cosign on my stupidity, telling me I have no business being here.

"You hold your breath a lot," she tells me, staring at me as though I should already know this. "Every time you drift off into space or wherever it is you go, you stop breathing."

I stare at her, confused. I have no idea what she's talking about.

"I know what you're doing," she continues. "It's written all over your face. You're daydreaming away your right to be here. Am I right? You're convincing yourself that you don't deserve to be here to talk about what you need to talk about. You blank out and go somewhere, only God knows where. And while you're gone, you hold your breath. You probably don't even know you're doing it either, do you?"

"Okay," I say, embarrassed to know my therapist does, in fact, read minds.

"Here, let me show you something." Dr. Linda inches forward in her seat situated opposite mine. Her knees bump the round table between us. "Mindful Breathing. It's a tool that I want you to learn. It will help you become aware, conscious, of what you are doing, thinking, feeling."

"Mindful breathing?" I say, my eyebrows scrunched together.

Dr. Linda waves off my uncertainty. "By becoming conscious of what's going on inside of you—of what you're feeling and thinking—you can start to recognize the triggers that cause you to hold your breath. Or really, what triggers your constant need to escape: to run away. To daydream."

She sits back. "I can see when you do it. I can see what triggers you. But I want you to find out. And tell me what it is."

"Triggers?"

"Trauma reminders. They can be anything that reminds you of your traumatic experience. A smell, a sound, a certain word—a name. They can be incredibly intrusive, bombarding your thoughts, making you relive the experience repeatedly, daily."

Intrusive thoughts, constantly reliving it all, day in, day out: It sounds just like me. I tune in, shushing the noises inside my head, wanting to hear more.

"Most women will use self-destructive coping mechanisms to escape their triggers, not wanting to relive the painful trauma. Hence, you zone out. Run away. Hold your breath."

"Hold my breath," I say, fascinated and perplexed.

"Triggers can result in panic attacks, prolonged anxiety, flashbacks, loss of self."

Loss of self.

I feel myself dissected, as though Dr. Linda has direct access to what I've been living with for the past ten years.

"This, in turn, causes emotional exhaustion, which can then lead to emotional detachment. Dissociation. Avoidance."

A light turns on in my head, highlighting a long list of people, places, and things I've spent a great deal of time and energy running away from. Avoiding.

Dr. Linda pauses, hinting to me. "Once I teach you how to breathe again, you can pinpoint what your triggers are, learn how to cope with them, and ultimately learn how to take control of them."

"Instead of them controlling me," I say to myself, getting it.

She nods with a smile. "It's hard work, but it can be done."

I feel myself space out. I don't quite follow what she means. "What's hard work?"

"Learning how to focus. How to breathe."

I shake my head at myself. Cover up my misstep with humor. "I thought I learned how to breathe the moment I was born."

Dr. Linda looks at me patiently. "I'll show you how to breathe better. How's that?"

The whole thing sounds a little too far-fetched for the serious expression on her face, and I want to laugh out loud. But I force myself not to smile.

"And that's another thing, Miss Matty Bell," Dr. Linda says, tapping her pencil on her notepad. "You keep your emotions to yourself too much. As if you don't feel you deserve to express yourself freely. Am I right?"

Hurt and embarrassed, I shy away from her questioning eyes and turn inward, unsure I want to continue. Tears well up in my eyes, though this time, I know I'm holding my breath. And it does help me control my emotions.

I don't want to cry. I don't want to feel.

It hurts too much.

"Matty, if you need to cry, cry," she says in such a soothing tone that I want to smack her. "Or if you feel the need to laugh at something, laugh. Scream. Jump for joy. Throw dishes at the wall even. Do whatever you need to do. Just don't ignore your feelings. Stop pretending they don't exist. You are worth your own thoughts, no matter how trivial they seem. Your thoughts, your instincts: They are you. They are a part of you. If you allow them freedom, then you are allowing yourself to be free."

I feel the corners of my mouth start to curl up at the thought of me being free. Yet I hesitate further, unsure I can see it or believe it yet.

Freedom is scary.

"That's a start," Dr. Linda says. "That is tool number three. Releasing yourself: releasing your deserved emotions. I want you to practice that, okay?" She writes something down on a bright green Post-It Note and hands it to me.

"Okay," I say, wiping my eyes with the back of my hand. On the paper is written *Tool #3: Deserved Release*. I'm supposed to stick this to my bathroom mirror, along with the two other tools she's given me since I started coming to see her.

"Now, back to breathing." She jots something else down and hands me another Post-it Note, this time with *Tool #4: Mindful Breathing* written on it. "I know it sounds cliché, but one of the best ways to combat fear, stress, anxiety—your body's gut reaction to triggers—is to concentrate on your breathing. Focusing on your breath not only helps you think before you act, but it will also keep you in the present."

"You mean keep me from flying off to La-La Land?"

"Exactly. You're getting it," Dr. Linda says, cheerful. "If you want to live your life in the here and now—in the present—you have to stop leaving when things get tough. When you have to think or feel or see or touch or even smell something you don't want to—something that reminds you of your trauma—your immediate reaction is to avoid it."

Run. Hide. Die.

"But stop." Dr. Linda reaches across the round table between us, giving my knee a double pat, enunciating the words. "Don't run. Instead, I want you to breathe. By focusing on your breathing, you'll become more and more conscious of yourself and your surroundings, and of what emotions are coming up inside you. Your breath will keep you focused: will help you remember your goal—that you want to be free from these things. And that will keep you from wanting to escape."

"Interesting concept," I say, trying not to sound too sarcastic. I take notice of the time and realize our session isn't anywhere close to being over. So, reluctantly willing, I decide to give it a try. "Alright, what do I do?"

"Close your eyes. Block out your thoughts, and I want you to really feel what it's like to breathe."

Eyes closed, I chuckle to myself, knowing that, if my father were here right now, he'd say Dr. Linda is a certified quack. He's definitely not the out-of-the-box thinker she's painted herself to be. Yet I wait for her instruction, and attempt to think about nothing and clear my mind, as if that's possible.

"Breathe in through the nose," I hear her say. "Feel the quick coolness of the air against your nostrils and hold it for a few seconds. Feel the fullness of your lungs. Now slowly let the breath out through the mouth. Slowly now. Feel its warmth pass over your lips."

I roll my eyes behind closed lids and breathe in through my nose. To my surprise, it does feel cool in a way I've never noticed before. I suppress a smile and concentrate on the air in my lungs. Feel the tightness of my chest. The subsequent lightness of my body. And then, as I move the air out through my mouth, it does feel hot as it flows past my lips.

"Neat."

"Again."

Eyes still closed, I breathe in and out, this time feeling as though I'm floating on an ocean wave. In, out. Up, down. I breathe again, smiling along with the sensation of the tide moving through me.

"Keep going."

Excited to feel the continued tranquility, I take in an even deeper breath this time. Start to feel myself stabilize in the present. I feel myself, my thoughts, steady on one solid idea. They stop branching off into insane, multiple tangents. This is new: this ability to concentrate and follow one thought to the end without interruption. Almost like freedom from my own prison.

Exhilarated, I continue to breathe deeply, feeling the coolness and the warmth: the in and the out, the up and the down. I can't believe how easy this is. I'm free. I'm done.

To think I wasn't even going to try.

"It wasn't your fault," Dr. Linda interrupts me with a phrase that doesn't need explanation.

I know what she's referring to. And I don't want to think about this now. I feel my throat tighten.

"You didn't wish it upon yourself."

I hate her. I can't breathe again.

"You need to stop hurting yourself for something you had no control over."

No control? Is she serious? I walked into that house. I walked up those stairs. I walked into his bedroom. No one held a gun to my head.

Sure he locked me in his room, wouldn't let me out. But I wasn't jumped in a parking garage. I wished upon a star for a man to change my life forever, and he did just that.

Plus, I didn't tell anyone he was a monster when I could have. I stayed with him. I enabled him to do it again and again.

It was me. I did it.

"It wasn't your fault that you were repeatedly raped."

I recoil from her words. I want to run, but I know I can't escape. I can never escape. I know I'm holding my breath now, but I won't let go. I don't want to feel or think. I don't want to be here.

I don't want to do this.

I don't want to live in my body anymore.

My lungs start to hurt and I'm reluctant to let go, but I'm unable to hold my breath in any longer. Opening my eyes, I see Dr. Linda nod all too knowingly, like she knows where I've been. What I can't stop thinking about.

Annoyed, hatred steams up inside me. "*Why?*" I stretch the word along my gritting teeth.

I despise her. She keeps making me feel things I don't want to feel. Think about things I don't want to think about. Everything keeps getting magnified when all I want to do is white it out.

The image of a blank, white canvas pops into my mind—a new beginning—and my anger dissipates a little. I hold my hands in my lap to keep them from shaking. Exhausted, a tired, old question comes to mind.

"When will I be able to let this all go?" I say, my eyes welling up with tears. I want to reach for a tissue, but my body feels heavy, weighing me down. I can't allow myself to feel that I deserve to want or need anything.

I was stupid. I let it all happen. I don't deserve anything.

"Soon," Dr. Linda says with such compassion that I want her to hug me. Hold me. "We're getting there. Just keep doing like I've taught you. Breathe. Be conscious of what you're thinking and doing, and make sure you stay focused in the present. That was then. This is now. You don't want to live backwards, do you?"

I shake my head, wanting to laugh at her silly response but too busy holding my hands to my eyes, trying to keep myself from crying.

"And cry, Matty," Dr. Linda says as she hands me a tissue. "Or scream. You really do deserve to have a reaction to the world around you, just like anyone else."

I grab the tissue box. Pull out a tissue and hold it to my eyes, soaking up the waterworks that have now turned on full-force.

She's right. I don't feel I deserve to show my feelings. But in the same heartbeat, I'm beginning to see that I do. I do deserve to feel. To think. But I haven't done so freely for so long that I don't know how to anymore.

My cheeks burn hot with a mixture of sadness and anger, the flood of emotions too great.

"Oh, my God. This is too much," I cry to myself. "I can't. I can't do this."

"And why do you think that is?"

Pushed over my limit, I don't resist the urge to raise my voice. "Why do I think that is? I don't know. You're the doctor! Why don't you tell me, Dr. Linda," I sneer, making fun of her effort to make me feel comfortable by letting me call her by her first name. "Isn't that why I'm paying you?" As soon as I spit out my anger, I want to take it back.

I open my mouth to apologize.

"Don't, Matty," Dr. Linda interrupts. "Don't."

"But—"

"No apologies."

I suck in my breath.

"And no holding your breath, either."

"You and the breathing!" I burst out laughing, albeit through tears. When she laughs along with me, I start to cry. "One step forward, two steps back."

"It's okay. You did a lot of work today. Don't think this is going to just happen overnight. It took you a long time to get this way. To become stuck."

"So it's going to take another ten years for me to get unstuck?" I sob, unleashed.

"No, no," my therapist soothes me with her gentle voice. "But it will take time. We've only met a handful of times so far. I think we're making good headway though. You're making good headway."

Dr. Linda waits for my new gush of tears to subside to a leak.

I dab a handful of used tissues to my eyes, trying to breathe through shaky, residual sobs.

"I want you to work on the two new tools you've learned today, Matty. Mindful breathing…"

"Mindful breathing," I repeat, looking at my now tear-stained note.

"And Deserved Releasing."

I nod through yet another installment of tears, knowing how much I want to believe her yet also feeling how hard it is to really do so.

"Okay?" she says.

I continue to nod, like an obedient, sniffling little girl.

"Good. Now," Dr. Linda reaches for a book on the table and flips open her date calendar. "When's a good time for us to meet next week?"

CHAPTER FOUR

Toolbox Matty

I always feel like I'm paying a prostitute for her services when I pay Dr. Linda at the end of our sessions. By the time I've told her some of my most intimate secrets, I'm practically lying naked before her. Transparent. Vulnerable. With all that emotional release, I'm primed and ready, baring my soul.

And then, *bam!*

Our time is up.

I pull out my checkbook.

Then comes the aftermath. The exhaustion is totally mental, but after so much hidden information pulled out and examined in such a short time, my mind drunkenly wanders afterward, unsure of what to do with itself.

So enters Dr. Linda's prescribed therapeutic tools, including the first of her Post-it Notes stuck to my bathroom mirror.

Tool #1: Run.

"Run outside. Run on a treadmill. Doesn't matter. Just run," is what she had said after I mentioned that I used to run long distance. She explained that the physical exertion helps unjumble a tangled mess of a mind.

I hate to admit it, but despite my lack of drive to start up again, by the time October begins—and I've actually started running every day instead of occasionally—I start to feel the benefits of mental defragging. If I skip a run for a day or two, I feel a definite difference in clarity. I'm foggy again. Trancelike. And I can actually start to feel myself slide backwards ever so gradually, slipping right back into my damned autopilot of work-eat-sleep-survive.

Running helps me open up and sort through all those old boxes in my head. And I love it. When I get off the treadmill that I now have up in my studio apartment, I always feel lighter, as though I've released some weight that was holding me down for far too long.

The more I run, the more free I feel. The more free I feel, the more I want to run. And freedom, by the way, is intoxicating. Even if I can only manage a ten-minute jog, I do it.

I'd love to run outside, but I'm afraid it's not safe. Baltimore was the murder capital of the U.S. at one point in time. Besides, I'm alone. And let's not forget the main ingredient—I'm a woman. With breasts. Can't hide that fact, no matter how baggy my jogging shirt is or how many sports bras I strap myself into.

Today, I worked fourteen hours straight at this new receptionist gig I have. No lunch. No breaks. I sat for fourteen hours staring at a computer screen. I'm not even sure my legs work anymore.

Yet, after a quick throwdown of leftovers when I get home, I can't wait to get running. I strip out of my work clothes, pull on my sports bra of choice—navy blue today— and put on my running shorts with the lime-green trim. I hurriedly tie my running shoes and start pushing buttons until the treadmill starts to move.

With my turquoise water bottle filled and placed in the cup holder, I once again start to jog with the lovely bare brick wall in front of me. First, a warmup to loosen the muscles. Then I get to increase my speed with a simple push of a button, allowing me to fall effortlessly into a nice solid rhythm.

Thump, thump. Thump, thump.

Left foot down, breathe in. Left foot down, breathe out. Breathe in, breathe out.

Thump, thump. Thump, thump.

The combined rhythmic sounds of my shoes and my breathing soothe me into a meditative state. Pulling my arms through the air at a ninety-degree angle, I throw my hands behind me as though I'm pushing through water. For the first half mile, I focus only on my form, further quieting any mental restlessness that lingers.

Scenes of the ocean pass by in my mind. I can almost hear the surge of ocean waves as I run past them, leaving all behind.

Thump, thump. Thump, thump.

Of the four tools Dr. Linda's given me thus far, running is my favorite. The breathing technique she taught me seems easy enough, although not as enjoyable when you bring triggers into the picture. And I'm still working on the deserving-to-have-emotions and-reactions part, too.

But there is that number two tool that she gave me that I've been ignoring and have yet to stick to the mirror. *Tool #2: Paint.*

She instructed me to get back to it when I mentioned I hadn't picked up a paintbrush since I dropped out of art college. *Touch the brush, and let it bring you back,* or however she had said it. Only trouble is, even though I started to do as she told me—I bought a new canvas—I haven't touched it since I brought it home months ago.

Not that it would do any good since I don't own the proper paint anymore nor have any clue as to where my brushes are.

Thump, thump. Thump, thump.

Left foot down, breathe in. Left foot down, breathe out.

Breathe in, breathe out.

Thump, thump. Thump, thump.

I know I could purchase a new set of brushes to replace my lost ones, but I don't dare re-enter the art supply store after my canvas-shopping trip fiasco. Riding high on the fumes of Dr.-Linda-says I-should-do-it, I went straight to my old stomping ground—*The Art Supply*—the store across the street from the art college I went to when I first moved here. I hadn't thought I'd be walking back in time just by going into that store.

Thump, thump. Thump, thump.

"Oh! My! God!" I had heard someone yell the moment I walked in, and I instantly froze.

Dear Lord, I thought to myself. It's Linus Montgomery. His high-pitched squeal was unmistakable.

Linus and I had had a few classes together during my year at MICA: Maryland Institute College of Art. Although a lifetime ago, Linus looks as though he's been lifted out of a page in my history. He still wears his black hair straightened over his left eye, with the right side standing straight up, its spikes dyed like the feathers of a peacock.

Linus also knows more about me than the fluidity of my painting skills or my prowess with charcoal. So when he called me out the way he did that day, I afforded him a weak, no-eye-contact smile and made a beeline to where I knew the blank canvases were stored: down the crooked stairs and to the left.

Canvas in hand, I headed to the register, hoping against all hope that Linus wasn't there. But he was. Bounding out from behind the counter, he jumped up and down like a lovesick puppy and hugged me tight.

"Wow, Linus," I managed to say. "You haven't changed a bit."

"I wish I could say the same for you, girl." He stepped back and punched me playfully on the arm. "Looks like you've been swallowed up whole by a trash bin. What's this drab garbage you wearin'?"

I looked down at myself, dressed in wrinkled, oversized blah. "Work clothes. You know the deal," I said, trying to sound on top of my game. "Professional casual."

"Professional shit," he joked back, eyeing me for a moment. Then he took my canvas and returned back to his side of the counter. But the transaction was too short, and so he went back to his inquisition all too quickly.

"O.M.G. It's been so long. How was Europe?" he asked, leaning on the counter, batting his eyelashes at me like we used to play. "Tell Linus everything."

"Europe?"

"Yeah. That big land mass over the ocean. Or wherever it was that you disappeared to," he chattered on. "How was it? Everyone thought it was Europe. I said South America, but that's only because I knew you better."

"What? I didn't go anywhere."

"Girl, don't lie to your Li Li."

"Seriously. I didn't go anywhere. I've been here the whole time."

"Right," he said, rearranging a stack of handmade cards and absentmindedly playing with his hair. When I didn't respond, he looked up. "Here, here? Like you didn't go anywhere, here?"

I nodded my head yes. Saw his jaw pop open without taking in any air.

The look on his face made me want to drop into a ball and hide inside myself. Too many questions were coming, I just knew it.

"You're shitting me! It's been, like, years, Matty! Where the hell have you been?" he asked, his voice a near shriek. "No, no, you jokester. I haven't seen you around at all." He eyed me again for another moment, studying.

I felt my skin prickle, heating up under his scrutiny.

"Shut up. You left. I know you did. Where, Matty? Spill. It's me, Linus. You can tell me."

Except that's the thing. Linus was only a fun friend. I never told him anything other than what time I'd meet him for drinks after class. Blame it on moving around so much as a military brat, but I've never known anyone long enough to divulge all the secrets of my mind. I'm a master of withholding.

That and I don't really want to talk about the dark spots on my soul. Even with Claire, I still hold back.

"How's Chip?" I changed the subject to his boyfriend back in college. If memory served me right, Linus could go on for days about how horrible men were, never getting back to the elephant-in-the-room topics I never wanted to discuss.

"Oh, Chip-schmip. We've been over longtime, honey. He bailed, too, you know. Dropped out."

Shit, back to me. "So, with anyone now?"

"Na. No one new." He blew a breath at the hair draped over his left eye. "Guys aren't the way they used to be. Chivalry is dead, ya know? They only want one thing."

"Like you don't?" I joked, feeling our old camaraderie rekindle.

"Well," he smiled, his eyes daydreamy. "I'm not the only one, Miss Run Around."

Rekindled spark gone.

"Don't tell me you don't remember. I know I sure do. That's all anyone would ever talk about when you didn't come back."

"Ah, yeah… I've got to go," I said, grabbing the canvas and heading for the door in hopes of saving myself from an old avalanche of regrets. "Nice seeing ya again, Linus."

But Linus was swift. He hurdled the counter and wedged himself between me and my escape, leisurely counting off on his fingers, like it was a game I wanted to play.

"Let's see. There was Brayon. Alex. Juan."

Linus, the encyclopedia mind. God, help me, I pleaded. Please, don't let him go on.

When he didn't, forgetting one, I pushed past him and out the door.

"Wait! Give me your number. We should talk. Hang out like old times!" I heard him shout as the door closed too slowly behind me. "Call me!"

Thump, thump. Thump, thump.

I pound the treadmill harder. Push buttons to increase my speed. I need to run faster. Farther. I need to get away before all my stupidity catches up with me.

Thump, thump. Thump, thump.

I run on, wondering why I feel like I've lived so many lives inside my one. Then the answer comes to me.

Reinvention.

The siren curse of moving to a new location every few years, providing too many opportunities to let go and test out new skins of personality, then moving away before anyone can get to know the real you. Most every military brat benefits and suffers from the power of reinvention. Every new base assignment. Every new group of friends. The recurring chance to be a new version of you, over and over again.

After finding myself in Baltimore with Claire, I decided to do something I always dreamed about: art school. Once in and situated in my new skin, I consciously entered a permanent state of euphoric denial. I closed off all ties to my old self and got busy enjoying my new life. I tested into advanced art classes and breezed through prerequisites. Made friends, took on extra classes, invited people over to hang out on my rooftop deck overlooking the Baltimore city lights. My insatiable state of giddiness had everyone fooled, myself included.

By second year though, I was bored with my happy-go-luckiness. That and the flashbacks hadn't exactly stopped just because I ignored them. So I switched gears. Cut class to hang out with a new cast of friends. Drank till I passed out so I wouldn't think about anything. Popped pills and turned a blind eye to haunting and humiliating thoughts.

I only wanted to concentrate on the new me-myself-and-I, forgetting all the trips and dips of the past.

Soon, though, I went a little crazy. Overboard with my impulsivity is more like it.

One weekend, I decided to surprise Claire with a full wall mural of her favorite canal in Venice. Took me the long weekend she was away with Greg, her then boyfriend. Burst my bubble when she said she was moving out soon to get married.

Thump, thump. Thump, thump.

The night I got back from their wedding, I Jackson Pollocked my entire apartment. Blasted the place with paint splatters and drip puddles. Didn't care that the colors were heinous and didn't really go together. Didn't care that I got some on the windows, floors, ceiling, my clothes that were lying on the ground. I'd had no intention of painting before I saw the extra paint cans just sitting there in the hall from Claire's move. I just grabbed them and did it.

Although it looked helter-skelter, it felt great to go a little wild.

Find release.

Then there was Alex.

He was my first, by insanity. I rushed into sex with him as though I would implode if I didn't. There was no chemistry between us. I had no desire to date him. He just happened to be the only straight guy I hung out with in college. And, deep down, I knew I had something to prove.

I couldn't pin it down, but it was there, just waiting for an opportunity to pounce. To devour.

Linus left us alone one night for a beer run with his boyfriend. And I jumped Alex before he had a chance to think otherwise. Thanks to pain pills mixed with alcohol, I didn't feel a twinge of discomfort from sex. And that fueled me. Because of the endometriosis, I had never had sex before that didn't hurt like hell.

But Alex was a quickie. Couldn't last long enough for me to get a thrill in also. So I moved on.

To Juan.

A cold night in March, I found him sitting on the curb in the parking lot after a late-night art history class. Poor baby, his girlfriend had dumped him. Needless to say, he was an easy lay. In the backseat of my Bronco truck, I rode him like one. Darkness around, I couldn't see his face.

Fine with me. It wasn't about him. I didn't need to see who I was with. I was erasing the used-up feeling inside of me by using someone else.

Then, as I was about to feel my first ever burst of pleasure, I saw his face. The jackass's face.

Instantly nauseated, I almost threw up in Juan's mouth.

I sped home with that asshole's face haunting me, obscuring my view of the road. And I did throw up the moment I got into my apartment. Cried until I fell asleep.

Then I met Brayon.

Brayon was a bad-boy sculpture artist with the hands of a god. And not only did Brayon have the moves, he had the stamina. And keys to the kiln room, resulting in hot, sweaty, messy sex. But I could never orgasm. Always, my abuser's face lingered in the hot air next to mine, eyes approving.

Unable to ignore it—and nauseated every time I had to deal with it—I bolted. Started skipping the class Brayon and I had together so I could get rid of them both.

And move on to Tom.

Thankfully, no one, including Linus, knew about Tom. I didn't know much about Tom either. He was a transfer student at the end of spring semester. Fresh meat. A few minutes after I met him at a party, I pulled him aside and told him I wanted to get to know him better.

Now.

Showed him the hidden shadows of a rooftop haven. Thoroughly liquored up, my numbness kept my abuser's face from appearing in my mind. And finally, I was about to have my first climax ever. Only the strain of making sure it happened brought about a voice in my head.

It whispered a name to me.

His name.

Jett.

I immediately slammed my head into the brick wall behind me, hoping the pain would make it go away. But the voice wouldn't shut up. It kept repeating his name over and over again, keeping in time with Tom's efforts.

Jett. Jett. Jett. Jett.

I closed my eyes. Used the force of my eyelids to crush the very thought of Jett out of my brain. Banged my head against the wall again and again to relocate my focus.

When that didn't work, I opened my eyes wide and kept them strained on Tom's, forcing the sweet swell of pleasure to build up inside me. I wasn't about to lose it again. Not for that jackass.

Except my inebriated self couldn't sustain such a heightened level of concentration.

"Jett," I sighed his name out loud along with a shitty taste that caught in my mouth.

"Jett?" Tom stopped fucking me. "Who's Jett?"

I stiffened and swatted at his name like the dirty fat fly it was, never leaving me alone.

"What are you doing?" Tom asked, ducking so I didn't hit him.

"Come on, don't stop," I pleaded to Tom, annoyed he'd stopped. "What? You do know how to do this, don't you?"

Yanking off my top to reveal that I wasn't wearing a bra, I stuck Tom's face into the middle of my breasts. Got him back in the mood.

My back rubbed raw against the brick wall, but I didn't care. Anything to keep that face from appearing before my eyes or hearing his name repeat in my head, out of my mouth, into the air.

And it worked, but only for a minute. Then there it was again. A broken record, tripping me up. I tried to ignore it. Avoid it. Pretend it wasn't happening.

Jett. Jett. Jett. Jett.

Over and over again, his name read out in my mind like an endless tunnel into oblivion.

Jett. Jett. Jett. Jett.

Nausea swelled in the pit of my stomach, then swarmed to my brain, keeping me from feeling anything but vile.

You don't deserve this, it told me. *You'll never enjoy sex. You're not normal.*

I didn't want to believe it, but the sick self-loathing only adhered to me more. Unable to take it anymore, I pushed myself off Tom and fumbled my clothes back on.

He stumbled back, his pants around his ankles. "Hey! I wasn't done yet."

"Fuck off!" I yelled before slamming the roof door behind me.

From then on, the flashbacks came in tsunamis.

Jett ...

I couldn't get away from the images.

Jett...

I couldn't breathe without hearing his name.

Jett...

I couldn't even paint without seeing his face fall over the canvas. Everywhere I went, I felt him follow me. Everyone I met seemed to say his name amid normal conversation. His stupid name was everywhere.

Out of fear I was going crazy, I soon didn't leave my apartment. Ended up dropping out of all my classes and missing finals. Lost the scholarship that enabled me to go to MICA in the first place.

Embarrassed and, more importantly, knowing I didn't deserve to follow my passion, I never went back.

Lifetimes ago. From then on, my day-to-day consisted of staying above water at whatever work I could find, with little want for anything else.

Thump, thump. Thump, thump.

Work. Eat. Sleep. Survive: my monochromatic, autopilot life.

I look at the clock on the treadmill and push the button to stop, realizing I've been running for over two hours. Consumed by all that's been locked away inside my head, I barely feel like I've run at all. Yet the sweat rolling down my face, legs, and arms is a key indicator that

I have indeed run long and hard.

Good. I needed it.

I step back off the treadmill and trip over a moving box that's been sitting there for years, acting in place of a nightstand. I tumble and land hard on my ass with my leg resting up on top of the old, never-opened container.

That's when I take a look around. See the other boxes. Have a thought.

I need to get rid of this shit already.

CHAPTER FIVE

Merry Chrismas, Matty

"Okay!" I barge in unannounced, too excited to care about my manners.

"Miss Bell, what are you doing here? We just saw each other yesterday." Dr. Linda turns to check her December calendar, a worried look on her face.

"Yes, but—"

"And we don't have a scheduled time together for another two weeks."

"I know, I know, but I couldn't wait. I had to talk to you today. Now," I say, still standing near the opened door. I'm antsy. Cannot contain myself.

"Matty, I was just on my way out. You barging in here without an appointment isn't how our relationship of trust works," Dr. Linda says, folding her arms impatiently.

On any other day, this sort of body language would not only have discouraged me but also gotten me all worked up to spout a million apologies for being selfish, only to go home to worry myself into a knot.

But not today. I'm not feeling like my old, timid self after six months of Dr. Linda's therapy. Plus, I know what I have to do now.

"I'm going to do it," I say with the biggest smile, eyes wide.

"Do what?"

"I'm reporting it," I say, and my breath catches. "I'm reporting him." Saying it gives me such a lift of energy, I have to clasp my hands together to keep myself from clapping. Tears come to my eyes. Happy ones.

"Now, Matty," Dr. Linda says as she stands, grabbing her quilted purse to go. "I don't think you need to rush into anything just yet. We've only broken the surface with everything. If you jump the gun, you can derail your whole healing process."

"No," I say without thinking. Her logic isn't working for me today. "I don't think this is something I can sit on. I want to do this for me. It's all I've been able to think about all day."

"Alright, but this is something that is going to be difficult, and I don't think you're ready."

"I'm not asking permission, Dr. Linda."

My therapist looks at me and then asks a serious, "Then why are you here?"

I start and stop, unsure why it is I've barged in on my therapist. I take a breath first and then think, like she's been teaching me to do.

"I guess I just don't have anyone else to share this with," I acknowledge.

It's such a truthful verbalization that I almost start to cry at hearing myself say it out loud. I could tell Claire, but she's heard it all before. All this healing from the past stuff is old hat to her. I can see it in her eyes when they glaze over any time I bring it up.

"Well, Matty, I still think it's too soon," Dr. Linda repeats herself, but I can tell she knows it's no use.

"I don't," I say. "With almost fifteen years since it happened, and in a totally different country, I know there's really nothing the police can do, but that's not why I want to do it. I don't care about him. I care about me, and I need to do this. For me."

Dr. Linda's facial expression softens, and I can tell she sees me differently. I know I'm feeling different. In a good way. Great way.

"I just needed to tell you."

She nods. "Well then. I don't agree with you doing it so soon in your recovery, but if it's what you want, then I'm in your corner, Matty. Good luck."

I contain my jubilation long enough to give her a hug, run down the stairwell, climb into my truck, and buckle up.

"Yes!" I yell, releasing my joy. I dig for my cell phone in my bag and dial the number to the local police, fingers shaking.

"Baltimore Police Department. State your emergency," a female voice says.

"Oh, no. No emergency," I say as I fumble with my mental notes, starting to feel silly all too soon. "I just want to report something," I say vaguely.

In the very next moment, I'm second-guessing myself and wonder if I should just forget it and hang up.

"Hold one moment, please. I'll transfer you to the officer on duty." There's a click and a pick up on the other end before my self-doubt has a chance to completely compute. And then a man's steady voice asks me what he can help me with.

I decide not to think, but to just do. Just do it, Matty.

"I'd like to report a rape." The power of those words propels me forward in mind, body, and spirit.

"Are you in danger? Do you need medical assistance?"

"No. I'm not in any danger," I say and stop, once again feeling stupid for calling.

"Are you calling for someone else? Do they need help?"

An imaginary lineup of all the girls and women in the past week who have just lived through this horrible event—who have just been sexually assaulted—conjures up in my mind, and I feel like a heel. Unlike them, I'm in no real danger now. No pain. I'm just being selfish in my healing and wanting to cleanse myself of this by taking up someone else's valuable time with something neither they nor I can do anything about now.

"I'm sorry, officer. I'm in no danger now. This happened," I swallow hard, "a long time ago."

I wait for him to berate me. When he doesn't say anything, I feel my confidence creep back again after all. "I know there's nothing that can be done about it, but—" *just spit it out, Matty!* "I want to report a rape that happened fourteen and a half years ago."

"Okay. May I have your name, please?"

I look around the empty parking lot and take a deep breath.

"Matilda Bell. Matty, for short," I say and slap myself silly on the forehead. As if he cares what my nickname is.

Don't change the subject, I berate myself. *Forward motion only.*

"I was sixteen when it happened, and I know it's been a long time and nothing can be done about it now, but I just needed to report it. For me,"

That mantra is the only thing keeping me safeguarded from what

I'm sure will be his immediate reaction: *Look lady, it's too late to report it now*. Or maybe even: *This really isn't a police matter, lady. Call a shrink*.

Only, I already see one on a regular basis. Which, I suppose, means I must be truly crazy.

"Well, Matilda Bell—Matty," he starts, and I hold my breath, my finger poised and ready to end the call. "I wish more women were strong like you. It doesn't matter how long it's been. Reporting a rape is the most important thing you can do, and I'm proud of you for making the right decision to call me today."

I blow out my breath with the force of disbelief. Strong? Proud? These two words stand out and repeat themselves in my head.

"Really?" Stunned, I don't know what else to say.

"Absolutely. I wish more women would come forward and report. Even if it happened three years ago—thirty years ago, even—it's very important to report rape. How else can we get these perpetrators off the streets? Besides, it's necessary to report it for the healing process. To heal from your trauma. You did a good job in calling, Matty. Thank you."

"You're welcome," I say with a growing smile that shines out through the front windshield. I shiver from both the excitement of reporting and the winter chill in my truck. Turn the key in the ignition. "Thank you for your time, officer," I say as the engine rumbles to life. A sense of finality washes over me.

"Oh, we're not done yet, Miss Bell. I need to get some information from you first."

"Oh, duh," I say and reach to kill the engine but decide against it. Although just a machine, I feel a little less alone with her on. I had come to Dr. Linda's office with the half-crazed notion that she'd be just as excited about my decision and want me to report it in her office, with her. But as it is, alone in my truck in uptown Baltimore with snow falling all around on this midweek, dusky, December day, I'm left to chatter away my nervousness with the officer on duty.

He asks questions. I give him answers.

Where did it happen? On a military base in Italy.

Who raped you? My boyfriend at the time.

Acquaintance rape? I guess. Yes.

How old were you? It was my sixteenth birthday.

He? Seventeen, I believe.

His name? I stall. Feel nauseated.

His name? I can't say it.

Can you spell it? J-e-t-t-i-s-o-n F-i-s-h-e-r.

I give the officer all the information he needs after that, no longer holding back. I don't want to, anyway. Letting it all flow out of me to this safe person feels like a godsend. A gift. Like I'm finally doing something that I was robbed of doing so many years ago.

I shake my head clear. Forget all the finger-pointing blame. Forget dwelling on everything I can't change from the past. Forget other people's reactions and avoidance.

This is my trauma. My experience. My healing. I'm not doing this to prove anything to anyone. I'm doing this for me.

And I'm proud of myself, too. That in itself is a gift.

Merry Christmas, Matty.

"Now, moving on to today. Are you in any danger from Mr. Fisher now?"

"No, I don't think so. Although he did say more than once that he'd kill me and hurt my family if I ever left him. But that was years ago, and he doesn't live anywhere near me now. Last I knew, he was living in Ohio."

"And that's not where the rapes occurred?"

"No, they happened overseas, in Naples, Italy. The base where it happened is closed now, otherwise I would have called the military police."

I had looked online for that information first, only to find out there was no one to call.

"Huh," the officer says. "Well, Ms. Bell. I thank you again for reporting. Like I said, it's a very good thing for you to have done so, and I commend you for your bravery. I know this must have been hard for you, going through all the details."

Hard, yet liberating, I think and exhale, the air in the cab of my truck finally warmed enough that I no longer see it.

"From what you've reported, I understand your assailant was a civilian, like yourself. Unfortunately, since this happened on a military installation overseas and on a base that is now closed, I think you will need to call the military police on the nearest military base to further the investigation. I only have jurisdiction for Baltimore City."

"Oh, I see," I say, my victory party coming to a halt. "Do you have a number I can call?"

When he gives me it, I thank him for that and his time before hearing once more how proud he is of me. This time, I can't help but cringe.

Running out of gas and daylight, and with a new installment of snow starting to flurry down, I drive home and dash up the stairs to my apartment, locking the door behind me.

From there, I steady myself on the couch. Do Dr. Linda's breathing exercise to calm my nerves. Center myself. I'm not sure I want to make another call and do it all over again, but to turn back now would only be suicide to my healing.

The number the police officer gave me is the local Army base's main line. Automated. When it doesn't transfer me to the correct location after the third time, I punch in zero for the operator, who sounds all too perturbed to be bothered to do her job. But she does give me the military police's number. Tells me to look at the base's website next time for direct lines. Cuts off my "thank you" with a click, transferring me immediately.

Army.

I cut my eye roll short when my phone call is answered. My heart races.

"I know this has been difficult for you to do, Miss Bell. I thank you for your bravery in reporting today," the military police officer says after I've gone through my story, and I'm floored for the second time in a day. More so this time than the last.

He sounds heartfelt and sincere. Yet I've only ever known MPs to be harsh and direct.

"What would you like to do from here?" he asks.

"What are my options?" I search my mind. "I figured since it happened so long ago, I wouldn't have any."

"Actually, you have a few options. Rape is in a category all of its own. A victim has eighteen years in which to report the occurrence. It would be on Mr. Fisher's permanent record and would help with any future cases should it happen again."

"Or if it happened in the past?"

"Yes. If he already has charges against him but, for whatever reason, that case didn't go to trial due to lack of evidence, the addition of yours would bring about justice for the victim. In that case, we would be dealing with a serial rapist. Not just acquaintance rape."

A sharp, queasy feeling rises up in me at the thought that he might have done this to someone else. Or that he could still be doing it. Knowing what I know about him, and what he's said and done to me, I don't have any doubt that could be the case.

Zero respect. Zero empathy.

"Now, you said he was seventeen at the time. Good news. Seventeen is not considered a minor. Are you thinking of pressing charges against Mr. Fisher?"

I imagine a courtroom with him in it and waver.

"No. I don't want to see him. I just want to get this reported and on file. I guess, on his record. In case there is another woman out there that could use my help in reporting him. Or child, for that matter," I say, nauseous at the thought.

"Okay." I hear typing and a long "hmmm" similar in tone to the one I just heard from the previous officer.

Dread rolls over me.

"Unfortunately, since you were both dependents, neither one of you lives on the exact military installation it happened on, and neither of you are involved with the military in any way, I'm afraid this is not my jurisdiction. I think your best bet would be to call the Maryland State Police and report it there."

Not my jurisdiction. I let go of the breath I've been holding. I use the one lead I have. Something Claire mentioned once long ago.

"I heard a while back that he was in the Marines," I say.

"Well, if he still is, then I can help you. If he's no longer active duty, you'll have to contact the civilian police. If you'd like to proceed, we'll have to locate him first."

I spell out Jett's full name and last known address.

"Ms. Bell," he tells me after I do. "One more thing. Take this name and number down. It's our liaison contact at the Naval Academy down in Annapolis. If he's Marines, then it's a Navy matter. The Marines are a subsector of the Navy."

I drop my head into my hand. The Navy. I'm a Navy brat! We were living on a naval base. His dad is Navy. My dad is Navy.

Why hadn't I thought to call the Navy instead of going through the civilian police first, and now the Army? I don't need Dr. Linda to tell me it's probably due to some subconscious mental block thing. More crap I have to work through, no doubt.

"Call her and give her his name and his last known location. She might be able to track him down. She's also a lawyer, so you might ask her for some legal advice while you have her on the phone."

"Oh," I say with a bit of nervousness. A lawyer.

"Ask her what your options might be at this point since the crime occurred so long ago."

"Okay…" *Crime.* New chills run along my skin. Scared ones. "Thank you. Thank you for everything."

Jitters follow me everywhere over the next few weeks after talking to the naval lawyer. Even more sympathetic than the male officers I spoke with—at one point, she choked up during my retelling—she vowed to help as much as she could.

The Marines don't put up with this kind of behavior, she said. If he's active duty and this is put on his record, he'll more than likely be discharged. Dishonorable discharge.

Unfortunately, after three months of waiting to hear from her, all I hear in the end is, "Sorry."

"Sorry, Ms. Bell. No one can locate him. Not the Navy. Not the Marines. Not the civilian police. No one. And charges can't be placed without a person."

CHAPTER SIX

One Last Breath

As I'm turning a stray strand of blonde hair around my fingertip and playing with my flipflops on my feet, a name pops into my head and I smile. Gabe, my skater boy.

My first kiss. My high school sweetheart. Maybe even my first love.

Unfortunately, there hasn't been anyone since Gabe who's tugged at my insides the way he did back then. None of the guys I hooked up with in college ever came close. Maybe that's why I've had him on my mind lately, the thought of him taking me on a much-needed mental vacation.

I do need the escapism. Sitting in the all-too-familiar waiting room for the umpteenth time in almost a year has my stomach in knots.

No, not knots. Butterflies, ever since last week's session.

That's when Dr. Linda finally asked me if I wanted to talk about it—the rapes—and I finally went into full detail. The release of all that held-down trauma has left me in a state of unquenchable restlessness. Heart pounding, mind racing, I feel both emotionally cornered and freed all at the same time.

I fix my gaze and all my energies on the door, willing it to open, but it's no use. It doesn't budge. Dr. Linda is incredibly attentive to her clients. If necessary, she'll go over the allotted session time. I know that to be true because she's done it for me several times.

Finally, the doorknob moves and I'm up, standing at the door before it's open. Dr. Linda greets me with her standard candid smile and hello before returning to her old wooden desk. I take my usual spot and, just like every other time, my tense body relaxes. This is a safe place—although the box of tissues reminds me it's also a painful one.

But not today. Today I feel something else. Exactly what though, I'm hoping Dr. Linda can help me describe. No longer beaten down by all the post-traumatic daze of living my life as a survivor, I've started to feel more and more like I'm beyond that. Like I'm almost thriving.

"So how are you doing this week?" Dr. Linda's voice interrupts my internal monologue.

"Great," I reply with a smile and then sigh.

It's my typical response, even when things were at their worst. No matter that the circumstances are bad, my life boring as hell, or I feel like I'm falling apart inside, I always reply with, "Great."

"Okay," Dr. Linda says as she sits opposite me. Crossing her long legs and laying her hands gently on her lap, she asks, "Is this a real 'great' or a classic Matty 'great?'"

I don't respond instantly like I used to. After all, Dr. Linda has taught me the importance and benefit of thinking before I speak.

"It's much easier to spit out a canned response," she's said, "than it is to think of an actual answer of what you really feel like inside."

Stomach butterflies quieting to a small fury, I sit back, take a deep breath, and contemplate.

"Yes, actually, it is a real 'great,'" I say. "How are you doing this week, Dr. Linda?"

"I'm doing okay. A little stiff from all this sitting," she smiles. "But thank you for asking.

So..." she introspects aloud while nodding her head. "This is an actual 'great.' That's wonderful. I'm happy for you." She pauses before adding, smile subsiding, "It's a far cry from where you were last week. Can you tell me a little about what's happened since then that's brought about this change?"

God. Last week.

To say I was a mess last week would be the understatement of my life. There weren't enough tissues in the box to dry all the tears from that session. Having spent so many months conversing about everything in the here and now, bringing my focus out of the past and into the present, Dr. Linda caught me off guard when she asked me to talk about being raped. If it weren't for the trust I'd formed over the past year—not only with her but also with myself—last week would never have resulted in such a cathartic event.

"I needed that," I say. "I have been over the details so many times in my head since I remembered, after mentally blocking it out— repressing the memory, as you say. But not like last week. Not like that."

"Not like what?" Dr. Linda asks, more of a statement than a question.

I uncross my jeaned legs and lay my hands on my thighs, tissue ready in hand.

"Before, when I would dwell on it—him, my sister, my mother, all of it—I felt as though it were happening to me over and over. All the time. Even when I tried to avoid thinking about it, I still managed to relive it somehow, some way. Probably because I had yet to identify my triggers."

Triggers. Like the mention of his name by a passing stranger, seeing a solitary man on an empty street, or hearing of someone else becoming a victim. Hence I never watch the news.

"But last week," I continue, "as I went into more detail than I ever have with anyone else, I felt somehow separated from it all. Like I know it happened to me but, for some reason, it finally didn't feel like it was happening to me all over again. It didn't feel like that big of a deal anymore."

"Rape is always a big deal, Matty."

"Yes, I know. I know. It was like I knew that. Yet at the same time... I no longer felt like it was happening to me. Does that make any sense?"

"Like something you lived through in the past but are no longer living through in the present?"

"Exactly!" I say, excited to feel the mental separation from it all. I blow out a breath of release. "Although..." My smile fades. I take a moment contemplating how best to say what's on my mind.

"Something else?"

"Well, actually, there's one final thing I need to talk about, only I'm not sure how to make sense of it."

Dr. Linda sits patiently, the look in her brown eyes and worn-yet-warm face seems to say one final time, You trust me, now trust yourself.

I close my eyes. Focus.

"During last week's session," I begin slowly, "I noticed something I hadn't quite noticed before. I mean, I've always felt it, but I didn't realize what it was until last week."

I fidget a bit from nervousness, but the calm, understanding expression on Dr. Linda's face reminds me that I'm in good hands.

Taking in a quick, full breath, I relax and let go. "As I talked to you about it, about what he did to me, about blacking out, about walking home afterward, everything... I felt like there was someone else with us in the room. Like a presence."

"A ghost?"

"No, not exactly," I say, allowing myself to feel a second of foolishness, then releasing it.

It's not foolish, I tell myself. I felt it. It was real.

"No, not a ghost. It was me." I close my eyes. Find the right words. "It was my old self. Me when I was sixteen."

When my therapist doesn't look at me puzzled and instead simply sits and listens, I take in another cleansing breath and press on. It doesn't matter to me anymore that, by speaking the truth of what's really on my mind, I might be prescribed a dose of crazy pills.

I need to talk. Talking is healthy.

"I felt like I, well, she... like she was actually here, standing behind me. And I had this vivid image of her walking home from that first time on my sixteenth birthday. I remember right after he said *'she said you'd do it'*, I felt myself fly up out of my body. I was on the ceiling, away from what was happening to me below. Then blackness."

I inhale and exhale again. "And then, all of a sudden, I was walking home, alone, and didn't even realize I was walking until I was halfway home. Thank God, I was dressed," I say, more to myself than to Dr. Linda.

I take another breath. Press on. "Last week, I realized something. She—me—we've been stranded in time ever since then. Walking, walking, walking. Never making it home."

I hold the tissue to my eye, soaking up a tear for that girl. "I've always felt a heaviness around me all these years since then, like something weighing me down. And last week, I realized it's been her this whole time. Her weight with me. Following me around for the past almost fifteen years."

"That's a long time," Dr. Linda sympathizes.

Nodding silently, I feel a surge of empathy and compassion come up through me like a gust of wind.

"And now that girl?" I say, standing up and turning to look at the empty space behind my chair. "She's gone. That heaviness I've always felt with me is gone," I say, happy for her. "I feel like she finally made it home. Like we finally made it home."

Finally, at peace.

Dr. Linda nods and smiles in her way, and I sit down and breathe deeply and peacefully. I start to feel a brilliant lightness shine through me. Like a smile at the middle of my being, warm, beaming up through my skin.

"Dr. Linda," I say, slowly, shaking my head from side to side, my smile increasing tenfold. It grows stronger, and I feel it inside and out.

"What?"

"I... Oh, my God, this is so odd."

"Yes?" Dr. Linda asks with a half-humored smile of her own.

"This is so weird." I smile some more, still shaking my head in disbelief. I feel it so definitively, I can't deny it anymore. "I'm fine."

A single tear slips down my face, its coolness gliding down my cheek and dripping off onto my lap.

"Good."

"But how can that be?" I question with a bit of uncertainty, only to test the new feeling. "I've been at this, trying to get over this, for so long. And now, all of a sudden, I'm fine? How?"

She looks at me with her unique, steadfast compassion, as though she can view human nature from far above the chaos and know wherein lies the peace, enjoying the moments when we humans finally find it for ourselves.

She motions for me to continue.

"I came here almost a full year ago—I mean, it's May, for crying out loud. And I felt so frustrated and infuriated and drowned and broken... and now, all of a sudden, I'm fine?"

"Give yourself some credit here, Matty. You've come a long way," Dr. Linda starts, leaning forward in her chair. "Think about exactly how far you've come, not forgetting all that you've learned. You know how to do this."

She pats my knee. "It doesn't need to make sense right this moment. Why? Because you have all the tools in you now. We started at the beginning, working our way up to where you are today. And all the while, you were learning how to help yourself. How to empower yourself with your own methods of self-ascertainment. How to find a problem and deal with it. And, then, how to be done with it.

"You know how to do it, Matty. You have the tools," Dr. Linda continues, teeming with self-brilliance. "And you have the confidence, too. I can see that in you today. You look different. Sound different."

"I feel different," I say, more to myself than to her. Hearing myself repeat it solidifies it even further. This gives me a much needed punch of self-confidence. She's right. This release has been a long time coming.

"Remember, healing is a process," Dr. Linda says. "One last tool: a mantra I use all the time. You can say this either in your head or out loud any time you feel you need to or want to. Take a deep breath—"

"You and the breathing," I joke, and we laugh together, reminiscing about old times.

Dr. Linda tilts her head to the side and raises an eyebrow, waiting for me.

"Okay, okay," I say and relax again.

She sits in silence for a moment, then imparts her healing mantra. "I have faith that healing is a process. I have faith that God cares about me. I have faith in my own power."

I like the sound of it, so I let go, accepting the fact that I feel a bit foolish saying it out loud to her. But that's totally human. And it's okay to feel human. I take in a deep breath, slowly release it, and take a moment to think, feel.

I recite, "I have faith that healing is a process. I have faith that God cares about me. I have faith in my own power." I feel another shift inside.

"There you go." Dr. Linda's face registers that she too sees the difference I feel. "Sometimes it feels like God doesn't care, but God-the-Creator, the universe, the divine energy flowing through and all around us does, in fact, care. Sometimes we want to heal right now and be done with it, but healing is a journey: a process. And we have to have faith in ourselves that we can endure or we'll never reach our destination. Thankfully, we all have the power in us to persevere. To learn. To heal."

She coaxes me to say the mantra again. And again. Each time, I find courage to let go more and more. And each time, I feel more at peace with the journey I've set myself on.

"I think I'm done here," I say. A calm fills my insides.

"I think you are."

Done. The word rolls over in my mind. "Can I call you if I ever need to?" I ask.

I know I probably won't need to, but it feels odd having had such a close relationship end abruptly. Call it transference, I don't care. I see Dr. Linda as a friend, someone who has been there for me when I needed someone the most.

"Sure you can," Dr. Linda says cheerily as she gets up and opens the door. "But you won't need to."

"No, I won't," I add confidently with a smile, feeling a massive shift, this one almost mechanical, as though my physical, mental, and spiritual selves bind together for the first time, totally in the present.

Not only does it feel good. It feels real. Like I am real.

And I haven't felt real in a long, long time.

CHAPTER SEVEN

Be The Change

On a beautiful morning in June, my cell phone rings, waking me up. Sleepy-eyed and groggy, I sit up and blink against the painful sunlight blaring in through my windows, my brain slow to come back online.

Sunny.

I wobble-walk over to the couch where I last flung my bag. Attempt to find my ringing cell phone without dumping everything out. After no such luck, I hang the bag upside down and watch all the junk fall out—crumpled papers, hair clips, and loose change roll off the couch and onto the floor.

Sunny.

Phone.

Which stops ringing. Hands still asleep, I use half-numb thumbs to unlock it. Stop short when my brain finally catches up with my single-word-morning-vocabulary.

Sunny.

Phone.

Work.

I'm late for work.

I check the time on my cell phone. It's ten o'clock.

"Shit!"

I scramble to full awareness and toss on the first pair of pants and shirt I find, forgetting that I wore them to work yesterday. I do a quick mouthwash gargle while I twist up my hair in a knot, spit, and clunk into my shoes. Grab my phone, unlock my door.

"Shit, shit, shit!"

I worry up a sweat as I hurl myself down the stairs, through the front door, and into my truck. It won't start.

I hear my phone ding, indicating that someone's left me a text message. I fish for it in my bag, knowing this is it—I'll be fired for sure. And just when I got myself back together again.

Only all worry evaporates the moment I read the message. It's from Claire: *Going to the birth center. Wish me luck!*

"Birth center? Wish me luck?" I say dumbly into the air of my cab. Did I miss Claire mentioning she was having another baby? True, last time I saw her she did seem a bit off. Unfocused, distractible. So unlike Claire. Elusive, too. But that was just a few weeks ago. She wouldn't just text me that she's pregnant. She doesn't do impersonal.

Then I remember. She's always felt uneasy telling me she's having another baby.

"Here I am popping them out left and right and you can't have any," she'd say, upset.

"It's okay, Claire," I'd lie, hiding my sorrow behind a perfect smile. "I get to watch your little ones grow up."

I call into work, apologize for being late—again—and walk back up to my apartment, not caring that I just got fired. No. Instead I'm thinking back to when my doctor told me I'd never have any children of my own. I was eighteen and had just had surgery to find the source of the mysterious pain that later was diagnosed as endometriosis.

"Good news, Ms. Bell," the doctor had said, snapping off his gloves after doing my post-op gynecological exam. "You're healing well. Not too much tenderness. That's good."

Although the word good came out of his mouth twice in one breath, I didn't see the same thought painted on his face.

"But?"

"But," he said as he sat on his stool while I righted myself on the examination table, adjusting the paper sheet to cover myself. "There was a lot of scar tissue from the endometriosis. I tried to remove and cauterize what I could, but removing scar tissue just makes for more scar tissue in the future. And there were many, many adhesions. Most of which have twisted and corrupted the tubes and ovaries."

"Okay," I had said, conjuring up a mental image of my internal anatomy.

"I'm sorry, Ms. Bell. We did what we could, but there was no reversing the damage that had already been done. I'm sorry."

Sorry.

That one little word means so much yet seems so small, so insignificant, to bear the weight it always delivers.

Another baby. Claire, my friend, is going to have another baby. Well, maybe. And maybe, if I'm lucky, I'll get to watch him or her grow up, occasionally even in my arms. I take a deep breath and send a silent prayer out to my friend for the good luck she wants from me.

As soon as I flop my bag back onto its spot on the couch, kick off my shoes, and strip out of my wrinkled business attire and back into my pajamas, an excited grin starts to pull at the corners of my mouth.

I change into my turquoise sports bra and black running shorts with the burnt-sienna trim.

After a few warmup stretches, I step onto my treadmill and run. But I start to feel antsy anyway.

Picking up speed, I breathe out the uneasiness and clear my mind of anything and everything. Except that an insistent irritation builds inside my mind and stays strong, even after my first mile. I focus on the sound of my shoes hitting the treadmill. Try to empty my mind.

But that's just it. It's empty. No longer filled with the task of sorting out emotions and making sense of them, my mind is bored. And it should be. There's no breeze here. No view. Just a bare brick wall, splattered here and there with old, crummy paint colors.

Do something! the impatience screams out loud in my head, and I stop the treadmill.

"Do what?" I ask, flabbergasted, then laugh at myself. This isn't how it works. The voice, as Dr. Linda postulated, is simply my subconscious speaking out to me. Pointing me in the right direction.

I just wish it would be more precise.

Stepping off the treadmill, I almost slip on a pile of papers that's next to another pile of boxes next to a pile of clothes. Dirty? Clean? Honestly, I have no idea.

Mess. That one word describes my life. No. Wait. Described my life. I'm no longer a mess inside. Though, looking around, I can see I wasn't only living with an internal mess. The chaos has also stretched over every inch of my external life.

"So I need to do something about it, right?" I ask myself out loud. My internal agitation simmers down with a satiated smile, and I get the hint.

And then get to work.

Piles of paper of unknown relevance go into trash bags for

recycling. Clothes on the floor are tossed down the steps to the second-floor laundry room to be washed. Bed sheets follow, as do all the cushion covers from the couch. Maybe a miracle will happen, and they'll stop being itchy if I wash them with a full bottle of fabric softener.

I move my bed away from the wall, clean under it. Pull out the couch, clean behind it. Cobwebs, garbage, piles of junk I don't even remember acquiring: disgusting mess after disgusting mess. I can't believe I haven't invited a rodent or bug infestation by now.

"This is so not me," I keep saying each and every time I find something new and revolting. I can't believe how lost I was. Thank God, I've been found.

I clean the kitchenette and bathroom. Open my closet. Start dragging the boxes out. I'd put some of them on the closet floor after that one fell on my head last summer. Now I line them up in the middle of the room. Uncover the three in front of the couch that have served as my coffee table. And the one next to my bed that's been my nightstand for almost eleven years now.

Opening the first one, I rip into it with such exuberance I almost tear into its contents. Stuffed animals and other odds and ends. I unpack the box and set everything out on the hardwood floor. Seeing nothing of significance, I repack it and set it by my door.

I open box after box after box. Old knick-knacks, papers, some clothes. Outside of a few things collected while living in Japan, Italy, Mississippi, and the nicer mementos my dad brought back from his other worldly travels, not much else is worth keeping. I set aside what I want to keep and place the repacked boxes with the growing pile near the door.

I stand and think.

"There's a consignment shop," I say aloud, remembering the

storefront I pass every day on my way to work. It's a few blocks up, near the art college.

I go into the closet to find something to change into. Only, back in the closet, there's nothing but polyester black slacks, baggy shorts, bland t-shirts, and ugly-ass shoes strewn about. I push through it all, looking for something with a little life to it.

Nothing.

"Nope. This won't do either," I tell myself on my way to the kitchen. "We're not dead inside anymore. You're done looking like a zombie, Matty Bell."

I grab a handful of garbage bags and head back into the closet, stuffing them full, hangers and all. Soon I have six trash bags full of clothes, shoes, and other whatnot that have fallen prey to my purging party. I drag them, one by one, like dead bodies, down the stairs and to my front door. And, after a great deal of effort and sweat, I have everything packed up in the back of my Bronco.

I put the key into the ignition and turn it. Nothing happens.

I turn it again.

"Come on, old girl. You can do it," I say to my truck as I try a third time.

This time, the engine turns on, and I make a mental note to take her in for the tune-up I've been promising her.

Driving up a few blocks, I pull around back to the alleyway behind the consignment shop. Having passed it for years and watched how Claire consigns her children's clothes and toys, I know how it's done. Bring in items you no longer want, the consignment shop sells them, and you get a percentage of the sale. Whatever doesn't sell, you can either pick up at the end of a certain time period or just leave it, in which case the store keeps all the sales.

I don't need the cash from consigning my things since I have some money saved up. And, from the look of the place—the sign reading "Ri hteous R peats Consign ent S op"—it's apparent the store could use the extra cash.

Sweat forms on my skin as I heave the bags and boxes from the back of my truck. Looking at the small mountain piled next to the shop's back door, I feel the weight of my past life dissipate into the June air. I tell the woman who comes out back that I'd like to donate everything. I help her bring it all into the store and accept my tax-deductible donation receipt.

Feeling lightened and relieved, I head back to my truck. That's when I see him, his peacock hair impossible to ignore.

Linus Montgomery.

"Hey, you!" I yell at the top of my voice, running to catch him. Out on the main drag, walking fast, he's about to cross the street.

I yell his name. "Linus!"

Mid-step, he turns around and sees me. "Matty?"

"Linus, wow. How are you?" I say, jogging up to him. I feel a big smile spread across my face.

He greets me with a half-smile. "Well, well. If it isn't the elusive Matty Bell," Linus says. "Are you really here or are you going to break my heart and disappear again like you did in my shop last summer?"

Unable to find the right words to explain myself, my actions, my past, I realize I'm holding my breath. I let go and breathe.

"Sorry about that," I say with a shrug. "I was kind of… stuck in a closet."

Linus's eyebrows spike up with interest.

"Not that kind of closet." I punch his arm in jest.

"No?" Linus asks, contemplating. "Then what kind of closet?"

I blow out a puff of air. Search for the right words. "A closet of my own making."

Linus nods. "Huh. And now you're out?"

"Yes, thank God," I say with a big, bright smile, realizing how true a statement that really is. "How have you been?"

"Been okay. Same ol' stuff." Linus checks me out with a mischievous smile. "But look at you, all sweaty. Been running?"

I peer down at myself. Caught up in the excitement of the purge, I forgot to change. I'm still in my running shorts and bra, and not exactly sure how I feel about being so exposed. "Kind of. Where you heading to?"

"Lunch. Had to fix an early-morning tragedy at the shop." He hitches his head in the direction of his storefront, his colorful spiking tower of hair unmoving. "No time for breakfast. Now I'm starved."

"Me, too," I say, finding a common thread. I blurt out, "Wanna do lunch together? It would be great to catch up."

Linus is a few seconds in responding, considering me with all the seriousness one with a tower of rainbow hair can.

"Wow, girl. I don't know what you did, but I like it."

"Huh?"

"You know what I mean," Linus says, cocking his face behind one shoulder, batting his eye lashes at me, his body language reminiscent of the way we used to toy with each other back in college.

I try on my old habit and flirt back with lowered eyelashes and a tilt of my head, delighting in the fun again. "No, I don't. Tell me."

Linus's eyes brighten, and he shouts out, "O.M.G! This is the Matty I remember," as he pulls me into a hug, forgetting my sweaty mess. "You're back!"

I smile to myself in his arms. No. I'm better than back.

"Wanna do lunch?" I ask again after he steps back. "I just have to go home and shower first. Promise I'm quick."

Excited, Linus walks back with me and climbs into my truck, his hair poking the ceiling. "I cannot believe you still drive this thing."

"Don't diss my girl. I love her."

"Oh, no. No dissin' meant." Linus buckles, trying not to touch the belt too much. He adds a sheepish smile, "Smells the same as it did back in college."

At my door, I'm a few minutes finding my keys, the endless junk in my bag getting in the way.

"You're next," I say to my bag, sentencing it to my next purging rampage.

"I'm what?" Linus asks from beside me.

"Oh, sorry. Nothing. Don't mind me," I say as I find my keys and unlock the door.

Once inside, I take my worn path to the stairwell and start to climb the stairs. But when Linus doesn't follow, I turn back to see him standing in the middle of the empty living room, dust slowly dancing in the air around him.

"Coming?" I ask.

"Is this your place?" he asks, a worried tone to his voice.

"No, I live upstairs. This used to be Claire's. My friend. Remember her?"

"Yeah. Met her once," Linus says, eyeing the emptiness as he passes it. On the empty second floor, he stops again. "This isn't yours either?"

"Still Claire's. Well, used to be."

"Did she just move out?"

"Oh, no. She moved out years ago," I answer, making my way up only to realize that Linus isn't behind me again. "You coming or not?" I call down the stairs.

Linus is a few seconds in following.

Unlocking the door to my top floor, I take a tentative Linus by the hand and bring him up into my place. Once inside, I lock the door behind us, drop my bag to the floor, and make my way to the bathroom.

"I'll just be a few minutes. Make yourself comfortable on the couch if you want. The cushions are a little damp, but they're clean. I just washed them!" I say with a proud smile.

I make a pit stop in the closet to find something to change into. No longer hidden behind a forgotten mess, I find my favorite, long-lost flip-flops I wore the day I left California.

"I've been looking for you," I tell them, picking up the pair.

Standing, I see a pair of jean shorts I forgot I had along with a paint-spattered aqua tank top I used to wear back in college. I grab it, knowing how well it brings out the sea hues in my green eyes.

On my way back into the bathroom, I see Linus still standing like a statue near the door.

"Dude, are you coming in or what?" I ask, laughing.

The look on his face is an odd mixture of fear and befuddlement.

"You're not going to kill me, are you?"

"What?"

"You're not, are you? Cause if you are, I've got lots of stuff to do first."

Dumbfounded, I shake my head. "What are you talking about?"

"Matty…" Linus looks at the mess.

"Oh. I was just spring cleaning before I ran out. It doesn't always look like this," I lie, starting to feel his unease.

"And what about," Linus says, turning to point downstairs, "all that empty space. Empty? For years? And here you are, cramped up here in this, this…"

"What? This is where I live. What's wrong with it?"

Linus holds my gaze with unspoken concern and, in an instant, I see everything through his eyes: two floors of vacant space gone to dust under me while here I am, closed up with my paint-splattered walls.

I see what he sees now. It looks crazy.

"Linus," I say, embarrassed. "I…"

"Sorry, hon," he says with his hand on the doorknob. "I'm outie." Sure enough, he starts to leave.

"Oh, no! Please, don't go," I say, darting toward him only to trip over a lamp I left lying on the floor.

Linus rushes to my side and helps me up.

"Please, don't go. Please. I'm fine. Really. I know what it looks like," I acknowledge as I look around, seeing my place with new eyes. "This is part of it."

"Part of what?"

"My closet," I say, rubbing my knee.

I stop short of explaining myself. Yet here is Linus, a friend from my past, who has no idea what I've been through or what I've done to myself in the name of staying safe. If I'm not going to tell him, thereby allowing myself to release and let go, what good was this past year of therapy? Or tossing out everything I own? Why go through with any of it if I wasn't going to take this one final step: full exposure.

Dr. Linda said it would be difficult. But I hadn't realized what she meant until now.

"Without knowing what you've been through, people aren't going to know or understand you at all," Dr. Linda had said. *"You don't have to go into great detail, but if you want to have any kind of relationship with anyone, you're going to have to give them some sort of insight into your life's struggles. Once they know that, everything—from how you react to situations to how you see things—will start to make sense to them."*

I take in a deep breath. Look up at Linus.

"I was raped on my sixteenth birthday."

There, I said it. I wait to self-destruct. Only I don't.

Forward motion only, I hear Dr. Linda say. So I take another deep breath.

"I never got a chance to heal from it, and it just swelled in my head into something so big that I… that I…"

"Oh, Matty," Linus puts a hand up to his mouth and one on my shoulder. "You never mentioned rape before."

The way he barely verbalizes the "r" word sends an eerie feeling down my back. I stand taller against it.

"I know. We never really talked about anything. It was all just fun and games, ya know?"

I wait for him to say something. His expression says it's still my turn.

"When you saw me last year at the art shop, I had just started seeing someone. A trauma counselor. I just lucked out that the closest therapist that had an opening at the time happened to specialize in sexual abuse trauma. But I had only seen her once or twice when I saw you last July. I was still stuck, you know? Still stuck in my closet, to stay safe."

Linus drops his hand from my shoulder to hug his middle, nodding his head. He takes my hand and gives it a gentle squeeze.

"I'm okay now," I say, tearing up from his empathy.

I take my hand away, the caring touch so foreign it's overwhelming. Swallowing hard, I switch gears to divert attention away from the past. That's not what's important anymore.

"Well, this morning, I woke up with this crazy restlessness that got me cleaning everything out," I say and twirl around, looking at the strewn-about mess left from my midmorning madness. "I know it looks horrible," I say with a helpless smile. "But please, don't go."

"Don't worry, Matty. Friends don't leave," Linus says, picking up the lamp that tripped me. "Friends help. Where do I start?"

CHAPTER EIGHT

One is Silver, the other Gold

After a trip to the store for some fresh ingredients, Linus and I make a spinach salad and turkey avocado sandwich to share. Both are his recipes, and I'm loving them. Then we spend the next four hours bagging and tagging the rest of the crap in my studio apartment.

By the time we're finished, and I've taken the bags downstairs to the recycle bin around the corner and made another trip to the consignment shop, my apartment feels fresh and new. In fact, it looks just the way it did when I first moved in eleven years ago.

"So," I say with a big sigh of finality after walking inside from my last bag drop-off, "What do you want to do now?"

When Linus doesn't answer, I look around and find him standing in front of my bathroom mirror, scissors in hand, the sharp jaws poised at the base of his peacock row.

He snips.

I scream. "Linus! What are you doing?"

"All this purging, cleaning out the past and coming into the present is contagious," he says as he takes another snip at his blue spikes. They fall like icicles to the floor.

"Linus, no! I love your hair."

"Me too, hon," he says, snipping at the reds. "But I've had hair like this since forever."

He snips at the greens. Then the yellows. And, slowly, a rainbow starts to form on the floor around him.

I watch with fascinated horror as he chops it all off, concluding with the long swoosh of black hair that lies flat in front of his face, unveiling an alluring pair of dark-brown eyes.

I feel something stir inside me.

"Are you sure you're gay?" I say before I can keep my mouth shut.

Linus stops snipping and looks at me. "What?"

"Well, I, uh," I stumble. "I just never noticed what gorgeous eyes you had before."

"And so now you're hitting on me?" He bats his eyelashes at me.

"Stop," I say, trying to quiet the warming sensation he's causing in my body. "And no. I'm not hitting on you." Although I'm not certain that's the total truth.

I fidget. Bite my lip. Blush. "I'm just saying you have beautiful eyes."

Linus eyes me for a long moment. "Well, if you need me to, I guess I can help ya, but just this once," he says, circling an arm around me and pulling me close.

It takes me a moment to get what he's suggesting. Sex.

"What? No way!" I laugh nervously in his arms, trying to get away but not really wanting to. It's been a great long time since I've been held.

"Just saying," he grins and mercifully lets me go. "Looks like you could use the lovin'."

"Linus, I wasn't hitting on you," I say as convincingly as I can.

"And I was just playing around…" He winks at me, then gets serious and goes back to cutting his hair. "You know what Native American tradition says, don't ya?" he asks, taking his time to snip here and cut there as though sculpting a new work of art.

"No," I say, thankful for the change of subject. I sit down on the closed toilet seat next to the sink. Feel my blush dissipate and my body come back to normal. "What does it say?"

"That you should cut your hair to signify any new beginnings in your life. As an outward show of how different you've become inside."

"Yeah. I read about that in history class once."

"Oh, no. It's not history, hon. Native people are alive and well today," he says as he cuts more hair off the back.

Linus steps back, turning his head from side to side, looking for anything else to snip. Then he puts the scissors down and proceeds to pull up and pinch at a new low-profile Mohawk—the color predominantly jet black, with just the slightest hint of color at the tips. He turns and looks at me.

"I'm Native, and I'm not dead."

"I can see that," I say with a tilt of my head, admiring his adoring smile.

"Yep. Don't know which nation though," he says, eyeing his new creation in the mirror. "That's the problem with colonization. Generational trauma. Tradition gets lost. But I care. Learning more about my roots all the time. Go to powwow at Patterson Park every summer."

"That's cool. I didn't know."

"Well, you would've known had you stuck around to be my friend all these years."

Lost for words, I fall back toward the quicksand of guilt before remembering not to lose myself in a world of self-torture again. Past is past. *Forward motion only, Matty.*

"Speaking of friends," Linus interrupts my thoughts with a sassy flash of finger snapping. "The guys at the Hippo aren't gonna know what hit them. Damn, I look good!"

"The Hippo?" I think back, recalling college. "You still go to that bar?"

"Oh, yeah, hon. Best dance club in Baltimore. It's gonna to be bitchin' tonight!" Linus struts back and forth in the tiny space that my bathroom affords, walking up and down an imagined catwalk in front of the mirror, eyeing himself up and down each and every time. "Oh, yeah. This is it. I'm gonna be the star tonight, bitches!"

I laugh out loud, enjoying his impromptu show. "You sound like the crazy one now."

Linus grabs me by the shoulders, pulls me up from the toilet, and holds me intensely in front of him.

"You'll have to come with me tonight. Be my date."

"Date? But I thought you were gay?" I joke, feeling heat start to rise again.

Damn his eyes.

"Does that mean I can't have a hot girl on my arm every now and then?" Linus winks at me. "But you'll have to do something with yourself first. You ain't goin' anywhere looking like that. Not with me, at least."

"Looking like what?" I say, looking down at myself, still in my now funky running shorts and sports bra. "Trust me. This is an improvement."

"Whatev." Linus leaves the bathroom and starts toward the door. "Let's leave the truck out this time, too, shall we? Don't want to go in there smelling like your ol' Bessy," he rolls his neck at me in playful disgust. "I'll pick you up. Ten o'clock."

"Ten? What about dinner?"

"Still thinking with your stomach, I see," Linus says, then seems to lose his train of thought, his hands touching the top of his head. Jaw dropped, he shouts, "O.M.G! This is sick! I just cut my hair. I have to go home and find something to wear."

His words start to get lost as he makes his way down the stairs. I run down after him and watch from my front door as he walks up the block.

"Don't you want a ride?" I shout from my stoop.

It's dusk, the blue sky giving way to the greens and yellows of the city.

"No way, hon. I look too good to hide away in that old thing." He points to my truck at the curb. "I'm letting it all hang out!"

Sashaying down the sidewalk, he bops his head to music only he can hear and yells out one last "Ten o'clock!" before rounding the corner.

I stare at the empty space Linus has left. It's huge. Feel my throat tighten and my forehead break out in sweat.

I'm going out tonight with Mr. Center of Attention. And it'll be my first time going out in years. Nerves spike fear, and even the butterflies run and hide inside me. I feel their tremble and agree.

I'm not sure I'm ready for a coming out party just yet.

Back upstairs, everything is fresh and new again, and I send a thank you up into the air to my helpful friend. I go into my closet for something to wear tonight. Panic.

I have nothing!

I call Claire. When she doesn't answer, I leave her a voice message. Then, when she doesn't call back, I text her. All my messages are basically the same.

Where the hell are you? I need you!

It has been a while since I've seen her. Maybe she really was off having a baby I knew nothing about.

I walk down to the second floor and strip out of my now dried yet smelly running clothes. I put them in the wash, turn it on, and walk back up the stairs naked. Step into and relax in a hot shower, taking my time to wash and condition my hair, shave my legs, and just stand, letting the water fall on my face and the back of my neck.

When I get out, I wrap myself in a towel and look at my reflection in the muted hue of the fogged-up mirror. I wipe at it so I can see myself more clearly.

Do something with yourself, I hear Linus's voice in my head. Looking down, I see I'm standing amidst the pile of Linus's colorful, pine needle spikes.

I smirk at myself and pull my hair back into a ponytail.

The resistance is thick, yet the sharpness of the blades are stronger. With a forceful one chop, two chop, three, I feel the weight of it—my past, my sorrow, my journey—all fall to the floor, all fifteen inches of it.

Wet, free, short hair falls forward toward my face. I feel the bare back of my head and realize I only have an inch or so of hair left. Uneven and not yet attractive, I take the scissors to my hair again and again, cutting away at my old self, revealing my new inner self. My true self.

No longer weighted down by length or pulled back into ponytails and messy buns, my hair starts to bounce back, curling under and flipping out. It takes on a new life of its own.

When I'm done, I look at my new hair style. My eyes water with laughter, and my face grins fierce.

I love it.

I clean up and play with my new short hairdo in the mirror. Call Claire. Wait until she finally answers, and I hear her unforgettable hello.

"Hey, Matty, what's up?" Claire asks nonchalantly, as though it doesn't sound like World War III is breaking out between her three children in the background.

"Sorry, did I catch you at a bad time?" I ask, knowing she enjoys this question.

"Please," Claire snorts. "You babysit these little maniacs enough to know it's always a zoo." But there's laughter in her voice. "Are you okay? Your messages sounded urgent. I just couldn't break free right then."

I hold my breath, then say a quick, "I've got a date."

"A date!" Claire screams.

"No, not really a date-date," I back-pedal. "Just, I mean, like, someone's taking me out."

"That sounds like a date to me!" Claire squeals.

I envision her jumping up and down. So, before she has the chance to get too worked up, I explain with whom I have this date.

"Is he the one with the hair?"

"Yep, that's Linus. Wow, you remembered. You're good."

"I have my moments." Claire's voice muffles, and I hear her direct her children outside. "Stay in the backyard, okay?"

"Claire, I need to borrow something to wear. Can I come over?" I invite myself without reservation. "I tossed out everything I own this morning, and now I really have nothing to wear."

"You tossed out everything? As in everything? Matty…"

"Long story short, my clothes sucked."

"Yeah, but what are you going to do for clothes now?" Claire leaves the question up in the air long enough for me to smack myself in the forehead, dreading what she's about to say. "You'll have to go shopping."

"I wasn't thinking about that while I was caught up in the moment," I say, my last words before the firing squad. "Can't I just swing by and pick something out of your closet for tonight? I don't think I can brave shopping on such short notice."

"Oh, I don't know, Matty." Claire's voice trails off .

"What do you mean, you don't know?" It's unlike her to ever turn me away, especially where fashion is involved. I remember her peculiar behavior as of late and her text from this morning. "Are you pregnant?"

"Pregnant?"

"Yes. Pregnant. Your text? Birth center and wish me luck kinda go together with baby on the way. Are you?"

"Oh no. I sent that to you? "

"It's okay," I say, remembering again how she has a hard time telling me since I can't have children. "Are you?"

I hear a whispered, "Shit," followed by a failed, pulled-together, "That wasn't intended for you."

"And? So what? Cat's out of the bag now, Claire... Spill. "

After a moment's pause, Claire states, "I thought that I might be, and although I'd love to have another, I don't really want one right now, and I thought that maybe I was, so I had to find out, but no, I'm not."

"Okay..." I say and wait for Claire to respond. When she doesn't, I add, "You've been acting funny lately. What's going on?"

"No, I haven't," she says quick. "Nothing's going on."

"Yes, you have. What's up?" When she doesn't answer, I put my foot down. "I'm coming over. You can tell me all about it when I get there."

"No, you can't come over right now. My house is a mess."

"Are you kidding me? Do you have any idea who you're talking to?" I say, knowing Claire's idea of a disaster is worlds away from my previous, embarrassing hoarder's mess. "What are you hiding?"

I park in front of Claire's house down in Annapolis. The unignorable rumble of my truck scares birds and squirrels away yet, at the same time, attracts Claire's trio. Her son Max clings to the inside of the white picket fence, crying because he can't climb over it like his big sister Molly and big brother Marcus have. The two of them jump like popcorn on the sidewalk right outside my passenger-side door, squealing with sounds of joy.

"Auntie Matty! Auntie Matty!" they both exclaim into the evening air and jump up into my arms, examining my head.

"What happened to your mermaid hair?" Molly asks, her eyes shinny with the threat of tears.

"Oh, honey, I cut it off. On purpose. Do you like it?"

"I do." Marcus puffs out his chest. "Now you look like me."

Swiping my hand through my shortened locks, feeling the silky ends glide fast through my fingers, I feign a concerned grimace.

"Oh, no! You don't really think so?" I ask with widened eyes, pretending to bite my nails. Molly and I giggle together as I put down the two and grab little Max on the way inside, kissing away his tears.

Letting myself into Claire's house, I sing out, "Hello, is anyone home?"

Claire's house is immaculate as usual. I stand still for a moment, tapping my toes in my brown flip-flops, not knowing whether to be annoyed or concerned.

"Matty, you're here." Claire rushes over, sweat glistening on her forehead. "That was fast."

"You did not just clean your house for me," I scold my friend.

A silent pause lingers between us as Claire stares at my head.

A rush of satisfaction floods my system at her reaction, and I go narcissistic. And smile.

"Hoooleeee shit!" Claire shouts, then clamps her hand over her mouth, looking at Max. "Sorry, baby. Mommy made a boo-boo," she says to her little boy in my arms.

I bend down and let him run off after his big brother and sister to chase them through the house.

Claire combs her fingers through my short, lazy curls. "Oh, my God, what did you do?"

"Like it?" I ask, knowing I love it.

"Yeah," she says, eyeing me. "Wow, it's so fun and… sexy." She pauses after the last word. "Oops. Sorry. Is that okay to say?"

I blush at the weight of her question yet feel the power of confidence brewing in me. "I was kind of thinking the same thing. It is sexy, isn't it?"

"Huh," Claire takes a step back and cocks her head to the side, eyeing me.

Molly and Marcus burst back into the foyer, interrupting us.

"Mom," Marcus whines. "Where are the moving boxes?"

"Moving boxes?" I echo.

"Marcus!" Claire shouts and then lowers her voice to a more sane volume. "Honey, Auntie Matty and I are talking."

"But you said—"

"Not now!" she cuts him short. "Um, go and, um, pop in a movie and I'll make you guys some popcorn."

"A movie?" Molly and Marcus ask in stunned amazement. "Movie!"

Max catches up in time to join them as they barrel down the stairs to the basement family room, chanting, "Moo-vie! Moo-vie!" With Claire being anti-TV mom of the year, it's not something you hear often in this house.

"Moving boxes?" I say again in case she thought I wasn't listening.

"You don't see any boxes around here, do you?"

"No. Then again, you look like you've just moved a mountain," I say of her perspiration.

Ignoring me, Claire walks into her kitchen, starts some popcorn, and pours two glasses of sweet tea. Hot from the ride over, with no air conditioner in my truck, I drink mine and momentarily forget what we're talking about. Sweet tea is one of my weak spots.

Claire eyes me for a second. A curious smirk develops on her face. "What?" I ask after I down half my glass.

"You usually ask me which glass I want first before taking yours."

I down the rest of my drink, the sugary sweetness lingering on my lips. I lick them, closing my eyes. Savoring the sweetness.

"You know, you need to show me how to make this someday so I can have it more often."

"I think I ought to, too," Claire says with an awkward grin. "And soon. Although it does involve a stove, you know."

"And?" I say, unwilling to accept defeat.

She nods her head, eyebrows gathered together. "Something's happened, hasn't it?"

"Exactly. Start talking."

"No, I mean you. You're different."

"Don't try to change the subject, Claire."

"No, seriously. I mean it. You've changed, Matty."

Before I have a chance to say something back, Marcus appears.

"Is the popcorn ready yet, Mommy? We're waiting, and I keep telling Max no, but he keeps trying to get into all the moving boxes."

"Out of the mouth of babes," I say to Claire with upraised arms.

Claire hands Marcus the bowl of popcorn.

"Here, I'll come help you." She rushes him toward the stairs, saying something else under her breath to her son. "Matty," she tosses over her shoulder to me, "go in my room and grab what's on the bed. You better get going or you'll be late."

I try to say something, but she interrupts me with a stern motherly, "You're going to be late!" as she closes the door to the basement behind her.

I look at the time. It's only seven o'clock. No way I'll be late. Annapolis is only twenty, maybe thirty minutes south of Baltimore. I've got plenty of time before I meet Linus at ten.

But I do walk down the golden-hued hall toward the bedrooms anyway. In Claire's room, I see a short, strapless, black dress laid out on the bed.

"Ain't no way," I say to myself and open her closet to look for something less revealing. Only her closet is practically bare.

"What the—?" I leaf through the half dozen items left hanging, then open Greg's side of the closet. It's completely empty.

"What are you doing?" Claire chastises me as she huffs into the room and shuts Greg's closet door. "You're going to be late. What's wrong with the dress I picked out for you?"

"What's wrong with the dress? Where are all your clothes, Claire?"

"We don't have time for this."

"Time for what? What's going on?"

"Listen, I'll fill you in later, okay? Just take the dress and get going." She thrusts the dress into my arms.

I want to press her, but the tired look in her eyes tells me to drop it. Reluctantly, I change the subject.

"I can't wear this. It's too short. And strapless."

"It's a date."

"Claire," I say, annoyed. "It's not a date-date. He's gay."

"Maybe he's Bisexual? Besides, is there a rule against not looking good?"

I take a second look at the dress. Form fitting. Shimmery black. With my new hair and the red pumps I see Claire's pulled out, too: I'm not sure I can handle being a knockout just yet.

"Alright, alright. I'm excited for you is all," she says crossly, yanking the dress from me and grabbing a hanger. "It's been quite a long while since you did anything remotely close to having a social life outside of me and my kids."

I open my mouth to say I resent her comment, only I stay silent. Truth hurts. I take the dress back out of the closet after she hangs it up. Hold it up to myself. Look down at it against my body.

Claire is shorter than I am. And skinnier, too. I'm not even sure it'll fit.

"Oh, no. Uh-uh," she grabs it back. "I'm not going to be the one forcing you into anything uncomfortable."

"You're not," I say, yanking the dress back. "I just thought it a bit much for what it is and… wait. What's that supposed to mean: uncomfortable?"

"Oh, like I have to spell it out for you. Everything makes you uncomfortable, Matty. The way people look at you. The way people talk to you. The way you presume people think about you," Claire says with all the snideness of a twelve-year-old. "Honestly, it's exhausting being your friend. I can't do everything for you, you know."

"What are you talking about?" I stammer, mentally taking stock of all the work Dr. Linda and I have done over the past year. I struggled down the long-road-to-healing hell and have come back liberated, changed, renewed. "I'm not that person anymore, Claire."

"Oh, you're not?" she says, eyes wide. "You can't just throw away all your shit and chop off your hair and fix everything in one day, Matty."

I take in a sharp breath. "You know what I've done today is just the culmination of all I've been doing for a long time. I may not have burdened you with a full run-down of everything I've talked about and dealt with over the past year with my therapist, but don't go treating this as some superficial thing I've done."

My heart is pounding. It was no picnic coming back from the dead.

"Look, all I'm saying is… I'm not going to be around forever to take care of you."

"What, are you dying or something?" I joke, trying to lighten the sisterly fight we've entered into. I pick up the dress she threw to the floor during her tirade, but I stop laughing when I see her face. "You're not dying, are you?"

"No, but…" Claire sits on the edge of her bed, which—now that I'm looking at it—is stripped down to the sheets.

Come to notice, the rest of her room is bare of knickknacks and personal touches, too.

She looks up at me. "Greg got a promotion."

"He got a promotion," I say back flatly. "What does that have to do with the price of eggs?"

"Well, we only found out last week, so it's not like I've kept the secret too long."

"What secret?" I ask, although I'm not stupid. I can put two and two together. They're moving.

"I didn't know how to tell you," she says, tears in her eyes.

"Claire, honey," I sit next to her and put an arm around her shoulders. "It's not like I'm some civilian who'd fall apart at the thought of a friend packing up and setting up camp somewhere elsewhere. We're military brats, remember? It's part of our life."

"But it's a big change, Matty."

Seeing as we both took up residence overseas numerous times throughout our lives with both our fathers in the Navy, I can't imagine what would be bigger.

I shrug my shoulders. "So you guys are moving. Big deal."

"I'm moving," she says with tears in her eyes.

"Oh," I say, seeing where her line of thought is going. "And you're thinking that..." I trail off, not wanting to verbalize her hesitation.

True, I've leaned on Claire for such a long time, it probably feels to her as though she has four children instead of three.

A swell of embarrassment settles over me at the thought of what I've been all these years: a child in a woman's body. Only I've moved past that and am not about to cling to this last shred of humiliation.

Forward motion only.

"Where to?" I ask. "Boston? Chicago? The moon?"

"Promise you won't freak out?"

This time, I'm the one who sighs with annoyance. But I cap it with a grin. "Pinkie swear."

Claire wraps her pinkie around mine and slowly spells it out. "Germany."

"Germany? Wow," I say, contemplating how on earth she's going to separate her parents from their grandbabies. "Your parents know?"

"That's why I hesitated telling you. They just about had two heart attacks right in front of the kids when Greg and I told them."

She and I both let out a short-lived chuckle.

She looks me square in the face. "Honestly, I wasn't going to keep it from you for very much longer. I just didn't know how to tell you. It's been crazy here since we found out."

I know from past experience just how fast things start moving when your family gets relocation orders. "Greg must be thrilled."

"Yeah, he leaves in a few days to get things set up for us and start at his new position."

"And when do you guys head over?"

Claire hesitates. "We leave next month."

"Next month?" I yell.

"See?"

"Claire," I say, eyes shut, shaking my head, assessing the situation. "You should have told me. I could have helped. How much more do you have to pack yourself?"

"Just our personal items, the stuff we want to be there when we arrive. Hence the clothes." She tilts her head toward the emptied closets. "The rest, the movers will take care of days before we leave."

Like second nature, I give Claire a hug to congratulate her on her next move. It's a familiar hug, commemorating the end of an era.

Claire and I have been friends, living in the same locale together, for longer than I've been with any other friend. Ever. If it hadn't been for my recent shift in existence, I'd be fearful right now, questioning what I'd do without her. Instead, I feel a brief internal sigh of relief that I, too, just like her, am getting another chance to reinvent myself.

"Or!" Claire does an about-face, bouncing us on the bed. "You can move with us!"

The idea lulls me in instantly—new place, new me. Maybe this is that big break I've been feeling restless for. I've never really felt at home in Baltimore. I don't have a job anymore, and I loved living overseas.

I very well could use a change of pace. Germany would be just that. More than that. A move like this could take me on a whole new path that I would never have imagined for myself at this point in my life.

"Then again," I add.

Claire looks just as surprised as I feel. I should be jumping at this opportunity. A year ago, I would have. Even a couple months ago, so cleaved to my friend as I was.

But now? "I'm not sure flying to the other side of the world with you is the best thing for me right now."

"Oh, I'll give you a valium. Mix that with a glass of wine, and the flight won't bother you a bit," she says of my fear of flying.

"No, it's not that," I assure. I do a quick feel around my internal hesitation. "I don't know, Claire. I mean, I'm about to turn thirty-one."

"What does your age have to do with it?"

"And I have a family that I haven't seen in years. I'd have to at least see them before I go."

"Then go see them. Fly out to California. Patch things up."

I toy with the idea, feel my nervous butterflies cower inside me. I haven't seen my family in over ten years. Flying out there to "patch things up" isn't going to be a quick endeavor.

Oblivious, Claire grins at me like a cheerleader ready for the big game. "And then come back here, pack up, and come to Germany with us."

Caught by Claire's excitement, I tell the butterflies to go away. Call Linus and tell him something's come up. I won't be able to make it tonight. But I do want to thank him proper for helping me so much today.

We make another date: dinner next week, my treat. And then I spend the rest of Saturday and all of Sunday helping Claire like she's helped me all these years. We work well together, always have. We even head out into Annapolis on Sunday, and I buy some clothes at a consignment shop while Claire drops off her unwanteds. After that, it's the mall to replace my "granny pannies," as she calls them, with lacy undergarments in all colors of the rainbow.

It's a great rest of the weekend, being productive and spending time together. However, something nags my mind every time I see Claire smile at me over a box we've just packed.

Do I really think following my friend halfway around the world to play nanny to her children and sister to her is really what I need to do right now?

It's not like ten years ago, when I came out here on a freaked-out whim. I have my own life now to create something wonderful from. A life that I just paid a year's worth of crying and trying for.

As nice as following Claire and her family to Germany sounds, it also feels a little like defeat.

CHAPTER NINE

Leaving, on a jet plane

"I can't do this," I say to myself and turn to leave.

"*Next?*" a man from the ticket counter calls out, and the word stops me in my tracks.

Exactly, I force myself to think. What next?

In a binding, split second decision, I suck in a deep breath and turn back, reiterating all my reasons, like how I can't wait another day, month, year to come full-healing-circle.

Shouldering my carry on, I approach the ticket counter and hand over my ID.

"Great," the check-in gentleman says with an award-winning customer service smile. He checks my ID. "Thank you, Matilda Bell."

"Matty Bell," I correct him. Force of habit.

"Ah, yes. Matty," he says. "New hair, I see," he says of the old photo on my ID and gives me a little smile. "Is this your only item?"

I nod. Say that I'll be taking it as a carry on. Try to calm the frightened butterflies in my stomach with a promise to worry about flying later. Thanks to Claire, I have a few emergency antianxiety pills deep in my jean pocket.

"You okay? You look a little pale."

"Oh, no. I'm fine. I'm good. No problem," I lie in quick succession.

He gives me a slow nod, hands me back my ID card and boarding pass.

"All set, then. You might want to run and hurry through security best you can. Flight boards soon."

"There should be enough time," I say, checking the time on my cell phone.

Seven o'clock a.m.

He gives me an empathetic, smiling shake of the head, and I start to get nervous. I haven't flown in a long time. Maybe things are different now.

I grab my shoulder bag and start walking with my head held high, doing my best to ignore my father's imagined voice in my head. He always used to say people need to arrive two hours early for any flight. Not the one hour I did today.

Told ya so, Tilly Bell, I hear him say.

At a standstill in the security line, I'm a ball full of firecrackers, just waiting to go off. I finger the pills in my pocket. But I'm not in full panic mode yet. I'm saving that for the flight.

Just get on the plane. Just get on the plane. I keep my mantra steady.

Every two minutes, we inch forward half a human length. I tippytoe for the hundredth time, looking to see how much longer it's going to take. Take off my flipflops as instructed. Squirm when I touch sticky spots on the floor with my bare feet. Pass over my ID and boarding pass. Check the time.

Seven twenty.

A woman with four daughters stands in front of me, a car seat strapped to her back and a double-stroller in her arms ready to empty, fold, and place onto the conveyor belt, along with the diaper bag on her shoulder and all the loose toys of her entourage. The older girls attempt to help while the youngest two wail.

I give the mom a hand, and she thanks me with tired yet happy eyes.

I place my flipflops and carry-on into separate bins and onto the conveyor belt. Inches away from the halfway mark between leaving and going, my heart quickens with the oddest mixture of nervousness and excitement. I half expect to be stopped and blocked from reaching my destination.

Yet I step through the metal detector without a hitch. And a confident smile crawls across my face for the first time this morning. I can do this.

Ensuring I still have my ID and boarding pass in hand, I slip my flipflops back on and notice the conveyor belt has stopped prematurely, keeping my shoulder bag hostage.

"Ma'am, we need you to move over to the side." A security woman from behind taps me on the shoulder. "We have to search your bag."

"My bag?" I ask, confused, as she directs me over to a holding area sectioned off by see-through, cubical-like walls.

"Hold your arms out to your sides," she says in an authoritative voice.

I do as I am told. After she swipes her metal detecting wand past my upper body, I check a clock on the wall. It glows a red seven twenty-eight.

"Thank you. Please stand over there." She points to a stainless steel table where another security woman is standing with my bag, yanking everything out.

My eyes widen in disbelief as I watch her dump out all my little bottles of shampoo and lotion onto the table. Unsatisfied, she follows with shaking out each and every piece of clothing I had folded ever so neatly so it would all fit, then tosses them all aside, one by one, into a growing pile of crumpled belongings.

Heat rises to my cheeks when she tops off the pile with my previously concealed new collection of bras and underwear that Claire insisted I purchase the other day. I'm only momentarily distracted from my flush of embarrassment by the sound of my running shoes hitting the floor.

"What the—?" I try to neaten the pile so my private items aren't on display for everyone to see.

"Don't touch that!" she snaps. "I'm not done yet."

"But do you really have to do it like that?" I plead, my face burning hot red.

Regardless that I can see all the other soon-to-be passengers are too busy with their own security disasters, I feel all eyes in the room zoomed in on me and my new, lacy underwear.

I toss an unconscious glance at the digital clock on the far wall and feel my embarrassment turn to alarm.

Seven forty.

I can see gate number one just beyond the edge of the security area and look down at my boarding pass. I have to make it all the way to gate number twenty-seven in ten minutes. Not to mention repack my things and get the hell out of here. There's no way I'm making my flight now.

Maybe this is a sign?

I inhale quick and try a more diplomatic, "What exactly are you looking for?"

"I'm not sure, but I can definitely see something on the scanner."

"Something? As in what?" I ask, impatient. Look at me! I want to scream. *Do you really think I'm a terrorist? Do I look like I have any clue how to make a bomb?*

Only I know better.

One mention of the "b" word, and I won't be flying anywhere today. Or any other day for that matter.

The woman moves at a snail's pace. She gathers everything up into her arms and then spreads it out impossibly thin into multiple bins, passing each one through the x-ray machine, careful to inspect each and every damned image on the screen. Last, she rescans the empty carry-on bag itself.

"Ma'am," she catches my attention.

I must look pathetic trying to pretend I'm still calm.

She sends a wiry smile my way. "I'm sorry, but I have to do this. I'm not sure where it is, so I have to check and recheck everything until I find it."

She picks up my running shoes, pries at the soles, and pulls out the inner lining. Not finding anything, she sets them aside.

I do my best to ignore the clock on the wall. Breathe, Matty. Breathe. All the passengers on my flight are probably already securely buckled into their seats by now, adjusting their overhead air vents, and deciding if they want to purchase earphones for the in-flight movie.

"Is there any way I can start repacking what you've already checked?" I press, displaying my boarding pass under my face as though I'm posing for a mug shot. "My flight is about to leave."

"Sure, this pile here can go," she says.

Only there's little I can do without the actual carry-on bag, which is still being held in the x-ray machine. Irritated but not able to do anything about it, I gather my clothes up into my arms, making sure to strategically hide my colorful, lacy bras.

"Here it is!" she announces in a loud, triumphant voice, holding a small, paint-spattered, zippered canvas pouch.

Although I haven't seen it in years, I recognize it immediately. It's my little art bag. I feel my soul twitch, and I break into a smile like I'm seeing an old friend for the first time in years.

She unzips it, revealing a small assortment of colored pencils, bits of charcoal, and paintbrushes, some of which tumble onto the floor at their new-found freedom.

The security officer digs into the little bag and pulls out one last object.

"Is this yours?" Glistening proudly in the stark, overhead, fluorescent light is my old, rusty pallet knife.

"Oh, wow," I say, as though I've found a treasure. "I didn't realize it was in there. I haven't used this duffle bag in years."

I reach to retrieve it from her hand.She overly dramatizes an accusatory glare as she yanks the small, innocent knife away.

"I'm going to have to confiscate this." She pushes my bag toward me, no doubt permanently impregnated with radiation by now, and says a quick, "Here you go. Have a nice flight," and leaves me to it.

Pausing for a beat—not sure I want my painting tool held hostage by someone who knows nothing of its prowess on canvas—I snap out of it, fish for my fallen paintbrushes, and push everything into my bag best I can, no concern for organization or neatness.

I keep myself from looking at the clock, knowing full well I'm more than late. But I hurry on toward my gate anyway, praying that they haven't left without me. Pumped up with nervousness, irritation, adrenaline, and more, I run as fast as I can, holding my flipflops tight to my feet with my toes.

Yet, with the air rushing past my ears, the feel of it on my bare neck, and the *flump, flump, flump* rhythm of my footwear echoing down the terminal with me, all my nervousness has chaffed away and I start to feel excited by gate fifteen.

"Passengers for flight 8972, service to San Diego," I hear over the loudspeakers.

My flight number. My destination.

You've got two seconds before we leave without you, Matty!

I sprint and see my gate just in time to watch a woman in glossy black pumps and a tight, black pencil skirt begin to close the door. Breathless, I hand over my boarding pass and ID.

"We were about to leave without you," the flight attendant says with a smile.

Thanking her with one of my own, I use the last leg of the ramp to the plane to cool down.

And I make it.

A proud bubble swells up inside me, and I smile inside and out. For years, I would've never dreamed myself capable of doing something like this. A perpetual child stuck in a woman's self-loathing mind, I thought my time was up to do anything else or become anything else.

Yet I was wrong.

And here I go.

CHAPTER TEN

Chivalry is Dead

The moment the flight attendant seals the airplane door behind me, I come to.

I'm on a plane. I'm on a plane!

My heart attempts a death squeeze inside my chest, and I white-knuckle the shoulder strap of my bag. Another flight attendant ushers me toward my seat.

Pushes me, really.

I had been so consumed in trying to get on the damned plane that I forgot to give in to the terror. And get over it. That had been my plan all along: do my breathing while waiting to board, calm my nerves, say a few fantastic mantras of serenity like, *God cares about me, right? God won't blast me out of the sky, right?*

Basically, I was going to give myself some time to get used to the idea of flying for six long hours in a steel deathtrap. That and swallow one of Claire's pills before I board to give it time to do its magic.

The flight attendant says a stern yet pleasant, "I need you to sit now, ma'am."

She tries to take my carry-on, but I yank it back: my security blanket. I gulp down hard when I see her pointing earnestly at my empty seat just ahead. So I walk to it, where I find an elderly gentleman sound asleep in the aisle spot and a mother-child duo sitting in the middle seat. I squeeze past them all to the window and flop down.

I feel like I'm sweating buckets as I stash my shoulder bag under the seat in front of me. Fumble nervously with my seat buckle.

The plane rumbles under me, and I glance over at my neighbor to see she's busy settling her child on her lap for takeoff. Grandpa next to her is snoring loud enough it almost drowns out the sound of my heart pounding in my ears. I lean back into my seat, a tight grip on the armrests, my chest rising and falling rapidly.

How can everyone be so damned calm? I want to scream.

A flight attendant hurries by, and I blurt out, "I need a drink!"— pulling out my pill, holding it up, as if he cares I'm about to take it.

He turns to me, his face a twist of frustration, and motions for me to sit down. He then starts his preflight safety instructions while the plane sways from side to side on our tour to the runway.

I look at the pill. Feel the squeeze in my chest and the lump pressing into my throat. I pop it into my mouth. Then think twice and spit it out into my hand.

I can't take it now. I've never taken Valium before. I don't know how it'll affect me. What if I lose my faculties and we go down? How will I get out of a fiery plane if I'm doped up?

Then again, maybe I won't feel the hell of a crash landing if I'm medically numb. I pop the pill in my mouth and swallow it dry.

I close my eyes. Try to think of Dr. Linda and all her tools. Attempt a few deep breaths. Try to see the situation for what it really is. After all, if Grandpa over there in the aisle seat can chill out, so can I. Right?

I lay my hands on my lap and try to still their shakiness. I pull out the safety instructions and memorize them and, for the tenth time since I sat down, take notice of where I am in relation to the nearest exits.

I jump and omit a small scream when a little foot plops down onto my lap, startling me out of my craziness.

"Oh, I'm so sorry," the woman next to me says as she tries to corral her little boy into a sitting position. "He's under two, so he's considered a lap child, but he's big for his age," she says with a gentle smile. "We don't quite fit."

After she gets him situated and facing forward, she coos into his ear, "Don't forget to say you're sorry to the lady.

The little boy looks my way, and I feel a massive sigh sooth over me. Deep-brown eyes set within a warm, sweet face, he's a moment in silence staring at me, then melts into his mother's arms, grinning from ear to ear.

"He's a bit shy," his mother smiles, all the while stroking his curly hair with a soft hand.

"That's alright," I smile back at her and then lean in toward him and whisper, "So am I."

With that, the little boy turns and nuzzles his head into his mother's chest, wrapping his little arms around her neck. Tight, dark curls spring up all around his small, adorable head. My heart trips a beat. I swallow back spontaneous tears and take a peek out the window without really looking at anything.

I can't believe how much not being able to have children affects me sometimes. And it's not some biological clock thing, as far as I can tell. It's just a sadness, really, at never being able to share life with a little joy.

I wait until my eyes are dry to turn back and extend my hand to the lovely mother sitting next to me.

"Hi, I'm Matty Bell."

"Tanisha Whilings." We shake hands. "Nice to meet you."

"*Prepare for takeoff,*" the pilot announces over the loudspeaker in a monotone voice, and I feel my chest squeeze. A swirl of last-minute seatbelt clicking sounds out in the cabin.

Dropping the flight safety manual in the seat pocket in front of me, I sit back and tighten my grip on the armrests, trying like hell to remind myself that people fly all the time. So what if it's a billion-ton, aluminum tube with wings.

It'll fly fine.

I'll be fine.

We're not all going to die.

I hyperventilate as subtly as possible—I don't want to totally embarrass myself—and actually look out the window at one point, for what insane reason, I don't know. Watch as the pavement moves by faster and faster. Watch as the trees move farther and farther away.

"Plane down! Plane down!" the little boy cries out, motioning toward my window. Tanisha and I exchange a look of marvel at him.

So young, yet he obviously understands that we are going up, up, and away.

"Hold on, sweetie," she says in a soft coo, and I watch as she maneuvers her son to a lying position on her lap so he can nurse.

Although I've seen Claire do it a couple hundred thousand times with her three children, it still amazes me. And just like Claire, the mother next to me exudes such a calm and knowledgeable presence that I too feel lulled into a soothing state along with her son. Within a few moments, the little boy is fast asleep, and I've totally forgotten to continue my freakout fest.

"I'm surprised he understood that we were taking off," I say to his mother in a hushed voice.

Tanisha nods and smiles back, letting out a long sigh.

"Yeah. He loves planes. This is our second cross-country flight. The first time, he was much smaller. But now, it's a bit of a tight squeeze. Next time, I think I'll be getting him a seat of his own."

I smile.

"Six hours is a long time," she adds. "Sorry if he kicked you while I was getting him situated."

"Oh, no, don't worry about it. Actually, I should have probably offered you the window seat, now that I'm thinking about it. That way he could look out the window, and you might have a bit more room." I kick myself for being so self-consumed with my own craziness that I didn't think of it before. "Maybe when he wakes up, we can switch."

"Thank you, that would be great," Tanisha says, then adds, "Actually, I had hoped the sleeping gentleman next to me would offer to switch seats. A little more room for kicking feet. Or that man a few rows up? He has a whole row all to himself. I'd like to ask him if we could possibly switch, but I'd be too embarrassed if he said no."

"Oh, yeah. Chivalry is dead. No doubt about that," I say, echoing Linus's statement about men.

And it's true. Men don't hold doors open for women anymore, offer up their seat, or move aside when a woman walks by. I know I've been bumped into many times by men, young and old, and for no good reason that I could see. It's as though the women's movement gave the males of our species the out they'd been praying for, thus lifting the burden of having to be extra sensitive—aka showing respect—to the opposite sex.

But I know men aren't the only ones to blame. Some women can be downright brutal if a man ever offers any assistance. I'd be a liar and a hypocrite if I didn't admit to being one of those women myself. I know I've given the sour look and scowled before when I clearly could have opened my own damned door.

Though, in my case, it wasn't that I didn't appreciate the help. Rather, I've just been afraid of men, which in time turned to hatred. Thanks to Dr. Linda, I know now it was only my rape radar—an involuntarily warning bell that goes off when a man gets too close. Any man, for any reason.

I turn and watch the clouds pass below my window. I'm glad that's not me anymore. Emotionally, physically, I've evolved. Changed. Every day, I feel it more and more. It's like my mental, physical and emotional selves are reuniting after a long time apart. I feel more and more whole again. In control. And free.

For that, I am truly grateful.

Turbulence jolts me out of my seat and out of my head. *Oh, my God, I'm in the air. In a plane!*

I feel a sudden heat rise up through my throat, and I grab for the barf bag. Hold it tight to my chest. Oh, how I wish it were a parachute.

I make a mental promise to myself to never, ever do this again. I'll just have to take a boat to Germany.

"Feel free to move about the cabin," the pilot states over the intercom in such a humdrum voice that he sounds like he's just risen from a nap.

I grip my armrests. Stay as still as possible. I'm not moving until we've touched back down onto sweet Mother Earth.

I silently curse Claire and her stupid pills. Obviously, they aren't ever going to kick in. Then I remember her saying something about drinking wine with them. Maybe that's how they work.

I careen my neck and look up and down the aisle for the drink cart. Finding none, I start to panic. Then, out of the corner of my eye,

I see Tanisha's little boy peeking at me, evoking sweet smiles on both our faces.

My tenseness fades.

"What's your name?" I ask him. He nuzzles closer to Mommy, giving me a wide, semi-toothed grin.

"His name's Camren," Tanisha answers with a proud, motherly smile.

As though the sound of Mom's voice gives him wings, Camren bounces up from his mother's lap, grabs for my hand and shakes it in both his little, soft hands.

My heart swells. "And how old are you?"

He holds up five fingers for me to see.

"He'll be two in a few months. I have another back home in La Jolla with her dad. She's seven."

"Oh, wow. You've got a big sister?" I ask Camren, and he hides a shy smile in his mommy's chest. I look up at Tanisha. "So you live in California?"

"Yes, and we have family back in Baltimore, so that's why we were just there. Right, little man?" she coos to her son. "How about you?" she asks me. "Where you from?"

I open my mouth to answer, unsure of what my answer should be, when I'm interrupted.

"Excuse me," a man's voice breaks in from behind us.

Turning in our seats, Tanisha and I look up, and I feel my breath catch.

Leaning on the top of our seats, his tanned arms resting under a five o'clock shadow, he's cause for drooling. I close my mouth. Swallow hard.

"I don't mean to interrupt," he continues in a smooth, sweet drawl, "but I was wondering if I could offer you my seat back here? There's no one sitting next to me, so your little man can have his own seat to play in if he likes." He looks at Tanisha with smiling, misty-blue eyes. "Could make for a more comfortable flight?"

A lovely thought pops up into my mind: I'd enjoy sitting with him for the next six hours. I bite my lip and feel heat rise up to my cheeks. So I turn quick to stare out my window until my blush simmers down.

I overhear Tanisha resist the seat change, saying her seat is fine, and I feel an internal push and pull, half of me hoping she'll stay, the other half holding back the urge to push her myself.

I turn to look at her, thinking the move would be good for both of us.

She gives me a wink.

My heart pounds.

"If you don't think it would be too much trouble?" she says to the man.

"I insist," he adds with what sounds like a smile.

Before I can formulate in my mind just what I'm going to do, think, feel with this knight in shining armor about to sit next to me— oh so close to me—for the next six hours, the older gentleman at the end of my row is up and standing in the aisle, groggy, smacking his lips.

With adrenaline-rich hands, I help Tanisha gather her things while the man behind us moves into the aisle, as well as the person sitting at the end of his row. We make the seat switch with only a mild bit of commotion, allowing little Camren to gain all the glory as he squeals for joy to find himself in his own prized seat behind me, looking out the window, full of smiles.

Standing aside in the aisle one more moment to allow the older gentleman to make his way to the back of the plane, my new neighbor-to-be is every bit tall, broad-shouldered, and dressed enough to give me a heart attack. Wearing a slate-blue t-shirt snug around tanned, defined biceps and dark wash jeans hugging just O.M.G so, his wavy, tousled brunette hair just cries *play with me* as he stands there and I stare. And stare.

I can't help myself. He's a buffet for the eyes.

When his eyes meet mine, they turn a shade of curious. And he grins. One of those knowing grins, as though he knows what he's doing to my insides.

I turn toward my window, bite my lip, and go weak in the knees. Thank God I'm sitting.

"Sir, you'll have to take your seat. We'll be serving drinks shortly," a female flight attendant says, and I glance back in time to see her lightly tap his shoulder.

Hands off, he's mine! I think in a knee-jerk reaction that I, for one, am not accustomed to having.

I shake my head at myself and watch as he moves in to sit next to me. I fidget in anticipation. In place of the afraid-of-flying jitters, I now feel invigorated, charged, vamped.

Whatever's gotten into me, I like it.

As he situates himself closer to me, I feel his heat on my skin. Or imagine it. Either way, again, it works for me.

Never more entertained, I watch out of my peripheral vision as he tucks his belongings under the seat in front of him, mentally letting my fingers trace his arm muscles as they tighten under the fabric of his shirt.

Engrossed in a real-life daydream, I follow his strong hands and watch as he puts in his earbuds. Our eyes meet again, his misty-blue, like a haze settling over the ocean. I feel my insides tighten, and I warm from head to toe.

"Hi," he says with a quizzical grin to his eyes.

The sound of his voice brings another bout of heat to my cheeks, but stare on I do, all the while enjoying the warmth permeating throughout my being.

If this is how it feels to be a woman, I'm glad to finally be one.

He lets out a soft chuckle, snapping me out of my body and back into my head.

Earth to Matty, I think to myself. *Staring is rude!*

"Sorry," I say and look out the window for a second, then think better of running from this. I mentally flip open my dusty book of *Quick and Hilarious Ice-Breakers,* then turn back toward him. See he's still looking my way and, holding onto my last thought, I just do it.

Tucking my chin behind my shoulder in jest, I say, "Look. I'm sorry for staring, but I was under the impression that chivalry was dead." I bat my eyelashes in grand finale style.

His eyes hold mine, and for a second I fear he doesn't get my humor. *My God! I'm such a dumbass. Blew it already in what, ten seconds? Got to be some sort of record, Matty!*

Then he leans in close, pulls out his earbuds and grins—a daring expression with the delicious curve of his mouth and intensity in his eyes.

"Actually," he says, "I overheard your conversation with the lady about chivalry being dead and felt the need to prove you wrong."

CHAPTER ELEVEN

Adult Conversation

I momentarily choke on my own spit and resume breathing.

Sense of humor? Check. He's got one.

He hesitates a split second before chuckling and saying, "Hi, I'm Ty Waters." He holds out his hand for an official meet-n-greet.

"Matty Bell," I reply, as though I've been open to adult conversation my whole life. As though I'm Miss Confident. Miss Comfortable in My Own Skin. Miss I've Done This Before.

I accept his hand with mine, feel his heat wrap around my fingers, palm, touch.

"N.. n... nice to meet you." I release his hand and feel the heat travel hungrily to the rest of my jealous body. I clear my throat. "So," I say, feeling the need to continue my joking ways lest I actually start drooling. "You were listening in on our conversation? Doesn't seem very chivalrous to me."

"Well, I couldn't sit back there and listen to y'all bash men, as if we're all alike."

I puff out a snort. "All men are alike," I say and suck in my breath, horrified I actually just said that. I shake my head at myself. I don't actually think that way anymore, do I?

Forward motion only.

"I mean…" I say, my wheels spinning, trying to fix up my mess. "So you did it to save mankind from being bashed?"

"And a young mom from six hours with a screaming, upset child."

The plane jostles in the air. I clamp my hands down on both armrests, white-knuckled.

"So," I say, jittery, losing my train of thought. "You mean you were saving all the men on this plane six hours from what we women have to deal with twenty-four-seven." I continue on with my humorous tirade, only it isn't turning out to be so comical anymore.

I sound snide. This is a train wreck.

"So you have kids?" he asks.

His question halts all mental processes in my brain. I press the recline button. *No*, I want to say, only the word no is caught somewhere between my heart and my throat.

"They're the best," he says. "Got two myself."

"Great." I nod and turn toward the window out of cowardice.

What the hell are you doing? I mentally shake myself by the shoulders. *Did you feel any of that? That excitement? Pleasure? Even if it's just for an inflight conversation, for the love of God, Matty. Please! Enjoy yourself for a change. Forget the blunders. Forward motion only!*

I'm in a boxing ring with myself. That's obvious now. A match between my old, coward-runner self and my new, confident-wanting self. And I do want. I want to feel again. Live again. Taste all that life has to offer without adding my own bitterness.

And that's what this trip is all about, isn't it? Trusting life? Trusting myself without giving in to old, hard-to-die, shitty habits? Maybe even learn how to trust others for a change?

I hadn't thought about it that way.

I turn back and look at Mr. Ty Waters. He's busy selecting a playlist from his cell phone. I look down at his left hand. The need to check is instinctual, with an added hint of curiosity.

No ring.

But he has two kids.

Married? Divorced? Single? Six hours is a long time to sit next to a man who probably thinks I'm an idiot. How to compete with technology and a bad first impression?

Humor.

"You know," I say with a hint of singsong, and he looks up, melting me. *Breathe, Matty.* "It's a long haul out to San Diego." I relax, letting my eyes travel the length of his long body, rather obviously, just for laughs. "It's a pretty tight squeeze in this little middle seat you've got yourself stuck in."

"Oh, yeah?" he jokes back, seeming amused. "You insinuating I can't hack it? Oh, I can hack it." He reclines his own seat.

"Oh, we'll see," I quip. "No bellyaching until we're at least over the Rockies."

Grinning, he leans back and puts in his earbuds.

I open some travel magazine from the seat pocket in front of me and attempt to read. Except my eyes are smiling too much. That and I feel his arm brush up against mine every so often, taking my attention away from my nervousness. I try to concentrate on what I'm reading. Destinations I can venture to now that I have the time.

Oh, who am I kidding? I can't stop thinking about him. I decide to just be myself, no matter what that looks like. Forget the funny flirting.

Just be me.

"Sorry about my, um, attitude there," I say in a soft voice.

"Come again? Didn't notice," Ty says, although I hear sarcasm, albeit nice sarcasm.

"I just, well," I start, knowing the whole truth and nothing but the truth is the best policy, "I'm afraid of flying, and I'm trying—really trying—to be a big girl about it. But, you know... I, um... Well, I guess I just..."

"Took it out on me?" he jokes back, and I want to pinch him, tackle him in a game of gotcha first. "No offense taken. Really, I didn't notice. Sort of in my own world, if you know what I mean."

"Yeah," I say, and it's the truth. After a few beats, I ask, because I'm intrigued and feel like a heel for acting so ridiculous before. "So you have kids?"

I look down at his ring finger, damn instincts getting the best of me again. Still naked.

"How old are they?"

"Five and nine. Lights of my life," he says, maneuvering up onto his left hip to pull a wallet out from his back pocket.

I watch as he unfolds his billfold to reveal a semi-faded photo of two children, a little blonde boy and a young redheaded girl, running up the beach from a small incoming wave. Pure joy on their faces.

"This was last summer at the beach near my mom's house. Kids spend a lot of time there."

"Looks like they're having a blast."

"That they always are. They're a handful. But I love them." He folds the photo back into his wallet and bends down to stash it away in his bag. "You got kids of your own?"

Dangerous territory. I push aside my urge to redirect my uneasiness with meanness, and answer honestly. It's the truth. Nothing I can do about it.

"No. None of my own. But," *let's lighten this up a bit,* "I have, for the past few years, stood in as mommy number two for my friend back in Maryland whenever she needed the extra help. She's got three under five."

"Ouch."

"Yeah, you could say that," I laugh. "Handfuls they are, too, but great to be around. Especially when you're a kid at heart yourself." I revel in how therapeutic having a good, honest conversation is.

See what happens when you give someone a chance?

"So you from Maryland?" he asks in a drawl I can't quite place yet have heard before.

"Me? No. Not exactly," I say slowly, thinking on the tricky answer. Too much information to go into detail, I decide. Besides, it's okay to be a little vague. I just met the man. "I'm between places. You?"

"From California, although I grew up a little in New Orleans. My grandparents had me for summers."

"Oh!" I halfway turn in my seat toward Ty, excited to give him my full attention. "I thought that accent was familiar. I grew up a little in Mississippi myself."

"Is that right?" Ty grins deep and friendly. Makes me feel right at home. "Just a little?"

"Three years when I was younger. Best food I ever ate other than what we had while we lived over in Italy."

"A regular world traveler, I see."

"Yep. Born and raised military brat. I'm Japanese-American to boot," I hear myself say and almost smack my forehead for being too silly too quick.

Ty grins. "I can see how that could happen," he says, the sound of his voice like a well-worn hug, pulling me in again and again. His eyes smile. "So what takes you out to Cali?"

"Family," I say because, damn him, he's too easy to talk to. "Haven't seen them in a while. And since I might be moving to Germany at the end of the month I, uh… just a quick trip." His face turns curious, and I switch gears with a quick, "What had you back in B'more?"

"Baltimore? Just a connecting flight. I was in New York for a book signing thing. Can't wait to get home though."

I thought there was something exotic about him.

"Book signing? You're an author?"

Ty fidgets a little, all of a sudden seeming to not fit in his seat. "Not exactly an author. I didn't write anything."

I raise an eyebrow in question.

"It's just a cookbook."

Food. I love food. "Oh, wow," I say, all of a sudden hungry.

"I'm just a chef, really. Got my restaurant back in San Diego, which is all good to me. The book thing just… Well, anyway, it's my second cookbook now and I wasn't really all that interested in going out to book signings, but my agent insisted because of this possible network thing. So we compromised with me doing a signing in New York and one back home for publicity."

He keeps going rapidly. "I just don't see my kids enough as it is. But they're with their grandmother, so it's all good."

"Huh," I say, not exactly sure what Ty means by his roundabout answer. No need to, though. I've got my hiddens; he has his. "So you're a chef with a restaurant and two cookbooks," I say.

Too good to be true, I hear the voice in my head spit out. My heart deflates a little. "Shouldn't you be up in first class?"

"What, with all the stuffies? No way."

Cute retort, just not sitting quite right with me. "Two cookbooks, huh?"

"Yeah. Hard to believe. First one caught us by surprise. Didn't think it'd take off the way it did. *The Big Easy.* I came up with the title for that one, although the book itself wasn't my idea."

"*The Big Easy?*" I say and stop. I've heard that before. Where? "*The Big Easy Cookbook?*" I add, remembering the back cover with the woman with red hair and green eyes. "Good try, Mr. Ty guy. Had me going for a while there."

"Beg your pardon?"

"I have *The Big Easy Cookbook*. Friend bought it for me for my birthday last year."

"Oh, really? That's great. Like it?"

"Are you serious?" I can't believe that this man, this ass grown man, is playing games with me. "You know, Ty Waters—if that's even your real name— if you're going to pretend you're someone else, you should at least make sure your genders match."

"Come again?"

"The cookbook? I have it. And the photo on the back cover?" With those green eyes I'll never forget. "You ever look at it?" I see him stiffen, and I press on with a victorious smile. "It's a woman."

"Yeah, that—"

"Yeah, that," I cut him off. "What, now you're gonna say you had a sex change? Well, they did one hell of a job, I can tell you that."

I almost laugh at my own joke, except self-pity intercepts and I feel sorry for myself. Falling so hard so fast for the first man that I bump into. I'm like an infant. I have no clue what I'm doing.

I stare out the window and start an internal flogging of myself for being so dimwitted. Only something interrupts my thoughts in the silence.

It's a slow creep at first. Like a trickle. Then a flood. So caught up in this man sitting next to me, I didn't realize it until now. I have to pee. Bad.

Only I'm not about to ever speak to this con artist again, no matter how good-looking he is. I might forget myself. Fall again. Besides, the moment I lock myself inside that tiny deathtrap of a powder room, we're sure to crash.

An image flashes though my head of my bare ass slamming into the ceiling as the plane plummets thirty thousand feet out of the sky.

"You know, there's a good reason Vanessa's picture is on the back cover of *The Big Easy* and not mine," I hear him say, as though our conversation simply took on a normal hiatus, one used for deep thought and reflection.

"Vanessa, huh," I say toward my lap, concentrating hard on holding it in. "At least you know the woman's name you're trying to pawn yourself off as."

"You're a funny gal, ya know that?" Ty says with a little chuckle, and I hear him take a breath and clear his throat before adding a soft, "Vanessa's my wife."

Wife? I turn toward him, try to concentrate on something intelligent to say in reply. But I've got other things on my mind. Other things that are too pressing. My eyes start to water.

I stare at the chair back in front of me. Cross my legs. Wiggle my dangling foot. Do some Kegels. I concentrate on the unlit fasten seatbelt sign above me, understanding that I can get up but knowing I won't. If I unbuckle now, disaster will happen.

I feel movement to the side of me. Look over and see Ty's bent down, digging around in his bag. He takes out a book. Hands it to me. Only, I'm not letting go of the armrests lest I pee my pants. Unfortunately, and he says as much, the slippery, new book cover is hard to handle, and it falls out of his hand and lands on my bladder. I whisper an, "Oh, God," with what I'm hoping is only the tiniest bit of pee.

"Sorry about that," he says, taking the book back and holding it up. "This here's my latest cookbook, Just Cajun. Take a look," he says, sounding genuine and a little proud. "It's me on the back this time, although I ain't too proud with the way they have me on there. Full of myself lookin' and sexy and whatnot."

"Yeah. That's great, thanks. Sorry I said you had a sex change," I say after a quick look at it, everything in my vision blurry.

"Do you need to get up for something?" he asks, more gentle and kind than I can stand at the moment.

I must be a sight, bouncing ever so slightly in my seat, holding my breath, wiggling my foot ninety miles an hour. I beg God to shut Ty up. He's so sweet and gentle that I might relax right now, and that would be a bad thing. A very bad thing.

Ty stands. "Here. I'll move out of the way so you can get out."

"No!" I shout, a knee-jerk reaction, and blush, feeling goofier than ever.

If I move now, I'll wet my pants for sure. That and the plane will plummet to earth the moment I unbuckle. Although right now, I'm not sure which will be worse.

"I'm fine. Really, just sit back down," I say, pleading.

He sits back down, a twist of concern and amusement on his face.

"Please stop that," I beg.

"Stop what?"

I hold my breath for a few beats, trying to ignore his sweetness. "You know what. Please. Stop."

"Okay, I'll stop. Don't know what ya mean, but I'll stop," he says, all charming still in that accent that just makes you want to hug him.

"But if you gotta go that bad—"

"You don't understand. I can't get up."

"Well, then I'll help ya," he says, half standing again.

I grab for his arm—nice, solid—and pull him back down. "Stop moving," I chastise him. "You'll make the plane tilt."

"Tilt?"

"Oh. My. God," I whimper.

Kegel. Kegel. Kegel.

"Here," he stands and asks the gentleman next to him to get up. Let me out.

"Please, I'm fine," I say, bewildered. "I can wait."

Ty looks at the older gentleman standing in the aisle and back at me. "Suit yourself. I'm going then."

"No, wait!" I call out and before I know it, I'm up in the aisle, walking fast behind Mr. Ty Waters. The plane hits some turbulence, and my knees buckle with the sway of the plane.

Ty looks back, his grin gone the moment our eyes meet. "Geez, you weren't kiddin'. You're white as a ghost. Here, let me help you."

He takes my elbow and guides me past him. We brush up against each other for a brief moment—a sensation I know I shouldn't enjoy since he's married, yet one I know I'll mentally revisit as soon as I empty my bladder.

A little girl exits one of the lavatories at the back of the plane, leaving it open for me. It looks like the standup death chamber I remember. But I feel Ty's hand on the small of my back, giving me a slight push.

"Uh uh. No way. I can't." I turn to him, about to explain in honest detail how this is all my mother's fault. She raised me with this fear of flying.

"I'll be here the whole time."

"But—"

"I won't let anything happen."

Although there's no validity to his statement, it's the sincerity in his eyes that gets to me. Just like that, I obey my bladder and get my ass inside.

The fact that Ty—a total stranger whom I've just met yet grown more than slightly fond of, although I shouldn't since he has a wife, and also someone whom I've just accused of faking a sex change, only to later relish in the feel of his body against mine—the fact that he's standing close enough outside the bathroom to hear me pee escapes me one hundred percent until I've zipped, flushed, and wiped the threatening tears from my eyes.

Only I don't care. Odd. Always mortified, I never use public restrooms. Ever. I've held out for endless hours over the course of my lifetime because of my undying fear of public humiliation. This all, of course, discussed in length with Dr. Linda and amazingly, thankfully cured. For that, I'm relieved.

Pun intended! the voice shouts out in my head.

I slap my knee and laugh out loud in the death chamber at the back of the plane.

CHAPTER TWELVE

So Cal

"Thank you for flying with us," the pilot says in a rather chipper voice for someone who sounded hung over only hours before.

Surprised, Ty and I burst out laughing. So consumed with our nonstop conversation since my survival of the bathroom ordeal, neither of us realized we were landing until we're actually at San Diego International Airport.

The first few jolts of wheels on the pavement don't bother me. I survived the flight, the plane didn't crash, and I've got Ty still sitting next to me. But then the plane sways, bucks, and kicks as the pilot slams on the brakes, burning rubber down the runway. At least that's what it feels like.

I grab for Ty's arm—not the first time during our freakishly turbulent flight, I might add—and hold on tight until the plane slows to a more sane speed and I can breathe again. I unclaw my fingers from his arm.

"Sorry," I say, my chest rising and falling fast. I resume my white-knuckled grip on the armrests, cursing Claire's pills that never kicked in, and vowing over and over again that, if I live long enough to touch sweet Mother Earth again, I will kiss her—oh, kiss, kiss, kiss her—no matter what part of her I see first.

"Rest easy now," Ty says in his hushed, soothing tone I've grown blissfully accustomed to.

I look at him out of the corner of my eye, suppressing the smile within. Although I feel safe and warm in his presence, touching down has brought about a reality check. He's married. He has two kids.

We were only a conversation in the air.

Once the plane stops, the cabin fills with the sounds of passengers gathering their things, calling family and friends to tell them of their arrival. Remembering why I flew to California in the first place, I do the same, although happy that Eleanor doesn't pick up. I didn't exactly get a response to the email I sent last week that said I was coming. Nor did she return the phone message I left this morning to say that I was on my way.

I leave Eleanor another message. I know at some point I'm going to have to talk to her about exactly why I'm here, only I want to hold out as long as I can. I want to fix our sisterly bond first. Build some trust. Then I'll talk to her the same way Dr. Linda did with me.

I truly feel it's the only way to make this all work again. Our family.

Although, I will admit it: I am excited to see her. It's been ten years. Things have changed. I've changed. Just in case she doesn't get my voice message, I leave a hopeful, smiley-filled text message—*We landed :) See you outside baggage claim! Can't wait! :) Love you :)*—hoping she'll soon be circling the airport, eager to pick me up.

With that in mind, I graciously retrieve my things and depart our row on the plane, Ty standing back to allow me to exit first.

What a gentleman.

I hold back a moment once inside the terminal to reunite with Tanisha, the woman who was seated next to me. She has her son securely wrapped to her body in some sort of sling, freeing her arms to hold onto their belongings. The three of us walk together toward baggage claim, Ty and Tanisha taking out their respective cell phones to call whomever.

I pull out mine. See Eleanor has yet to return my call or respond to my text. I leave her one more quick voice message and text, then wonder if it's overkill the moment I hit send.

Maybe I should take a cab instead.

My anxiety takes a brief trip when Tanisha, with her little boy snug to her chest, dashes out in front of us toward a man holding a bouquet of flowers. She turns and says a quick, "Thanks again," to Ty and waves goodbye to us both. The reuniting embrace with her husband takes my mind off my sister completely. And I notice something I've never given much thought to before.

I love Love.

The baggage claim area is a wreck and, within seconds I'm lost amid a rather tall crowd of who I presume to be female volleyball players. They seem to be equally lost within a crowd of hollering foreigners who stand shoulder to shoulder with a crowd of everyone else in the world who's looking for their luggage. Safe to say, I lose sight of Ty.

Since I didn't check any baggage, I wade through the endless sea of people, about to have a hysterical, claustrophobic fit, when I see the glass doors and make a lifesaving dash outside.

The Californian sun sets itself onto my skin, and I feel it: warmth without humidity. Here, you can breathe in the summer air and not feel like you're constantly being mugged by a wet sock like back in Baltimore. My body rejoices, and I sit down on a concrete bench and wait for Eleanor.

I sit, still and quiet. I know this bench well. Just outside the baggage claim doors, it's the one my father instructed anyone he was picking up to sit on to wait for him. And since I always stayed glued to my dad whenever he was home, I always rode in the car with him to pick whomever up.

I don't remember now who any of them were. The only importance to me was being with my dad.

Dad, the superhero celebrity in my life. At least, that's how Dr. Linda put it. How I'd always put him up on a pedestal and thought the world of him, even though he was never around, just as unattainable and absent as my mother.

For months, I countered everything negative Dr. Linda had said about him. But she finally got me to listen, although not accept it right away, when she asked, "Then why didn't you just go talk to him like you wanted to? Why let one comment from your mother stop you?"

I dwelled on that one for another few weeks before relinquishing.

"Because he wasn't someone I ever talked to either," I remember admitting.

I press back the tears with my fingers. Talk. As anxiety-ridden a thought as that used to be for me, I know it's what I have to do now. Open up. Tell the truth. Be the woman I know I am, not the child who used to hide and run away. And maybe we can start fresh. Me, my dad. Maybe even my mom. And my sister, Eleanor. That's what I want, isn't it? A family, held together with acceptance, honesty, understanding? Forgive the past, all of us, and move on. Forward. Together.

Two weeks. I've got two weeks to do it—one for Eleanor, one for my parents. I think I can make this happen.

No. I know I can.

"Mind if I sit here?" The accent is unmistakable.

I peer up into the sunlight and see Ty standing next to the bench, a huge duffel bag slung over his shoulder. My heart busy skipping a happy beat, I smile and nod.

He plops his bag down on the ground and sits next to me. "Phew! What a mess it is in there. Got to help an elderly lady get her bigger-than-day bags up on a cart though."

"Well, that was mighty nice of ya," I say with a smile, then lean closer and say in jest, "Just so you know, you've already won the knight in shining armor award, so you can stop now."

"Is that right?" Ty says with an eye-squinting grin in my direction. After a beat, he looks down and fumbles with his hands for a minute. "Matty, there's something I…" he starts to say and then stops.

Not being able to stand a grown man at a loss for words, I interrupt his silence with, "Thank you for not laughing at me over the past six hours."

"You're really stuck on that number, aren't ya?"

"It's a long time to be holed up in a plane you can't escape."

Ty's laughs and then is a while thinking to himself, holding my gaze.

"Well, it was my pleasure. Not every day I get to sit next to a half-crazed, funny yet captivating woman like yourself, Matilda Bell." He smiles at me, then looks down, which is a good thing.

I'm working on decoding what he's just said. Crazed? Yes, that's me, no doubt about that one. Funny? Yes, I always succumb to humor when I can't find my way out of a situation.

But captivating? I'm not sure I'm ready for such a heavy compliment. And worrying about that makes me miss the first part of what he says next.

"I'm sorry. What did you say?" I ask.

"I said it was my wife, Vanessa, on the back cover of *The Big Easy Cookbook*."

Red hair. Green eyes. How could I forget?

"Yes, I know. You said so on the plane. She's beautiful," I say, although my eyes again fly down to his left hand next to me.

It's bare. No ring.

Two kids and a wife? Maybe Ty's a little weird like my old art history professor back at MICA who said he didn't like wearing his wedding ring yet insisted his wife wear hers.

"*Matty!*" I hear my name yelled and look up, only I don't see anyone looking my way. "*Matty!*" I hear my name yelled again.

Screamed, rather. I squint in the direction my name came from and scan the cars parked along the curb in front of me. I don't recognize any, not that I have any clue what Eleanor drives these days.

"*Ty!*" I hear a woman's voice singsong from the far left, and both Ty and I turn to look over at her. Long, auburn hair billowing behind her, she's got one arm raised, waving and wearing a big, wonderful smile on her face.

"Excuse me," Ty says to me, and I watch as he stands, grabs his bag, and walks over to greet her with a warm hug.

Before I know what I'm seeing, I hear two long horn blasts, followed by my name being shrieked by a madwoman parked directly in front of me.

"*MATTY!*" Bleach blonde, she's banging on her steering wheel and searing my skin off with her glare.

I blink. Squint. Is that Eleanor?

"*What the fuck?*" she yells toward her windshield, arms raised in the air. Barreling out of her pearl-white Mercedes sedan, she slams the door behind her and stalks over to me. "Are you deaf?" she hollers at me. "I've been calling you for over five minutes. I've got to get back to the office. Let's go!"

"Eleanor?" I look past the new hair color and anger and see who it is.

El.

My sister.

Although she's obviously pissed, I stand and stretch out my arms for that long-awaited hug, my heart filling the space between us. I didn't realize how much I've missed my sister until she's standing right in front of me, close enough to smell her still favorite floral perfume.

Ignoring my reunion gesture, El grabs my bag.

"Let's go! I've got to get back to the office for a meeting I'm supposed to be in right now!"

She stomps, then drags my bag behind her and tosses it into her trunk, gets in the car, slams the door, and buckles up. Her only pause is to yell a flabbergasted, "Are you coming?" at me out the passenger side window.

"Excuse me, ma'am," a California state trooper taps on her driver side window. "You have to move your car. This is a no standing zone."

"I'm quite aware," El tosses attitude at the police officer, then follows it up with a semi-gratuitous, "Thank you, officer. We're moving as soon as she gets in."

She glares at me.

The raised-eyebrow look on the officer's face tells me to get in the car. Quick.

"Hey, sis. How are you?" I ask as I belt myself into the car, although I'm not sure I want to know gauging by El's outbursts.

When she doesn't respond but instead shifts the car into gear and starts to speed away, I turn back quick to see Ty.

He waves a hesitant see-ya-later my way, all the while hugging the woman beside him.

CHAPTER THIRTEEN

Confused, I am

I know this might sound goofy, but sometimes I like to "pull a Yoda" to help me make sense of things or a situation: talk in backward, philosophical lines. Emphasize the feelings inside with an odd shakeup of language. Like, Good, it is. Or, want, I do not.

Well, this is one of those times.

Confused, I am.

Ty took my mind and body on a whirlwind detour to an outpost I'm not quite sure I've totally returned from or ever will. I know it's wrong, and I plan on flogging myself later for falling for a married man with two kids. But right now, I just want to simmer in the remaining warmth of our brief yet delicious time together.

Of course, I'm finding it hard to hold onto any feeling with Eleanor driving like a lunatic. She peels wheels out of the airport and onto the highway, weaving in and out of traffic, yelling at people and flipping them off along the way.

I watch my sister while bracing myself with one hand on her headrest and the other holding fast to the Holy Jesus bar above my window. I want to ask her how she's doing. If she ever thinks of me like I've been thinking about her. How her twin daughters are that I've never met. Only, I don't dare interrupt her driving concentration.

I didn't come to California to die.

After a while, highway traffic becomes thick and El is forced to drive more sanely. I roll my window down to feel the refreshing ocean air as we travel alongside the Pacific. Watch as some familiar and other not so familiar landmarks pass by.

The breeze filters through my shortened hair and tantalizes my skin with its warmness.

"Roll that up. I have the air on."

"Since when do people in Southern California use air conditioning?" I joke.

The July sun might be baking, yet with zero humidity and a light breeze off the water, being outside in sunny Southern California is the most beautiful feeling on earth. I want to keep the window down to enjoy it more, but the glare El shoots me kills that idea.

Window up, I watch my sister as she drives. It takes a while for the excitement of being home to simmer down, but when it does, I really look at her. She looks different, although I knew she would. It's been a long time since I've seen her, outside of the photos she sometimes sends me at Christmas. I'm pretty sure I look totally opposite of what she expected, too, although she has yet to say so.

However, unlike my change for the better, Eleanor doesn't look so good. That's not something I was expecting. Always proud of her luscious, silky, brunette hair, styled with big rolling curls with layers cut in just so to show off its fullness, El's hair is now shoulder length, blunt cut, and straight blonde.

She's overly skinny, too. Not in the gym-nut way, but more in the anorexic way. And there's a pale, gray hue to her skin. I didn't notice it at first, but I can't deny it now. Minus the red hair that Georgette Bell always has, she looks just like our mother.

I watch as her chest rises and falls with quick, steady breaths. After what feels like forever of stop and go traffic, she seems to calm down, and I can see the tenseness in her jaw relax. Not wanting to let any more time go by without talking, I jump right in.

"So, El, you have a new hairdo."

"Yeah, about two years ago." She rolls her eyes. "Not so new now."

"You look different blonde," I say, casting my line into the dangerous waters of I'm-not-sure-how-she'll-react.

She gives me an odd look that makes me ask, "Do you like it?"

"What do you mean 'do I like it?' It's blonde. What's not to like?" A few beats pass, and El glances my way, adding, "Besides, Mark likes it."

"Looks nice," I lie,

Thankfully, El's already turned her attention back to the road. Had she been looking my way, she would have seen right through me. Although we haven't seen each other in years, I'm sure my sister still knows me. I don't wear a poker face. Growing up, I always got stuck with telling the truth while Eleanor got away with hiding it.

My sister, the professional liar.

I shake my head at myself and pocket the image of El from the past. It's time to make a fresh start. I'm sure in the time we've been apart she's changed, just as I have. And to that note, there's so much to talk about.

Ten years is a long time.

"It's so nice to see you after all this time," I say, placing my hand on her shoulder.

She lets out a sarcastic chuckle that pierces my heart, and I pull back my hand, not sure what she's about to do or say. But then she sends a small smile my way that looks to be genuine.

"Yeah, it has been a while. Why are you here, anyway, Matty?"

"Well, I wanted to—"

"And why the hell didn't you at least call before you came? I mean, shit. I do have a life, you know?"

"I know. I'm sorry. I just thought—"

"You thought nothing, Matty. You don't think. That's the problem with you. You just jump."

I sit quietly and stare out the front windshield, knowing my sister is right. I've always been impulsive. I watch as buildings go by.

"Listen. It's been a long time," I say, finding strength to keep my voice steady. "Can we start over? I want us to be sisters again. You know, get to know each other again."

"You do, do you? You didn't even fly out here to see my daughters when they were born, Matty. That was five years ago. Why didn't you come out then? Sisters. Yeah, right."

"Listen. We both messed up. Can we just start over?"

El pulls the car over in a rush and slams on the brakes.

"We both messed up? We? You ran out on my wedding and made a big fucking mess of everything when you disappeared." She's furious.

I don't know what to say, which is good for her since she keeps going.

"We? Who the fuck do you think you are, showing up and pointing the finger at me when you're the family fuck-up. Always have been, always will be. I can't believe I missed a meeting to pick you up. What the hell was I thinking?"

Our eyes lock, and I can only fill my lungs halfway. I force my breathing to steady. Think of what Dr. Linda would say. Hold off on the truth. I force her voice to speak up in my head. Fix the trust bond first.

I know that's the best course of action. But I wish, for once, I could throw it back in her face just the same as she's always given it to me.

"I would like us to start over, El," I say, using the nickname I only use with my sister when I like her. "I love you, and I want us to be close again. I'm sorry I wasn't here when Allysa and Allysn were born. That was my fault."

"They don't even know you other than from photos," she fumes at me. "And what about Mom and Dad? Do they know you're here?"

"No," I say, my heart feeling sick. "I didn't want to see them just yet. I just want it to be us first." Eleanor stares at me and doesn't blink. Then she drops her head and faces out the front window.

"I've got to get back to the office. I'll have to talk it over with Mark first, but I think he'll be okay with it if you stayed in our guestroom."

"Oh, thank you, El. Thank you."

"Mark and I do have plans, though. Going to a wine tasting later tonight. You can either stay at the house or join us."

"A wine tasting?" I say, my ears perking up with interest. "That sounds like fun. I've never been before."

El nods, puts the car in gear and pulls out into traffic.

"A mutual friend of ours opened a new winery in Encinitas," El says. "It's not a dressy occasion. However, you might want to freshen up and change into something a bit more fitting before we go."

Fitting. Nice. As though I know what that means.

As though reading my mind, El rolls her eyes and lets out a little huff. "If you need to, you can borrow something of mine."

"Cool. Thanks, sis," I say, my throat choking up a bit at that last word. It doesn't feel quite natural yet.

When she doesn't continue, I ask, "So how are the girls? From the looks of their pictures, they're getting so big."

"They're good. They'll be five next week."

"Can't wait to meet them," I say, jubilant. "I hope you don't mind, but I brought them a few gifts from Maryland. A little stuffed crab for each and, oh, you have to see these little shirts. They're so cute. They have this big crab on them and say I'm Crabby."

"That's fine. But you'll have to wait until they get back."

"Okay."

"They're not home."

"That's okay. I'll wait until later tonight, no problem," I say, trying to not sound insulted.

With it only being Thursday, and Mark and Eleanor both at the office running their business, I'd have to be a socially inept person to not understand that the girls are either off at some summer day camp or out with a nanny.

She exits the highway and turns onto a familiar road that, after a few new turns and dips, comes out into the town of Del Mar where she and her husband live. We enter the upward winding streets and soon reach the tree canopy, my favorite part as it shades the road and homes while allowing sunshine through in tiny increments here and there.

El lets out another huff. "I mean, they won't be back home for a while. I just dropped them off at Mom and Dad's this morning before work."

"Okay, then I'll wait until they come back," I say, annoyed, although nervousness takes over at the thought of seeing my parents so soon. "Or are they staying the night at Mom and Dad's? I'll just hang at your place and see them later when they get home. No prob," I rattle on.

I hadn't planned on surprising my parents with my presence until maybe sometime next week, after I had a chance to work things out with El and maybe even enjoy a bit of my vacation with her, too.

I've missed out on a lot, holding onto my anger. If I want us to be the sisters I've always wanted us to be, it's going to take some time. That, and I'm not sure exactly how to talk to two people I've never really talked to before.

Pulling into a private driveway, I watch as El's villa comes into view, set far off the road and high over the valley below. Last year when I read El's Christmas letter, it mentioned that she and her husband had renovated a soon-to-be demolished Old Spanish Revival style villa into a breathtaking piece of art. And it is. The espresso tiled roof glimmers in the afternoon sunlight, setting off the crisp-white adobe walls enclosing their home.

"You're not hearing what I'm saying," El says, matching my annoyed tone and cutting into my artistic appreciation. "The girls are gone on Mom and Dad's grandparents' trip. They'll be gone for the next two weeks while Mom and Dad's house is being fumigated for termites."

"Wow, that sounds nice," I say, lost in a dreamy vision of what that will be like—my parents and the girls, hiking through the woods during the day, roasting marshmallows around a campfire at night. We did that once or twice ourselves when we were little, before things started to fall apart.

We hit a bump in the driveway.

"Wait, what?" I ask. "Two weeks? I'm only going to be here for two weeks." Then I'll be leaving for Germany.

"Yep. That's the plan. Dropped them off just this morning," El says and laughs, shaking her head. "You really should have let me know you were coming."

She stops at the end of her gravel drive and takes the key out of the ignition, staring over at me in the spotted sunlight. Shakes her head again, chuckling to herself.

"Look, I really need to get back to work." She takes the house key off her key ring, hands it to me, and hits the button release for the trunk lid.

At a loss, I take the key, walk to the back of the car and grab my stuff. Then, before I can say anything, I watch as my sister puts the car in reverse, makes a turn toward the road, and drives away.

I turn around and start walking toward El's house when I hear her slam on her brakes, drive in a quick reverse up the gravel driveway, and stop within one foot of me.

I let out a sigh.

This is all a joke. It has to be. Everyone's just playing a trick on me. El told my parents I was coming, and everyone's inside about to yell a great big "Surprise!" when I walk through the door.

My head hangs for just a second as I take it all in, including the quick turn of emotion. I can't believe I was such a sucker. I smile and look up. Drop my bag in preparation of the warm, sisterly hug El purposely held back at the airport.

But instead of getting out of the car, El leans her head out the window.

"I forgot to mention about the dog."

I barely hear her. I don't understand how this fits in with the surprise.

"Dog? What dog?"

"Yeah, got him a few weeks ago. His name is Shadow. Mark had to have him, although I don't remember Mark ever liking dogs before," she says, mumbling to herself. "Anyway, Shadow's a doll baby. Don't worry though. He's usually out in the backyard. And although he can get into the backroom, he's locked out of the rest of the house. So don't worry. He won't bother you."

After this, she adds in a whimsical, "Ciao!" and speeds away.

CHAPTER FOURTEEN

Locking the door behind me, I drop my bag on El's marbled foyer floor. I'm visually struck with the amazing abilities of my sister and her husband. Their home looks as though it's a photo pulled from a magazine.

Beyond where I stand is a step down to a living area drenched in dark, silky wood with white, contemporary leather sofas and a handblown glass table between. Just beyond is a wall of floor-to-ceiling windows overlooking the cliffs and ocean.

Leaving my bag in the foyer, I walk over to admire the view. The middle window, which is actually a sliding glass door that leads out into the backyard, is wide open. I envision the upstairs with windows and verandas open, overlooking the same beautiful views, sheer white curtains billowing in the breeze.

I stick my head outside. Look around.

No sign of the dog.

Heading back up the steps to the foyer, I hoist my bag onto my shoulder and climb the spiral staircase to the right, finding my way to the second floor. From the way El wrote on and on about the remodel, she and Mark added the second floor, creating three extra bedrooms in the left wing and a guest wing of sorts in the right. The middle area, directly above the foyer and living area below, is open space, viewable from the indoor, wrap-around balcony that acts as the hallway for the second floor.

Before I snoop—what are sisters for?—I decide to take my bag into the guestroom. So I walk to the right and go down the long hallway that leads to the guest suite. The room is a masterpiece.

Overlooking the ocean, to El's credit, it's beautifully decorated with flowing white fabrics and dark mahogany wood contrasting against pale-blue-green walls. The queen-sized bed, outfitted in luxurious white bedding and a multitude of pillows, faces an open veranda that welcomes in the salty, arid breeze from outside.

I drop my bag onto the bed and walk past the open veranda to another room on the right: the kitchenette. Stocked and decorated to match the rest of the guest suite, it's a huge improvement from what I had as a kitchen back in Baltimore.

Next to the kitchen, on the far right wall, is a door. Which I open and see there are steps that lead down to the garage directly below.

Walking back into the bedroom, I stop at the foot of the bed and look up at the wall above the headboard. There, in stark colors that clash with the hues of the room, is a half-finished painting of a beach scene.

The ocean is blue. So is the sky, I'll give it that. And the rocks are brown and the trees have green leaves, but it's flat and two-dimensional. There's no shading. No depth. And the scale is all wrong, with the palm tree being half the size of a nearby rock and the beach a monochromatic, flat side note under a simple sky.

I halfway expect to see a yellow ball sun in the corner, thinking maybe my nieces had a hand in the painting. I lean over and see the artist's signature: a swirly, elaborate E.

E.

Eleanor.

My sister painted this?

To the left of the guestroom door, the bathroom holds a mess of opened wall paint cans with a variety of cheap paint brushes left haphazardly out to dry.

I walk back to the guest kitchen and fill myself a glass of water, drink it down, and flop back onto the bed. I stare up at the vaulted ceiling with exposed wood beams and watch the ceiling fan circle round and round.

I had thought two weeks was just enough time to resolve my issues with my family. I had childishly figured I'd have one day for the shock and awe. Another day for the screaming and crying. And then a day to heal, come together, and enjoy the rest of my vacation before rejoining Claire and her clan.

Now it seems too short. Especially since neither of my parents will be here until I leave.

I close my eyes and drift back and forth, with the faint sound of the ocean pulling and pounding the sand. Feel the sensation of its breeze on my skin. Soon, I'm warm and calm, both inside and out.

And, against my better judgment and the assortment of other things I need to sort out, I think of Ty.

His kindness tangled in ruggedness. The way he made me feel safe and desirable. I'm not sure when the last time was that I felt both. Or when I've felt so alive. Intoxicated.

So what if he's married, I think to myself, running my palms along the silky duvet cover. There's no harm in thinking. I can still wish he were here while I drift off to sleep and dream.

The sand, warm beneath my feet; the ocean, cool to the touch.
I run barefoot, my long hair flowing behind me.
Alone and free, I run all day.

Arrrwoof! Arrrwoof!

The guttural rumble of a dog barking penetrates my dream world. I open my eyes and hear a far-off door slam and then more barking closer, louder.

Scrunching up my face, I roll over to my side. Try to go back to sleep. Return to my favorite kind of dream: running atop the ocean water toward the dipping sun.

Arrrwoof! Arrrwoof!

I sit up. From the resonating sound that rumbles the bed and rattles the windows, even in my dream-daze, I reckon the size of the bark matches the size of the dog.

Another door slams, and I hear voices below. More barking booming down the hall toward my room. I rush to shut the door to keep the dog, wolf, bear, whatever, from greeting me. Claws, even from a happy dog, can scratch and scrape. I used to be a dog walker. I rather enjoy the smaller variety.

I find my cell phone and check the time. It's well past seven p.m. Crap.

I'd had every intention of showering before El and Mark came home from work so I'd be ready to go to this wine tasting thing. However, I can't remember the last time I slept for so long and so hard. It felt good.

I stand and smile, stretch my arms upward toward the ceiling feeling renewed and refreshed, albeit a little airplane dingy.

I dump all my belongings out onto the bed and fumble for fresh underwear, bra, jeans, and a shirt. Everything is wrinkled to hell due to my airport security fiasco. But I don't have time to do anything about it. Even though I haven't been in my sister's vicinity in a long while, I know El's about to announce it's time to go. She's never late, always on time, always in a rush.

I have to hurry.

After a quick Navy shower, I pause only long enough to think to style my hair. I open the cabinets and look under the sink. All men's stuff. I grab for a tube of men's hair gel—thankfully, it doesn't smell like men's hair gel—and work a small amount of the sticky gunk into my hair. Scrunching here and there, it's enough to help my loose, natural curls take shape.

Soon my hair looks just how I've always wanted: soft, sweet, and sexy. And not a moment too soon.

"Ready?" El says, poking her head into the room, her tone tinted with annoyance, making me feel like a rushed child. She looks at me and tosses a pair of green sandal wedge heels at my feet and leaves back down the hall. "Wear these instead of those old flip-flops, please."

I steady myself on the stilts and take one last, quick look in the small bathroom mirror. I'm no child, that's for sure. Looking back at me is the image of a confident woman.

In my new burnt-orange V-neck blouse with the capped sleeves, my green eyes sparkle, complementing the glow I have about me. Add that to the sleek, fitted jeans Claire insisted I buy, and I actually agree with Ty's sweet statement now.

I am captivating.

"Matty!" El screams for me from the front door.

"Why does she think she can treat me this way?" I ask myself out loud.

I grab my phone, stuff it into my back pocket, and think to mention that her abrasiveness could use a little chill pill. Then I hear Dr. Linda's voice in my head to let it go and tell myself to pick my battles. There'll be time for confrontation later. For now, festivities and fun. Maybe it's just the start we need to get to know one another again.

The spiral staircase going down is a bit more difficult in strappy, green heels, yet I manage to make it down in one piece and stand tall, my self-esteem boosting itself up another notch. The slow-setting sun outside the wall of windows blares golden rays into my eyes, and I close them, soaking up their warmth.

That's why I don't see him until he's on top of me.

All I see is a large mass of dark marbled fur before something heavy and slobbery knocks into me. I grab hold of the stair railing just in time to keep myself from falling backward into the steps, except the dog is too much. Too demanding.

"Shadow!" El screams. "Down, boy! Down!"

Not satisfied that I haven't succumbed to his happiness yet, the dog jumps up onto me again, this time slamming me back into the iron stairwell after all, the brute happy to be on top.

"Shadow, down!" Mark yells in the sternest voice I've ever heard him summon.

The dog's ears perk up and, in a swiftness I didn't think possible for such a big piece of furry meat, bounds over to Mark and sits at perfect attention—albeit drooling—on the floor. Mark grabs the dog's collar and escorts the big, furry, black-and-brown beast to a room beyond the kitchen, where he's promptly locked in.

Rubbing my back, I try to stand up.

"What kind of dog was that?"

Heels clicking on marble, El rushes to my side.

"Matty, are you okay?" she asks while helping me up to my feet.

Struck confused by her all-of-a-sudden care for me as a human being, I barely register her saying, "Shadow's a brindle fluffy mastiff. Rescued him a few weeks ago from someone who didn't want him anymore. I swear, that man. Mark!"

I cover my ears as El's voice echoes around the marbled foyer.

Mark walks back into the room sans dog, and I stand, happy to see him again. Only Eleanor cuts me off.

"Mark, why the hell did you let the dog out here knowing Matty hasn't met him yet? You know you're supposed to have him meet her in a neutral way so he doesn't feel threatened."

My heart stops, and I stand, shocked. My sister is yelling at her husband. The two of them, always the picture of true love, always showing off just how in tune with each other they are. I never once witnessed a disagreement, squabble, or raised voice between them when they were dating.

Guess ten years of marriage and twins changes things.

Eleanor throws her hands up in the air and turns to me, brushes dirt off my new jeans, straightens my blouse. I can't tell if she's acting in a sisterly fashion or a motherly one, but I don't care to analyze the moment. I'm just glad she's no longer yelling at me.

As if something else comes to mind, she whips her head back around.

"Why do I have to be the grown-up in this, huh? He's your dog. Your responsibility." She pauses, back stiff, then turns and looks at me, half-whispering, "I never wanted the damn thing anyway."

I let a small smile slip, halfway thinking this omission feels just like something should between sisters. A secret, just for the two of us.

"She's fine," Mark says loosely. He comes over and gives me a sideways hug. "Well, this is a nice surprise seeing you here, Matty. Didn't know you were coming. Been a long time."

"Like I said, I didn't know, so that's why I didn't tell you," El says to Mark, as though I'm not standing between them.

"I wanted to surprise everyone," I say, ignoring her tirade and returning his hug.

I'm so touched by the gesture—the welcome I have yet to get from my sister—that tears burn my eyes, and I let a few slip down my face. I wipe them with the back of my hand.

"Well, I wish we'd known you were coming, Matty," Mark says, giving El an eyebrow raise and slight shake of the head. "We're leaving tomorrow for our anniversary."

"Wait, what?" I spin around to El. "You're leaving, too?"

"You didn't tell your sister we were going?"

"El, I came here to see you."

"I can't believe you didn't at least mention our Mexico trip to your sister. I mean, El—"

"Stop!" Eleanor screams at the both of us. "Why am I the bad guy here, huh? I didn't just show up and think everyone would stop their life for me."

"That's not fair, El," Mark says, calm. "Matty's here now, and that's what's important."

"Yeah, but—"

"And it's perfect, actually," Mark says, looking over El's head, thinking. "You can stay here for the first week with Matty and then fly down next week to meet me in Mexico."

"Stay?" El asks, incredulous.

"And instead of waiting until we get back, you two can fly up to Seattle on Tuesday to go over the proposal."

"But—"

"Then, Friday you can take care of the meeting in L.A., which should make those New Yorkers happy."

"Mark—"

"And then spend the rest of the time doing what girls do and fly down to meet me in Mexico Monday morning."

"Meet you in Mexico," El says flatly. "While I work on our anniversary vacation and babysit my sister."

"Babysit?" I balk.

"It's perfect, El," he says, pleased with himself.

Eleanor's a moment alone with her thoughts. I can tell she's trying to keep it together with fake calm. "And what exactly will you be doing alone in Mexico?"

"I won't be alone. I'll take Eric. That way we can talk business and voila! We expense half our trip."

El stares at her husband, not breathing. The silence in the foyer magnifies the intensity of the moment, with El's disbelieving momentum giving way to anger. I can feel the charge radiate off her skin.

But unlike myself, anxious of the bomb about to go off, Mark is unfazed. Rather he seems cocky in his brilliance, as though he's used to getting his way with my sister.

Although the feeling of my sister being bowled over so easily doesn't sit well with me, the thought of being with her for a whole week—together with no husband and no kids—leads me to act quick, hoping to solidify his plan.

"I am only here for two weeks, El, so it would be really great to get to have that time together," I say in my sweetest, kindest, most honest voice.

I take hold of both my sister's hands in mine. She feels cold to the touch and rough on the skin. But I hold her gaze long enough that her grip weakens just a bit and she seems to start breathing again.

"Maybe when we leave for LA, I'll continue the drive up and meet Dad and Mom with the girls for their last camping week."

"See, El? Perfect," Mark smiles, sure of himself.

El is a moment before taking her hands from mine. She forces a smile up at Mark, which seems to settle the plan, although I can sense she's fuming just beneath the surface.

"So how've you been?" I ask Mark, breaking up the fight or at least changing the subject. "You look great."

"Oh, thank you. Been working out."

"Yeah, if he's not at the office, he's at the gym," El interjects under her breath.

"That and running on the beach," Mark continues, ignoring El.

"You should give that a try while you're out here, Matty."

"Oh, I plan on it," I say with a grin, remembering all the times I've run on these very same beaches growing up. "Got my running shoes upstairs."

"Yeah, about that," Eleanor says to Mark. "That room is atrocious. I don't know who you had up there, but they left a huge mess and it needs to be straightened up." She adds a hand gesture my way and a semi-sweet yet sarcastic, "We have a guest."

With that, she stilettos out the front door.

I gingerly step over to the floor-to-ceiling mirror to the right of it and check myself for damage from my dog collision. Hair, face, clothes: fine. Not a trace of slobber to be found. I do a little half spin, admiring myself, totally forgetting Mark's still standing in the house with me.

Walking up behind me, he straightens the back of my shirt, brushing off what I assume might be dust or whatnot from when I was knocked down.

"You look good, Matty," he says in the same sweet mannerism I remember him by. "It's nice to have you home."

With that, he leaves a gentle kiss on my cheek before walking out the door.

CHAPTER FIFTEEN

The Cat's Meow

The drive to the wine tasting is at least refreshing. Mark wins the quick battle between the two lovebirds, and the car windows are down to welcome in the breeze while El pouts quietly from her front seat. We head north from Del Mar to Encinitas, which takes us right alongside a sun-kissed ocean view, and I watch as the sun slowly starts its descent toward the horizon.

Taking in a deep, cleansing breath, I sit back and just gaze out the window.

Mark pulls into a graveled parking lot at the far edge of Encinitas, and both he and El get out. The two haven't spoken a word since the window discussion, their hostility toward each other thick enough to taste. Yet, by the time I manage myself out of the car and find my high-heeled footing over the rocky parking lot, the two are arm in arm, happily greeting another couple as if nothing turbulent has transpired between them over the past hour.

The warehouse building doesn't look like much from the outside, especially after what I envisioned a winery would be. However, once inside, I'm greeted with rows upon rows of wine barrels stacked high to the ceiling, with a sea of people mixing and mingling about, holding plates of food and sipping from wine glasses.

As we make our way around the warehouse-turned-winery, we pass through a multitude of loud, chatting-it-up people, some standing in one of many lines for food, others waiting for wine to be poured. Everyone is talking, eating, and sipping in gatherings of family and friends.

Following behind the meandering Eleanor and Mark as they make their way around the room, we pass an open door to an outside area, complete with a live bluegrass band, a whole lot of kids running around, and even more people mixing and mingling about.

Definitely not what I expected, especially from how El had boasted about knowing the owners as though she and they were royalty. Looking around, I notice the majority of people here are casually walking around in flip-flops. I do a little stomp-pout and almost lose my balance in El's stiletto sandals, wanting the comfort of my own.

The introductions begin, and I feel myself blush deep red even before I've started to drink. Excuse myself to the bathroom to collect my nerves. Normally, I would shy away from such situations, as they overwhelm me. But I need to show El, and myself, that I've changed. I can handle a social situation.

Upon my return, El and Mark introduce me to a young couple from Seattle who are building a new restaurant east of San Diego. Clients. Then an older gentleman remodeling his office buildings downtown. Another client. Next, a pair fresh from New York who are opening up a new clothing store in La Jolla and in need of design help.

Again, client.

Between Seattle and New York, I start on my first wine tasting. It's a semi-filled glass of light-pink sparkling Moscato called Pretty Kitty. I start to feel the alcohol-induced ease of confidence seep in with each sweet sip. And I begin to relax into the introductions to more of Eleanor and Mark's clients/friends.

As the evening sun sinks behind the ocean, warm indoor lights illuminate the room, and vibrant songs echo in from outside. I excuse myself a few times to get some breathing room. Grab a plate of food or two to go with my wine. Only El won't let me out of her sight. She tags along with me, grabbing two glasses from each winetasting station for herself, and strongarms me back into her group—however elegantly—to meet more and more people.

Soon the introductions start to mount on the side of excessive, and I begin to feel like an expensive piece of jewelry she just has to show off to everyone she knows.

Come, meet our out-of-town guest. Doesn't she look marvelous? Yes. My little sister. This is then followed by details of their Mexico excursion.

We walk by a table with small shot glasses filled with something simply called Curiosity, and I watch as Eleanor and Mark each shoot back a few shots with their friends, laughing and half-falling into each other.

I take one and shoot it back too. Feel it burn straight to the pit of my stomach. Grab for another wine sample when I can't find water, this one a golden-blonde pinot grigio called Fat Cat. When sipping it down doesn't help cool the burn, I load my tiny plate with seared bison skewers and a nicely buttered piece of ciabatta bread topped with an olive tapenade.

I stand on the periphery of El and Mark's ever-growing group and eat, drink, and watch. Nod and add my two cents when it feels El wants everyone to hear what I have to say, then go back to chewing when she takes back the reins of conversation. She's pushy with a side note of snide to just about everyone, although she does it in such a coy and delicate way, like our mother, that no one seems to notice or mind but me.

I shake hands and exchange pleasantries with yet another couple of clients-turned-friends. Then Mexico is brought up, and I take a few steps back until the crowd swallows me whole. Watch as El and Mark walk away with their friends/clients and forget to take me along.

At last, I'm free.

I wander for a bit before realizing I have to pee. Walk my way around the warehouse until I find the women's room.

Once relieved, I freshen my lip gloss and do a once-over before walking back out into the crowd. Finding myself thirsty, I notice there's a short line for another Moscato called The Cat's Meow. It's sweet and bubbly and the perfect complement to the coconut macaroons I add to my plate.

With those in hand, I venture off toward the outdoor area El and Mark routinely dismissed while making our rounds. The cool of the night air chills my arms and soothes my wine-warmed face.

I recognize the bluegrass song the band is playing and decide to lean against a nearby post to listen and sip my wine along with the beat. Enjoy my alone time. Only half a day into my visit, and I'm already exhausted by Eleanor and Mark's game. I'm almost relieved about Mexico.

I close my eyes and take a relaxing breath, glad to be away from them. Glad to not be like them. If I had love, I wouldn't waste time playing games.

Feeling the calm of the night seep in, I let my eyes wash over the crowd. That's when I see someone.

My heart stops. And I blink a few times and squint, thinking my eyes are playing a trick on me from too much wine. But then I push away from the pole and follow who I think I've seen.

I make my way around semi-dancers and a flock of children whirling around the outside dance floor to stalk my way back into the warehouse. The crowd inside is thick and full of laughter, and I walk half tippy-toed to see overhead.

Finally, I fall back on my heels with a sigh. It was a wine-induced mirage. My mind just wants to see Ty again.

Only, he's married. And I'm sure he's here with his wife.

What am I thinking?

I find an abandoned wine station with one lone glass left to taste: a deep-red sauvignon called Kitty Like. Over in a corner near the entrance, I see El and Mark, arm in arm, talking loud and obnoxious with a group of new arrivals. My sister and Mark wave me in.

"Matty! Matty!" El shouts, which is totally unnecessary as I'm less than two feet away. "This is Ron Peterson!"

Unsure why the man deserves such an exclamation, I extend my hand. Nice solid handshake. Nice on the eyes. Very nice.

El shoots me a sly smile, winks, then shouts with glee, "He's getting married this weekend!"

"Oh," I say. "Congratulations."

I try to smile. A little numb from too many tastings, I'm not sure my face is responding. I don't have the tolerance I used to. I stumble through a round of introductions with more clients, friends, clients of friends, friends of clients, and feel as though I might fall asleep standing at any given moment.

"And this is Dana." My sister bounces while holding onto Dana's arm. "The bride to be!"

"You seem familiar," Dana says, looking at me as though

she's trying to locate my face from memory. "Do I know you from somewhere?"

"I don't think so," I say although, now that I think about it, she seems familiar to me, too.

"Oh! There's my brother," Dana says over my head. "Hey! Over here!" she shouts and waves. We all turn to look.

Although a few aisles of wine barrels away, I see and recognize him immediately. It's Ty.

I spin back around and stop breathing. My guilty pleasure of flirting and enjoying the company of someone's husband chokes me.

Vanessa.

I feel her presence immediately behind me. I don't dare turn around. She knows. She's got to know. I was drooling over her husband for six hours on our flight from Baltimore, and now she's here to kick my ass. I feel the burn of her red hair on my bare back as I'm sure she and Ty are making their way over to our group.

I gulp down the last of my wine. Pop a piece of seared bison on a stick into my mouth, and chew and chew, eyeing any and all potential escape routes.

I'm such a fool. All Ty was really doing was just rolling along for the ride, enduring my quirks and smirks. And me? I'm just the giggly, blonde chick he told his wife about. The one he had to endure for six long hours. The freak who kept crying about flying and wouldn't get up to pee.

Oh, dear God. I'm such a weirdo. I've got to get out of here.

I see Dana's expression go from search and rescue to here he is before I have the chance to run.

I freeze. Hold my breath. Dana's looking right past me. Behind me. I see everyone's lips move and bodies rumble with laughter as Dana mouths what seems to be some spirited introductions. My heart is pounding so hard in my ears, all I can hear are my own thoughts.

Run, Matty, run!

"Matty," I hear my name. Feel all eyes on me. I don't move. Can't move.

El gives me the look of death and turns me around, her grip painful on my arms.

And there he is. In the flesh, yet alone. There's no redhead on his arm.

I let out the breath I was holding. Then Ty grins, and I momentarily forget about his wife. I just can't help it. He melts me.

"And lastly," Dana says to Ty, "this is… oh my." Dana turns to me, apologetic. "I've forgotten your name already. Sorry."

"Matty Bell," Ty says in his sweet 'n' spicy accent, tossing back a hardy laugh. With a self-amused smirk, he shakes his head while taking and shaking my hand. "Again, pleasure's all mine."

The skin-to-skin contact with Mr. Ty Waters sends a flurry of warm tingles throughout my body. Blame the wine. Blame him. I travel off to la-la land, imagining how the way a man meets a woman's hand tells a story of how it might feel to have those hands elsewhere.

Everywhere elsewhere.

Heat escapes up to my cheeks, which tells a story of its own, I'm sure. Ty grins anew, and I can't help myself from laughing a little as well. Of course, this is all happening unbeknownst to the looks we're both getting from our respective sisters.

"You two know each other?" Dana and Eleanor say in unison.

"Ah, yes, we, um," I stumble, still trying to catch my flurried breath, my hand still in Ty's shake.

"We were on the same flight this morning," Ty says with a smile at me that both calms my nerves and fills me with hope that I really oughtn't be thinking about.

He grabs a plate of food and a glass of wine from a nearby station.

"Well, isn't that a coincidence," Eleanor says, eyeing me, then Ty. She turns to his sister and says an overdramatic, "I didn't know you had such a handsome brother, Dana."

"Yes, well, he doesn't get out much, do you, Ty?"

"Busy with the kids and the restaurant. You know how it is."

"Yes. Yes, I do," Dana says with a momentary sad smile at him. She looks over at her fiancé, back to Ty, to me, back to her fiancé, and then smiles at my sister. "You know, Eleanor," she tells her with a conspiratorial hint, "I was quite upset when you and Mark made your plans for Mexico without regard to our upcoming wedding."

"Oh, I know," Eleanor pouts and takes Dana's arm. "I forgot. I'm sorry. I messed up."

"Yes, you did," Dana says with a wink. "Well, maybe there's a way you can make it up to me. Besides, we should make Matty's stay in California as memorable as possible, don't you think?"

"Memorable?"

Dana pulls Eleanor in close for a whisper session. They giggle to themselves like schoolgirls, shrieks and all, and I watch as El almost falls into Dana.

My sister really should limit how much she drinks.

"It's settled then," they say in goofy unison. Dana takes Ty by the arm and Eleanor grabs for me. They push us together.

"Matty, I'd like you to come to my wedding," Dana says to me. "As my brother's date."

"What?" I cough out, my stomach doing a flip. Are these two nuts? I see silent Mark catch my eye, and I give him a help me look.

All he does is shrug.

"I insist," Dana says.

El is still pressing me into Ty. Dana is still pressing him into me.

I find enough breath to ask, "What about his wife?" but it comes out so hoarse that I can't even hear my voice above the crowd. Caught in a monsoon of utter lunacy, I yank Eleanor by the hand, through the crowd, and push our way out to the front door.

"Are you out of your mind?!" I scream when we're finally outside, heading for the car. "I can't be his date!"

"Why not?" she whines, eyes almost rolled up into the back of her head as I drag her behind me. "You are such a party pooper," she slurs.

"My God, you are so drunk," I say, infuriated.

"What are you talking about?" Eleanor raises her voice. "I'm not a drunk!" she yells in inebriated fashion and pulls free from my grip, again stronger than she seems, then makes it back into the crowded warehouse full of mingling winos.

"Fuck me!" I curse under my breath and lean on the side of the building, searching for my sanity.

I juggle with the idea of breaking into Mark's car, hot-wiring it, and racing away. Or just closing myself into it and dying from lack of oxygen.

Both ideas are wine-induced. Neither one is good.

I slip through an open gate just outside the back patio area and spot a vacant bench behind the band's stage next to where they've stashed all their stuff. No crowd here, and so I sit.

Within minutes, night falls around me. I wait, enjoying the chill in the air until I feel my wits come back. That's when I remember why I stopped drinking in the first place.

I hate losing control.

I lean my head back, eyes closed, and decide to just enjoy the rest of the night. Alone.

"Guess I'm not the only one trying to escape," says that oh-so-familiar voice.

I will myself to keep my eyes shut. Use my humiliation to glue them tight.

"Mind if I sit here a bit with ya?"

I shake my head no, wanting him to leave. Feel him sit next to me, all warm: stupid clean warmth pulling at my senses, his cologne perfect. It tingles my brain and kills my defenses.

"Look, Ty," I say, opening my eyes and getting up. "I'm sorry. I think your sister may have had too much to drink. I know mine has. You're nice and all, but you're married, and I don't date married men."

"God, I really messed this up, didn't I?" he says, rubbing the back of his neck. "I'm sorry. I should have told you, and I almost did back on the plane and then again after baggage claim. But it just didn't seem like the right place with all those people around."

I shake my head, confused. "Tell me what?"

Ty takes in a deep breath through his nose. I watch his chest rise and then fall. "I'm a widower. My wife, Vanessa, died five years ago."

My hands go to my heart. "Oh, my God. I didn't know."

"How could you? I hold onto that knowledge like it's my own... And it is," he says, nodding to himself while looking up at me. "I never tell anyone right away anymore. I used to just let it all spill. How she died. How life was without her. Raising the kids by myself. But then I started drowning in other people's pity, you know?"

Ty looks up into my eyes. "They were all so sorry, and rightfully so. I know that. Everyone meant well. It's just... I needed to figure how to get on in my own way, you know? And I did. Learned I didn't want all that pity and 'sorry' following me around everywhere I went. That's why I don't say much about it anymore to anyone new unless I feel it's a good time. And it has to be the right person, too. It's my sorrow to share."

I sit back down on the bench, blown away. My mind swirls with images of this tall, strong man, weeping over a gone Vanessa. His children, the smiles in the photograph, lost without their mother. The thoughts are enough to make me weep along with them.

But this isn't my heartache. It's Ty and his family's. And he's decided to share it with me.

I take in a deep breath. "I'm glad you told me," I say, taking his hand in mine just for a moment. It feels right.

Then I let go, something else that feels right. I feel like saying a whole lot of things: That must have been devastating. Or I'm so sorry. Or I'm at a loss for words. But I keep all that to myself. I'm sure Ty's heard it all before.

Didn't he just say as much?

"I'm glad you told me," I repeat, this time a little more upbeat. "Now I'm not so confused."

"I'm real sorry about that. I know on the plane I mentioned Vanessa as my wife. I have yet to call her my late wife. I don't know why."

"You don't have to explain it to me, Ty."

"Oh, but I do. At least I feel like I do," he says with a smirk. "You were just so damned serious, thinking I was pretending to take credit for the cookbook. You shook me up. Made me laugh."

"Great. Laughing at my stupidity."

"Hey. There's nothing wrong with having a good laugh at someone else's expense once in a while," he chuckles.

I punch his arm in jest. Laugh at myself along with him. It is pretty hilarious how my paranoia can sometimes render me clueless.

"Where are your kids?" I ask, my heart hurting for them, knowing they're motherless.

"Went home with my mom after the wedding rehearsal. Guess they didn't miss me much while I was away. Besides, their cousins are in town for the next little while. Eh, Grandma's house is always more fun."

"Probably." I smile, although I never knew my grandmothers.

Ty stares at me for a moment, unsure.

"I. Um. I would, you know… I mean, I uh." He rubs the back of his neck again, chuckling under his breath. "Damn, I'm really bad at this."

"Bad at what?"

His eyes sparkle. "Hold on," he says with a grin, standing up. "Let's start over."

"Start over?"

Ty walks away and disappears around the corner of the stage, only to come back into view on the opposite side, walking toward me as if we hadn't just been talking to each other.

"Well, look at what the cat drug in. If it ain't Matty Bell from the plane. How the heck are ya?"

I shake my head. Laugh. Decide to play along.

"My, my. If it ain't Ty Waters. Well, I'm just peachy," I say, digging out my ol' Mississippi accent, happy to oblige. "Mind sitting with me again for a spell?"

Ty's eyes dance with delight, and I feel my heart skip a triple beat. He looks down, pushes gravel with his flip-flop.

"I'd love to," he says and raises his eyes to meet mine. He seems excited, on edge, not sure what to do.

But he sits down next to me anyway and grins, melting me again. Damn those misty-blue eyes.

I hold my breath in anticipation. Say something! my heart yells at me, but my brain—my good-for-nothing brain—can't seem to make my mouth move.

Frozen, I just sit like a lovestruck idiot.

"I'm glad I bumped into you 'cause there's this thing I've got to go to on Saturday," he starts, and I realize what he's talking about.

I can't help it. I let go and hold my breath again, this time in joyful anticipation.

"See, my sister's getting married and if I don't bring a date, she's sure to read me the riot act. So I was thinking, if you're not already doin' something, that maybe you'd like to accompany me to her wedding?"

Ty looks at me, hopeful. "I know it's really short notice 'n all, and I totally understand if you've got prior engagements—"

"Yes."

"Yes, you do you have something else to do? Or yes, you'll go with me?" Ty asks, looking and sounding like a schoolboy.

I resist the urge to wrap him up in my arms and rustle his hair.

"I'm sorry, it's been such a long time since I've done this."

"Yes." I smile and nod. "I'd love to accompany you. It's been years since I've been to a wedding."

CHAPTER SIXTEEN

Just Flow with It

Seven a.m. the next morning, I'm again shaken awake by the house rumbling beneath me. My first thought is earthquake. Then I hear Shadow, the slobbery beast, barking his head off down below.

Other noises take over—voices—and the barking stops. I roll over. Hear the faint ocean surf in the silence from the open veranda. Feel its pull. Remember how the sand used to feel underfoot. Soft. Warm. Then remember it's been days since my last fix.

I need to get up. I need to go for a run.

I stare for a moment at my sister's half-done, lame excuse for a mural above the bed before stumbling over to dig in my bag for my running gear. I stand, clothes in hand, which is the moment Mark appears in the doorway. He's dressed for the beach and is holding a cup of steaming coffee.

"Breakfast is on the table." And then, just like that, he's gone.

I hurriedly dress in my running shorts, bra, and t-shirt and head downstairs.

Down in the kitchen, I see El sitting at the table. Although her hair and makeup are done, she's in her housecoat with an untouched plate of food in front of her and a similar cup of coffee in her hands. She's looking over toward the backyard and doesn't look at all happy to be awake.

Hangover. From the way she was carrying on last night, and tallying up the amount of tastings I saw her drain, she's got to be at least hurting a little. I know I am.

I hear the front door close, followed by the subsequent roar of what I'm guessing is Mark's truck going down the drive. El visibly relaxes. Shaking her head, she tips the coffee cup up to her mouth and takes a sip.

"I just got a phone call this morning, and I need to leave for Seattle today without you," El says to her coffee.

"Okay. Then when you get back, we'll—"

"Not exactly," El says. "I canceled the L.A. meeting. I'm just going to fly straight down from there to meet Mark in Mexico. No sense letting my husband enjoy our anniversary vacation without me."

As usual, perfect Eleanor has managed to make sense of the insensible, and I'm at a loss at how to keep her here with me. The look on my face must say as much because my sister visibly softens.

"Oh, Matty. I just feel awful about leaving you here all alone."

"No, you don't," I say, honesty coming out before I have a chance to censor myself.

I'm glad for it though. It feels good to let it out. There's so much I want to say to her. Need to.

"You've done nothing but complain about my being here since I arrived. And that was just yesterday."

"Oh, Matty, no." My sister waltzes over, putting a soothing

motherly hand to my cheek. "You just caught me off guard is all. And I've been under a lot of stress lately. People act badly under stress. Forgive me?"

I open my mouth to say something, but I know better. Narcissistic with a tinge of the bipolar, she's just like our mother. She's covering up the catastrophe from the day before by purchasing a blank slate today with love and affection, however artificial. And it's something I've fallen for a million times over.

Today will be different, their sweet behavior says. Today I won't hurt you.

Like the enabler I was brought up to be, I instinctually ignore this unchangeable characteristic of my sister and carry on our conversation as though, yes, nothing has happened.

"I'll be fine," I say. "I think I'll stay for an extra week or so, so I can see you when you get back."

"Oh, good. That'd be nice."

"And I'll think of something to do until you guys get back."

"I'm sure you will," she says with a sly look in her eyes. "You have a date."

"Yes, but I'm not going because you set it up," I say, trying not to sound too rebellious. "I'm going because he asked me himself."

"Oh, really?" El says, walking away. "That man asked you?"

"Yes, he did," I answer, ignoring her renewed condescending tone. "It was actually quite sweet. He found me sitting over by the band and—"

"Well, make sure you don't do anything stupid or childish," El interrupts. "His soon-to-be brother-in-law is an important client of ours."

Before I have a chance to think or say anything, she hurries on with, "My cab will be here shortly, so do be a dear and walk with me so I can tell you about the dog."

"Wait, what?" I rush after her up the kitchen stairs that lead to the master suite. "Oh, no way. I may have been a dog walker before, but I've never taken care of a beast like that."

"Don't worry," she says, hanging up her robe in her walk-in closet and dressing in a blue silk blouse with a gray pencil skirt and jacket to match. "I don't expect you to be able to take care of Shadow. I have it all taken care of."

Slipping on gray stilettos, she shoulders her briefcase and purse and hands me her already packed carry-on. "The dog walker will be here daily. She has a key. And so does the groomer, who should be here once a week."

"A key?"

"Yes, Matty. A key. You're just like my daughters, repeating everything," Eleanor says, annoyed, clicking heels back down the kitchen steps. "They'll let themselves in, just like any other day, through the front door. You can lock your guestroom door if you're that bothered about it."

"I'm not bothered—"

"And here are keys to my car if you really need to go anywhere," she says with a raised eyebrow. "Don't wreck it. And the house keys." She holds three keys in front of my face labeled front door, car, and guest suite, respectively. Hands them to me and cocks her head to the side. "Don't lose them."

My hand muscles tighten. One smack would do her good.

I grit my teeth instead. "I won't."

"And don't think you can just do whatever you want in my house. You're a guest, remember. Don't trash the place."

I open my mouth to speak up in my defense when I hear a car horn honk out front.

"Taxi's here! Gotta go!" El sings as she takes her carry-on from me, gives me an odd, quick hug, and is gone before I can eke out a goodbye.

Left in the silent house, my mind tells me what to do and I don't question its wisdom. Don't think. Just run.

I dash up the spiral staircase to the guest wing, lock up, and run down the outdoor guestroom stairs that lead to the backyard. I hear my cell phone ring from my open window upstairs and decide to answer it when I get back. Could be my sister with more instructions.

Well, guess what? She can wait.

I stretch in the early morning sun and trot to the backyard's far fence, where there's an opening. Original to the house, the steps are made of split Torrey pine wood that guide me down the steep face of the hill El's house stands on. It's an adventure trying not to fall.

At the bottom is a small, new housing development with clean, paved roads that lead right to the railroad tracks. And after that, the beach.

There is a mixture of runners out already. Hesitant for just a second, I do a slow jog north along the beach to warm up and get over my jitters. Soon enough, I find myself at a dead end, blocked by a watery inlet joining the inland lagoon: the same inlet I tried to drown myself in after El's wedding.

Don't Think. Just run.

I trek back to where I entered the beach and leave the sand behind to run up along the road. Jog my way up to Camino Del Mar. I'm almost certain it will lead me to the bridge over the next inlet. Within a couple minutes, I'm over the bridge, through residential side streets and back onto the beach, heading north again.

Even though the beaches my father and I used to run are still a ways away from here, I can feel them. Remember the countless times

I ran with my dad, him waving me on ahead, pushing me to go faster, reveling in the pure enjoyment we both got from doing something we loved. Together.

My heart feels like it solidifies in my chest, solid as a rock. I miss my dad. Us. We used to be a team. Then I let him down. Left town.

Or did he let me down, letting me go?

Don't think. Just run.

But it's hard not to think being so close to home yet so far away. Ten long years, and what do I have to show for it? A lost decade where I almost buried myself in denial and guilt. Anyone seeing me now, running past me now, wouldn't even have a clue how far I've come from that lost world of mine: the one I built to keep the real one out.

But now that I am out, what am I? Where do I fit in? Here with a family that's nonexistent? Here on the beach with the vast wide ocean to my side that, although beautiful and soothing, is really just water filling a void?

My void. My life. Or really, my old life was the void. My life now? Well, I've got to fill it up. Use it up. Do whatever it is I want with it. Be with whomever I want to be with.

Live. Love. Run.

Run.

My shoes hit the flattened sand near the water's edge with every step, and I lose myself in it and soak it all up—the sound of the surf, the feel of the cool breeze, the sun warming my skin. I feel my stride open. Feel my body yearn, wanting more. And I take more.

No hesitations. This time is mine. All of this. Right now. And I can do whatever I want and take away from it whatever I feel. I own it all.

I own me.

I run on until I come to another inlet. Stretch a bit, taking in the view—it's not every day you get to run alongside a beautiful ocean—and head back south toward Del Mar, running along towering seaside cliffs and warming sand.

It's then that I see a pattern up ahead. It stops me. Not natural by any means, it's a huge, elaborate drawing of intricate swirls and precisely angled lines etched in the sand. A brilliant work of art, the beach its canvas.

About the size of half a football field, I'm surprised and a bit embarrassed I didn't see it the first time I passed by. So consumed by my own internal ramblings again, I ran right over it. Someone's artwork.

Someone's love.

The ocean spills up onto the beach, simultaneously wetting my running shoes and erasing some of the beach art. Whoever the artist was, he must have been out early to set such a wonderful stage. Now the tide's about to reclaim it.

Yet the artist obviously didn't think anything of it. He just wanted to create and did. No permission asked.

That gets me thinking.

A beach. What a wonderful place to start.

Excitement bursting through me, I race back to El's, manage my way up the rickety wooden stairs, and fumble with my key to the guestroom. I'm no less than a minute inside when I start. I can't help myself. I don't want to.

It's been so long that I cry happy tears.

CHAPTER SEVENTEEN

Down & Dirty

Completely satisfied like I haven't been in a long, long time, I sit back and take a breather, gazing up at my just-started work of art. Not only have I covered over every last centimeter of the previous painting in the guestroom with my own, I've stretched its dimensions to include not only the whole space above the bed but also the entire wall. From the doorway that leads to the hall all the way to the wall that separates the sleeping area from the kitchenette, deep blue hues blend with light ones to create a vast ocean mirrored by a bright-blue sky.

Between the two, a swath of soon-to-be beach and painted cliffs will stretch along the entire length of the wall as well. It was tricky working with the colors left behind, but when determination crashed into creativity, nothing could stop me from figuring it out.

I was careful to not get any paint on the floor thanks to the left-behind paint cloth. But as for myself, I'm decorated head to toe in all hues of turquoise and deep sea.

I make a list on my phone of all the colors I'd like to pick up new at the art store, excited to watch the vision in my head dance along with my renewed joy to be painting again. And now that I'm breaking from the insatiable drive to paint, I realize what time it is. I ran this morning, painted all day, and it's now four in the afternoon. Yet I didn't stop once to eat, let alone shower.

I'm starved, and I stink.

Taking a nice, long shower, I emerge wearing some of my new undergarments—a deep-purple lace bra and matching… panties.

Ugh. I hate the word. It's so…

"Panties! Panties! Panties!" I yell to myself, then flop onto the bed, laughing. It's just a word. "Panties, Matty. Panties!"

I jump off the bed at the sound of my phone ringing, startled for a split-second that the person calling heard me chanting. The caller hangs up before I have a chance to accept the call.

The number isn't familiar, yet it's local. And it's not the first time this person has called. The screen on my phone indicates this is their third attempt at reaching me.

Maybe it's Ty?

I call the number back. No answer. So I sit on the bed, staring at my phone, wondering where I should go for food.

That's when it rings again. Same local number.

"Hello?"

"Hi, can I speak with Matty Bell, please?" says a woman's voice.

"This is Matty. I'm sorry I keep missing your call. Who is this?"

"This is Dana Waters, Ty's sister. I hope you don't mind my calling. Eleanor gave me your number."

Of course. "Oh, Dana, hi. It was nice to meet you last night at the wine tasting."

"Likewise. Hey, listen. I know this might seem a bit odd and sudden, but seeing you're coming to my wedding tomorrow and you probably won't know anyone there except us and Ty, I was thinking it would be great if you came to my bachelorette party tonight."

"Bachelorette party?"

"Yeah. What do you say? Honestly, I don't know what we're doing. My maid of honor is setting it all up, and she's a bit of a wildcard, but I'm sure it'll be harmless. That way, you can meet some of the people who'll be at the wedding. So when Ty has to be busy doing something groomsman-related, you'll at least know a friendly face or two."

I bite my lip. I would love to hang out with Dana. She seems like someone I could be friends with. And she's Ty's sister, so doubly good.

On the other hand, a bachelorette party? Set up by a wildcard friend? What's that supposed to mean? Bar hopping and strippers?

"Wow, Dana. That's very generous of you, but I don't want to intrude."

"Oh, come on. I'm the one who's inviting you. Besides, you're dating my brother. You have to come."

I chuckle. "Well, I don't know that we're dating so much as—"

"Oh, come on, it's going to be fun. And I insist."

The bride-to-be insists. Can't say no to that.

"Are you sure I won't be in the way?"

"Absolutely not," Dana says with what sounds like a genuine smile. "Oh, I'm so excited! It's going to be fun. I'll text you what time after I find out more of what's going on tonight. Oh, and text me El's address so I can use GPS. You're staying at her house, right? I've only ever been to her office. See you soon!"

With that, she hangs up.

My cell rings again.

The sound of Ty's voice calms me like nothing I've ever known before. "So. Just get off the phone with my sister?"

"Yeah. I've got to say, she doesn't take no for an answer."

Ty laughs out loud, which warms my heart.

"You don't really have to go. She's just doing the take-charge, micromanaging bride thing."

"As she should," I say with a smile. "No worries. I actually had no plans for tonight, so this'll be fun. Although I wish it were you I was going to be with," I hear myself say before I have a chance to censor myself.

However, I find that I like my mouth having a mind of its own nowadays. It doesn't lie.

I hear Ty chuckle again, and I picture his grin. Sweet energy fills me, and I lie back onto the bed in my purple lace, silently wishing. Wanting.

"Hey, listen. I can't talk long, but I wanted to let you know I'll be by tomorrow to pick you up for the wedding. Say four-ish?"

"Sure. Sounds good. See you then."

After we hang up and my heart subsides, I pull on some jean capris and a green, cap-sleeved shirt and walk downstairs for a quick bite to eat. Looking in the fridge, however, I find a few things shy of nothing.

Chewing on some milk-less vegan cheese, I expect to see the dog locked up out back or in the mudroom off of the kitchen. But there's no sign of Shadow the Humongous anywhere.

Funny, I almost feel sorry for the big guy, even though he did almost try to eat me yesterday. Here he is alone in this big house, waiting on a once-a-day dog walker and a once-a-week dog groomer. With their busy family schedule and business, I wonder just how much love and attention El and Mark pay poor doggie Shadow.

Does he ever gets to play at the dog beach I passed on my run this morning?

Back in my room, I see Dana's texted me that she'll be by to pick me up soon. I swap out my green t-shirt for a deep-purple summer blouse that I thankfully bought just last week with Claire, and don El's green strappy heels from last night that I've grown to love.

That should do the trick.

"Wow." Dana's standing in front of my painted wall, staring. "All I can say is, wow."

"Thanks." I smile, feeling proud of my accomplishment, although it's nowhere near done. Right now, it's just blended blues all across the wall. "I'm not finished. Hope to finish it by the time Eleanor comes home."

Then I add a sheepish, "She doesn't know I'm doing it."

"Well, she sure will be surprised. I love the way the colors just melt into one another. You do this professionally?"

"Oh, no. This is just a one-time thing. You know," I say, as if Dana knows my life story.

"Think you can do something in my house after Ron and I return from our honeymoon?" Dana asks, totally oblivious to what's going on in my head.

"Uh, sure," I answer, artificially mirroring her enthusiasm.

I'm about to take it back, when I see the excitement on her face. For some reason, I can't say no to this woman. Besides, I don't have much else to do while I'm waiting for El and my parents to get back into town. El's guest bedroom mural is expansive, but it won't take me more than a few full days to complete.

"You'll have to let me know how much you charge."

"Oh, I'd do it for free. I couldn't charge you."

"Are you kidding? Don't sell yourself short, Matty. I'm paying you." She looks at me for a moment, then softens her expression. "Ready to go?"

By the time everyone arrives at Dana's maid of honor's house, there's a nice sized group of women. We spend a good hour making cocktails, begging for details of the night to come, and not getting any from the hostess. Instead, we fill up on wedding details from Dana.

From what I can gather, her wedding doesn't sound like it's going to be anything like the typical, conveyor belt matrimonial deal. Simple, casual, and straight to the point. I plant a few questions here and there to see what the others are planning on wearing and make a mental note to raid Eleanor's closet when I get home.

The doorbell rings.

"Ooh, ooh, stripper!" Dana says, laughing.

"No, no. Not this time," her maid of honor, Gale, says as she emerges from the kitchen and trots toward the front door. "You ladies make yourselves comfortable out on the deck. I'll be right back."

When no one moves, she insists with a boisterous, "I'm serious. Go!"

The view from the deck is something you'd want to paint, making my fingers tingle. Situated on a hilltop in inland Escondido, the backyard has a wonderful vista of the town below and the surrounding hills. With the sun starting to set, the sky and hills are blanketed in soft pinks and the air starts its promise of a coolness coming.

We sit around an inlaid firepit in the center of the deck and continue sipping our cocktails and chatting with each other.

Maybe it's the drink or these Southern Californian women. But other than with Ty, I don't remember ever feeling this at ease with anyone outside of Claire.

Then I realize something. A truth. That it never had anything to do with not feeling comfortable with other people. Rather, it was me.

I didn't feel comfortable with me.

Everything feels so much easier and not as worrisome since I finally started liking myself again. Loving myself.

"Everything's ready," Gale sings out to us. "Come on, everyone, back inside."

"Oh, I hope it's a stripper," Dana says with a wink.

"It's better than a stripper," Gale says as she ushers us back in. "Come on."

As we walk through the kitchen and down a short flight of steps into another living room area with tall windows to the backyard, Dana continues talking, "Better than a stripper? What could possibly be better than a stripper?"

Wondering that myself—not that I've ever seen a stripper—one of Dana's friends shouts "Toys!" with as much enthusiasm as though they've found buried treasure. Everyone in the room is invariably full of lively talk as they find a seat or refill their drink. That is, everyone except me.

I'm standing at the bottom of the stairs, a little taken aback. I've never seen items such as the ones that are proudly set on display. And when I say proudly, I mean proudly. Standing big-and-large.

Up the stairs I go. I need food. Water. Fresh air out on the back deck. Anything to keep me busy.

I walk back inside and make myself a plateful of food despite how everyone else stays downstairs to chitchat and ogle the toys. It is, after all, a bachelorette party.

I take a few breaths. Feel my heart slow its pace. Gain some clarity. This really isn't that big a deal. No harm with a group of women laughing it up about some heavy machinery.

I push my nervousness aside as I walk back downstairs and situate myself in the last seat available, a lone chair near the bottom of the steps.

"I'm excited you all could make it to Dana's bachelorette party," Gale says, centering herself before us. "As you know, I've known Dana all my life and I couldn't be happier for her as she solidifies her life with Ron tomorrow."

Cheers and applause erupt from the room.

"However, first, I think we should all have some fun tonight! Don't you think?" And with that speech, she passes the conch on to a polished woman who I'm assuming brought the arsenal.

"Thank you, and hello," the woman begins. "Before we start, I want to share a little bit about myself and why I'm with this company."

I roll my eyes and refrain from putting a finger down my throat. Having been dragged to an insurmountable number of home parties with Claire, I know the drill. Be bored while being shown an assortment of crap. Fill out a form to order the crap. Then be told how I can become a real-life entrepreneur by selling the crap.

Blah. Blah. Blah.

I start to tune the woman out until I hear her say, " That, and I'm a sex therapist."

Sex what? Just like that, she has me hooked.

"I sell these products on the side mostly because I believe in them. Not all the products here are toys."

The announcement is unfavorably received by a few in the crowd.

But the saleswoman-turned-sex-therapist adds with a wink, "Don't be discouraged, ladies. We'll get to those soon enough. But for the most part, these products are informative: books, personal care items, DVDs." Another wink. "And they're all about empowering women to enjoy their sexuality."

I feel heat rise to my face and hide behind my martini glass. Yet no one is looking at me. Of course they're not. They don't know what's going on in my head. They don't know that the mere mention of sex makes me freak out. That I feel like this woman has been brought here just for me, and I'm not comfortable with it.

"By day, I'm Dr. Miles. By night, I'm Luscious Loraine and a consultant for Demure, a woman's private line of personal items and," she raises an eyebrow, "accessories."

More excited chatter comes from everyone else in the room.

"How many of you have ever been to a Demure party?"

Everyone raises their hands but me.

"Wonderful. So you all have your Demure names, I presume? Who would like to go first? Oh, and for those of you who haven't been to one of my parties before, just know that when you're here, you acquire a new name," she adds with a wink.

Gesturing toward the women seated on the couch, a volunteer stands and introduces herself.

"Hello, all. I'm Randy Rhonda." Someone outright bursts into laughter. Others nod with approval. I'm confused.

"Wonderful to meet you, Randy Rhonda. And you?" she points to Dana.

"I'm Delicious Dana."

To which maid of honor Gale adds, "Oh, how about Deliciously Daring Dana!"

The change is well received with hoots and laughter, and so it goes around the room, everyone saying their name.

"Good-for-you Gale."

"Down and Dirty Daniela."

"Multiple O's Melanie."

"Doggie Style Dorothy."

"Aroused Angela."

The next victim stands. And then the next. Only they don't seem so much victimized as I initially felt when they started this charade. They're actually enjoying the game. The attention. Playing up their sensual, sexual sides.

I'm just starting to get it and relax again when it's my turn, leading to a not-so-clever, "Um, me? I'm Matty."

Seems everyone else had a name preplanned except for me.

Honestly, I couldn't think of anything other than nothing.

A word that starts with M that describes me?

Misunderstood? Mistreated? Motionless?

Slightly embarrassed, I shrug my shoulders.

"No problem, we can help you out," the sex-therapist toy-dealer says. "Matty. M. Anyone?"

"How about Misbehaving?" someone says.

"Or Midnight?" says another.

"Ladies, remember," Dana slyly interrupts as she stands before everyone. "Matty will be my brother's date for the wedding tomorrow."

"Shut up! You got him to date?" one woman practically shouts, followed by another who whines, "I've been working him for years." Another says, "Oh, the things I would do to that man."

"Okay, so you're dating Dana's brother," the consultant brings the group focus back as Dana sits down amid pouting friends.

"Well, not exactly dating," I speak up. "I only met him yesterday. Dana set us up."

The room explodes.

"Dana!"

Apparently everyone, including the sex therapist, wants Ty. Somehow, this makes me feel empowered, and a twinge of confidence sparks.

"Must-be-the-one Matty." I joke with a wink of my own. After a few half-hearted laughs, the room quiets enough for me to really think.

I try on "Mysterious Matty" for size. And with that, the show moves on.

And wow. Do I get a real education: nipple creams, tickling feathers, things that vibrate, others that warm. Although I know I've got at least five years on everyone else in the room, if not more, I see I've been the only one left in the dark.

I continue to take it all in, leaning in with my mental note pad.

"Now, I want everyone to make a tight fist with your left hand," Luscious Loraine instructs. "And then, with your right index finger, I want you to try to push your finger into the middle of your left hand through the opening on the side."

Everyone does as instructed.

"See how hard it is? Not a very smooth ride, is it?" the sex-therapist saleslady says with a chuckle that everyone seems to get but me. "Now, with this cream on your index finger," she says as she makes her way around the room to adhere a small glob of some peach-smelling cream to our fingers, "I want you to try to insert that same finger again. Only this time, it slides in effortlessly."

"Oh, yeah, Dana! You need to get some of this for tomorrow night!" someone hollers across the room at the bride-to-be.

"And it's edible, too, ladies."

Dana and her friends all seem to be in on the joke, but not me. Oh, I laugh along with them as best I can. But I notice, again, I'm getting further and further away from knowing what the hell this doctor chick—or anyone else in the room, for that matter—is talking about. My head's swirling from all the added info, much of it not knowing where to land.

Then it happens. It's my deer-in-the-headlights moment of all time. Because, being passed out and handed around is the first of her "toy" items.

"Seeing that I have you all pretty loosened up and having a good time, I'm going to start at the top," the woman says as she produces a monstrous, double-headed faux penis. While sliding her hand from the one end to the other, she adds a throaty, "and work my way down."

The maid of honor falls off the couch laughing out loud, and everyone else actually cheers for the penis. Again, I play the part as best I can but then become a tad bit alarmed when the woman places it between Dana's knees.

"Every time I say the word pleasure," she instructs, "whoever has this big boy has to pass it to the next person. Only there's a catch. You can't use your hands."

Thirsty, but not really, I dash back up to the kitchen for a glass of water, a refill of my plate, and a gander at the mountains and the city of Escondido. I check my phone to see if anyone has called while I was downstairs.

I do know I should be doing my breathing thing again, but I don't care. This is nuts. No one ever told me about double-headed fake penises before. I wasn't prepared for this.

Feeling as though I've wasted a sufficient amount of time, I rejoin the women downstairs. Thankfully, big boy is nowhere to be found.

I sit down and let out a "Yow!" from the vibrating, gyrating, spinning things set on my chair.

"Looks like you were the absent end of the sharing line," the saleswoman says, pointing at the pile of sex toys I just sat on. "Feel free to play with them a bit—get to know them—before setting them on the table next to you. I'll get them a little later," she says with a grin.

With a mixture of curiosity and unsettledness, I find each off button and then set them all down on the table next to me, making sure to point them away so they're not staring at me.

Leaning away from the table of toys though, I realize something all over again. Everyone is having a good time but me. Everyone is comfortable with all of this but me. Everyone knows what they are doing but me.

I have to pee.

Drying my hands on the bathroom towel, I take a deep breath, look at myself in the mirror, and am overcome with emotion. I can't quite explain it, but it's so instant, so intense, that I have no choice but to give in. I cry as quietly as I can, all the while trying to figure out why I'm crying at all.

Knock, knock.

My heart leaps. "Someone's in here," I choke out. "I'll be done in a sec."

"No worries, I'll use the one upstairs."

I look at myself in the mirror and mouth to myself, "What the hell is wrong with you?" Another stupid burst of tears pours out of me, and I can't find a way to get a hold of myself.

Breathe, damn you, breathe, I hear a mixture of myself and my therapist say in my head. I force myself to, each breath doing a better job at helping me regain control than the last.

Finally, I stare at my reflection and it hits me. "It's not fair."

More tears come, only this time I know why. I sit on the side of the tub and quietly sob. Hold onto myself.

It isn't the lotions or the nipple cream or the heavy machinery. It has nothing to do with the toys and everything to do with me. And I know why. I didn't get a chance to grow into my own sexual knowing on my own terms. I was forced. And then, because I didn't heal from the trauma, I ran and hid. Lived in a bubble of motionlessness to drown out the noise in my head.

It's not fair.

Here I am, a thirty-something woman, crying alone in the bathroom while a room full of twenty-somethings are having a great time with each other and themselves. They're okay with the fact that they're women. They're happy with the fact that they're female, have all the necessary parts to enjoy themselves, and not only want to but talk about it openly, no reservations.

It's not fair.

All I've ever known sex to be is a weapon, either used against me or by me against someone else. I don't know what it looks like or even feels like to start something you want—really want—with someone you want. Someone you love. And if I ever get to the point where I think I can be involved with someone on my own terms, will it dredge up the past and keep me from enjoying the moment?

The person I'm with: Will I ever be able to be with someone and not see him when I close my eyes? Will I ever get to be normal again?

It's not fair.

And yet…

I've traveled a long way to solidify my stance as a newly reclaimed person in this life. I am a new woman. And although late in the game, I felt the heated rush in my body when Ty looked at me that first time. That second time. Third.

Every time.

I, too, can imagine what I would do with him right now if given the opportunity.

I can't change or fix what happened in the past. But I can take charge of what happens from now on. And I don't want any more of this run and hide mess. I want to enjoy all that life has to offer. As a woman.

I just wish I knew what my triggers were before they hit me in the face.

"Or I sit on them," I whisper-laugh to my reflection. Big penis toys. Who knew they'd be a trigger?

I take in a cleansing breath and fix my smudged makeup. I can do this. I just need to move at my own pace and not lose myself.

I open the door, ready for whatever, and walk out to an empty room. The saleswoman is packing up her arsenal while the rest of the party is up on the deck, laughing it up around the firepit.

"You okay?"

"Ah, yeah. Got some of that peach stuff in my eye… eyes," I lie. "Good to go now. Thanks."

"Well, that's good," she says in a way that reminds me of Dr. Linda and how she'd gear up to dig into something I didn't want unearthed. "I don't want to pry, but you seemed a bit overwhelmed back there."

I restrain myself. Force of habit. Hear Dr. Linda's mantra in my head.

Forward motion only.

"Oh, well, yeah. I've never been to anything like this before."

"Great. I love first-timers. Do you have any questions about any of the products? While everyone else is busy outside, I can go over some of them again for you."

"Ah, no, thanks. I don't think this stuff is for me. I'm not really, you know…"

"Comfortable with sex?"

I grit my teeth. I hate when people can read my thoughts.

Breathe, Matty. Breathe.

"The thing is," she starts, and I stiffen when she puts her hand on my arm. "All this stuff is pretty overt. Sex on overdrive, if you will. It's not for everyone. But that doesn't mean that someone who's not into over-the-top sexual exploration isn't comfortable with or can't enjoy sex—"

"On her own terms," I say before I realize my mouth's done it again.

"Yes. Exactly," she nods knowingly. "On her own terms. And at her own speed. Don't worry. You'll get there."

You'll get there.

This statement relaxes me inside and out. I guess it's what I've been waiting to hear for a long time. I can be normal.

I thank her and find my way out to the deck.

With the fire crackling as we're seated on a semicircle bench, we talk and carry on into the night. Soaking up the atmosphere, I gaze off over at the city lights. Watch them twinkle off in the distance. See the stars are crisp and bright.

Stars.

They always remind me of the wish I made before we moved to Italy. The one where I wished for a man who would change my life forever.

Remembering the wish has always crushed me, making me think the wish came true when I was raped and traumatized when I was sixteen years old.

Yet...

Maybe that wish didn't work out the way I've always felt it had. He surely wasn't a man then. And certainly not the kind of man I was wishing for, either. Maybe that wish upon that star hasn't come true yet.

Or maybe it just has.

CHAPTER EIGHTEEN

Forget Plans

The moment my eyes see sunlight, I vow to go easy on the alcohol for the day. I groan, rolling out of bed. Dress in my running gear. Refill my water bottle. Grab my cell phone. Head out the door.

Sounds of the ocean pull me in, and I'm awake and ready by the time I hit the beach. I head south this time, not wanting to run on the street.

I want to be alone. And at this hour, I am.

Not a soul is in sight, minus the occasional fisherman sitting by his lines. My mind jumbled and tumbled from last night and anxious about the night ahead, I've got to run. It's the only way to sort everything out.

The coolness in the breeze coming off the ocean prickles the skin on my right as the rising sun warms my left. Competition. Let them have it. I don't have any control over them.

I fill my mind with peace and quiet. Quicken my pace. Pound the sand beneath me.

I don't have to be in control to be in control.

The thought passes through my mind, and I don't stop to analyze it. I just let it pass. But it does something. It adds to the peace I feel. I don't stop to analyze the peace, either. I just let it be and enjoy it.

It's eight o'clock by the time I return home. I'm not sure how far I've run, but I'm not stopping to calculate that either. I feel good.

It was a good run.

Then I see the wall—my wall—and start piecing it together in my mind: what I want to do next. What I want to add. To redo. I search on my cell phone for a local art supply store and head out, still dressed and sweaty from my run. Find everything I need and more. And by the time I get back, I can't wait to grab my paints and get to it.

A long beach.

Towering cliffs.

Children playing in the sand.

Burnt reds, bright yellows, dark greens. My hand glides the paintbrush effortlessly over tiny imperfections in the wall and brings to life the hidden beauty of my daydream. Brush strokes romanticize. Highlights focus. Deep hues hide.

I lose myself in a trance until my cell phone rings.

I rub paint-spattered hands on my running shorts and flip open my phone. It's a message from Ty. I feel a warm tingle rise, only to go instantly cold when I read his text: 15 minutes out. Got directions from Dana. See you soon.

Fifteen minutes out? Directions from Dana? See you soon?

But it's only eight in the morning!

At least that's the last time I remember looking at the clock today. So engrossed in painting, I did it again. Painted all day. No breaks. No sanity. No sense of the real world outside of this one wall filled with my passion pouring out.

I look at the time. Three-thirty. Reread his message. Slowly come back to reality.

"Oh, my God! The wedding!" I scream to myself, stumbling up, running toward El's closet. "He's coming to pick me up for the wedding!" I scream again out into the house, and hear the dog locked up downstairs howl in response.

I can see the disaster about to ensue. Not only is the entire room destroyed from my sporadic Mad Hatter painting style, I am covered from head to foot in multicolored paint splatterings that would make a rainbow jealous. And, doing the armpit check, I am disgusting from my morning's run.

My God, don't I ever stop to take a shower? I'm such a gross animal.

Then I remember. My brushes. They'll be ruined if I don't wash them out!

I turn and run back to the guestroom. Fill the kitchenette's sink with water. Drop all my brushes in. Gather up all my paint trays covered in pools of waiting-to-be-used paint in multitudes of colors. Slipping them into and sealing them in Ziploc bags, I put them in the guest kitchenette's fridge, glad there's only a few bottles of beer and nothing else crowding up the space. Chilled paint doesn't dry out as fast as left-out-in-the-room-uncovered paint. I'll be able to use most of it again tomorrow.

The room though is destroyed. If Dana gave Ty directions, that means he'll be coming up to the guest suite door, not the main door. He's going to walk right smack into the middle of my chaos.

I toss the bed together, getting paint on El's pristine white sheets, shove all my loose clothes and duffle bag under the bed, push all remaining paint supplies close to the wall and make a sane pathway to the only orderly spot in the room: the open veranda.

Frazzled but with no time to dwell on it, I do a mad dash to El's closet. Last night, I had planned on rummaging through her closet for something to wear after maybe getting my nails and hair done today. Something remotely close to getting ready to go to a wedding. Now, I don't know what to wear. I don't even know if I'll fit into anything she owns.

"Stupid, stupid, dumb, dumb," I ream myself. At least my sister is superbly anal, and her clothing is organized by color and hung by occasion.

"Breathe, Matty. Breathe," I say to myself and look around her closet. I feel just a tad bit under control until I hear the dog bark. Ty's here.

"Fifteen minutes my ass!" I yell, then throw my hand over my mouth. At least I'm a house away from where he stands outside the guestroom door. He can't hear me.

At least I hope he can't.

I run around the U-shaped hallway to the guestroom. Hear him knock again. The dog's going insane downstairs. There's no time to collect myself. Ty's just going to have to deal. He's early.

I open the door. And, at the sight of him, I let out the breath I'm sure I've been holding ever since I knew he was minutes away. Lost in his eyes, I see his signature grin: that damned, wonderful, knowing grin.

He says a quick, "Sorry, I'm early. Drove fast. Couldn't wait to see you again and…" He looks me over. "Are you painting?"

"Yeah. I'm so sorry. I just got so taken away," I say, rushing back into the room. "I can get ready quick. Honest."

Ty casually looks at his watch and makes me sweat, hiding his reaction. Then he smiles with his eyes, and I wish we didn't have anywhere to go.

"I'm the best man, so I have to be there soon," he says, walking in. "Can you be ready in twenty?"

I disguise my fear and internally scream. I have to shower, find something to wear, do my hair, my makeup, and all this while Ty is only steps away. After I persuade him to sit on a comfy chair on the veranda, I dash to El's closet. If I had known I would've been doing this much running around the house, I wouldn't have bothered with my morning run. Then again, if I hadn't forgotten about reality and ventured off to la-la land and painted the day away, I wouldn't have to be running around.

Stop it, Matty. No time to argue with yourself. Find something to wear.

I rummage through El's assortment of evening dresses, sundresses, and elegant pantsuits. Everything is black, white, and gray. Everything. I can't wear black or white to a wedding, can I? I frantically search the room—yes, her closet is an actual room—hoping to find something that doesn't scream out I'm going to a funeral or I'm going to sue you.

Then I see it. Tucked in a corner at the end of a rack is a deep-emerald-green dress, short to just above the knees, sleeveless, high-waisted with a nice V-neckline. I hold it up to me to determine if the length is good and grab a pair of strappy turquoise heels. And a pocket purse thingy of a muted metallic gold that, as magic has it, has a skinny gold necklace tucked inside with a pair of hoop earrings to match.

First thought? It all goes together. At least I'm hoping it does. I don't have time to second-guess at this point.

I run at full speed back to my bathroom, holding the dress away from me so as not to drench it in my grossness. Hang the dress on a bathroom wall hook, drop the shoes to the floor and proceed to vigorously rub and scratch off every millimeter of paint that is also, after looking in the mirror, in my hair.

Not to worry. I have at least fifteen minutes to go.

The heat of the shower and the scent of the chamomile shampoo help settle my nerves enough to realize I need undergarments. Translation? When I'm finished getting clean, I have to leave the bathroom in a towel and walk past the open veranda to get to my bag that's stuffed under the bed.

Second translation? I'll have to walk past Ty practically naked.

A subconscious genius, I may have done this on purpose.

Finished with the shower, I towel off, wrap myself in its fluffiness, and quickly but quietly walk across the guestroom. Confident, I am, right? I hurriedly crouch by the bed, rummage through my bag for a bra-and-panty ensemble, when I realize I'm not alone. Ty's been standing inside the room the entire time. His back is turned to me, but he's only inches away.

"Breathtaking," he says in a hushed voice.

The sound of his voice steals mine. I stand, holding my undies in one hand and securing the towel in other.

Electrified, I manage a whispered, "Really?"

"This is absolutely breathtaking. Did you paint this?"

I nod, only momentarily confused. He keeps his gaze on the wall. Moves closer to inspect some detail. I shimmy back to the bathroom and slam the door.

"I'm practically naked, and all he wants to do is look at my painting?" I pout to myself in the mirror. In a moment of defiance, I drop my towel to the ground, wondering if something is—as I've always suspected—wrong with me.

I take in a good look at my reflection. Head, shoulders, breasts, tummy, legs. I'm not a misfit. I fit, as does everything on my body. I sway to the side. Turn to see the back of me.

Nice tush.

Ty's voice is soft against the door. "You okay in there?"

"Uh, yeah," I snap out of my self-approving moment. "Almost ready."

I slink into the dress, put on the heels, scrunch gel into my hair, and dab on a little peach lip gloss and eye shadow. Then I place any essentials I think I might need for touchup in the pouch and take a step back.

I hadn't quite calculated the depth of the V-neckline when I held the dress up to myself in El's closet. It's plunging. Revealing.

Stunning.

If I had time to second-guess myself, I'd add a cami underneath to hide my femininity and ruin the whole look. Yet, really, I like it. No hiding. No running. Glamorous.

I look like a woman who's not ashamed to be a woman.

I emerge from the bathroom with a puff of steam at my back, like a goddess coming forth from her own prison of self-loathing. Catching a glimpse of myself in the full-length mirror at the opposite end of the room, I don't stop myself from doing a twirl and a twist, enjoying what I've managed to pull together in such a short time.

I spin around and see Ty. "Ready to go?" I ask with a flirty grin when I see he's speechless.

He's a moment in responding. "If that's what you look like in twenty minutes, I'd love to see what you could do with more time. You look wonderful."

After Ty opens the door to his car for me, he slides in behind the wheel and starts the engine. The rumble sends excited ripples through my seat, and I bite my lip.

"I have a confession to make," Ty says softly over the sound, and

I barely hear his almost whisper.

Yet I notice it's the first time I've heard his voice without the ease of his grin. I look at him. He's looking down in his lap.

"I got here real early because I wanted to warn you."

I raise an eyebrow. "Warn?"

"Yeah," he says, turning toward me, a strong crease visible on his forehead. He kills the engine. "You're about to be thrown into a lion's cage. To be honest, this isn't my idea of a good first date."

The seriousness on his face is unsettling. "If you don't want me to go, Ty, I understand."

"Oh, hell no, Matty." He puts his hand on mine, smiling, although forced. "No. I mean, it's my family. All of them. And my kids. It's just, well… no one's seen me with another woman since Vanessa."

"Okay," I say, understanding his logic and beginning to be infected by his worry.

"They're a lively bunch, not opposed to asking and prying, if you know what I mean."

"No biggie. We're on a first date. Set up by our sisters. I think we can handle that," I say with an easy smile.

When he doesn't respond with his usual grin and chuckle, I get it. "It's your kids," I say, seeing from the look in his eyes that this is the real issue.

He takes his hand away from mine and rubs the back of his neck. "Yeah. Baz and Maia. They're not accustomed to seeing me with anyone, much less on a date. I'm not one for sheltering them, but this is all real sudden."

"Ty, I understand." When he lets out a reserved sigh, I reach for his hand. "Really. It's okay. We can do this another time."

He holds my gaze for a moment. "Damn," he says under his breath, and the worry crease in his forehead vanishes. He chuckles.

"Dana told me you would understand and that I was working myself up for nothing."

"So we can just go out maybe tomorrow if you want." I trail off, getting the gravity of the moment yet not wanting to leave his side.

"No. No. I want you to go. Us, I mean, to go. God, I'm horrible at this," he says, staring at the steering wheel then looking over at me. "I just… This is all new to me. New to my kids."

I send him a gentle smile and squeeze his hand. "Me, too."

The drive to the wedding is quiet. With the windows up and a slight breeze coming from the air vent, I relax back in my seat and enjoy the ride and the comfortable quiet between us.

"So," I finally ask, "how long have you known the groom?"

"The groom? Oh, well…" Ty pauses. "Well, Vanessa, my late wife, she worked with Ron. She knew they were going to be a perfect fit. So she set them up. They've been together ever since. 'Bout nine years now."

"Nine years? Wow. Why so long to tie the knot?"

"Oh, well, Dana wanted to finish college first. Then grad school. She always wanted to be a therapist. Felt if she got married, she'd start having babies too soon and, well, the whole career thing would be put on pause. Now that's she's got the career thing situated, all she wants to do is be a mom. Funny how it works out."

"Dana's a therapist?" I say.

"Yeah. Don't worry none though. She rarely tells anyone when she first meets 'em. Feels people are uncomfortable knowing they're talking to a shrink."

"Oh, not me," I blurt out. "I've talked to a therapist long enough to know they're harmless."

I almost slap my hand over my mouth, but I don't want to bring any more attention to myself. I feel my heart rate speed up, wondering if I've let the cat out of the bag too soon. That I'm nuts.

Well, not nuts now. But was nuts, and not too long ago.

I peek over at Ty from the corner of my eye. See him smiling at me.

"Me, too," he says with a light squeeze on my hand. "They're mighty good to talk to when you need 'em."

CHAPTER NINETEEN

This is Crazy

Dana and Ron's nuptials take place on a beachside grassy knoll with the sun setting behind the ocean. Just about everyone seated is wearing sunglasses.

Ron walks up with Ty, his best man and the two stand side by side. One sends a wink my way. The other fidgets and sweats in the late afternoon sun.

An acoustic band consisting of guitars, a banjo, an accordion, and a harmonica play a soft, lovely tune as maid of honor Gale strides in to take her place. Dana follows gracefully. Dressed in an elegant, pale-white dress with cap sleeves and a scoop neckline, she lights up when she sees Ron.

After their vows and a rather raucous burst of celebration that follows, everyone joins the freshly married couple for a round of kisses and hugs, all caught on various cameras. I stand with a few of Dana's friends on the outskirts of the crowd and enjoy watching the scene. Flutes of champagne are passed around, and we all partake in a little libation as a few loud souls shout out their toasts and good tidings to the newlyweds.

It's not the lion's cage Ty warned me it would be. People are warm and friendly, and a few introduce themselves. I watch with amusement as Ty tries yet fails many times over to detach himself from his family to join me. He catches my attention, often with waves and smiles, yet is held captive by various adoring family members and friends who only want to hold his attention a little while longer.

A handful of children play together on the grass, running around in circles. Some try darting off toward the beach, never making it far though.

As for me, I continue to make small talk with Dana's friends, all the while glancing around to see if I can spot Ty's kids. The photo he showed me on the plane was a few years old, yet I can at least make a guess from what I remember.

His oldest, Maia, I spot right away. Although taller now and a little leaner, she looks just like her picture. She has on a just-below-the-knees yellow sundress and a pair of white flip-flops adorned with tiny daisies by her toes. A barrette trailed by white and yellow ribbons stands out against her long, brilliant-red hair.

Watching her, I notice she's keeping a close eye on one little boy in particular, who, now that I see him, looks just like Ty. He runs around the grass barefoot in a white, button-up, short-sleeved shirt with green shorts. The same dark, tousled hair of his father's frames his little face.

Baz is adorable. If I knew him better—or at all—I wouldn't think twice to whisk him up in my arms and hug him.

I spot Ty at the other end of the crowd and smile, warm from the inside out. Again, he heads my way. Only, as usual, his arrival at my side is circumvented by kisses and hugs from family and friends sharing in the excitement and love.

"Everyone!" Gale yells, clapping her hands loud. "Everyone, attention please!"

She grabs Ty's arm and directs him toward the bride and groom, who've moved over to the right edge of the crowd.

"We're all going to do a processional to the restaurant," she yells, then adds a happy, sing-songy, "So everyone, please, get in line behind the newlyweds!"

Ty looks back at me from his spot up ahead and bends down to pick up his son. I follow from my place in the back as we all walk behind the bride and groom in one big party line. Drinks in hand, the band trailing behind playing a tune, and some guests singing and dancing along, it's a sight to be seen.

Two blocks up, on the back deck of a restaurant reserved for the wedding party, I sit up at the bar with some of Dana's friends. Ty attempts to sit with me, yet is pulled away every time.

The look on his face seems pained, yet I can't help but laugh inside. It's endearing to watch him being tugged to and fro between his family, friends, and kids. It's obvious he's loved.

The band plays on as dinner is served, followed by a light dessert and toast after toast after toast to the happy couple. The guests are a lively bunch. Kids run around the deck, and everyone joins the newlyweds dancing, stealing the bride for a song here, the groom there.

I'm so busy enjoying myself as an onlooker, I don't realize someone's close beside me until I feel his breath on the nape of my neck.

"This is crazy," Ty breathes into my ear.

"I actually find it refreshing," I say, trying to not melt in public from his hot touch. "No bouquet tosses. No garter belt. I do miss the cake smashing part. But, hey, that's just me."

"No, silly. Us."

I look up at him and get it.

"Well, it's working out that we don't need to keep a low profile in front of your kids," I muse. "I don't think they even know you have a date."

"Still," Ty starts, the strain in his voice noticeable. He leans down, whispers in my ear, "Not being with you is killing me."

I let out a breathy laugh. Feel the heat of his hand on the small of my back. Revel in his touch.

But my heart quickens. "What about your kids?"

"They'll be okay."

"And the lion's cage?" I ask, worried, seeing all eyes in the room start to focus on us.

"They won't bite hard," Ty says, a glimmer to his eyes. "Would you care to dance?"

"Here? Now?"

"No. In the coat closet." He grins.

"Well..." I flirt back with a sly smile. Me, Ty, alone in the dark. That's not a bad idea. But I know he's putting himself out there, so I don't leave him hanging. "I'd love to dance."

The band is playing an upbeat country version of an oldie, but goodie: Louis Armstrong's What a Wonderful World. Once we reach the dance floor, Ty slides his hand behind my back and pulls me close. And for a moment, the whole room quiets to total silence.

But it's not my imagination. Everyone has, in fact, stopped talking. Dancers have even stopped dancing.

I feel momentarily uncomfortable until I see the look in Ty's eyes. He's enjoying this, and so I relax. Waltz around the floor with him leading.

After a lingering moment, the room starts to regain its normalcy. Dancers reunite and twirl. Conversations buzz.

Ty's gaze softens and, just like that, I'm back on that plane, meeting him for the first time. Only now, I get to melt into his arms.

"Dad," Ty's daughter whines, breaking the spell. "You said you'd dance with me."

Before Ty can say anything, his son, Baz, jumps in asking, "Can I dance with the pretty lady, too, Daddy? Can I? Can I?"

"Baz," Maia stomps at her brother. Obvious from the glare she tosses at me before wedging herself between Ty and myself, her intention wasn't to include me.

Ty sends me a worried half-smile. I shrug my shoulders with a wink and let little Baz whisk me away.

"That's my name," says a proud little voice above the music, and I look down at my dance partner. "My real name is Basil. But I like it when people call me Baz. It's spelled B-A-Z. I'm Baz the Taz!"

"That you are," I coo down at him.

All too soon, the band announces its last song and I watch from across the dance floor as Ty dances with his daughter again. Dana and Ron climb up onto the stage where the band is playing and take over the last half of the song, singing and laughing together while everyone joins in dancing.

Even the older guests meander around the dance floor, some with their canes, tossing a hip here, a shimmy there. People come up to me off and on and introduce themselves, full of questions.

Through it all, Baz continues to dance on like any little boy would: wild, crazy, and full of life. I try my best to keep up with him, but alas, I'm being pulled every which way.

And loving it.

"Everyone," Ron says into the microphone after the song ends, "I want to thank you all for coming to our wedding. I hope you had a great time?"

Cheers follow.

Dana takes the mic and adds, "Ron and I are going down to San Diego for a night on the town, so anyone who wants to join us for a little afterparty, let's go!"

"And for those of you calling it a night," Ron says, sharing the mic and taking Dana into his arms for a hug, "thank you again so very much for making our day so special and loving. We love you all!"

Just like that, as the sun ducks down beyond the horizon, the party is over. And the afterparty begins.

"Matty," Ty calls over the crowd, and heads turn in my direction. I watch as he ever so diplomatically makes his way through to me.

"Dang, it's like a zoo in here."

"Lion's cage," I joke. "Get it right."

"Nice one," he grins at me. "So. You ready for our first date, take two?"

"Take two?" I wonder, then get it. "The afterparty?"

"Yeah. My family can't be contained to party in one spot all night. What do ya say? It'll be a hoot."

"A hoot?" I laugh. "Sure. Sounds fun."

"Great. Listen. I have to get my kids set and off with my mom, so, um—" He looks around. "You mind hanging here for a bit and I'll come getcha?"

I wait for Ty while members of his family file out of the room, of course after coming up to me for a quick hello and goodbye that has more to do with finding out who I am and what I'm doing with Ty rather than social etiquette. When they all leave, I mildly obsess about my quick interaction with Ty's kids.

Although I seemed to have hit it off with Baz, I'm not so sure how it's going to go with Maia. Her glare at me on the dance floor had been a tad bit torturous. I think letting them ease into the idea of their dad being in a relationship will be best for everyone.

Relationship.

It's just a first date, Matty, I hear from the doubtful voice in my head. Don't get ahead of yourself. Could be all there ever will be.

When Ty returns, we're the last two remaining in the room. I'm borderline wondering if this is going to work out for everyone involved when our eyes meet.

He grins. Takes my hand in his. And I warm at his touch, all the butterflies in the world migrating back to me.

Go away, self-doubt. I'm enjoying this.

"Hey, Dana," Ty says into his phone as soon as we get into his car. "Tell Ron to head to the corner of J and Fifth Street... Yeah, I know... No, not yet... What do ya mean, why?... Well, I want it to be a surprise... Okay, sis. Bye." He disconnects. "Sheesh."

"What's the surprise?" I ask, wondering what he's got in store for Ron.

"You'll see," he says with a wink, and I get it. The surprise is for me.

As we get closer, the city lights start to sparkle against the clear, darkening night sky. We park in the last spot available in front of a three-leveled, old-style brick building that's been freshly painted a dark slate blue.

I glance up and admire the ornate, off-white gingerbread details that trim the windows and roofline as we walk over. Dana, Rob, and a whole group of others from the wedding are gathered on the sidewalk.

"So you're the boss," Ron says to Ty, slapping him on the shoulder, "Where to?"

Ty chuckles, holding my hand, "We'll follow you guys into the lounge."

Ron nods with a grin and takes Dana's hand.

"Let's go, troops!" With that, we follow the bride and groom around the building to the front entrance.

I hear live music, similar to the music the band had been playing at the wedding. But Ty stops walking, holding me back with him until everyone has disappeared inside.

He turns toward me, takes both of my hands in his. "Matty?"

"Yes, Ty?"

He inches closer. "Thank you for accompanying me to my sister's wedding. I had a great time."

"I had a great time, too. Thanks for inviting me," I say, stepping in closer myself.

The air surrounding us energizes, and the busy city disappears. And just as though we're closing out a first date, Ty leans down and kisses me softly on the lips, an ever-so-sweet kiss that I've never had. The feel of his lips on mine lingers warm, then hot.

He pulls back, the feel of his touch fuzzy on my lips. Electrified. I reach up and touch them. Watch as Ty's eyes linger on my mouth.

I want to dwell on the feeling, hold onto it forever, and see where it might lead. But the food aromas coming from the building smell so good. My greedy stomach growls loudly.

"Hungry?" he chuckles in a hushed voice, just for me.

"Always."

"Well, it's a good thing we're having our date number two at my restaurant," Ty says, his eyes all grin.

"Oh, goodie!" I say with more excitement than I would have at any other establishment.

"This is my home away from home." Taking a step back, he

lifts his arm and points to the sign above the doorway. "Boudin, my restaurant."

"Nice," I say, looking up at the heavy font script of the neon sign. "Boudin. Isn't that some sort of meat?"

"Cajun sausage: pork, rice, love of my life," Ty says with a wink. "Come on in."

The entryway leads to an open gathering area with three options to choose from. One, walk through the sliding glass doors to the left and you'll be seated in a casual, outdoor dining area with a deck and a live band. Option two, go to the right and up a grand staircase to where the silverware clinks on plates and conversations go on in the distance. Or three, walk straight ahead and into a darkened tavern filled with laughter and camaraderie.

"V's Lounge," I read the small sign above the door, knowing.

"Yeah. Vanessa said the place lacked style and sophistication. That's what she was all about. So I gave her this. Free range to do it up right." Ty looks up at the sign and then back down to me. "It's nice. Come on."

Taking my hand, he leads me in and I walk behind him as he edges his way through people, saying hello, shaking hands, and giving half hugs along the way. He does a quick introduction to a few people here and there, trying to keep things short as we work our way to his sister and the rest of the party at the back of the lounge.

Although I am warmed from the outside in by the feel of Ty's hand in mine and the linger of his kiss on my lips, I still feel enveloped by the presence of Vanessa in this place. Dark walnut wood, plush violet velvets, modern yet beautiful stained-glass windows. Her selection of paintings on the wall. Her selection of spirits on the shelf.

Strong. Independent. Confident.

If I had known where we were going, I would have waned,

thinking it might be too much. Too her. Yet, being here and walking through, it's not as confrontational as I would have imagined it to be. Her sense, her taste, her persona. She's here. Everywhere.

Yet, so am I.

"To the newlyweds!" Ty cheers as soon as we each have a drink in hand. "May they know happiness together and love forever."

"Happiness together and love forever!" everyone repeats and drinks, bottoms up.

I take a nice gulp of my glass lamp martini, a sweet, yellow concoction with swirls of red liqueur.

I listen in on the conversations and look around at the décor and artwork. Laugh wholeheartedly at the jokes. Accept a second martini and drink it up. Feel Ty's fingers intertwine with mine.

A third martini finds its way into my hand. I feel warm and fuzzy all over. My mind swims, and I start to mentally wander.

And wonder.

Wonder how Ty can live and survive in a world that still lives and breathes Vanessa. His children, his sister's happiness, even his business: They all owe themselves to her existence.

I look on as Ty talks to his new brother-in-law, the doctor. Married to Ty's sister, the therapist. And Ty, a renowned chef and business owner with multiple cookbooks published, once married to a beautiful, successful woman who was also at the top of her game.

And he has a family. And a car. And a house.

He's lived lifetimes around my one.

My stomach tightens, and I try to quiet the doubtful voice that creeps into my head. Only I'm too liquored up to stop the thoughts.

Who can I possibly be to him? Sure, I own a few new outfits and a handful of boxes in a storage unit back in Baltimore. But outside of that, I'm homeless and jobless. Even family-less. There's no way I fit into his life.

What was I thinking?

Excusing myself, I find my way to the bar and order a tall glass of water. Maybe it'll ease the burning in my stomach and the pain in my heart telling me I'm no good. I internally battle the monster of self-doubt, but it's no use. It's right.

I am useless.

"Hey, Matty," I hear Dana's voice behind me and turn around to see her standing stark against the crowd in her beautiful wedding gown. "Ron and I are about to scoot out of here, hopefully unnoticed." She wiggles her eyebrows and swishes her wedding dress. "But I wanted to just say a quick thank you."

"Oh, no. Thank you, Dana. Really. I had a great time. Your wedding was lovely."

"Ah, thanks. But I meant thank you for my brother, Ty. I haven't seen him this happy in years. Totally has the spark of life back in him, if you know what I mean."

I look over toward Ty, cautious.

"Oh, and one more thing. Here," she says, handing me an envelope. "This has directions, the key to our house, and a picture of what I'd like painted on the wall right above the kitchen table. Just do your magic."

"Key?"

"Just let yourself in, and if you don't get done by the time we get back from our honeymoon, that's okay. I just want it to be a surprise for Ron. There's a check in there for you, too."

"A check? But Dana—"

"Thank you, Matty, for everything," Dana says once more and gives me a hug before disappearing into the crowd and out of sight.

I shove the envelope into my clutch purse and down my water. I feel a warm hand slide around my middle. I look down. Notice Ty's arm around me.

He rests his chin on my bare shoulder.

"The group's headed out to a dance club next," Ty says into my ear and then swivels me on my seat to face him. "I'm not sure if that's my speed, but up to you."

"Oh, well..." I say uncertain, the alcohol making a tangle of my self-conscious thoughts, Dana's thank you, and the feel of Ty's hands that are now both on my knees. I breathe. "Maybe we could go somewhere quiet?"

I see relief and excitement wash over Ty's face. He leans in.

"I know just the place."

Engulfed in pure silence, the elevator ride is like a vacuum suck to my ears. I feel my head spin a little and chastise myself for not taking it easy with the martinis. Three floors up, we walk out onto a rooftop deck, surrounded by twinkly, white lights. It's quiet up here, with the city sounds and music from the band below muffled and a wonderful, quiet breeze blowing.

"The roof's closed for another few days to complete the addition," Ty says as he guides me around. "But this is it. Boudin's latest and greatest. What do you think?"

A rustic wooden pergola sits in the center of the roof deck, creating a seating area with tables and chairs for dining. Situated to the side of the elevator is a small kitchen-like bar with stools set around.

"Nice," I say, not knowing what it looked like before. "Looks great."

Ty directs me over to the kitchen-bar area. "This here is where groups can sit and watch their food prepared. You know, interact with the chef." He pulls out a stool for me. Sits on the neighboring one. "Funny thing, I'm not sure what to call it yet. But I'm thinking that giving it a name will make it less casual. I just want it to be an experience."

"Then don't complicate it," I say and lean my head back, eyes closed, to bask in the coolness of the evening, a liquid smile on my face.

"That's basically what I was thinking," I hear Ty say, and I look at him. See his grin.

It's nice being here with him. Comfortable. Like I've known him far longer than I actually have.

"Sorry if my kids gave you a scare back there," he says, the worry crease marking his forehead again.

"No worries. They're cute." My smile slides into a frown, and I sigh. "Your sister gave me a key, you know."

"I know."

"I don't know what she's thinking giving a total stranger a key to her house."

Ty chuckles at me. "She trusts you."

"But she only just met me."

"I trust you."

I laugh under my breath. "You hardly know me, Ty."

"Then talk," he says in his singsong drawl. "Tell me about yourself. What's your family like? You know all about mine now, that's for sure."

"Well," I start, wondering if I have a worry crease of my own now. I know my stomach feels like one big worry knot. "I don't really have any family to speak of."

When Ty leaves me space to fill, I take a shallow breath and say, "There's me, my dad, my mom, and my sis. That's it."

"Okay."

Expand, Matty, I hear Dr. Linda prompt in my head.

I look down at my hands. "I'm not really in good standing with my family at the moment. That's why I'm here. In California." I look up, bite my lip.

Ty nods, says nothing.

"I've talked to them here and there over the years, but I haven't seen my family in… ten years." When Ty doesn't flinch, I add, "My father was a Navy captain. Just retired back in May."

"Go Navy."

"Ha. You sound like my friend Claire back home."

"In Baltimore?"

"Annapolis, just south of Baltimore. Although, this time next week, she and her family will be heading to Germany. Her husband got a transfer. They'll be there for at least five years. Maybe more. Really great opportunity."

"Germany. Pretty far away."

"Yeah. They want me to stay out there with them."

"Stay? That's pretty nice of them."

"Yeah, but I'm not really sure where I want to end up just yet."

Ty seems to ponder this a bit, then adds, "And your mom? Sister?"

I twist on my stool. "Not much to tell. I'm basically estranged."

"So you're alone," Ty says, more as a statement than a question.

"Sad, huh?"

"It happens," he says, inching closer to me. "I tell ya, after Vanessa passed away, I just about swallowed myself up inside. Wanted to die. Didn't want anyone around. But they—my family—pushed their way in and helped me get along."

He takes both my hands in his and sets them on his lap. "Nothing wrong with being alone. It's life. Gives you time for other things to enter in."

"Yeah," I say, although I don't quite follow.

"Like painting," he says with a sparkle to his eyes. "That was pure passion I saw up on that wall. Like you gave it your all."

That last part comes out with such wonderment that I want to laugh at myself. But tears start to build in my eyes instead.

I try my damnedest to suck them back in. "I like that. Passion in life. Knowing what you want and going for it."

I blink tears back. Swallow hard.

"Like food," he says. "I have a strong passion for it, and it's become my life."

My stomach rumbles loudly, and I laugh, thankful for the lightening of the moment.

"Hungry?" he asks with a laugh of his own. He texts something into his cell phone. "I'm gonna have them bring us up something from the menu before the kitchen closes. Anything you like."

He leans over the bar, grabs a menu, and hands it to me. "Whatever you want, go for it."

CHAPTER TWENTY

Surprise, Surprise

Excited energy carries me through Sunday. I run in the morning, paint all day… remember to eat way too late at night.

I get a few texts from Ty during the day that I instantly reply to—reason one why my phone is now a multicolored paint mess. He and his children are together for the day, and I get the feeling that Sundays are a special time for their family.

Just the three of them.

As much as Ty insisted I join them and I want to be with him—with them—I need a day to process. We had a grand first date last night. And a wonderful second-try first date, too. Add to that his good-night kiss when he dropped me off: another light brushing of his lips on mine.

Yep. I need a day to bask in the daydream of it all.

Then it's Monday, almost one o'clock on a cloudless afternoon, and I'm halfway finished with the mural in El's guestroom. Although

I have plans to paint something on almost every wall, even adding small elements to light switch plates and above doors, the mural is already beginning to flow with the space perfectly, never competing with any of the other details in the room.

Question is—am I getting carried away? Emotionally, that is?

I take a step back and a deep breath in. Yes. Yes, I am. And I don't feel the tiniest bit of guilt about it.

I know what I'm doing. Even though it's beautiful and, really, just paint, I'm doing it as a punishment. To her. For what she did to me. As quirky as it may seem, I'm standing up to my sister in my own way.

Then again, maybe I do feel a tad bit guilty. Maybe I shouldn't have done anything without her formal consent.

Oh, well. Too late now.

Besides, the painting is perfectly orchestrated, if I say so myself. Plus, I'm enjoying painting again, and it does look professional. Like a muralist has been hired to do the work.

An effortless expression of art. That's how my father had once coined my talent. I hadn't given him much credit or really understood what he meant until today. But he's right. As is Ty.

This is who I am. This is who I've always been. This is me.

"And it looks so damned professional," I repeat out loud with pride and amazement.

Dana had said it, hadn't she? That I could do this and make a living? I toy with the idea for a few minutes, adding brush strokes here, details there.

Although it would be awesome to do something I love and am good at, and get paid for it, I know better. Art careers don't always pan out. I could start big and end up small if people found they couldn't afford extra touches to their finances, like decorative painting. It is an extra expense, after all.

However, it could be possible. I could at least try and see where it goes...

For starters, I'm related to two people who own and operate an architectural and interior design company. Eleanor and Mark could help me start my business with contacts of known clients who would want murals or decorative painting in their homes or offices.

That is, if Eleanor doesn't kill me first.

I step out of the room, pace a few lines in the hallway, and walk back in for a fresh look. It does look nice. Spectacular, really.

El might be upset with me at first, but she won't be mad for long. She'll see the true beauty I've created and not the nasty aim I did it with. She'll forgive me. Might even recommend me.

At least I hope.

My stomach rumbles.

I take a quick shower, dress in cut-off shorts I've had since college and a new scoop neck, bright-blue top I bought with Claire, and head downstairs for lunch. Only, there's nothing in the fridge still. That, and I don't feel like eating alone.

I text Ty a quick: hungry? with a winking smiley, then think better. It's Monday. He's working. He has a job. He has a business to run. I'm sure he's hustling around doing whatever restaurant owners who happen to also write cookbooks on the side do.

I wish I could take back my impromptu intrusion into his busy day when I receive his quick reply: Always. Late dinner okay?

I do a happy dance and text back: Absolutely.

And grin. A stupid, face-erupting, ear-to-ear grin. Dinner with Ty Waters. It doesn't matter where or when. I just can't wait to be with him again.

Yet that doesn't do me any good for now. I'm still hungry. When I don't hear back from him right away, I assume he's busy—as I'm sure he is—and don't bother him with any more texts. I trust he'll get back to me when he has the chance to let me know when and where.

In the meantime, I jog back up to my room, grab my stuff, and head for the garage. El had left me instructions that, if necessary, I could use her car while staying at her house.

If necessary. What did she think? That I'd hole myself up inside their house alone for two weeks? Not only is Southern California beautiful, but I have a lot of catching up to do. For my entire twenties, I didn't really spend any time enjoying myself. For my thirties, I want to start treating myself to simple pleasures again.

And going out for lunch is first on my list.

I drive down through Del Mar and hop on Highway 101, which is less like a highway and more like a main street that makes its way straight through every beachside town north of San Diego. I head north with the windows wide open and enjoy the view. Make a U-turn somewhere past Cardiff by the Bay and head back through Solana Beach.

Nothing catches my eye, so I continue on and return to Del Mar. Park right outside a dark-brown, German-styled building with white trim. I lock El's car and ask for a table on their roadside patio.

"Good morning," A cheery waitress walks up. "Have you had a chance to look over the menu? What would you like to drink?"

I glance at the menu and find my favorites. "I think I'll have a glass of grapefruit juice, the big plate of huevos rancheros, and a large bowl of fruit salad. Extra berries, if possible."

As soon as she walks away, I see someone on the sidewalk and feel my breath catch. It can't be, but I stand to get a better view and then, without hesitation, dash out onto the sidewalk.

It can't be. But it is.

"Sara!" I call out. "Sara!"

Immersed in conversation with those around her, it's a delayed reaction. She pauses, stops, and turns around.

"Who called my name?" she says in the heavy English accent I remember so well.

"Sara, it's me, Matty," I say as I run up to her. "Matty Bell from Naples, Italy. Remember?"

Tall and dark mocha with a short-cropped 'fro, she looks almost exactly the same as the day she and her family moved back to the States a month before my family.

"Matty?" she asks, looking at me. "Blow me! Is that really you? I would have never recognized you."

Oblivious to the odd looks coming from her companions and others passing by, we jump around like a couple of teenage girls at a boy band concert, everything out of our mouths high-pitched and exaggerated. We hug and bounce and giggle and laugh. And why not?

It's been more than a decade since we've last seen each other. That, and when you're a military brat, goodbyes usually mean forever, even if your heart never forgets. After a while, we calm down a bit, both of us wearing mild-wide smiles.

"Wow, didn't expect to see you ever again," I say. "Do you live here?"

"No, just fannying around. We were in La Jolla for a conference and decided to stay on for a bit more. Gander around. It's brilliant here."

"Sure is," I say. I get an idea. "Hey, if you're not too busy, would you like to join me? I just sat down for lunch. We could catch up. My treat."

"Smashing! Oh, I'd love to catch up," she exclaims and turns to her group, "I'll take a taxi back. Ciao!"

We walk arm in arm the way we used to back in Italy.

"I cannot believe it," I say, sitting down. "I just looked up for a second, and there you were."

"I'm so glad you did. I would have never guessed this bald chick in front of me was my long-lost friend." Sara laughs, rubbing a hand over my short-haired head. "Matty Bell. The runner from hell. How are you?"

I laugh out loud. "No one's called me that in a zillion years. I totally forgot all about that." I shake my head, jog down memory lane.

"So you living here now?"

"No. I don't live here, although I used to. I'm sort of between places. Sort of visiting," I hear myself say and stop short. I don't really want to get into all my historical detail. Not now. I'm too happy.

I change the subject. "How about you? What have you been up to since high school?"

"Oh, the usual. Got married too soon. Divorced too soon. Then married again," she laughs with a head shake. "Then found myself and realized what I really wanted to do. Went to law school, and now I'm a tax attorney. Don't ask me why. I just love it."

"Good Lord, someone has to," I jeer back.

We soon start to reminisce about our high school days, living in Italy, being military brats, running around base together with Claire and all our other friends. It was a totally unique experience. We talk about the sport trips and traveling all over Europe. The food, the fun, the friends. Everything we wished we never had to leave behind.

And that's when we come to the part about who all each of us is still in contact with. When I tell her that Claire and I have basically lived next door to each other for the past decade, Sara cocks her head and squints at me.

"Wonder why she never told you about everyone keeping in touch online?"

Although it pains my heart to hear the deception, I don't have to give it much thought and ignore the know-it-all voice in my head pointing out the obvious. She knew you couldn't handle bumping into him online. She was protecting you.

"Oh, I basically lived in front of a computer at work." I laugh it off and wave a mental hand at the voice in my head. "She probably thought I'd rather not spend any more time in front of a screen than I had to."

Thankfully, my nonchalance about it satisfies Sara, and the subject is dropped, only to lead into a lull in conversation. My wheels start to spin in a different direction.

There has to be a reason why we bumped into each other. I don't want to, but I know I have to do it. I have to ask. My police report can't go any further until someone locates him. I guess I had hoped, by reporting it, someone else would do the work of finding him.

"Hey, Sara, do you by any strange chance know where… you-know-who lives?" I ask, still unable to say his name.

She stares at me. "You mean him him?" Sara asks, seeming to not want to say his name either.

"Yeah. I don't really want to know, but I need to know," I say, hoping she gets it without me having to go into detail. "It's complicated."

"Complicated," she says quietly to herself, then looks up at me. "He's not online, if that's what you're asking. Not that I've seen anyway. I never understood why you went out with him in the first place. You stopped coming around, hanging out. Hell, you dropped out of track and cross country, too. Totally disappeared."

"Yeah, well, if everyone hadn't pressured me into it, I wouldn't have. Everyone knew I was still in love with Gabe," I say, as though we're back in time: back in high school. As though I can stop it all from happening.

I close my eyes. Take a deep breath. "I," I say and stop.

When I don't start again, she takes a deep breath herself before saying in her lovely accent, "Well, on about it, then."

This is a test, my little voice friend speaks up in my head. A test to see if I can get it all out without falling apart. Sara may have been a good friend years ago, but she's a long-ago friend now.

How much is too much to tell someone you haven't seen in years? How little is too little to leak?

"I'd rather not get into it here," I confess, which is true. I might be okay with her knowing, but it's too much information for strangers' ears.

"Well, I would like to walk a bit on the beach," Sara says.

The beach turns out to be perfect. The normalcy and peace of the ocean is all I need to come out of my shell. With Sara's silence stretching out in front of me, I start talking about how it was all innocent at first but then how I later felt trapped. Couldn't get out. How he isolated me from my friends and threatened to kill me if I left.

The mind games. The mental abuse.

The rapes.

After such a long time with it being so big in my life—so overwhelming. So all-consuming—after I get it all out, it feels small. Like a page in my history that needs no dog-earing. No need to go back to it anymore.

It's over. Gone.

When Sara doesn't interrupt, I gain a hurried momentum. I talk about how, after I remembered the rape, both my sister and mom shot me down: made me feel guilty for it. How I had to leave home, not wanting to be around those who wouldn't believe me, hear me, or see me. But then how I never really did any healing on my own until just recently.

All the years wasted, and for what? And now how I'm finally at a place where I don't feel fearful or shameful about the past, but instead how I feel like this superpower full of life and confidence, and ready to take on the world.

Rejuvenated, I snap out of my wired monologue when I notice Sara's no longer walking by my side. I turn. She's a few steps behind me with a stricken look on her face.

"Are you okay?" I ask.

Sara lets out a breath as if she had been holding it the whole time I was talking. "You say he… raped you?"

Selfish in my own need to express all that was bottled up inside, I hadn't given much thought that the person on the receiving end of my hurried speech would need time to adjust. To digest.

It had taken me more than ten years to overcome it all. What was I thinking?

"I am so sorry, Sara," I say, walking the few steps back to where she's standing. "I just can't believe how over it I am now that I am."

I chuckle, wondering if I'm making sense. When she doesn't seem to lighten up, I collect myself. Get serious.

"Yes. He did. And more than once. Enough times that I got to a point that I just let him do it so he'd leave me alone and not hurt me more. But I'm okay now."

Sara doesn't respond. Nor does her skin pigmentation, which is frightening given her usual mocha coloring.

I place my hands on either side of her arms, feel her skin cold.

"Sara, it's okay. I'm okay," I say, worried that I've overwhelmed my friend of old. "Sorry I let it all out like that. You just opened a door, and I haven't really told anyone other than Claire and my therapist."

Sara, her dark-chocolate eyes locked on mine, is a minute before speaking. And then she's barely audible over the surf at our side.

"Matty… he raped me, too."

CHAPTER TWENTY-ONE

Testa Dura

My head swirls with my overactive imagination. Images and sounds, like movie trailers, sprout involuntarily in my mind, and I can't help but envision Sara in the same abusive scenes I've been reliving for years.

I don't know where to land. Sara and I were both raped by Jettison Fisher.

It's a while before I feel the ground under my feet again. Find my voice. Tell Sara about the case I'm trying to bring up against him.

The case. Now that I know he hurt more than just me, it has to be a case. I can't just leave it at reporting it now. I have to bring him to trial. I try to get her to be on board with me. The more power we have, I say, the better. But Sara doesn't know where to land either.

In her own way, she healed from her trauma years ago. She's okay now, too. She's just not sure she wants to go down that road again.

And she wants to go home.

Both of us in shock, I say goodbye to her and watch her cab drive away. Then I drive back to El's house, drowning in my own buzzing thoughts.

My silence. What if it came with a price? I know I couldn't have saved Sara. It happened to her months before it happened to me.

Still. What if, because I didn't report it when my memory first came back to me, someone else has endured the same fate as we did?

My stomach pinches deep. I could have reported it ten years ago, and I didn't. Instead, I allowed others to make me feel guilty for something that I definitely did not want to happen. And, in turn, I ran away from my number-one responsibility: to protect others from suffering the same fate.

I should have reported it.

With newfound determination, I do what I should have done right from the beginning. I call the sexual assault hotline on the Navy base near San Diego. When no one answers, I leave a message. Ask that my call be returned as soon as possible so that my Naval lawyer in Annapolis, Maryland, can further my case.

As I walk up the stairs to the guest door, I feel my phone vibrate. Hold the railing for support. Stand tall and answer my phone. I tell the woman at the crisis center how I've called and reported my rape to civilian and military police alike, yet have gotten nowhere.

"I sympathize with your frustration, Ms. Bell. How can I be of service?"

I cross my fingers in hopes I'm talking to someone who can actually help. Give all the details. Explain the previous reports and the lack of the restitution I now want.

"I want to make sure that I've exhausted all potential avenues of getting something in the form of permanent charges brought against this person," I say. "I want it on his permanent record."

"And exactly why didn't the military do just that? I don't suspect that time should play any role in disallowing it. You're well within the statute of limitations on this."

Feeling relief, I take in a deep breath to steady myself before foraging on. "The reason no charges were ever brought against him is because no one can find him."

There's a pause on the other side of the phone, then, "That doesn't make any sense. The military couldn't find him?"

"That's what they said. That they had done all they could, but that they couldn't find him. So the case closed there."

"I see."

"And right before I left Maryland, I called to see if I could get a copy of the report in case I wanted to resume my search, and they said they couldn't find it. That they had moved offices and lost the paperwork."

"Sounds to me like someone didn't want to do the work," she says.

I drop my head, defeated, and sit on the top step.

"I don't want you to get too excited because, like you said, this is an old case. However, I'd like to see what we can do for you before you decide to fold again. Do you have his name?"

"I do. And his birthdate, too, if that helps."

"And this is the same information you gave to the Army's military police?"

"Yes, ma'am."

"Humph." I hear her snort. "Is there anything else you can tell me before I start making calls?"

Jogging my memory for any pertinent information, I can't scrounge up another morsel. That is, until I recall something Claire mentioned in passing. "Actually, he is or was at one point in the Marines."

After a moment of silence, she speaks again. "Thank you, Ms.

Bell, for all the information. I will see what I can do."

Consumed, I try to fight thoughts about a potential resolution. I don't want to get my hopes up though.

I let myself inside El's guestroom door and pick up a paintbrush. Dip it in crimson red. Swirl it around and around. Let my fear and frustration out on the wall. Grab for blues and greens to force calm into the scene.

Before I know it, I've been painting through the rest of the day and haven't thought about anything at all like I'm in a trance. The sun starting to set outside, I wash out some of my brushes. By now, I feel miles away from caring what will happen. If anything happens at all.

I've done all that I can, which was more than I ever thought I'd do. And I did it for me.

I feel the freedom of relief wash over me every so often, reiterating that I've done the right thing: to try. And then to let go.

Then I hear my phone ring.

I rush to answer it and speed talk, half-thinking.

"Hello. So glad you called. I was starting to wonder. I hope it's good news."

"I hope it's good news, too," I hear him say. It's Ty. "Calling to see if you were close to ready for dinner. Sorry if I interrupted something. I can call back."

"Dinner?" I ask and smack my forehead. I totally forgot about life outside of trauma healing after I bumped into Sara.

"Yeah," he says through what sounds like a halfway grin. "If you've got other plans, that's fine."

"No! I, um. I mean, yes. I mean…" I scramble, trying to form an intelligent response to my absentminded one. "I'm ready when you are." I let that simmer for a split second before adding, "Sorry for the momentary forgetfulness. I've had a hell of a day."

"Maybe you can fill me in when I get there. I'm about five, ten minutes away."

CHAPTER TWENTY-TWO

One Minute, Please

I shower and dress, buttoning up my capris jeans and slipping on a silky, sleeveless, red blouse along with my brown suede flip-flops just as Ty knocks on the door. I tie the blouse's neck strap at the back of my neck and feel the long ties dance on my bare skin. Open the door and see he's on the phone.

He holds up a finger and goes to say something when he sees me. Instead, a stunned yet pleased look fills his face and he stands speechless.

I blush. I've never been so adored.

He shakes his head at me, mouths a "Wow!" and smiles sideways before calmly yet firmly barking some sort of orders into the phone.

Work stuff, clearly.

Not caring to be nosy and happy I stole his breath for a second time, I leave the door wide open and walk across the room and out onto the veranda. Again, it's the only clean, orderly spot in the guest suite. Overlooking the ocean and hillside below, feeling the evening air glide through my short hair, I think it's just become my favorite part of the house.

I do a few deep breaths like Dr. Linda taught me, although I do them for the mere enjoyment of taking in this moment and enjoying myself in it. Sara and the report linger on in the background, but there they stay.

I have a say in what takes control of my mind. My life. I can feel safe and happy even when things aren't perfect.

I hear Ty end his call and turn to see him carry in a cute little bouquet of flowers.

"Baz picked these for you," he says as he walks out onto the veranda with me. "He says you're a good dancer."

"Oh. What a cutie," I say, breathing in their aroma, enjoying the scents of lavender and basil mixed in with others I can't place. "Please tell him thank you for the flowers. And he's a very good dancer himself."

I walk inside with the bouquet toward the kitchenette, placing the flowers in a glass of water and leaving them next to the sink. I spin around to ask where we're off to, except Ty's not there.

"Ty?"

"Over here," I hear him call from the bedroom area before I hear, "This is amazing!"

Ah. The mural. I walk into the guest bedroom to find him standing at the end of my bed, admiring the ocean and cliffs that I've added.

"Dana can't wait to see what you do with her place."

Excited and nervous to be taken so seriously as an artist again, I smile and stupidly change the subject.

"So where are we off to?" So much for feeling empowered just seconds ago.

"Well," Ty claps his hands and rubs them together. "Seeing as this is technically our fourth date—the airplane ride being our unofficial date number one, Dana's wedding our official date number two, and our after-wedding date-redo our unofficial date number three—well, I figure something a little low-key with just the two of us would be nice."

Doing the math along with him, I laugh at his attempt to add logic to our whirlwind romance over the last few days. "A quiet evening, just the two of us, would be nice."

"Only thing, we need to head back to my place for something. Forgot the blanket."

"Blanket?"

"Crap. That was part of the surprise. Sheesh," Ty says, rubbing the back of his neck. "I did mention I'm bad at this, didn't I?"

"Depends," I say with a slight blush and sly smile. "What's the blanket for?"

Both of us standing at the foot of my bed, close enough to touch, I'm no longer the only one blushing.

"For the beach," Ty spits out, and I bite my lip and smile, seeing I'm not the only one nervous and excited.

He changes the subject quickly with feigned dismay. "Might as well tell ya now. Dinner on the beach okay with you?"

"Absolutely," I say, my thoughts still on the sheets next to us. "But we don't have to go all the way back to your place," I say, although I have no idea where his place is. "I'm sure my sister has a beach towel or something in the garage."

"If you think she won't mind."

I'm halfway down the hall on the way to the garage with no care of what my sister minds. "Bring your car around front, and I'll meet you in a few," I call back to Ty.

I hear Ty shout an "Okay!" as the guest door closes behind him.

Down in the garage, I find Eleanor's fancy for organization has no boundaries. Labeled bins and cabinets line the walls, and there are racks of hanging bikes, beach chairs, and anything and everything gardening requires. This clean, streamlined, color-coordinated organization would render Martha Stewart breathless.

Except there's one flaw: Mark's area.

I can tell it's his one-and-only corner to be free in El's domain because it looks like my place back in Baltimore did before I cleaned it up. I walk over to a cluttered metal desk pushed up against the wall under overflowing cabinets, where I see there's a nice quilted beach blanket on his desk chair.

A plastic bag full of photos of the girls with Mark and El are on top of the blanket, as well as sandy beach toys that look as though they were deposited there after a long day out in the sun. I look through the photos and feel tugs at my heart.

The girls are so beautiful and spirited, running along the surf. El looks amazing in a two-piece and healthier than she does now. Reading the printed digital date on the back of the photos, these pictures were taken two summers ago.

I take a deep breath and wipe away a tear. I have no idea what has happened to my sister in that time. Nor do I even know what my nieces look like now. I hate that I've been away for so long. No matter the obstacles that still stand between us, I'm just as much to blame as everyone else in my family for letting us fall apart.

On that self-deprecating note, I pull the beach blanket out from under the sandy toys and, seeing it's also sandy, shake it out before folding it under my arm. As I pick up some of the toys that have fallen, I notice a crumpled piece of paper on the floor. A flashback of the note I found in my closet on my birthday a year ago pops into my mind's eye.

Yet I bend down anyway and read it before I think better of it.

Mark, I had a magical time with you this weekend. Cannot wait to spend more time together soon. I love you. ~ E

I stare at the note and notice the script of the E matches that of the mural above the guestroom bed that I just painted over. Although, now that I see the rest of the words written out, this doesn't look like my sister's handwriting.

A honk from Ty's car jolts me, and I drop the note and run for the front door. Remember my stuff left up in my room and run up the spiral staircase, grab my sunglasses and keys, lock the guest entranceway, and speed toward the front of the house and out the front.

"Did you get lost?" Ty asks in his sweet drawl.

"Here," I say. "Beach blanket."

"Great, thanks," he says as he tosses it in the backseat. "That'll do just fine. You okay?"

"I'm fine," I say and think it better not to say anything about the note. It's none of my business. "Ready to go," I add with a forced smile.

The five-minute ride to the beach is spent mostly in silence because my mind won't stop spinning. But setting up the beach blanket and food he brought for us is a good diversion. And by the time we're sipping a tart merlot out of stemless, beach-safe wine glasses, I've wholeheartedly forgotten about Mark's note, my note, Sara's visit, the phone call to the sexual assault hotline… everything.

It's not that Ty's presence is the antidote. Well, maybe a little. I just don't know how to bring it all up. Or if it's even relevant.

Then he brings out the food, and all reality is postponed. For us, Ty brought spicy crawfish boudins that, he says, are made from his family's secret recipe. Simple, delicious, and portable, it's the perfect beach food.

"Squeeze the boudin stuffing into your mouth with your fingers," Ty says and demonstrates his technique of transferring all the flavor into his mouth while the juices trickle down his hand. I do the same, enjoying the spicy crawfish and juicy rice.

"Here, let me get 'dat mess." Smiling, he reaches out his cloth napkin to my chin. I warm inside as he tends to me with sweet tenderness. And, as the sun descends closer to the ocean, Ty refills my glass and holds his own out.

"A toast. To new beginnings."

I let out a relaxed sigh and echo his toast with a smile and a blush. "Yes. To new beginnings."

Listening to the ocean, breathing in the salty air, and watching the setting sun's hues dance along Ty's profile, I can't help but wonder at the fate that's played in bringing us together. Replaying the past few days in my mind solidifies my resolve to postpone telling him anything that would ruin this moment.

Besides, I want to enjoy this Californian vacation I've fallen into. We're alone on a beach, warmed by the setting sun, good food, good wine, and each other's company. There's nothing more that I'd ask for.

"I have a surprise," Ty says with a twinkle in his eye as he turns and reaches into the cooler behind him. "Now, don't get mad at me. It's really not my fault."

"What?" I chuckle and wait as he hides behind him what he's fussing with. When he finally turns around, the world stops turning.

"Happy Birthday," he says, holding out a plate holding a piece of chocolate cake with decadent chocolate icing pooling around the sides.

And a single lit candle.

My heart stops beating out of habit and I force myself to breath, staring at the flickering flame. Years of practice. I had totally blanked on today's significance.

I forgot it was my birthday.

"H—how did you know?" I loop back through all the conversations I've had with him. On the plane. At the winery. Dana's wedding. In the car and at his restaurant. Never once do I recall saying anything about my upcoming birthday.

Like I said, I totally forgot about it myself.

"I'm telling you, honestly, it's all Dana's fault," Ty says with a pleading smile, but I hardly hear him past the rush in my ears.

"Dana?"

"Yeah. You left your purse by one of her friends at some point during the wedding. I think when we were dancing."

"They went through my purse?"

"I told them they should be ashamed of themselves," Ty jokes on, not realizing I'm having a small panic attack. "But when they gave me this little tidbit of information from your driver's license, well, how could I possibly be upset?"

He grins, his eyes crinkled and warm. "You didn't mention you had a birthday coming up." The twinkle in his eyes dances with the single flame, but I can't tell which way is up or down. Can't breathe.

"Blow it out," he says, and I do with what little breath I can manage.

Ty turns back and grabs two forks. I blank-stare at his hand movements, trying desperately not to go where I know I'm going. Back there. To the place I've worked so hard to get away from.

But it's today. It happened today. He raped me today. I was screaming today. I couldn't get away today. I lost myself today.

I vanished today.

My hands shaking, I take the plate of chocolate cake and place it on my lap. Try to find my breath. This isn't how I want to be.

Not now. Not with Ty.

"Now this cake," Ty says, "is a specialty of mine. The icing is all homemade from scratch, of course. But it's what's inside that makes it special. So be careful bitin' in. It's sweet with a nice note of spice." He takes a forkful and holds it up for me to take a bite and smiles. "Happy Birthday, Matty."

Before I know it, I'm in the water, almost knee-deep and splashed by the incoming tide. But I don't feel the chill of the Pacific waters nor it's shimmery sand swirling around my feet. It takes me a few forced breaths to calm down, but then it happens and I can't stop.

Tears fall in fast streams down my face, and I can't believe I've wrecked this beautiful dream. I don't want to do this. Not now. Not ever again.

Only I can't stop. Big gulping sobs spill from me like a dam has been broken. I thought I'd already done this. I thought I had already opened all the doors of my closed-up mind. Went through all the boxes of ignored memories and sorted them out, dealing with what needed dealing with and tossing out the rest.

I reach up and grab onto my shortened hair. Remember all that I've done. Been through to get to where I want to be. I hug my middle and squeeze tight, the exertion somehow giving me back a semblance of control.

It takes a few tries, but I manage to quiet my sobs with big, deep breaths. Wipe my tears away. Breathe, calm and relaxed. Let my shoulders go. Drop my head back and sigh.

That's when I realize Ty's standing behind me, holding on to me.

I close my eyes against the embarrassment I feel when my head rests on his shoulder, wondering what kind of a mess I must look like to him. I don't even know what happened to the cake on my lap. Let alone the glass of wine I was holding.

I lift up my head and try to move away from him, but Ty wraps his arms around me tighter and I feel his body firm behind mine. Strong. Attentive. Supportive.

Pushing away the coward inside me, I turn toward him.

"I'm so, so sorry I ruined our dinner," I say, shaking my head, unable to look up at him.

The threads of his shirt stare back at me, and I feel his finger under my chin lifting my face up to see him. So he can see me.

"It's not ruined if you talk, Matty," he says, hushed against the waves. "You said you had a hell of a day. Talk to me."

And it's in his arms, with the darkening sky surrounding us and the ocean pulling at our feet, that I tell him. Everything. Everything that happened before. Everything that happened today. Everything that makes my birthday so difficult.

I tell him, and he takes it all in. Who I was. Who I am now. Who I want to be.

When I'm finished, I feel weightless enough to float away yet still anchored to Ty. And thankfully so. He leans down and kisses me so softly on the lips that a few fresh tears spill from my eyes. Only they're tears of joy at the ease of being able to speak, being heard AND understood.

"I'm sorry all that happened to you, Matty," Ty says as he wipes an escaping tear off my cheek with a warm thumb. "But look at what kind of woman it has made you. You're strong—"

"Crying like a baby," I joke, wrapping my arms around him.

"God gives us tears for a reason," Ty says, and I nod.

"This is true."

"And it takes true courage to open up to someone and show them your heart, no matter how painful. I love that about you."

My breath catches at the word love, but it's not because someone's forcing it onto me. The sound of it is sweet, more comforting than I ever thought it could be.

I almost say what I've always feared to say back. I almost say I love you. Only Ty's mouth is on mine, moving to the tune of love that needs no utterance. I wrap my arms tighter around his middle and welcome his kiss with a deepening of my own. I feel his hands glide along my bare back and up into my hair.

Finally, I'm breathless for all the right reasons.

With the incoming tide, we're interrupted by a wave as it crashes into us, letting us know it's time to make our way back to the beach. My jeans are drenched, and the bottom of my shirt is dripping. Ty's no better. We laugh as we slosh back to the beach and jog over to our blanket on the sand, hand in hand.

I note he's got a pretty good stride and say so. Ask him to join me for a run tomorrow morning. He says he might be up for it so long as I don't leave him in the dust.

Shivering from the chill of the night, we pack up what's left of the cake, stretch the blanket across both front seats of his car, and head back to my place. After a body-warming good-night kiss, Ty walks down the guest suite stairs backward, never taking his eyes off me, almost tripping after he misjudges the number of stairs down to the landing.

I laugh with him only after I see he's okay and note that I, myself, have never been so okay. I bite my lip as he drives away.

Holding onto my leftover piece of chocolate cake, I know it's sandy but I don't want to throw it away just yet. Ty made it himself, especially for me.

CHAPTER TWENTY-THREE

Gone Fishing

I awake, reveling in the sweet dreams I've just left. Notice the sandy feeling I must have brought to bed last night. Look at the time.

It's nine a.m. I overslept and missed my and Ty's seven a.m. run meet up.

"Shit," I say and reach for my phone, only to breathe a sigh of relief when I see he texted me hours ago that there was a problem at home so he couldn't go for a run today.

Maybe tomorrow? his next text asked.

I text him a quick sure with a smiley-wink, then take a shower, strip the sandy bed, and do laundry while I eat leftover Ty-made chocolate cake for breakfast, minus the sandy parts.

Cake for breakfast. And why not? I'm on vacation.

Heading back upstairs with an armful of warm, clean clothes and linens, I hear my cell phone ring. I drop a pillowcase as I sprint down the hall and don't bother going back for it. It could be Ty calling, and

I can't wait to hear his voice.

"Hello," I say, breathless.

"Hello yourself," I hear my friend say. "Fall off the face of the earth or something out there?"

"Claire! Oh, my gosh. I'm so glad you called. How are you? Have the movers arrived yet? How are Molly, Marcus, and Max? Are they excited about flying over the ocean? I sure hope they didn't get my fear of flying. There's really nothing to be worried about," I ramble on, happy to hear my friend's voice.

"My, my, Matty. Something going on? Or is that California air really that good?"

"Huh, what?" I say and smile at how well my friend knows me. "Only the best thing ever. But first, tell me how you are."

"Oh, no you don't, Matty Bell. Fess up. What's going on? Not only haven't you called at all like you said you would, but I haven't heard you this excited since they discounted your favorite ice cream. And really, that's only a fraction of how excited you sound now. Tell me."

So I do. "I met someone."

I leave it at that and let Claire formulate a response. When all I hear are shrieks and exclamations, I join in with some of my own, and we both ramble on in giddiness. Then she fills me in on all the woes of having to move out of the country on a month's notice, along with living apart from her husband while she handles everything, with the added benefit of having to deal with grandparents who just can't say goodbye to their grandbabies.

At the end of our nonstop, catch-up conversation, I hear Claire sigh over the phone, and I feel just as relieved as she. I felt like something had been missing these past few days: being able to talk to her. Only, I've been under such a sweet spell, it hadn't occurred to me to call her until I heard her say hello.

Claire tells me about her final preparations for their move to Germany and, even despite hearing all about my new-bloom relationship, still begs me to go. "Just until we settle in. It would be such a help to me. And the kids."

"Claire," I say, not sure what I want to do, "I think I'm going to stay here longer than the two weeks I planned."

"Alright. But you need to at least get your ticket soon before the prices get too high."

We hang up, and I sit on the stripped mattress with the pile of clean linens beside me for a long while. I hate to disappoint Claire, but I'm not a kid anymore. I need to make my own life, not follow others around like a lost dog.

She helped me when I left California and continued to help me for a good long decade of her life. I know I owe her for all her support and understanding. But move away overseas with her family?

I have a family of my own that I need to take care of. My own life.

My phone rings again. It's Ty, making my skin warm as it always does at the sound of his voice.

"Something's come up," he says in a worried voice. "Can you do me a favor?"

He gives me the address to his house. So I type it into the GPS on my phone, start up El's car, and head over.

After explaining how his kids were staying at his mother's last night, only to have Baz call crying around three in the morning because he wanted to come home, Ty picked them up and decided to take the day off to be with them. But his agent just called with a surprise opportunity and needs him in Los Angeles. Pronto.

"Ty, relax," I say when he opens the door and looks about ready to have a panic attack. "I'm good at this. They'll be okay."

"Yes, okay. Good, good," he rambles. "I know you'll be fine. Just everything is happening so fast."

Not sure what he's referring to—me being in his life, me watching his kids, or the impromptu meeting up in LA—I say a calm, "I've got it," followed by a good-humored, "May I come in?"

"Oh, right. Sorry. My mind is going a mile a minute." He walks toward the kitchen. "I really appreciate you doing this, Matty. I'll make it up to you."

"Oh, you don't owe me anything," I say, excited to spend the day with his two kids. "We'll have fun."

Ty visibly relaxes and grins. "I just don't want you to think I'm dating you so you'll be my babysitter."

"Well, if that's the case," I tease, "I charge a pretty hefty salary, just so you know."

Ty laughs. "I just don't know what I'm going to do. Cooking is the easy part. Talking: I talk all the time. I'm a people person, so what can I do? Even in front of the camera, I'm calm, sure, relaxed. But my kids? I'm already busy all the time. What am I going to do with my kids?"

Seeing his's distress, I take a jog down comedy lane to lighten the mood. "Never know. You might fail miserably, and you'll never have to worry about being on TV again."

"This is true," Ty grins and takes a deep breath, all the while holding my gaze.

He takes my hand and walks me past the kitchen and through an open sliding glass door that leads to the backyard patio. I watch as he gives each of his children a hug and a kiss. They're all smiles, just as excited as him at his impromptu opportunity to shoot a pilot for his own cooking show for the Eating Network Channel.

"Maia. Baz. You remember Matty? From Aunt Dana's wedding?"

They nod—Baz all smiles, Maia with an eye roll.

"Well, Matty's going to watch you while I'm out today."

"Great!" Baz cheers, hugging my legs.

I hear a groan escape from Maia.

"I'm old enough to watch myself," she says.

"But not old enough to watch your brother," Ty answers.

"Then why can't we just go back to Grandma's?" Maia pouts.

"Maia, you know why," Ty says in a fatherly tone. "It's in the total opposite direction of L.A., and I'm going to be late as it is."

He looks at me, then back at his kids and back to me, nervousness seeping through. "Do I at least look okay?" he asks.

The kids shoulder shrug and head back into the backyard. He looks at me, expecting, hoping.

"You look handsome," I say with a warm blush. "Knock 'em dead. Or, um, break a leg or whatever cooking thing you chefs say. Good luck."

When Ty just stands there, I add, "You're going to be late."

"Right, right. I'm stalling."

I follow him back inside to the kitchen, where he hands me a piece of paper. "Here's a list of emergency numbers in case of chaos."

I nod and follow him to the front door, watch him pull on a blazer and then, thinking better, take it off and drape it over his arm. "Oh, and whatever you do, don't cook for them. Order pizza or whatever if they don't want what's already in the fridge, and I'll pay you back when I get back."

"Okay," I say, wondering what don't cook for them means. Are they food snobs?

"Thanks, Matty," Ty says, not noticing my worried look. I give him a quick good-luck kiss. With that, he's out the front door.

I stand there, watch as he backs out of his driveway, and wave goodbye as he drives off. Then I make my way to the backyard patio to find the kids.

Edged with an extensive vegetable garden, the patio is the only place in the backyard to sit or play. The garden itself spans the entire length of the house and stretches all the way to the back fence at least twenty yards away. It's neatly maintained in four-foot by four-foot sections, separated by clean foot paths between each.

On the patio, there's a brick fireplace, its chimney protruding up out of a wooden pergola that shades the sitting area from the sun. Maia and Baz, meanwhile, are nowhere in sight.

Hoping I haven't already lost his kids, I holler out, however cheerfully, "Hey, you guys? Where are you?"

"We're over here next to the Mexican sage," little Baz pipes up.

Not knowing what Mexican sage looks like let alone what plain old sage looks like, I follow the sound of hushed whispers. Finding them sitting contently among the foliage, I ask, "So what do you guys want to do today?"

"Nothing," Maia drones.

"I want to go to the zoo!" Baz leaps up.

"I am not going to the zoo," his sister snaps.

"I want to go to the zoo! I want to go to the zoo!" Baz chants, jumping up and down.

"Okay, okay," I laugh along with Baz, keeping in mind I'd like Maia to at least not hate me. "We'll figure something out. First of all, do you guys need anything to eat? I haven't had breakfast yet. Want to go out somewhere?"

"Breakfast is the most important meal of the day," Baz says like a teacher leading his students in a lesson.

I smile down at him, and he jumps out onto the path and hops around like a frog, complete with frog sound effects.

"I am not going anywhere today," comes another hostile complaint from Maia. "She can just eat something here."

"Ooh! Ooh! I can make you an omelet!" Baz grabs onto my legs, bouncing. "Wanna omelet?" He grabs my hand and starts pulling me toward the house.

"Oh, sweetie, thanks. I'm good. I'll get something for myself," I say, but before I can convince him of the fact, he's inside in the kitchen, pulling out pots and pans and all sorts of things from the pantry and fridge.

"You better just let him do it. He likes to cook," Maia says, staring at the ground.

"Okay… I guess…" I stammer, not sure it's okay to let a five-year-old cook. "Would you like to come in and cook with us, Maia?"

The look of death she gives me says it all.

"Alrighty then. Enjoy the sun," I say, masking my uncertainty on how I'm going to reach her. It's been a while since I've been in the vicinity of a preadolescent attitude.

I rush inside to find Baz wreaking havoc on a pair of cracked eggs. Surprisingly enough, outside of the spot of milk on the counter and the use of way too many dishes, bowls, and utensils, he hasn't made a complete disaster.

Together, we make a wonderful omelet, complete with two cloves of chopped garlic, half a dozen scoops of tiny capers, three five-year-old handfuls of mozzarella cheese, a sprig of fresh basil that Baz zoomed outside to get and, after it's plated, a puree of roasted red bell peppers drizzled over top and a sprinkle of toasted pine nuts that mostly make it onto the plate. All under the direction of Baz.

I would have never put any of these ingredients together. Apparently though, Baz has taken a few notes being the son of a master chef and restaurateur.

Aside from the powerful saltiness of too many capers and the additional bite of the potent fresh garlic, the omelet hits the spot. And I tell him as much.

"You did a fantastic job. Thank you, Baz."

Beaming with pride, he puffs up his chest like a superhero and runs out to tell his sister all about it. The children stay outdoors most of the morning, running around the garden and playing on the patio with various items ranging from shovels to soccer balls to sidewalk chalk. While watching over them through the kitchen window, I work on the disaster Baz the Taz left behind.

Not that I mind. Unlike my tiny kitchenette back in Baltimore, Ty's kitchen is open to the eat-in area and, beyond that, the family room. It's all joined by a long wall of windows and sliding glass doors that open to the backyard patio area.

The kitchen is loaded, too. He's got all the latest and greatest kitchen appliances and gadgets, more than half of which I've only ever seen on TV while watching cooking shows and none of which I know how to use, sans the ones Baz just introduced me to. It takes some effort, but I manage to clean the kitchen and transform it back to its pre-Baz polish and shine.

Before heading out back, I sit down on the nicely aged leather couch in the family room, ease my legs up onto a nearby ottoman, let my head lean back on the back pillows, and close my eyes for a relaxing moment.

"Wanna go fish with me?" a little voice pops up next to me.

"Fish? Where?"

"In the garden! Come on!" Baz pulls me by the hand, dragging me from my lounging position through the open slider and out to the garden.

He informs me of the varying species of fish they have as we walk through a maze of raised garden beds. I enjoy his imagination until

I see it. At the back of the house, opposite the patio, is a huge, gray cistern with piping that leads to a small pond situated amongst the flowering vegetable and herb plants behind the house.

Manmade, of course, but here it is, complete with water lilies and koi fish of all sizes and colors.

"Wow."

"Yeah, my Uncle Dr. Doug—who's not really my uncle but Dad's best friend—made all this. He's a sustainable engineer."

"Oh," I say, unsure what that means.

But judging by the mile-wide smile on Baz's face, he loves it. I watch as he sits down next to the pond, grabs a long stick with rope attached at one end, and tosses his line out into the water.

"Don't you need a hook?"

"Oh, no. I'm just pretending. I don't want to eat these fish. They're not for eating," he says seriously.

Nodding in acknowledgement with feigned seriousness to hide my smile, I look around for my own stick. Baz hands me a wad of string and, after working out a multitude of knots, I attach it to my stick turned fishing pole.

And there we sit in the morning sun. Fishing.

It's pleasant fun, sitting and chatting pondside. I could spend an entire day like this, I think, and tell him as much. Until I hear a crash come from inside the house.

Jumping to my feet, I dash in through the patio doors. "Maia? Are you okay?"

Hearing another loud sound coming from the hallway at the other end of the house, I run to see what's going on.

Slam! goes a door at the end of the hall.

I jog toward it and knock. "Is everything okay?"

"Go away!" I hear Maia yell.

Relieved that she's at least able to speak, I ask through the door, "Do you need any help?"

"Are you dense? I said go away!"

"Oh, she gets like that," I hear Baz say from behind me. "Just leave her alone. She'll come out later."

I turn to see Baz, the informer, standing behind me, stick in hand, soaking wet.

"Why are you all wet?"

"I fell in. But I'm okay."

"Fell in?" I smack my forehead for leaving a child waterside, alone. I guide him to the nearby bathroom, leaving him with instructions to strip, put his wet clothes in the tub, and wrap himself in a towel. I wait outside the closed door until, five minutes later, he emerges.

"Which way is your room?"

After finding him some dry clothes, I return to the bathroom and clean up the disaster of wet clothes strewn all about. Then I mop up and dry the line of water that Baz dripped along the hallway floor, only to be interrupted by a little naked butt running down the hall.

I redirect Baz back to his room to get dressed. "For real this time," I say, amused yet slightly exhausted.

By the time the house is back in order and Baz dressed, it's noon.

"Where did the time go?" I mutter to myself as I resume my relaxing position on the couch.

My feet don't even touch the ottoman this time.

"I'm hungry," Baz whines.

He looks about ready for a nap. I know I am. Yet, heaving myself up off the couch, I follow him into the kitchen.

"What would you like?"

"A tuna sandwich."

"Okay. Tuna… tuna…" I search the pantry.

Ty's don't cook for them instructions linger in the back of my mind as I try to look like I know what I'm doing. But Baz, true to his nature, does it again. He shows me what he wants, tells me what to pull out and, with my added help, makes three huge tuna sandwiches, complete with toasted rye bread and a dipping sauce made of sour cream, more chopped garlic, and fresh cucumbers and dill from the garden.

I try to keep a lid on the number of dishes and utensils and gadgets we use, but it's no use. The kitchen is a disaster again.

I sigh. If I can clean a whole kitchen once, I can clean it again.

"I'm gonna get some cherry tomatoes. Be right back," he says and dashes out the back.

Setting the table for the three of us, I walk back toward Maia's room and, as nonchalantly as I can manage, ask, "Hey, Maia. Are you hungry? We made a tuna sandwich for ya."

When no answer comes, I knock with one hand and put my other hand on the handle. "May I come in?"

When no answer comes again, I worry. Knowing it won't be a welcomed gesture, I open the door anyway.

"Maia?"

Her room is a brilliant yellow, touched here and there with hues of green and purple polka dots. And, curled up on the top bunk of her loft bed, Maia is holding herself, crying.

My heart breaks. "Oh, sweetie, are you alright?"

In less than a second, she bolts up and jumps down off the bed. Before I can ask again, she runs off down the hallway, slamming the door and locking herself into the newly cleaned hallway bathroom.

"Oh, Miss Matty!" comes a singing little boy voice from the table, followed by a proud, "Do you want lemonade? I can make it myself."

Eyes wide, imagining more mess, I speed off toward the kitchen.

Luckily, he hasn't started without me. Torn, I help Baz not make a huge disaster and, with my thoughts still on Maia, quickly eat my tuna on rye with Little Boy Wonder.

Maia eventually emerges from the bathroom, eyes swollen from crying. Before I can ask, she holds up an opposing hand and walks the other way, slamming herself once again into her room.

Remembering back, I think about the things that would have made me act the way Maia is acting now, hoping to find some sort of bridge I can use to reach out to her. In my teens, on occasion, I did act a bit vile toward my parents. However, I will confess, they were always hormone-induced outbursts.

Maia is only nine and far from those.

Besides, who am I to her? Her dad's girlfriend. She was cold toward me at the wedding once she realized her father's intentions. Perhaps this whole charade today is part of her own inability to accept her father moving on.

In which case, it's totally acceptable and understandable. Maia lost her mother when she was four and, most likely, has fond memories of Vanessa. From a child's perspective, things between her dad and I might be moving too fast.

However, all things considered, I've been given a whole day to spend with his kids. Maybe, if I try, I can be someone Maia can talk to.

Cleaning up the dishes with Baz's gallant help is a snap. Before I know it, he's out the patio door, romping around the backyard garden.

"Do not go near the koi pond, please," I call out through the open window over the kitchen sink. I listen to his playful noises as I finish cleaning up the rest of the kitchen and dining areas.

Knocking on Maia's door, armed with her sandwich and lemonade, I enter into enemy territory.

"May I come in?" I ask, prying the door open just enough to peek inside.

Again, she's curled up on her top bunk.

"I've brought you some lunch and Baz's homemade lemonade. I'll set it here for you on your desk." Setting down the peace offering, I start my retreat when I hear a muffled whimper.

Instantly alarmed, yet as delicately as possible so as to not step on any land mines, I walk over to her bed.

"Maia, are you sick? Do you want me to call your dad?"

Hitting a nerve, Maia spits out, "No! Don't call him. He's busy, and he doesn't need to be worried."

"Worried about what, sweetie?"

"Stop calling me sweetie," she growls then, much less vehemently, cries into her pillow, "I'm not your sweetie."

Frustrated, I feel at a total loss as to what to do. She sounds like she wants to be left alone, but she's acting like she needs help. My gut instincts tell me to pry.

Forget trying to be friends. I'm the adult here.

"Maia, you're really worrying me. What's wrong?" It's a statement more than a question. "Are you sick? Have you thrown up? Are you upset that I'm here?"

When she doesn't answer with anything more than another muffled cry, I reach over and gently rub her back. "You need to tell me what's wrong. Otherwise, I can't help you."

Stiffening at first to my touch before relaxing a little, Maia rolls over to face me.

"I—I'm—" she tries to speak, but tears jump the gun and she's crying into her pillow again.

Smoothing her hair away from her face, I don't know what to do. However, she isn't shooing me away like before, so I take that as a sign

I'm on the right path.

Twisting her head to face me once more, the expression on her face is total despair. With tears and an almost inaudible voice, she ekes out, "I'm dying."

"Dying? From what?" Although I haven't known Ty long enough to know everything about his family, I'm certain he would have mentioned something as important as his daughter having a terminal illness.

Suspecting that this is not really the case, I ask, "Why do you think you're dying?"

"Because... because..."

From out back, I hear a screech. Rolling my eyes, I say a quick, "I'll be right back," and run out to see what the commotion is all about. Before I make it past the kitchen, I to run into a little boy covered from head to foot in what looks to be mud.

"What? How?"

Through the mud, Baz smiles bright, white teeth at me.

I sigh. "Forget it. I don't want to know."

Bewildered yet entertained, I direct him to the bathroom again and, after successfully cleaning him up and getting him dressed in a new set of clothes, I ask him—no, beg him—to sit. Stay.

"Would you like to watch a movie?"

"Yippee!"

While he picks out his movie from a vast collection, mostly talking to himself more than to me, he finally sets his mind to watch a movie about a rat who likes to cook.

"This is Daddy's and my favorite movie."

"You don't say," I smile.

While he cues up the movie, being more technically inclined than myself, I make him some popcorn. Then I set him up on the couch and head back to the bathroom to clean up the muddy mess.

Only, upon finding more than mud to clean up in the bathroom, I quickly finish the job and make final sure Baz is content enough to leave us alone for a bit.

I go to Maia's bedroom and shut the door. She's sitting on the floor, aimlessly staring at her sandwich. Joining her, I say, "Maia, I think I know what's going on. Would you like to talk about it? It's totally natural."

"Natural?" She looks at me, distraught. "I know dying is natural!"

"Maia, sweetie—I mean, Maia, I don't think you're dying."

"Oh, really? What makes you the expert? It's my body, you know."

Holding strong to my own knowledge, I keep my composure steady. My words kind.

"Yes, it's your body. But when I was just in the bathroom, I saw something. Is it yours?"

"Is what mine?" she stabs back.

Not wanting to be too direct, I hedge, trying to find a more subtle way to say it. But there's no way around the fact, so I say it as understandingly as I can.

"The green panties. With blood."

Eyes wide, Maia seems as though she wants to bolt, yet her body revolts against her, freezing her in place. Obviously battling with herself—one side clawing at me with angry words, the other crying her eyes out—the crying side wins, and she doubles over, weeping.

Rubbing her back, I say a soothing, "It's okay, Maia. I know it's scary. It's really early to be happening to you, but you don't have to be worried about dying. I think you just started your monthly cycle."

Unsure what a nine-year-old is educated about these days, I ask, "Do you know what a menstrual cycle is?"

Through tears mixed with embarrassment and resentment, she

manages a heartbreaking, "No."

After explaining what it is and giving her time to digest the information, I watch as her expression slowly goes from confused to understanding. And then to tears again.

My heart reaches out to her and, without thinking first, I hold her in a hug. We sit there on the floor together for a little while, me just holding her and the nine-year-old girl who is becoming a young woman letting her tears do what they were designed to do.

Her crying subsides and, guard down, she looks at me with red rimmed, searching eyes.

"It's going to be okay," I smile back. "You're becoming a woman. This is something to celebrate. Does your dad know?"

Her reaction answers my question.

"Don't worry. If you want, I can tell him."

When she nods her head, smiling beautifully for the first time I've seen, I smile back. "Okay. I'll tell him. In the meantime, why don't we go get you some things from the store to make it more manageable, okay?"

By the time Ty returns home, it's well past eleven at night. I hear him close the front door gently, put down his things, and walk over to the back side of the couch where we three are sitting cuddled together, eyes closed. The patio door is still open, affording the room soothing sounds of the outdoors and a cool, gentle breeze.

I stifle a giggle and continue to relax with Baz and Maia snoozing on either side of me.

Feeling his eyes on me, I lean my head back more and open my eyes. "How'd it go?" I whisper.

"I was going to ask you the same thing, but it looks like you guys had a good time?" It's a question more than a statement.

"Yeah. Great time."

In an instant, Ty leans down and gives me a gentle kiss on the forehead. "Thank you."

"Oh, it was easy," I joke and see amusement in Ty's eyes.

He is, after all, their father. He knows what a day spent with them is like.

"Here, let me help you," he says, walking around to the front of the couch and heaving Baz up into his arms. "Maia likes to walk. Just shake her gently, and she'll wake up enough to make it."

Making his way to Baz's room, I see him watch me out the corner of his eye as I wake Maia and, after a few hushed whispers between her and myself, I walk her first to the bathroom then toward her room. See the astonishment in Ty's eyes.

No fights. No slamming doors. No angry words.

Ty's waiting for me just outside Maia's door at the end of the hall. I whisper a, "Good-night, Maia," to which his daughter responds with a sweet, "Good-night, Matty," as I gently close the door.

With a quizzical look on his face, Ty asks, "What did you do to my daughter?"

Patting his chest, I smirk to myself and walk past him toward the kitchen, pull out a tea kettle, fill it with water, and turn on a burner.

"Would you like some tea while you tell me about your day? Or," I pause, adding a little sexy sass, "are you going to keep it all a secret?"

When Ty doesn't respond but instead stares at me, I add a quick, "Oh, geez. I'm so sorry. You're probably tired as hell. I should go."

"No. stay. Please."

"Oh, no. I couldn't impose. I've been here all day," I say before I realize what he's said. Stay. Too tired to know how to respond just yet, I add a quick, "They missed you, ya know?"

I yawn.

"It's, what? A twenty-minute drive back to your sister's place?"

"Five. But that's if you don't obey the speed limit," I say with a bit of sly humor before emitting another lengthy yawn. "Oh, wow. Sorry. I can't help myself."

"Don't apologize. Stay."

There it is again. Stay. We stand looking at each other for a moment, neither of us moving nor speaking. From the look on Ty's face, he knows what he's saying. And me?

All of a sudden I forget I'm totally spent. I don't want to go. I want to stay with this man.

Wanting to break the silence yet not wanting to break the electrifying connection, I move closer. Ty meets me halfway.

Without a word, we kiss. And kiss. And kiss. Ty moves his hands gently over me, slowly at first, like a warm hug after a long day. Then, feeling a mutual need for more, his hands become quicker, stronger. So does our kiss. I struggle to remain quiet, knowing his kids are only down the hall.

Ty pulls back, questioning me with his eyes. Too fast?

I don't stop to think of an answer. Instead, I let my hands do all the talking. Our mouths meet in time to muffle a guttural moan from Ty.

In a moment, we melt to the kitchen floor—kissing, arms around each other, hands touching here, touching there. My fingers move to the buttons on his shirt and, after undoing a few, I let my hands glide over his warm chest and push the material away from his shoulders so I can bury my face in the warmth of his chest while I undo the rest of the buttons.

My mind rushes forward, tossing out statistics and facts, timetables and crazy formulas, shouting too soon, too soon. But my body slams the door on my mind and goes back for more.

How long has it been since I've felt the skin of a man on mine? Too many years to count. And none of the men I'd ever been with ever made my body sing and my heart melt.

Feeling Ty's hands find their way under my shirt and toward my shorts, my body locks the door on my mind for good. No woman should go years without a man's touch. Not only does it feel good. It feels right.

Pulling at his tucked-in shirt, Ty reaches around me, finds the clasp of my bra, fumbles for what feels like forever. I pull away from our heated kiss and, eyes on Ty, reach back myself to undo it.

He starts to say sorry, but I put up a finger to his mouth, feeling the moist heat of his lips before leaning in to kiss him again. I emit a breathless, soundless oh, my God against his mouth as he cups my breasts.

Ty sits back onto the kitchen floor and I lean forward, straddling him. I hear him send up a whispered thank you to the Man upstairs. I move against him ever so slightly, teasing him until it's too much and he presses me against him, hard.

Then I jump up. Not only is the tea kettle whistling at full blast, Baz, half asleep, has walked into the kitchen.

"What are you guys doing?"

Being the only one fully dressed-ish, I corral Baz back to his room with a hushed, "Looking for something we dropped. Let's go back to bed, sweetie," before Ty can move or say anything.

I walk Baz back to bed after a quick pit stop to the bathroom. He falls fast asleep.

I hear Ty move the tea kettle off the burner. Meet him at the pantry door and say, "He fell right back asleep," then think better of myself. "I guess I should have let you handle that. Sorry."

"Actually," Ty looks down at himself, then up at me, with his Matty-body-melting grin. "I don't think I could have gotten up and walked him back to bed the way I was."

"Oh," I bite my lip and do my own version of Ty's grin as I lean in close, reach past him and grab something out of the pantry.

I hold up the box of tea bags. "Tea?"

CHAPTER TWENTY-FOUR

Celebrate

After a slow-sipping cup of tea, Ty graciously lends me his bed but I insist on sleeping on the couch. He tosses me a pillow and a few blankets from the linen closet and, with a sweet kiss goodnight, agrees that it would be best not to start anything else lest little Baz wake up again.

It only takes me a few minutes of adjusting myself on the couch and Ty tripping up the stairs to his bedroom for us to realize that neither of us is tired.

"I'm not going to be able to sleep," he whispers down to me.

I look up at him from the couch and smile. "Me neither."

So instead of sleep, Ty grabs us a few beers and we head out through the sliding glass door to the covered patio. He flips a switch and white twinkly lights illuminate the patio, much like on his restaurant's rooftop.

"My inspiration," Ty says in response to my acknowledgement of the similarities.

"Nice," I say and take a seat next him on a cushioned sectional under the stars. I sip on my ice-cold beer and feel it hit the spot better than the tea I just drank. Cool and refreshing, it's the perfect complement to a long day.

It's then that I let Ty in on a little secret.

"She what?" He asks, shocked.

"She's a young woman now."

"But she's nine years old."

"Yeah, I know. She thought she was dying. Says that's why she's been acting out lately. This was the second time it happened. The first one last month."

"Wow." Ty rubs his mouth with his hand, then his head, then the back of his neck, finally resting his hand on the side of his face. "Her period?"

"Some women prefer the term 'monthly cycle.' It's not so curt. You know, more personal. Besides, that's what it is: happens every month."

"But she's nine!" Ty quietly exclaims in despair. "Isn't this… too soon? Is she okay?"

"If I didn't have a friend who started at nine, I'd think differently. But that was Claire's story. And she now has three children. She's fine. I guess when it's time, it's time."

"But…"

Sitting sideways, facing Ty, I put a gentle hand on his shoulder and, in the words I used earlier in the day, repeat, "It's going to be alright. This is something to celebrate."

Taken aback, Ty looks at me sideways.

"Celebrate?"

Patting him on the knee, I lean in with a smile. "Yes, it is. She's becoming a young lady."

"Wow," he says, rubbing the back of his neck.

I trace a soothing line over the worried one on his forehead.

Ty sighs and looks up at me. "This is not something I was expecting at all."

"Neither was she. But now that she knows what's going on with her body and understands it a bit better, she's really excited to become a young lady," I explain, excited myself for Maia's newfound sense of self. "Oh, and I mentioned to her that I see a midwife myself for my yearly well-woman visits."

I pause and wait for the new worry line on his forehead to fade a bit. "She and I searched online together and found a local midwifery group that she'd like to go see. Oh, and don't worry, we took a trip to the store and got her all the necessities, so she's all set for a while. I got her a few different kinds of everything so she can test them out, see what she likes."

I have more to say on that note, however the deer-in-headlights look in Ty's eyes stops me short. Glazed over, he seems on the brink of overload on the subject.

Feeling sorry for the guy, I lean back, take a sip of my beer and say, "So… are you ready to tell me about your day?"

Ty sighs and shakes his head with a weak smile. "Thank you, Matty, for helping her out."

"It's what we women do." I smile, thankful for all the work I've put into becoming a woman comfortable in her own skin. I can now help others out. "Come on now. You have to tell me everything. How did it all go?"

So Ty tells me about his whirlwind of a day. Meeting after meeting with representatives from the Eating Network Channel and then, without a moment to waste, the filming of his totally impromptu cooking-show pilot. There were a few starts and stops, but he finally got the hang of it and was later told he's a natural in front of the camera.

After that, the time remaining was spent celebrating with his new team of producers, managers, and, of course, his agent, without whom the opportunity would not have been possible.

After going into more detail about his new deal, it's apparent that Ty, although excited, has reservations about life in the spotlight. Not only for himself, but for his children. However, as he also explains, it's an outstanding opportunity and one that, if not taken by him, will be snatched up by the next person in line.

"You know, Vanessa is probably astonished I even agreed to do it," Ty says, his eyes on mine. "She was such a driven woman. Career and success were her thing."

"I bet she's happy for you."

"And probably plotting out my next move," Ty chuckles, and I see his eyes light in the reminiscence.

I listen as he describes his late wife as the pulse behind moving his simple Louisiana-style takeout grill into the full-scale restaurant it is today, all the while gaining culinary stars and fans from far and wide.

"The cookbook was her idea, too. I already mentioned that on the plane, didn't I?"

"Yep. Right before I called you a liar and said you were faking a sex-change." I roll my eyes at myself, then soften my voice. "If you don't mind my asking, how did—? Never mind," I say when I feel Ty tense under my touch. "Sorry, I don't mean to pry."

"It's okay," Ty says and takes a deep breath. "It was real sudden. Right after Baz was born. Complications from a repeat C-section."

I keep myself from saying sorry, as he already mentioned how he doesn't care to hear it. Instead, I put down my beer and hold his hand in both of mine.

Ty takes a good-sized swig before adding, "She had this all-important meeting she wanted to attend. Same as for Maia. She just didn't have the patience for pregnancy," Ty chuckles, although not at all lighthearted.

"There was always some important meeting she was missing. So she scheduled the C-section with Baz earlier than if he had come on his own. She had it all mapped out. Pregnant just enough, maternity leave just enough, then she'd make it back to work in time. I told her she could go even though she was on leave, but she wanted to be back in full swing. Didn't want to miss a beat."

"She sounds like she was very determined and focused. Like she knew what she wanted and how to get it."

Wasn't that exactly what I thought about her the first time I saw her picture on The Big Easy Cookbook? That she looked like the type of woman I wanted to be? A tiny chill runs down my spine until I look at Ty.

He eyes his beer, then looks up at me.

It is mournful that she left this world and her family so soon. And after learning of the woman Vanessa was—determined, driven, and loving—I have no doubt that she had something to do with our finding each other. I can still feel the love Ty has for her; yet, surprisingly, I don't feel guilty for being here in her place. There's no bringing her back.

But I am grateful to her for guiding me here, and I say so to her in my heart.

Unable to sleep long on the worn leather couch, feeling

overwhelmed with all the thoughts and images in my head, I know what will help me sort them all out.

Run.

I fold the blankets and set them and the pillow on the couch where I slept and skip out of the Waters' household before anyone else wakes. By the time I reach El's, I feel guilty at how I left —without a word or even a note. I text Ty just before going out for my morning run. By the time I return, I have two text messages and a voicemail on my phone, all from the Waters family.

The first one is from Baz: come back!—Bazzzz the Tazzzzz.

The second one, sent only moments after the first, is from Maia: pls cm bk. dnt wnt 2 do ths aln alreD.

Translation? Come back!

The voice mail is from Ty.

"Matty, the kids are upset that you're not here, and" – I can hear his grin through the phone. "I'd be lying if I didn't say the same. If you aren't busy, please come back for breakfast. Unless, of course, you're sleeping, which I don't blame you. Call if you're coming. We leave at nine for me to drop the kids off and get myself to the restaurant by ten. Either way, can't wait to see you again."

Smiling at their combined sweetness and desire to have me back, I check the time on my phone. If I left now, by the time I got there, it would be time to leave.

Bummed, I text back saying I can't but thank them for the sweet invite.

I shower, dress in my paint-spattered clothes, and stand back to get a good look at my progress. So far, I've got the base colors and blending done. I've got the red of the cliffs too dark and daring, so I know I need to soften those before I move on to the beach and other details.

I pull out my paints, prep the area, and start to paint, making a mental note to add some soft, rolling waves and breezy Torrey pine trees to the cliffs.

I hear my cell phone ring.

"So, you're blowing us off, huh?" Ty jokes.

"Sorry. You guys are super sweet, but I've got to get this painting done before El gets back. Chances are she's going to kill me anyway since I never got permission, but," I say, dabbing sienna onto the wall, "if it's at least done, there's a slight possibility she'll forgive me in the same instant she threatens me with death."

"No need to apologize," Ty answers. "I've got to get the kids to my mom's and head to work for a bit, then a noon meeting, and then back to the restaurant."

"Wow. Sounds like a busy day."

"Business as usual," Ty says. "But if I have a moment to spare, mind if I stop by and see you?"

"I'll be covered head to toe in paint, so be sure not to touch me unless you want paint on ya," I joke.

Ty gives a deep, hearty laugh, and I can feel his warmness over the line.

"Oh, I think I can handle a little paint."

CHAPTER TWENTY-FIVE

Anywhere but Here

After painting for hours, I make a quick trip to the art supply store for some additional tubes of acrylic in all the colors I think I need—and a few more that I want, just in case. I also grab a few new professional-grade paintbrushes to replace some of my old ones.

I don't know if it's from the chaos of the day before or the energizing night that followed, but after my morning run along the beach, I've got a slew of new ideas bursting in my head just waiting to make their appearance in the mural.

I dump out all my newly found treasures and enjoy the feel of the new, smooth bristles along my fingertips. Measuring out enough white, aqua blue, and sea green onto my palate, I dip my paintbrush into the water to wet it, dab it off on the junk towel I have lain out on my lap, and make the perfect color of the three to work on my incoming, rolling waves.

The silkiness of the paint medium glides fine onto the wall. I push and pull the paint until I get the result I want—smooth ripples building up to a foamy topple of water at the top of the wave crests. It's a picturesque Californian dream: a surfer's paradise, with cascading waves rolling in under a crystal-blue sky.

As I paint, I feel the tide pull at my legs as it did while I spoke softly to Ty about my past. Remember the feel of his strong, understanding arms around me. Remember how those same arms and hands felt on my skin last night. His mouth on my neck. His heat radiating all around me.

A low, simmering blush builds up inside me and I bite my lip. Take a few breaths to help steady my hand. And it works for the most part, although I can still feel where his hands were on my body, like warm coals lying in wait to reignite the fire.

The feeling stays. And lingers. And builds.

That's when I realize something wonderful and exciting and breathtaking. For the first time in my life, I know I won't have a problem hitting all the high notes when the time comes. There won't be any elusiveness to that hard-to-reach orgasm anymore. Instead of my usual run-and-hide response that got me nowhere, I'm setting out a welcome mat for all the passion a romantic relationship with Ty has to offer.

Personally, I can't wait to finish what we started last night.

Rinsing out the white-hued, blue/sea green mixture from my brush, I get up and take a step back. See what's missing. Only, I can't see anything that's missing. I can only feel what's missing.

Ty.

Knock, knock.

Not knowing anyone else who would be knocking at El's guest bedroom door, I feel my body amp up in anticipation. Through the peephole, I see him and feel a visceral heat ignite.

"Hello!" I open the door breathless, as if he knows what I've been thinking about all morning long.

His answer says he's thinking the same thing. "My lunch meeting was canceled, so I'm free for a while. Are you busy?"

I blush, knowing what's about to happen. I can't help it, and I don't want to. This man does things to me that I like, and I'm going to enjoy it all. I open the door wider and let him in. I take his hand and guide him into the bedroom area. As he gawks at my painting and takes in all the new additions, I hear a voice go off in my head.

Are you really considering this?

Before I can answer mindfully, my body parts pipe in. Oh, yes, we are.

My mind, obviously the instigator here, adds its own two cents. You've only known this guy for what, a week? If that?

And? My body answers with an eye-roll attitude.

And? Are you kidding?

No, my body says. Go away.

Excuse me? I have a responsibility here.

And you've done your part. Now go. It's my turn.

I let them hash it out while I join Ty in front of the wall. He's kneeling on the floor, admiring my newly painted waves.

"Wow. This is so much more than a view. I can feel the calm and beauty in what you've done here."

"Thanks," I say and take a seat next to him. "By the way, you're going to get paint on you from the drop cloth."

"Oh," he looks under his folded knees and smiles. "I think I'm safe, for now." He looks at me expectantly. "Mind if I watch you for a bit? I promise I won't make a sound."

"Oh," I say, surprised. "You want to watch me paint?" Both my mind and body stop their bickering for a moment to see what I'll do.

"Okay. Sure."

I pick up a brush, fully aware that it's been a long while since someone's taken me so seriously as an artist. Me included.

Yet I scoot myself closer to the wall anyway and, seeing a few waves I can touch up, pick up my brush, dip it in paint, and set to work. The waves roll in, and I feel at ease with Ty behind me. Not that it's painting that I want to do right now. But if he wants to watch me paint, I'll paint.

It's quite endearing.

Cleaning off my brush in preparation for a new color, I feel Ty's warm breath on my skin. Then his moist lips as they kiss the nape of my neck. Enjoying the lingering effects left behind by both, I mentally step in on the battle between my body and mind to silence them both. I want to be fully present in this moment. I don't need a background of anxiety and doubt clouding in.

So, says my mind to my body, you're saying you're ready?

We are thirty-one years old, you know, my body replies. Do you know how many orgasms we've missed already, waiting this long?

I chuckle with a raised eyebrow. My body has a point.

Well, waiting this long really wasn't part of the plan, my mind says.

Exactly. Don't you think it's time for her to make her own choices? And not be held back by what others say, think, or do to her? When is it her choice?

I feel a peace come from the common ground they found, and they come back to me, with my spirit, as I focus on the warmth of Ty's kiss on my neck. Shoulder. Fingertips.

I lean back and greet his lips with my own and find myself— mind, body, and spirit—transported to a place of languid bliss.

"I don't have to go back to the restaurant if you want me to stay,"

Ty whispers into my ear. "I pay plenty of people to manage things."

I turn fully toward him and, mounting him as I had last night, kiss him with all the passion stored up inside. When I pull away, I look into his eyes and say a breathless, "Stay."

"I'll take that as a yes," he says and kisses me so softly I don't stop myself from begging for more. Only, he teases me with gentle kisses as he undresses me, first my shirt, then my bra. I reach down to undo my jean shorts.

"No, slow," he says with a twinkle in his eyes.

"No, fast," I say, breathless.

"No, Matty… Slow." He teases me, softly placing his lips against my bare breasts. Showing me how slow can feel.

It's more pleasure than I can take in all at once, and I drop my head back yet lean my body into him, begging. He pauses. Pulls back.

I look into his eyes. "Faster, please."

Ty kisses me slow, then stands up. "Medium?"

He reaches a hand down to me, to help me up, and it's his soft joking that calms me enough to realize something: This is our first time together. And Ty is a romantic. I reach up for his hand and let him pull me to my feet.

We kiss and touch and kiss and feel as we free ourselves of the rest of our clothes. Standing naked against his warm body, I pull him close to me. Feel my knees weaken at the sensation of all of him against me. No barriers.

Breathless against his chest, I take his hand in mine and lead him toward the bed.

He holds back. "I don't want to mess up your painting."

Endeared, I hold a hand over my bared heart and shake my head with a smile. "You are such a wonderful man." With a noisy heave-ho, I pull the bed far from the wall and ask with sassiness in my eyes,

"Far enough?"

Ty grins at me. "That'll do."

We ever so slowly take our noonday rendezvous to the bed, interchangeably kissing, touching, and mouthing a variety of delectables that could satisfy any appetite. Spread out on the sheets, pillows falling to the floor, my mind, body, and spirit race around the room, savoring every touch. Every sound. Everything increasingly more vivid and more pleasurable.

Ty begins to savor the beauty of my breasts with his hot tongue, and I'm about to lose it in a good way. I'm reaching that point of no return. I move along the length of him with my body. Every inch of my being speeds ahead, swirling together. Every part of me. All at the same time.

It's a rush like no other. A spinning whirlwind of sensations and emotions all rolled up into one. I'm almost there, almost to my own nirvana.

"Matty!"

"Yes, Ty, yes," I urge him on. "Don't stop."

Only he has. "Matty, I think someone's here," he says.

"Matty!"

"There it is again. Do you hear that?" he asks.

Actually, I do hear it, but I don't want to. I want Ty back, moving to the rhythm of the ocean with me. But instead, he's moving to the side of the bed and sitting up.

"I don't care," I say, half-begging. I roll over, get up on my knees, and straddle him on the side of the bed. Pulling him closer to me, I can feel his fire hasn't completely died out.

But the voice from downstairs isn't downstairs anymore. It's in the hallway right outside the guestroom door.

"Matty? Are you in there?"

Unbelievable. It's El. I see the door handle twist. But only slightly, and it doesn't open. Thankfully, I locked it out of old habit.

"Matty? I saw a strange car outside. Why is this door locked?" Banging on the door, El yells through the door, "Matty, are you in there? Are you in the shower? Matty!"

Jiggling the doorknob more fiercely, she manages to jostle the lock out of place, and the door starts to open.

In an instant, I'm up, draped in a fallen sheet I pick up in my flight to catch the door from flying all the way open. Then I swiftly open and close the door behind me, which lands me standing in the hallway with my sister.

"El," I say between breaths, holding the sheet around me. "I thought you weren't supposed to be home until next week."

"That's the plan, but I needed to get my things for Mexico first. That and Mark wanted me to get a few things he left in his haste to get on the cruise ship with his friend. So much talk about palling around, he forgot most everything, including his toothbrush and bathing suit."

I wonder why Mark can't buy a new toothbrush and swimsuit in Mexico and, more importantly, I wonder what Ty's doing in the room without me.

I sigh in frustration at El's interruption. "Is that all?"

Brow furrowed, she gives a start.

"Is that all? What, like you've got better things to do?" A moment passes between us in the low-lit hallway before I see a twinge of recognition run across her face when she notices the sheet I'm holding to myself. "Oh! Oh, my gosh. Do you have someone in there?"

I can't help but grin.

"Oh, I'm so sorry. I had no idea."

Feeling full of myself, I nod and give my sister a sly wink.

Seeming of like mind, El returns my wink with one of her own as she takes a step back down the hall. My hand on the doorknob, I start to open it to return to my haven when she snaps.

I first see it in her eyes and then hear it echoed in the hall. "Wait! You have someone in there?"

Caught off guard by her sudden change, I stumble, "Um, what? Um, yes."

"You. You have someone in my house?" El storms close to me. "What do you think this is? A brothel?"

Stunned, I can only repeat her last word. "Brothel?"

"Yeah, a brothel," she says. "You think you can come in here and bring guys back to my house? My house! And have sex with them? In my house?!"

"Well, technically, we actually haven't had sex yet, only, you know," I say, as though I'm having a conversation with a sane person.

"There are children in this house!" El explodes.

Knowing full well her two girls are somewhere north of the Redwoods with our parents as we speak, I start to shake my head in defense.

"They aren't here, El. They're with—"

"They sleep right down the hall from this… this…" She looks at her hands with disgust. Then, all of a sudden, she snaps her head up, the look in her eyes full of anger and betrayal. "If anyone— anyone— should be having sex in this house, it should be me!"

Driven by rage, her last word echoes through the hallway. My initial reaction is to hold my hands over my ears, only I'm still holding tight to the sheet around me. That and I'm taken aback by what she's just said. Likewise, she too seems horrified at herself for having said it.

Mumbling something to herself, El stumbles backward down the hall and, before turning around, gives me a look I'll never forget: self-pity. She's down the hall and out of sight before I can formulate a thought.

Hand still on the doorknob, I stand stunned in the hallway, her words echoing in my mind until I hear a noise come from inside the guestroom. I open the door just in time to see Ty zip and button his pants.

"What are you doing?" I ask, bewildered. "Don't go. We were just getting started."

"Restaurant just called."

"What? You're going? I thought you said you could stay? That you have capable people managing the place," I say as I knee crawl across the bed toward him.

"Yeah," he says, and I don't hear the usual grin in his voice. Fumbling with his shirt, he doesn't look at me. "Sorry, but I have to go."

"Are you sure?" I ask, dropping the sheet to the bed, revealing my naked body. I reach for his hand.

"Matty, please. I can't," he says, shielding his eyes.

"What the hell do you mean, you can't?" I ask, wounded that he won't look at me after all we have just done—and almost done—together.

"Matty, please. I'm sorry. I have to go," he repeats, pulling on his shoes. "Go talk to your sister. She seems pretty pissed." He still won't look at me. "I'll call you."

With a soft close of the door then, he's gone.

I kneel naked on the bed, goose bumps flaring over my body from the brush of cool air that flows in from Ty shutting the door. My stomach turns sour and, in a moment of absolute vulnerability, I feel it.

Shame.

Only I'm not about to feel shameful about something I wanted to do. No. I throw that useless feeling away and instead come up with a better replacement.

Rage. Total, absolute, fire-breathing rage.

She said you'd do it.

Through clenched teeth, I roar, "Eleanor, you stupid bitch!"

Grabbing my clothes, I pull on my shorts and am halfway down the hall, punching my arms through each armhole of my blasted shirt and pulling it up and over my head. The spiral staircase may as well be a hole in the ground. I make it down so fast I don't even feel the individual steps beneath my feet.

"Where are you?" I yell, standing in the foyer. I walk toward the living room, my voice bouncing off the high ceilings. "What the hell do you mean 'brothel'? Do you have any idea—any idea—what the hell you're insinuating?"

Flashbacks from El's wedding fuel me further, and I yell out, remembering what she said to me on her wedding day when I confronted her.

"At least I can wait, you said to me. Maybe you wanted it to happen, you said when I told you Jett raped me!" My eyes blur as I stride through the glass doors out to the backyard, then back inside when I don't find her there.

"He raped me, El. Rape! But you? You said that I wanted it to happen! 'Girls do it all the time, Matty,' you said. 'You had sex, changed your mind, then cried rape!'"

I hear my mother's words come out of my mouth. "What? Did you and Mom have a meeting about me? Did you two come up with the same explanation as to why I wasn't raped so it wouldn't be your fault and her problem?"

My heart feels like a wrecking ball pounding out of my chest.

"I went to you with something so big, so excruciatingly painful for me to even talk about. And you! You insisted that I wanted it to happen!"

Looking in the garage, she's nowhere to be found. The kitchen is empty as well.

"Where are you, you coward?" Fire pulsing through my veins, I've had enough of her carelessness. "I don't give a flying fuck whose house this is, Eleanor. After what you did to me, you have no right—no right—to talk to me like that!"

Taking two steps at a time up the side kitchen stairway, I search the upstairs.

"El!"

She isn't in the girls' room. The playroom is empty. So is the laundry room. After seeing that her home office isn't where she's hiding, I only have one place left to search: her bedroom.

"And please apprise me of the situation, dear sis," I call out, seething. "What the hell do you mean if anyone should be having sex, it should be you? You're married! You get to have sex all the time if you want to," I say, then chuckle to myself. "That is, if your husband wants to have sex with you."

Hearing what I've just said and the evil slant that's taken over my soul, I sound light years away from the type of person I know myself to be. I pause in the hallway and try to calm myself down. This isn't how I wanted this conversation to go with my sister.

Only the moment I see Eleanor as she opens her bedroom door, it all floods back to me. All thought of civility evaporates. "I want to know why!" I storm at her.

"Matty, this is stupid. I shouldn't have to apologize for some foolish thing I may or may not have said when I was a teenager."

"May not have said?" I scream.

I boil inside and out. Hold myself back from lashing out. Walk back and forth in the hall for what feels like eternity, waiting for her to respond. I try to breathe. Try to look at her with anything other than disgust.

Eleanor sighs. "I was just. You know," she says nonchalantly and then stops.

When she doesn't go on, I restrain myself from choking her. The look on my face must say as much because she finally spits it out.

"I was jealous, okay? I was just jealous."

Confused and shocked, I force myself to speak. "Of what?"

"Of you. You had a boyfriend."

My hands reach up and strangle handfuls of my hair. "What? El! You had a fiancé!"

"But it wasn't the same."

"Wasn't the same?" I pace again, my hands pulling at my hair. "What, that yours was waiting for you back in the States, waiting to marry you, and mine was on base in Italy with me? I don't get it. You had more than a boyfriend. You're married to him still!"

"Yeah, but it wasn't the same."

"Wasn't the same? Wasn't the same? El," I try, kneeling before her, clenching my teeth, folding my hands in prayer to keep them under control. "Please explain it to me because I feel like I'm going crazy here. What wasn't the same?"

"Jett wanted you, and I was jealous. Okay? That's it."

"So you…" I shake my head back and forth, eyes blinking, trying to understand. "I don't get it. You were jealous that a jerkoff wanted me and not you?"

"No. Not that. I just—Forget it." She walks past me.

I slam my hands on the floor and scream.

"'Forget it'? Are you out of your mind?" I get up and run after her, yelling. "He raped me! El!" I grab her arm, swing her around. "Do you have any—any—idea what it's like to be forced to have sex?"

"No, but at least he wanted you!"

"What the fuck?" I drop her arm, disgusted by the feel of her skin on my hand. "You are insane. You are fucking insane."

With that recognition, I stalk back to my room.

"At least you know what it feels like to be wanted!" She yells after me. I hear her catching up to me, her damned high heels clicking in the hall.

"Get away from me," I growl at her. I grab my bag, my things. "I don't care if Mom and Dad's house is crawling with bugs; I'm not staying here. You are out of your mind."

"Matty, please. Let me—"

"No!" I snap, gathering up all my stuff. "You don't get to talk to me!"

The sound of the door slamming behind me a minute later doesn't quite hit the right note. It doesn't have the right amount of force or loudness or deafening roar that I need to hear. I want to crash. To outrun this insanity.

At the bottom of the stairs, I almost trip on the leg of a pair of jeans dangling from my arms. I take two seconds to repack, restuff, and then I'm off. Down the steep hill steps at the back of the yard. Through the newly paved streets at the bottom. Toward the beach.

Anywhere but here.

CHAPTER TWENTY-SIX

Healing Journeys

Sleeping on the porch swing in my parents' backyard wasn't as comfortable as I thought it was going to be. Not that I could sleep. I tossed and turned all night, replaying the events from the day before.

Head spinning from a whirlwind of emotions and the fumes I must have breathed in being next to a house tented with pesticides, I grab my bag and leave again. I don't know where I'm headed, but I start walking anyway like the hobo I am.

My legs ache from all the walking I did yesterday to end up at my parents' house in Oceanside from all the way down in Del Mar. But I decide walking more today will help ease the pain, and so I head for the beach. From there, I can walk as far north or south as I want.

The ocean is just as welcoming as ever with its serene understanding, but I want to stay mad at my life. Myself. My sister. Even Ty. Only I can't.

Up all night thinking, I've calmed down enough to see what I couldn't see yesterday. I should not have gone crazy like that with Eleanor. That's not the way I wanted the conversation to go. I traveled a long way to be where I am today—able to talk about my trauma and not fall prey to the shame and pain it's always caused.

Blowing up at her and basically having an all-out evil tantrum was not how I envisioned sitting down with my sister and making her understand just how her actions hurt me. I had planned on letting her know that, despite it all, I still love her. That I forgive her.

I've also realized that, while I enjoyed every second of it and would do it all over again in a heartbeat, I rushed things with Ty. That has to be why he left the first chance he got.

Maybe I forced him farther than he wanted to go. Like I had been forced in the past. Hadn't he said more than once that I needed to slow down?

My stomach clenches at the thought of me pushing him too far, and I start walking south, knowing Ty's house is just a few blocks up from the beach in La Jolla. I don't know if he wants to see me, but I have to see him. I have to apologize.

After walking for hours on end, the smell of a taco truck parked just off the beach should be able to entice me out of a coma. But at the moment, I'm too sick to my stomach with guilt. By the time I'm at Ty's house, it's well past dark, my legs are stiff, my shoulder is killing me from the strap of my bag, and my feet are rubbed raw from the sand trapped inside my shoes.

It's all torture I needed.

I knock. No one's home. Exhausted, I lie down on the bench in his front yard. Thankfully, the front of his house is shielded from the street by brick walls and fencing that encircles a desert garden and stone pathway to the front door. The bench isn't comfortable, but I think my behavior the day before deserves just one more bout of pain before I can forgive myself.

Somewhere between the sun setting and the night air chill, I fall asleep. It's well past midnight when I wake to the sound of a car approaching, followed by headlights and the garage door opening.

"Matty!" Ty calls out, stopping his car short of entering the garage. He jumps out and rushes toward me. "Where have you been? I've been trying to find you all day."

Groggy, I rub my eyes, unsure where I am.

"I went to your sister's house and found your phone out back. Or rather, the dog did." He reaches into his pocket and hands me a pile of mangled electronics.

None of what he's saying registers because I have only one thought. My fault.

"I'm sorry," I whisper hoarsely.

Yet Ty talks over me, rushing on with his words, not hearing what I've just said. I look down and see him take my hand in his, although I feel nothing.

"Matty, I'm so sorry. I wish I'd handled that situation better. Your sister startled me is all. And then the restaurant called. I have no idea why I acted that way. I'm so, so sorry. Please forgive me."

"Forgive you?" I ask, wide awake now. "Ty, I came here to ask you to forgive me." I take my hand away from his, unsure of my place in his world. Hear my stomach grumble.

Ty puts a soft hand to my belly. "Sounds like you're hungry. How about we talk over something to eat. I've got some steaks—"

I put space between us. "Forget food! How can you think about eating at a time like this? I forced you," I cry. "I forced you to almost have sex!"

"Sex?"

I recoil at the word, afraid of it. Then tears sting my eyes, and I let my shoulders slump. This is a far cry from where I want to be. I don't want to be this kind of woman anymore: the kind of woman undone by everyday words such as sex and panties. I thought I was over all this. I thought I was healed. A survivor, now thriving in my new world.

Hadn't I told him as much on the beach? That I overcame and healed and am now enjoying my second chance at life?

I'm no good for him. I can't be. Ever. I grab my bag and start to leave. Ty grabs my hand.

"Matty, what's going through your head? That you somehow forced me to be with you? Matty," he says again in his spicy drawl.

My stupid stomach speaks up again, grumbling despite the drama going on.

"That's hunger talk. Come on inside and—"

"I'm serious, Ty! You couldn't even look at me," I cry.

His bout of humor dissipates. "You're serious," he says, albeit a bit baffled. "Matty, there's no way you forced me. I got spooked by your sister walking in on us, and I didn't think." He moves to stand so close to me it hurts. "Then the restaurant called and I—"

Embarrassed that I'm not the woman he thinks I am, I can't bear to look at him. I drop my head.

"Are you sure I didn't force you?" I ask, feeling a tear crawl down my cheek. I hear his soft sigh, and I snap my head up, eyes searching for a better answer. "I need to know. Did I force you or not? Because the way you acted seemed like I did something wrong."

"There's no way in hell you forced me," he says. "Is this all from what you told me at the beach? About…"

I groan from all the redundancy, my mind always going back to the same thing: mental abuse, rape, surviving. Will I ever be normal again? Will I ever have a day go by when I don't think about it?

I nod yes, admitting to the obsessiveness I seem to have yet to overcome, then shake my head. "I'm sorry, Ty. I have too much baggage for you."

"Baggage? You? I'm the widower who can't seem to keep up with being a single dad who has this crazy career that keeps running away with itself. If anything, maybe you need someone who's not got so much baggage as me," he says.

"You don't know me," I say, ignoring the tug he makes on my heart. "I don't know what normal is. I don't think I'm good enough for you."

"How about you let me decide that?" he says, alarmed, then softens. He lifts my head up with a finger under my chin. Wipes my tears away with a rough thumb. "Besides. I think I'm…" He stops, leans down, and kisses me ever so softly, making my eyes fill again with tears.

I try to pull back, but his sweet touch holds me still. How can this man still want me? Here I've just made a fool of myself. Am in need of a major shower. Even I don't want to be with myself at the moment.

But Ty doesn't seem bothered.

He kisses me again. And again. Softer each time until, against my better judgment, I kiss him back. He takes my bag off my shoulder and lets it drop to the ground, wraps his arms around me, warm and strong.

I fight with myself inside and out, feeling like a disaster as always but wanting to be free of it all. The movement of his mouth on mine, the gentleness of his kiss, the warmth of his body holding mine: I feel my barriers dissolve.

I finally pull back and stare up at him, wanting to say something but not sure what. See him grin in the dark as he picks up my bag and walks me into his house.

"Why don't you take a nice hot shower, and I'll make something for you to eat. After that, if you want, I'll drive you back to your sister's house."

I walk with him up the stairs to his master suite above the garage, and he points me in the direction of the shower before he heads downstairs. I stand in the steady, hot water stream, trying to think of nothing and unable to think of anything but the last thing Ty said before he kissed me out front.

I think I'm…

What was he about to say? That he thinks he might be in love with me? I smile, then frown at myself. Shake my head. I don't want to push any meaning into it.

Yet that's exactly how it felt when he kissed me. That he loves me. Then again, how could he love me? He hardly knows me. After how I reacted today and yesterday, I'm not sure I even know myself.

I step out of the shower and towel off. Walk out into the bedroom, set my bag on Ty's bed, and open it, only to realize, in my haste to run away from El, I only stuffed it with the wrong things. A few bras, a pair of jeans, and the drop cloth.

Hoping he won't mind, I look for and find one of Ty's shirts and slip it over my head.

Putting on my jeans, I walk down the stairs and right into the aroma of something my stomach needs no time to know it likes and wants. Embarrassingly, its maddened grumble is loud enough for him to hear over the sizzling of whatever he's got cooking.

I take a seat at the breakfast bar and watch him at work.

"I knew it. I know a hungry woman when I see one," he smirks and places a nice-sized steak along with a fresh salad in front of me.

"Let me guess. Fresh from the garden?" I ask as I sidle up to the counter.

"I heard all about Baz's adventures cooking for you."

"With me," I correct with a smile. "Though I think he might have taught me a thing or two. I'm not much of a cook, but he's a great little one."

Ty smiles warmly. "Try this. Let me know what you think," he says as he cuts a juicy piece of steak and holds up the fork for me. "I didn't know how you prefer it, so if you don't like this, I'll eat it and make you a new one."

After tasting his cooking again, there's no way he's getting it back. I devour half the steak and salad, along with a glass of wine, before I realize I really haven't come up for air since the first bite.

"When's the last time you ate?" he jeers good naturedly as he leisurely cuts into his own steak and eats. He hands me a slice of warmed bread with butter.

I shrug, not remembering, and force myself to slow from devouring mode to savoring mode. I take a few sips from a second glass of wine. Feel my brain come back online. Find my sense again.

"Ty, about what happened. I hope you don't think I'm… I'm…" unstable, the voice in my head helps me finish my thought, and I just want to slap its mouth shut.

But I know it's right.

"Matty. I get it. You have a different history than I do when it comes to intimacy."

I internally cringe from the word intimacy and then get it. Words. They're triggers.

I close my eyes, remembering Dr. Linda's advice about triggers. Breathe deep and relax. Knowledge is power. If I know what triggers me, I can help break the cycle and heal.

I open my eyes when I feel him put his hand on mine.

"I should never have left the way I did."

"The restaurant—"

"Forget the restaurant. I should never have run out like that. I hope you can forgive me." The sincerity in his eyes helps me focus on the fact that I'm not the only one here who acted in a not-so-normal way.

My embarrassment lightens. People mess-up, and sometimes mess-ups look crazy. Maybe this is what normal looks like after all.

I smile. Squeeze his hand.

"It's okay," I say and lean over to give him a small kiss on the lips. "I just hope you don't think I'm crazy for thinking I forced you."

"About that." He looks at me and grins. "How about we leave it up to you to say when. I'm a man, after all."

"That's for sure," I say, blushing, remembering.

Ty grins at me. "No pressure. No rush. Just know I'm ready to go whenever you are." Ty winks at me, and I blush again and smirk at him, understanding where he's coming from.

"Although," I say, letting my finger—and thoughts—softly graze over his hand. "I really liked being with you, Ty. I didn't mind," I say before I know what I'm saying.

I feel that visceral rush build up inside me again. Too fast! Unsteady! yells out in my mind. I slowly take my hand away from his and internally pout. I don't want to hear it, but maybe it's right.

Maybe I need to take things slower. Take my time to get used to being normal so I don't go off the rail again.

I clear my throat. "I think I'm going to start on Dana's painting tomorrow," I say, changing the hue of the night. "That is, if I can get back into my sister's place so I can get my supplies."

"Don't think she'll let you in?" Ty asks.

"Well, I think she was only home to grab a few things before heading down to Mexico to meet up with her husband."

When I see confusion on his face, I explain.

"Interesting," he says and drains his wine glass. "Sounds a bit odd, if you ask me." He takes my plate, now empty, and sets everything in the sink. "I hope you don't mind, but I'm beat. I can drive you to your sister's now—"

"How about in the morning? It's late, and you look really tired. I can sleep on the couch."

"Oh, no you won't. You can sleep upstairs in my bed. It's a hell of a lot more comfortable. I'll sleep in Baz's room."

I bite my lip. The thought of sleeping in his bed is exciting when I know the sheets will smell of Ty. The pillows will speak of him. Even wearing one of his t-shirts, I already know I'll feel as though I've spent the entire night wrapped up in his arms, close to his body despite being separated by walls.

When our eyes meet, I know in my soul I don't want to sleep. I want to be with this man. I almost say as much, but I stop. I don't want to rush into anything and risk messing up like I did yesterday.

I take in a jagged breath, place a lingering kiss on his cheek, and head upstairs without looking back lest I change my mind.

CHAPTER TWENTY-SEVEN

A trip back from insanity

Thankful I forgot to lock the guestroom door while fleeing El's insanity—and even more thankful she didn't lock it after me—I walk into the guest suite and pack a bag full of my paint things, change into my paint clothes, find the keys, and wave goodbye to Ty as I drive in the opposite direction in El's car.

Dana's home is east of San Diego. Set far inland, you can't see nor hear the ocean. However, once inside her front door, there is no mistaking that she lives near one. Local artist paintings of the ocean and beach scenes hang on almost every wall.

I take a look around to see what kind of style she and her husband have. Most every piece of art is naturalistic, like painted photography. No pretense. Nothing contemporary. Just natural and serene.

The kitchen is decorated in plum-wine colors, with added accents of sandy beige and sage green. I find a sticky note on the wall above the breakfast table that says paint here.

The space is much smaller than El's guest bedroom wall, so I don't foresee I'll be painting for five days straight. I can probably be done in a day or two depending on the amount of detail work I add in.

I unload my supplies, move the table set away from the wall, lay out my drop cloth, and get to work. With the postcard that Dana left me in the envelope with her key, I get the picture set in my mind's eye. With momentum at my side, I spend the next eight hours painting her vineyard mural.

It's exactly what I need to feel back on track.

I paint the hills rolling in from the left and on to the right, drifting away in lighter and lighter hues while the sun blazes the sky with bright yellows and soft pinks in the distance. I blanket the deep-burgundy grapes and spindly vines in leafy greens all on a ground the color of damp earth.

Before I know it, my neck is stiff, my back is tight, and the clock reads six o'clock. I'm close to finished, if not finished already.

I step back and look. Walk out of the room. Come back and look. With such a small space on the wall, I don't want to overcrowd the view with too much detail. I place the table and chairs back. Sit and pretend I'm having a morning coffee looking out over the vista on the wall. If it weren't for the paint smell, it would almost seem as though I was sitting on a hillside villa overlooking vineyard fields below.

Perfect.

I hope Dana and Ron will enjoy it for years to come.

Packing up, I can't help but think about the business side of this gig. I could potentially do this. No more dog walking. No more waitressing. No more random jobs that drag on and on and drain all life from your veins. I could actually do something that I enjoy. That I'm good at. That people pay me for.

Knowing this is what I want, I make a mental list of things I might need for the business venture, including a new phone. Business cards. Website. Portfolio. And I'll need to take photos—good ones—of my two murals so far.

Although, knowing the design rule of three, I feel I need one more painting to make my venture more appealing to a potential client's eye.

I pack up my paints, thinking of business names I could use. Matty's Murals. Murals by Matty. Matilda Bell Designs. Bell Designs. Designs by Bell.

Shouldering my supply bag, I walk to the front of the house and open the front door to find Ty, hand raised, ready to knock.

"This is my sister's house. I have to inspect," he says lightheartedly as he starts to walk past me.

"Nice to see you, too," I say and kiss him hello.

Warmth curls up my spine, and I take a step back. I don't know how I'm going to take it slow with this man.

I move away from him toward the front yard. "I'm gonna put my stuff in my car."

The smell of pizza oozes from Ty's car as I pass it, and I feel the rumble of my stomach. And remember. As usual, I painted all day and forgot to eat. Ignoring the growl, I venture back inside and find Ty standing in the kitchen, looking at my freshly painted mural.

"What do you think?" I ask.

Hand rubbing his chin, he turns all business. "You have to charge her. I don't care if she's my sister. This is too good."

"No way. She can pay for supplies only. That's it. Besides, I didn't get them a wedding gift."

"Matty," he chides.

"Ty," I play back and capture him in a hug. He smells of cheesy pizza, and my stomach begs to know. "Pizza?"

"Friday is pizza/movie night at the Waters' house," he says. "You joining us? My mom drops the kids off in a few, and you know Maia and Baz are expecting you to come."

"They are?" I ask.

"I told them you'd come," Ty admits with a nonchalant shoulder shrug. "So, you coming? Answer quick. The pizza is getting cold while we speak."

"Well, I can't be the cause of cold pizza," I say, happy to comply. I miss his kids. "I'll follow you."

After a few slices of phenomenal pizza and a fresh tomato basil salad from Baz's and my harvest out back, I fall into step with them once again, watching a movie of everyone's choice and then talking afterward with Maia in her room about her past few days. Her grandma loved the idea to celebrate Maia's entrance into womanhood. They'd like to know if I'd join them next Saturday for an all-ladies luncheon.

Besides, since I'm the one who gave her the idea, Maia won't do it without me.

"I wouldn't miss it," I say, giving her a hug.

Close to ten at night, the Waters family waves goodbye as I ease out of their driveway. My heart overflows and aches at the same time, filled to the limit with love. Even the sight of El's house and memories of my brief yet horrific run-in with my sister don't quench it.

After a nice, long, hot shower, I head off to bed. My dreams are filled with sweetness and light, and I wake Saturday morning full of anticipation to see them all again.

Then I hear the dog, Shadow, bark downstairs. My heart breaks, knowing he's home all day with no one to play with. Here I've been holed up in my own little world this past week, and I haven't even once checked in on him.

I know El said to not worry about Shadow. That she hires a walker and a groomer to take care of everything. But what if he needs a little extra water or food? Or just someone to love him?

I find my way downstairs to the mudroom and am looking at the beast through the sliding glass door before I think twice about it. His ears perk up the moment I'm in eyesight. Tail wagging, he stands to full height, and I realize he's even bigger than I remember from our brief run-in. The top of his head is almost at my shoulder height.

Slightly afraid for my life, I change my mind. Walk away. But he starts barking and begging with doggie whimpers, and my heart hurts.

I stop. Turn around. He's got to have some form of good behavior to be walked every day by a dog walker.

I stand at the entrance to the mudroom, a single-paned glass slider separating me from the slobbery beast who's quite obviously happy to see someone, anyone. It's a small space he's in, and looking out to the side yard that's fenced off to keep him out of El's entertaining patio area, Shadow's room to roam out there is a tiny speck too for a dog his size.

Poor baby, my heart speaks up. He has no room to play. He needs a run.

"Look," I say, hand on the slider door handle. "I'm going for a run. Not a walk. Not a roam-all-over-creation peeing and pooping on everything in sight. A run. Do you understand run?"

Shadow tilts his head from side to side as I speak, and I take in a deep breath, hoping he won't eat me. I slide the door open about an inch. Then an inch more. He bolts toward me, excited.

"Sit!" I command.

Slobbery tongue hanging, tail wagging, he barks loud and clear, and my ears ring from the volume he's exuded in such a small space. But sit he does.

"Stay," I say, and he does. I walk over to where I see his lead hanging and grab it. This excites him, and he's up, bounding around the room, knocking things over in his exuberance.

"Down! Sit! Stay!" I yell, half afraid he's going to accidentally kill me in his happiness.

Thank God, he sits and stays put.

"Okay. Okay. Lie down."

Shadow lies down.

"Sit up."

He sits up.

I try something else. "Give me your paw," I say with my hand outstretched, and the dog hands me his big, heavy paw to shake. I laugh. "Well, someone did something right by ya," I say of his obvious training. "Now listen. I want to go for a run. Do you know run?"

More bouncing around. More knocking things over. I can see he understands plenty. And he's ready.

With an audible prayer to God of, "Please, don't let me die. Please, don't let me die," I attach the lead to the dog's hefty collar.

At the back of El's yard, the wooden steps down the face of the hill are tricky on their own. With Shadow, who doesn't take his time to wait for me, I slip and almost fall twice, fearing the worst. But Shadow's at my side both times, using his body mass to hold me back from falling all the way.

Each time I give him a hug, feeling the mass of his body under his shaggy brown-and-black marbled fur, and tell him he's a good boy. By some miracle, we make it down in one piece. Of course, he immediately heads for mailbox after mailbox to mark his new territory. But this is part of our deal.

Urinate now. Run later.

The beach is scarcely populated, and I take Shadow down to the water. Tell him to sit as I do a few quick stretches. After being cooped up in El's mudroom all day, Shadow seems to take a cue from me and does a few doggy yoga stretches of his own, complete with a grand downward-facing dog and a few slobbery yawns.

"Ready?"

We run south toward the Torrey Pines State Park Beach, me in my usual distance runner form, Shadow blissfully beguiling at the end of his lead.

Fisherman avoid us. Runners go to the extreme and make huge barrier circles to keep their distance from us. I start thinking I should have brought Shadow for a run with me while I was back in Baltimore. I could have run outside without worry. No need to hide inside on a treadmill when you have the ultimate weapon leashed to your hand.

Together, we run. Well, I run. Shadow bounds and flops and skips and jumps. When he needs a break, he trots next to me at my pace, my running speed just a tiny notch above his normal walking gait. I stop a few times to see if he wants to go back, but he runs ahead, pulling me along.

It feels amazing to run, as usual. My legs and lungs are overjoyed by the stimulus. My mind, too, making use of the time to divulge and sort out all that's transpired.

By the time we arrive back at El's, Shadow is spent. He drinks about ten gallons of water before flopping down onto his billowy dog bed in the mudroom. There's a happy curve to his mouth as he heaves a deep sigh and sinks in for a morning nap.

I give him a big hug and belly rub, hang up his lead, set out some fresh food, and head upstairs for a shower.

In the shower, I remember I need three solid paintings to showcase in my portfolio for potential clients and decide where to start my next project. And again, I don't care what Eleanor's going to think.

It's not for her.

CHAPTER TWENTY-EIGHT

Breathe

It's Tuesday morning before I come up for breath. Ty and his children spent the weekend together and, although they insisted, I resisted their continued invitations to join them.

Not that I did so willingly. My heart cried out each time I had to say no. But I knew Ty hadn't spent much time alone with his children since he arrived back on the West Coast. Plus, I don't know how I fit into their lives if I'm not going to be around come next week.

Not that I really want to go with Claire and her family to Germany. But to stay in a hostile place if things go south with my family?

Much to think about.

Sunday, I spent another morning run with Shadow. Rather, a quick jaunt on and off the beach. With more people out than the previous day, most running the other direction when they saw Shadow coming their way, there were a few brave souls who came within speaking distance to point out that dogs aren't allowed on the beach, leash or no leash. That there is a dog beach up in Solana Beach instead, so please go there.

Please.

So we ran along the side streets and sidewalks until we made it to the dog beach. The little inlet is a perfect spot for dogs of all sizes. I didn't let Shadow off leash at first, but as we got more and more accustomed to the surroundings and all the other dogs and people, I let him go on a few fetch missions to see how he did.

Monday morning, I let him stay off leash the entire time, there being fewer beachgoers at the dog beach than during the weekend. He did so well playing with the other dogs and coming back to me on command that I found the number of the dogwalker Eleanor employs and told him to take the rest of the week off.

As for my time spent alone at El's house, I started a new project. Again, a small part of me feels guilty for not asking her or Mark for their permission to paint in their house. But I want to do something special for Allysa and Allysn, my two nieces. Something special to make up for the lost time I haven't spent with them.

Knowing the girls will be home by the end of the week, I took a look around their room on Saturday after I got back from my first run with Shadow. Pale-yellow walls, white trim. Store-bought, matching bedspreads.

Yes, the room was fashionable and streamlined and could have very well been in a magazine. But it said nothing of little girls. Even their toys were in bins, organized away from looking like anyone played with them.

I leafed through the books by their bedside and the toys in the bins and dress-up clothes they had hanging in their closets. I could see there was a theme to what they liked, and it didn't seem at all forced, as though planted in their room to "look good" by their designer mother. No. I could tell that these were the treasured toys, books, and winged things of two little girls.

That was all it took. I could already see the painting come to life.

After a trip to the art supply store for some more paints, I took a giddy breath and started. First with the leafy greens, then with the dark blues, adding a hint of a pink-and-golden sun setting in the sky between the two.

A magical fairy garden at dusk.

I paint tall, wise trees above and beyond their bed wall, each with hidden hollows for fairies and furry friends. A multitude of colors dance from my paintbrushes to the wall, creating shimmery-winged fairies peeking out of nooks, lying on sleeping flowers, whispering secrets over little girls' beds.

The darkness of the dense trees and coming of the night sky set the room in low, dark hues. I do this so I can highlight here and there the auras of the fairies, their wings giving off light and sparkles, thus illuminating the hidden treasures of a sleeping forest.

And let's not forget the immense expanse of the fairy village itself, lit up with tiny lanterns and warm home window lights throughout the trees of the room.

By the time I pause to take a step back Tuesday night, not only am I wearing my customary array of paint splashes all over my body, clothes, and hair—a bit famished too, as I don't seem to like to stop my imagination at work to feed myself—I am otherwise completely satiated, inside and out.

I thought finishing the beach mural in the guestroom was rewarding enough, since it turned out fabulous. Even completing Dana's small window mural overlooking the vineyard was a delight. But neither was for the joy of a child.

Memories of Max, Molly, and Marcus come to mind, and I smile.

To bring happiness to children has always warmed my soul.

I step back and look at the creation covering all four walls of their expansive room, including the ceiling. Looking over it all and up at the starry sky peeking through the trees, I breathe it all into my heart and feel it.

This is what I'm meant to do.

A calling to paint. To bring joy. To inspire. To create. I make a mental note to look further into the business side of things later. For now, I just want to enjoy my nieces' new room.

I hope they love it as much as I do. I hope my sister likes it as much as she should. This is a child's room, after all. And now it's full of wonder and life and magic.

I clean up my paints, gather up my drop cloths, and set all my brushes in the guestroom's kitchenette sink to soak. I push Allysa and Allysn's beds back into place and set out a few toys on top of the bins and around on the floor, making it look as though some fairies from the wall mural have come out into the room and want to play.

Three days till they get home. Three days till they see what Auntie Matty got them for their birthday.

I can't wait.

With the new phone I purchased back on Monday, I snap a few pics and send them to Claire and Linus back east.

Since I instantly get a You're alive! response from Linus, I call him. Talk about everything and anything for the next three hours. He wants to come out to California to see me soon. Needs a vacation from the store now that classes at MICA are at a lull, mid-July to August.

"Please! Please! Please!" Linus begs over the phone, and I remind him—and myself—that I need to figure out what I'm doing after my few-week stay here in California ends. I might be going to Germany still. I just haven't decided for sure what it is I want to do.

Although, if I'm honest with myself, I do know.

After I hang up with Linus, I call Claire. "How's it going?" I ask, knowing they leave for Germany in two days.

There's a long pause on the other end, and I'm afraid Claire is upset that I haven't given her a concrete answer yet. Am I coming with them or not?

I hear Claire sigh. "It turns out Greg's parents are going with us now. They put their place up for sale here in Maryland and already rented a place just down the street from where we'll be staying in Germany."

"Oh, wow," I say. "Well, you knew this was bound to happen. They can't be away from their grandbabies for five years."

"That's what they said," Claire groans, although it sounds forced. Like she's not really all that irritated with the idea of them coming. Still. "They're retired, Matty. They have nothing to do. They'll be with us. All. The. Time."

"You don't know that. They like to travel, don't they?" When I hear her resigned yes, I add a lighthearted, "Well, then living in Europe is perfect. Think of all the places they get to go now that they'll be so close to everything. Just the two of them. This is perfect for them. And you. You won't be alone over there. You'll have family very close by."

"I know," Claire says with a sigh and then adds, "It actually won't be a bad thing. Greg's relieved, and the kids are ecstatic. But what about you?"

Instead of answering her right away about my not moving to Germany, I tell her about my brief run-in with my sister and my apprehension about seeing my parents after all these years. Although I've got a few days before they arrive back in town, I haven't even formulated a gameplan of how I'm going to talk to them about anything.

I don't even know them anymore. They don't know me.

I'm just starting to know me.

And then there's my painting. My love for California rekindled.

And Ty.

"Matty, I don't want to tell you what to do—" Claire starts, but I stop her.

"I'm not asking you to, Claire. I know what I want," I say with all the assuredness I feel.

"I know you do. I love you, Matty."

"I love you, too."

CHAPTER TWENTY-NINE

No Time Like the Present

Spent from our Wednesday morning run and play time at the dog beach, I have to practically drag Shadow up the Torrey pine steps at the back of El's house. However, the moment we get to the top of the guestroom stairs, he seems to instantly revive, almost knocking me over.

"You goofball," I say, unlocking the door as fast as I can. "Don't knock me down the steps, or you'll never get in."

Rolf! Rolf!

The moment we manage to get inside, the echo of his bellow is like a blowhorn at close range. Covering my ears, I laugh as I watch him leap into the house like a huge, lopsided gazelle. He skids across the hardwood floors, trying to run past the bed and out into the hallway full speed.

Such a joyful sight.

I jog after him just to enjoy the craziness of his freedom in the house. I follow as he skids around the next corner at the end of the hallway, making a hard right toward the girls' room. But he doesn't stop there. He runs past their room and makes another hard right, rounding the U-shaped hall of the second floor.

I stop cold when I realize he's headed for the master suite: El and Mark's room.

Before I can envision the kind of mess Shadow will make in El's immaculate room—and how Eleanor will kill me for allowing the dog to run havoc in her house—I hear a shriek. It only takes me a millisecond to register who the horrified sound belongs to—my sister.

Alarmed, I run toward the noise.

"Get off me, you stupid dog!" I hear El scream, and I make it into the master bathroom just in time to watch her try to get big ol' Shadow out of the bathtub she's soaking in. But it's no use. Shadow's overwhelmed with excitement at his owner's return.

Gasping for air, she catches sight of me. "Damn it! Get him out of here!"

Although I want to move past the past—and be the woman I know I am, here in the present—the sight of my sister being drowned by the dog brings out my need for evil revenge, and I resolve to let the canine enjoy his bath atop my sister.

Only when I see a glint of despair in her eyes do I come to my senses, grab Shadow by the collar, and help heave him out of the tub. Covered with bubbles and dripping wet, he shakes off to dry, drenching me and the room in a mixture of bath water, bubbles, slobber, and what smells like vodka.

"Shadow! Sit!" I yell, grabbing hold of him when he attempts to take off. I reach for the nearest towel and wipe the slobber off my face before I attempt to dry him off.

"That's my good towel," El snaps, although a bit slurred.

"Excuse me?" I snap back. "Would you rather me let him run through the house soaking wet?"

In all honesty, I want to let the brute loose, to teach her a lesson in reality. Let her clean up the mess. But I don't have it in me to be so cruel. At least, I don't want to be anymore.

So instead, I say a pointed, "The towel can be washed, El," before wiping the dog down.

When Shadow is good enough to be let loose, I give him the command to "go to bed," which he now knows means I want him to return to the mudroom, lie down on his dog bed, and stay put. As I mop up the bathroom, I watch as El sinks down into what water is left.

"Thank you," I barely hear her say as she slips beneath the water, submerging herself.

One part of me thinks I imagined it, yet there's no mistaking what I just heard. She thanked me.

Stunned, I wait, staring at the bubbles, until she comes up for breath. When she does, I can only see her face amid the bubbles. But when she looks up at me, I see it again: that look in her eyes. Self-pity.

For a brief second, I forget myself, forget my plans of confronting her, and ask a concerned, "What's wrong, El? Why are you home so early? Where's Mark?"

"Would you stop with the questions, already?" she snaps, sitting up in the tub. "So I'm home alone. Who cares? What's the big deal?"

Not caring to be scolded by my half-naked sister, I clasp my hands together and let out a long, "Okay," as I back out of the master bath and shut the door behind me. Smelling of sweat, dog, and vodka, I'm in dire need of a bath, anyway.

Well, shower. Back in the guest suite, I try to relax as the water washes over me. Try to force my mind to wander in sweeter directions than my last few minutes of reality.

I don't want to think about my sister. I want to concentrate on Ty and his luscious lips. His hands, warm, all over me. Only I can't help but wonder about Eleanor. She and Mark weren't supposed to be back from their Mexican anniversary vacation for another two days.

Why is she home so early? And alone?

By the time I'm dressed, I've had enough with trying to ignore my instincts and forcing myself to fly off to la-la land. I decide to seek my sister out and talk to her. If I want to have a close relationship with my sister, I'm going to have to work at it.

No time like the present.

I take a deep breath to center myself. Focus. I don't want to go off on a tirade like I did last time. Knocking softly, I poke my head into the master bedroom. Say a cautious, "El? Are you in here?"

When I get no reply, I enter, reiterating to myself that I will not dash for the door when she starts yelling at me. I will stand my ground.

Even though the light in the room is dimmed from the heavily curtained windows, I can see that the bed has been hastily stripped naked, the sheets and pillows strewn all about the room. I take a step closer and bump into the king-sized mattress that's half off the bed, half on the floor.

Concerned, I ask a louder, "El?" as I step over the mess and into the bathroom.

The tub now empty, there's no sign of El, although the stench of vodka is so strong my eyes sting. Walking back out of the room, I hurry down the hall toward the spiral staircase when movement in the girls' room catches my eye. Coming closer, I see her curled up on one of the beds in the unlit room, head buried in a pillow.

Bending down, I ask a soft, "El, are you okay?"

She's a moment in moving, but when she does, my heart hurts at the sight of her needful eyes. And I know. Something is horribly wrong. My sister never needs anyone.

I sit down beside her on the bed and brush the hair from her face. When she doesn't stir nor speak, I ask, "Can I get you something?" Even though we're sitting in an unlit room, I can see the unease in her eyes: the unease at allowing me in. And I don't blame her. I'm uneasy myself.

"El, I know we haven't been close in a long time, but if you need me, I'm here." With that, I stand to leave.

"Don't go." She sits up and pulls me back to sitting on the bed. "I…" she says and then stops, seeming unsure.

"El. What happened?" I ask, seeing if being direct will help coax her out of her hesitation.

"I don't know what to do," is all she says before she bursts into tears, burying her face into me.

I hold my sister, feeling her sobs come and go. Even though I'm grateful she's not pushing me away as usual, there are still parts of me that recoil at her touch, wanting to back away from her and make her pay for what she did to me. But I consciously extinguish them in the same instant they come up.

In all these years, I don't think I've ever envisioned my sister as anything but a monster. Now, I see she's just like me. Human.

"How could I have been so blind?" she says, although more of a question to herself than to me.

The smell of alcohol is repulsive, but I stay.

She sits up. Hugs her knees to herself. "I mean, how could I not have seen it? From the beginning? How could I not have known?"

With this last question, she bursts into a new set of tears, and I hold her again, but she pushes away.

"No, no. I don't want pity," she says, getting up and walking down the hall toward the back stairs that lead to the kitchen.

"It's not pity, El," I say after her, following her down the stairs.

"What is it then?" she says when she reaches the kitchen, snapping back to her old self, distancing herself from me.

Millions of responses rise up in me, but only one makes the most sense.

"Love." I watch my sister's stiffness dissolve. "I love you, El," I hear myself say.

"That's all I ever wanted to hear," El cries, but I know she doesn't mean from me. "He used to say it all the time, you know? When we were engaged and newly married... 'I love you, El. I love you.' But that only lasted for a few months. Then he stopped. Stopped kissing me. Stopped touching me."

Sitting at the kitchen table, El bends her head into her arms and cries—big, heaving sobs—every so often letting out verbal hints of her sorrow. How Mark works all the time, so she does, too, just to be with him, but how he never really seemed to want her around. How he's made comments like, "Your hair is too dark," so she'd go bleach it blonde just to make him happy, or get skinnier and skinnier when he said she was too fat.

"Too fat? El," I say, wondering if Mark needs glasses or a lobotomy.

"After the girls were born," El says, raising her head up to look at me. "He said I was too fat. That he couldn't think of being physical with me ever again. Then he said the girls were taking all my attention away from him. That they were on me too much. So I stopped breastfeeding. Hired a nanny. Lost all connection with my own daughters to make him happy. And still he wouldn't touch me." She cries on, covering her face with her hands.

"Oh, El, I'm sure your daughters feel connected to you," I say, kneeling down beside her. Although the moment I say it, I know I don't know what I'm talking about. I haven't been here at all.

"No, they can't stand me. Just like their father," El says, stiffening. "I'm such a fool. What a waste of my life."

"Oh, no, El. Don't say that," I say, not sure what else to say.

"It's the truth, Matty. It is." She looks at me dead-on. "I enabled him to treat me the way he did. When he said jump, I jumped. When he said mean things like I'm too fat and it's my fault he won't touch me, I took it to heart and did everything I could—including starving myself—to make him happy. And for what? For what?!" She screams. "Instead of having the real thing, I wasted years faking the perfect marriage!"

"Oh, El," I say, seeing how the brief interactions I saw between Mark and El a few weeks ago make more sense now. How they were at each other's throats behind closed doors yet, once out in the light, acted as though everything was just fine. Perfect, in fact.

I recall the note I accidentally found and read in the garage.

"Is this about E?" I ask before I think better of it.

What do I know? I shouldn't be sticking my nose in other people's business even if the other people happen to be my sister. I'm just here to listen and be a shoulder to cry on. Only, I know my sister's handwriting, and that E on the wall—and in the love note in the garage—was not written by my sister.

I know I've struck a chord when I see El's face.

"You knew, too?" she shrieks and throws her hands up in the air, getting up to pace the kitchen. "Why was I the last to know?" she slams her hands down onto the kitchen countertop, breathing heavy and seeming to stare at the granite but not really seeing anything.

"I didn't know, El," I say in a quiet voice. "I only found a note in the garage the other day by accident. How long has Mark been seeing her?"

She shoots me a look and snorts. "Her? So you don't know." This seems to give her strength: a slight glimpse of the old, snide Eleanor. "Matty, dear, Mark has been cheating on me for years, but not with a woman. He's gay. Mark's been gay since the day I met him."

"Gay?"

"Yes, Matty. Gay," El says, again seeming to gain strength as she's no longer the only one left in the dark. "Now… now it all makes sense. The long weekends away with Eric. The reason why Mark didn't want to touch me and his preoccupation with the gym."

"El, don't you think that's a bit cliché?"

"Well, if the shoe fits." My sister stalks off, flabbergasted.

I follow her as she walks through the living room and out through the sliding glass doors to the back patio area.

Shadow bounds out of the mudroom and runs along the fence blocking him from the rest of the backyard, barking jubilantly.

"And the dog!" El yells, pointing at him. "Mark brought that damn dog home all because Eric loves dogs! But it's not Eric who has to take care of said dog, is it? No! It's me!"

About to say that paying for someone else to walk and take care of your dog isn't really taking care of your dog, I hold my tongue and try to see things from her perspective.

She may not take care of Shadow as I would if he were mine, but she's the one who probably has to make all the arrangements for him to be walked and groomed and taken care of. That on top of running a business and faking a perfect marriage, not to mention outsourcing her mothering duties to a nanny, too.

"And that room you're in!" El screams at me, and I panic, a knee-jerk reaction, thinking I did something wrong. "He's been at it all this time. Right in front of me!"

El paces along the fence line, in step with Shadow on the other side. "You know this Eric of his? He's the one who did that painting up there that I hate. He was here for months, Matty. Months! Living up there in that room. Do you know what that means? Mark and he were playing house up there with me and the girls just down the hall. Makes me sick."

"I'm so sorry, El," I say, then think better of myself.

Ty said it, and I've thought it many times myself. Sorry just doesn't cut it sometimes.

"Me, too," El says. "I should have known. Probably did know. Just didn't want to know."

She sits on down with a plop onto a streamlined chase lounge under the sun. I see what little time she did spend in Mexico with Mark added just a hint of tan to her skin. Although I know she's distraught, and I won't say so out loud right now, the added color helps her look not as sickly as before.

"I caught them together, you know," El says.

I sit down next to El and take her hand in mine. Rub her bare arm with my other hand. Let my actions say I'm here without saying a word.

"When I arrived, Mark was all handsome and attentive to me. Like old times." She stares off into the backyard. "We held hands walking on the beach. We laughed together about old times. We even kissed. Hugged. Made love." El chokes back her words. "It was the first time we've made love in years.

Seeing her face twist, I feel my gut do the same.

"He made a spa appointment for me. A full day of pampering and relaxing, he said. I was in awe of who I married. He was finally stepping up to be the man I always thought him to be. He said he missed me and wanted me to feel wonderful for the night he had planned. That he was sorry for making me stay back from our anniversary trip."

Her face twists in agony. "But when I got to the spa, they didn't have me on the books for another hour, so I went back to our room. I didn't want to be away from him, even for a second. I was so full of love and life and the renewal of our happy marriage."

El cries for a while, then sighs, resigned. "That's when I found them. Together. In bed. So obviously in love they couldn't wait to be together. And there they were, with me only out of the picture a mere ten minutes."

"Why did he marry you then? If he knew he was gay all this time?" I ask, upset for my sister.

"That's the thing," she says, looking at me. "I didn't even have to ask. It's been there all along. I've only ever been his decoy. And I played right into his hand this whole time."

She looks down at her hand in mine and then looks back up to me. "I've always been the perfect match for him. Pretend everything is perfect, and no one will ever know. Never wonder. Never ask. Me included."

CHAPTER THIRTY

Lessons Learned

I remember the words. What El said of why she told Jett I'd have sex with him—that I wanted to lose my virginity for my sixteenth birthday.

At least he wanted you.

I grapple with it all: How everything starts to fit together. But I don't want it to. I want to be mad at my sister. I want to punish her for what she did. For her carelessness. At least there's a small part of me that still wants to.

A very small part.

"And that's why you told Jett," I say, knowing this is a bad time to bring it up but also knowing in my gut that there's never going to be such thing as perfect timing for this.

When El slowly nods, holding my gaze as if to say, please, don't hurt me, I blow out a breath. Let go of her hand.

"I'm so sorry, Matty. I had no idea what kind of person he was. I didn't know he'd force you."

"But you told him a lie, Eleanor," I say, standing up, putting space between us. "I never once said that I wanted to lose my virginity when I turned sixteen."

"I know."

Even though I'm looking directly at my sister, I do a double take. "What? You admit it?"

"Yes," El sighs, looking up at me. "Do you remember staying the night at my friend Patricia's house back in Italy before I left for the States to be with Mark?"

I flip through the pages of history, vaguely remembering an all-girls sleepover where I was the youngest: a fifteen-year-old in a room full of senior-year high school girls. I nod, not sure why El is bringing this up.

"Well, we were all sitting in a big circle on the floor that night, talking, when my friend Patricia started a topic question that everyone answered in turn. 'When did you—or do you want to—lose your virginity?'"

I stiffen at the memory. I remember feeling panicked and seeing a kindred panic in my sister's eyes that night. We had always said we wanted to save ourselves for marriage. We had even made a pact. Yet there we were in a room full of girls we knew were more inclined to explore and experiment.

I could tell then El didn't want to be ostracized.

Unsure of what my answer was going to be when it came my turn, I remember El had put her hand on mine, the look in her eyes calm and collected. She had it under control, I remember thinking. She's going to take care of this.

"When it came to be your turn, I answered for the both of us right away," El says to me. "I lied for the both of us. I said that I was planning on having sex with Mark when I got back to the States, and that you wanted to have sex when you turned sixteen."

"Which was my next birthday."

"Yeah, I know. But in my defense, I thought you and Mom and Dad would have moved back Stateside by then, and that it wouldn't have mattered. I was so caught up in my engagement and college, I knew dad had gotten orders."

"I don't get it. How does this have anything to do with Jett?" I ask, but I can see the answer in my mind's eye before Eleanor spits it out.

"The day before I left, I was out with all my friends and we happened to bump into him. In my defense, Patricia is the one who said it first. That you wanted to lose your virginity for your upcoming birthday. When everyone agreed, Jett turned to me, asking me if it was the truth. And I said yes. That you'd do it."

"Oh, my God," I say, feeling the world spin around me.

"Then that's why everyone pressured me into dating him. So they could see what happened."

"I'm sorry, Matty."

"Sorry? Sorry?" I stammer, unable to make an intelligent thought as all the pieces of my puzzle start to fit together. I walk back into the house, through the living room, and up the spiral staircase, not once looking back. I don't know what to think, feel. It wasn't just my sister who set me up. The whole senior class was in on it.

Did they know what Jett did to me? Did they know what their drama-seeking stupidity did to me?

I close the guestroom door behind me, pack for real this time. Gather up all my painting supplies in a bag, then stop, look around. I can't run away. Not again. But I can't stay, either. Not now.

Then what? Stay here? Talk to my sister, who I can't even look at? Or leave until the anger dissipates? The hurt subsides? The questions stop?

"No wonder Claire didn't want me to go online," I say to myself, staring at nothing. "No wonder she didn't want me reconnecting with all those people from on base in Italy. Does that mean she knew, too?"

My heart hammers in my chest. I feel like there's a noose around my neck, not allowing air in or out. I force myself to calm down. To breathe.

No, Claire couldn't have known. She wasn't at that all-girl sleepover. If she had been, if she had known, she would have told me long ago. She would have told me well before anything bad happened to me. Much like if I had known anything that could have prevented it, I would have warned Sara from suffering the same fate as me.

Raped by Jett.

"Ugh!" I groan out loud. I don't want to go down this worn road anymore. I'm so over rape. Yet it will always be with me. Right around the corner, hiding out, waiting to pounce back into my mind when unsuspecting triggers tempt it. I hate this world that they've painted me into.

I hear the door open behind me.

"Why?" I demand of my sister. "Why now, after all this time? Why didn't you tell me the truth when I confronted you before your wedding? Why now, after all the time I've wasted being angry, hurt, betrayed? Why at all?"

"Matty, I'm sorry."

"Sorry. Sorry. That doesn't do anything for me now. Stop saying it."

"Then what do you want me to say?"

"What? You want me to tell you to jump like Mark always has so you can ask how high and make it all better? No way, El. I'm not telling you how to do anything."

"Then what do you want?" she asks in earnest.

"I don't know what I want!" I yell at her with all the force my pain can produce. I grab my things, shouldering my bags.

"Where are you going?" El asks, frantic. "You can't leave. I need you here, with me."

"You need me? Need? Oh, El, come on now, really. You don't need anyone," I say, making my way to the door.

"That's not true, Matty," El almost sobs. "I'm human, too."

This stops me, my heart overriding the pissed-as-hell part of me. I stand with my face almost touching the door, my bags pulling heavy on my shoulders.

"I don't know what I want," I say, more to myself than to her.

"I know. And I know I can't make it up to you. Not just yet. But I need you, Matty. Mark's leaving me. He says I can have the business and the house and the girls and even the stupid dog."

"He's not stupid," I say, spinning around to face her.

"Okay, alright. But Mark's moving out. To be with him. I'm going to be all alone."

"You have your girls, El," I say, rolling my eyes. I'm in no mood for alcohol-induced dramatics.

"Yes, I know. But all on my own. I need you. We need you," El pleads on, clinging to me. "Oh, please, Matty. You can stay here. Live here. It'll be yours, all this," El says with a sweeping hand in a long arc, her gaze following along the entire length of the guestroom. "You can stay here for free and…"

When she doesn't continue, I see what's taken her breath away. The beach mural.

"Wha—? What the—? Who—?" she stammers, and I prepare myself for the outburst I'm sure is to come. That snide part of me can't wait for the full-on battle to ensue.

Hadn't I painted it so she'd be angry with me because I hadn't asked permission to deface her home?

I widen my stance, drop my bags to the floor. Bring it on, sister, I hear that voice within me speak up in defiance. This is the battle I've been waiting for.

Only, my heart steps in and slaps the voice in the face. Enough, is all it says, and we both know it's right. I did what I did, and I don't feel bad for it. But I'm not about to have World War IV over it. Or anything else for that matter.

What's done is done. It's time to move on now.

"You?" El looks at me, and I see genuine awe and confusion in her eyes.

"Yes. I painted it."

"When?" she asks.

"While you were in Mexico."

"But it's so… so… big!" she says as she walks from one end of the room to the next, looking over my masterpiece.

"Yep," I say, looking my sister in the eyes when she stops gawking.

She seems to get it. My intent. This was meant to hurt her somehow, some way. Only I see the opposite in her eyes.

"My God, Matty. You should do this for a living. I could help you. Get you clients," El says, rambling on.

Not sure if it's the alcohol talking or my sister, I hold up a hand. "How about we talk about this in the morning when you're not drunk. I don't want you promising me the world today and tearing out my throat tomorrow," I say, not allowing myself to get excited just yet.

That is, if I even take her up on her offer.

"Matty, I'm not drunk. I always drink this much."

When she doesn't go on, I feel the wheels in my head clicking pieces together once more.

"You get hammered often?" I ask, angry, remembering back to when I first saw her a few weeks ago when I flew in from Maryland.

Remembering she looked just like our mother. Our alcoholic mother.

El lets out a long sigh. Sits on the bed. "Yes. It's been the only way to deal."

"After living with our mother that way, always drinking, you went and did it yourself, too?" I yell. "How long?" I ask, only it's a not a question. It's a demand.

"A long time. But not until after the girls were born."

Allysa and Allysn.

"Oh, God," I say, sitting on the floor. My heart hurts for my nieces, knowing how it was to grow up with an emotionally vacant mother. "How could you?"

I ask it, but I don't want to know. I already know. Life was too hard, and she did what she knew best. What our mother taught her to do. Hide in a bottle.

Hadn't I done the same? Maybe not with drinking, but with hiding, running?

"This is all too much," I say, not knowing where to land.

"I know. I'm sorry."

Sorry.

"Please. Stop. Saying. That," I say, shaking my head, not looking at anything.

I'm trying to grasp the enormity of ten years of lies and miscommunication and estrangement and misunderstandings. I look up at my sister, knowing I want so much but not sure I want it from her.

"Okay. Okay. I'm… I don't know what to say, Matty."

"Just shut up for once."

El nods her head, seeming to get it. I get up, grab my bags. Set them down again. Pick them up.

"I don't know what to do," I say pointedly, mad that she's put me in this situation: this state of caring for someone who I want to stay angry at.

Then there are the girls. My parents. Even the dog, for crying out loud.

And then there's Ty. And his family. And my painting business, if I want it.

Overwhelmed, I flop down to the floor. Bury my face in my hands.

"I don't know what to do," I say, feeling all the battles within me.

"Then don't do anything," El says, her hand heavy on mine, holding me still. Holding me in place.

CHAPTER THIRTY-ONE

Landing

Turns out doing nothing means staying at El's house. Listening to her cry whenever she thinks she is alone. Then, when Mark arrives later in the afternoon, not only listening to El yell at Mark, but also being dragged into the screaming matches as some sort of sane observer.

As much as I try to accommodate my distraught sibling, I want to distance myself from her, too. I need to think. I take Shadow back to the dog beach for a few hours just to get away from the chaos of reality. Call and talk with Claire for a long while. Then Linus. Try on their lives for a bit and listen in as only a friend can.

But it's no use. My mind is too full.

Do something.

Bringing Shadow back to the home of World War V, I fill his water and food bowls and give him a few treats for being such a well-behaved dog at the dog beach. Rub his belly and say goodbye as he lays his head down for a nap.

The house quiet, I tiptoe my way back up the spiral staircase to my room. Close the door quietly behind me. Reach for my phone and text Ty.

Are Baz and Maia staying with your mother tonight? I text.

Ty's response is instant. I pick up at the first ring.

"Whatcha have in mind? They won't be home till Friday."

I hear his sweet drawl over the phone, and I breathe a heavy sigh of relief. Ty. He's the landing pad I want.

"Oh, I love your voice," I sigh into the phone. "I'm sorry if you're busy and I'm bugging you at work, but I just need to hear your voice right now."

"I take it something's going on."

"Yeah. My sister..." I start, then think better of it. "You know what, I really don't want to talk about it. It's not that I don't want to talk to you about it. I just don't want to talk about it anymore. I'm done. I'm good. I just want to get out of here."

"Well then, whatcha have in mind?" Ty asks again, and I know exactly what I need.

I need to be with him. Away from here. But not like I'm running away; instead, I'm running toward something. "I'm sorry to be so pushy, but I need to be with you."

Ty chuckles softly into the phone, and I can hear his grin. "No need to apologize for that."

"Good, because I'm coming over tonight. What time will you be home?"

"I'll be home close to ten tonight. But if you want to come over earlier, I'll give you the entrance code for the garage and you can come over whenever you want to. Make yourself at home."

"I like the sound of that," I say, feeling relaxed already.

I shower again, this time to get rid of the dog beach and slobber. Stand in the hot water, enjoying the chamomile scent. Wrap up in a towel and rummage through my bag for something to wear.

Before I know it, I find myself unpacking, placing all my belongings in dresser drawers and hanging a few items in the closet.

Breathing free, I'm satisfied at how nice and organized things can be when you make a commitment to land. No need to overthink things. No need to run away. I'm setting up camp right here, right now. And I feel good about it.

Seeing my things hung, I select a silky sundress of all shades of fuchsia and green and enjoy the softness of the fabric as it lays over me. I don't bother with undergarments. No bra. No underwear. I feel like being free tonight.

I lock up and head down to the taxi that's waiting for me. Pay after it drops me off at Ty's. Punching in the numbers and watching the garage door rise, I feel at peace. Like I've finally come full-healing-circle.

I know what I want and how to get it.

I pour myself a glass of wine and walk through the garden out back. Feel the leaves as I let my fingers glide over them. With dusk falling softly, I sit out on the back patio and watch the clouds play with the palate of a setting sun. When the chill of the night starts to set in, I go inside.

I'm only half startled to see Ty waiting for me.

"Benefits of running your own business," he explains. "I told them I'd see them in the morning."

I put a finger to his lips, not needing to hear the rest. With an alluring smile, I let my hand roam downward, gracing his chest, finding buttons on his shirt that need little coaxing to open. Ty bends down to kiss me, but I step back, slowly shaking my head side to side.

"Slowly," I say with a soft smirk. Lacing my fingers up under the straps of my dress, I move them off my shoulders, the whole time holding Ty's gaze in mine. "Slowly… slowly… slowly," I say, each time letting the dress inch off of me, farther and farther.

I bite my lip, smile with my eyes. Finally let it fall to the floor.

It's past three in the afternoon when I wake the next day. Well, it's the second time I've woken today. The first was around eight, with Ty leading me into a warm morning shower after our brief three hours of sleep. He could have slept until nine then gone in to work, but he wanted to be with me a little while longer, he had said.

Sore from the night before, I was still ready and willing, but Ty had other ideas for our morning shower together. Remembering the view of the top of his head bent down low on my body, I warm from head to toe just thinking of it.

Rolling over, I see a note along with a flower from the garden resting on Ty's pillow. I read the note.

Sleep late. Stay longer. I can't wait to see you again. Love you.

If it had been the first time he said it, I would have minded him saying "I love you" in a note. But after having heard Ty say "I love you" in person before we made love last night, I wouldn't want it any other way.

I was a little longer in saying it back, however, Ty didn't mind. Another trigger. The words were screaming out in my head, only I couldn't make my mouth work.

Then I climaxed. First. Time. Ever.

There was nothing left to hold me back.

"I love you, I love you, I love you," I kept saying over and over again, the luscious surges of ecstasy rolling over me in an endless succession of waves.

"I love you, too, Matty," Ty breathed into me, his hot breath curling around me.

"Oh, I do, I do, I do. I've loved you from the moment I laid eyes on you. I knew the moment I saw you that I loved you. Only you said you were married and—"

That time, Ty put a hushing finger to my mouth then his lips to my mouth with a soft kiss. And another. And another. Answering him with hungry kisses of my own, those were the last words we spoke until sunrise.

Pulling my sundress up over my head, I find my shoes by the front door and, with one final sigh, climb into the taxi.

Dropped off at the front of El's house, I see the front door is open. "Hello?" I call when I enter. "Anyone home?"

After having a day to themselves, I'm hoping Mark and El have come to some sort of stasis of calmness. Their daughters will be home tomorrow, after all.

When I don't hear any response, I close the front door behind me and make my way upstairs to my room. Only, it's not empty when I get there.

"El, hi," I say, seeing my sister sprawled out on the small couch opposite the bed. "You okay?"

"I am," she says, although with a heavy slur. "I've been staring up at your painting all night, and I just have to say, I like it a whole great bunch." She raises an almost empty bottle of vodka up in a toast. "To Matty, my sister, the brilliant."

She tosses back the rest of the vodka. "This, Matty. This is me drunk," she laughs.

Before I can formulate a response, I hear her start to snore.

"Oh, Eleanor."

I grab the blanket off the bed and drape it around her after taking the bottle out of her hand. The fumes reek as she breathes up into my face while I tuck her in.

"When did you get home?" she slurs awake, forgetting we were just talking.

"Rest," I hush, pulling the blanket up around her.

"I can't. I have forty-five guests coming tomorrow."

"Guests?" I ask, then remember. The girl's birthday party.

"Forty-five. Wow, why so many?" I say, then stop. Take a breath. "Don't worry about that now. I'll help you tomorrow."

"No, I have to do it now. I forgot to call the caterer and get the moon-bounce," she says, attempting to rise.

"I'll take care of it, El. Lie down. What time is the party?"

"One. Tomorrow . . ."

"Okay, okay. Rest. I've got it." Seeing my sister lying on the small guestroom couch, I add, "El, let me help you to your bed. I think you'd be better to sleep this off there."

"I am never sleeping in that bed ever again." She raises her voice, then falls back against the couch, mumbling, "All I can see is him. Us. Making love… And now?" she trails off, starts to snore.

"Alright. Stay here, sis," I say, tucking her in again and drawing the curtains to dim the room. Realizing how good it feels to finally say it.

Sis.

But the good feeling subsides when I see the state of the kitchen downstairs. Destroyed.

Forty-five guests. Tomorrow.

I start to sweep up piles of broken dishes and glass that were apparently thrown at the wall. After I clean it up, I do a quick wipe down of all the bathrooms and straighten up as best I can.

Granted, I'm no Martha Stewart. However, by ten that night, I deem it to be a job well done and shower and go to bed.

Touching up the kitchen the next morning—there's always more to clean when the sun shines bright—I watch as El comes down the kitchen steps, nicely dressed with her hair done, too. Her eyes are puffy red however. And she's holding her head.

"Looks good, Matty. Thank you," she manages before sitting down at the kitchen table. When that doesn't seem to help her swirling headache, she adds, "I'm going to sit out back for a while. Get some fresh air."

About to say okay, Shadow bounds past me, barking his head off at the arrival of someone at the front door. Knowing the catastrophe that will happen if he gets out, I call out, "One second! Be right back!" to who's at the door while I drag Shadow back to his section of the backyard.

"We're having a party today, boy. I'm sorry, but you have to stay here. Okay? Stay."

Breathless and delighted, I open the front door.

"What the hell was that?" Ty asks, not seeming to want to enter the house.

"Oh, that was Shadow. El's dog. He's a doll baby. Don't worry. Got him locked out back."

"Sounded like a freight train barreling through the door," Ty says, walking into the house. He stops to give me a kiss hello.

Smiling inside and out, I take one of the huge bags he's carrying.

"Where do you want me to put these?" he asks.

"Follow me. I think we'll set up the food in the kitchen."

I help him spread out a wonderful buffet of food from his restaurant. Then I tiptoe to give him a kiss on the cheek.

"Thank you so much, Ty."

"You owe me now, you know." He winks.

"A payment I'll happily make in full." I smile against his lips, pressing my body into his.

"What's all this?" El asks from behind us.

"Food for the party," I say of the spread. "Don't worry about it. My treat."

"Oh, my goodness." She rubs her forehead. "I forgot about the food." But then she looks up at me and stops berating herself to give me a hug, complete with a sweet, "Thank you, Matty. This would have been a disaster without you."

It takes me a second before I hear what she's said because I'm feeling what she's finally done: hugged me. Welcomed me home.

Sisters again.

El backs up and, staring at me with puppy-dog eyes, asks, "You wouldn't happen to have thought about the moon-bounce, too?"

"All taken care of, El," I say and feel my sister squeeze me in a warm, sisterly hug again.

El still seems to feel as though the world is spinning, so I send her out back to sit and relax before her guests start arriving. With some last-minute searching through the house, I discover party decorations and, with Ty's valiant help, we set to blowing up balloons and hanging streamers here and there, creating a festive atmosphere.

Hearing the doorbell ring and Shadow's subsequent barking, I go to get the door. It's my second planned surprise of the day, and I delight at the astonishment in Ty's eyes when he sees his own children walk into the house.

"Thought they'd like to join in the fun," I say with a smile and a wink as Maia and Baz give their dad a hug hello. "I called your mom. She's happy to have the rest of the day to herself."

I watch as Ty rubs the back of his neck with a humored look my way.

"Matty!" Baz exclaims as he gives me a hug before darting off.

Maia walks up to me, all serious. "Tomorrow. Remember," she says to me point-blank.

"I wouldn't miss it for the world," I say of her celebration at entering into womanhood.

She visibly relaxes and gives me a warm hug, too, before running after her brother.

Ty scoops me up in his arms. "You are one hell of a woman, Matty Bell. You know that, right?"

Wrapping my arms around his neck, I sigh and smile. "I'm beginning to."

One by one, guests start to arrive. Food is starting to be eaten. Kids are laughing and playing and having fun. All that's missing are the birthday girls.

"Hello, hello!" I hear come from the front foyer, and I know who it is. It's my dad.

Running, I don't even know I'm pulling Ty along behind me by the hand until I've got my dad in a long-awaited hug that includes Ty.

"Oh, sorry," I laugh, seeing the two men of my life meet. "Dad, this is Ty. Ty, this is my father."

"Mister B—Bell," my dad stammers with his hand extended out, his eyes never leaving mine. "Matilda? When…? How…? You're home," he manages, astonished.

"I am, Dad. I am," I say, giving him another long hug.

"And what about me?" asks a voice I know, too. My mother. Only her words aren't as guilt-ridden as usual. They're casual, as is the look on her face.

"Matilda, darling. Let me look at you," she says, taking me into a quick hug. "My, my. I'm not sure that hair is befitting of a young lady."

"Woman, Mom. I'm a woman."

"Ah, that you are," she says to me, although her eyes are on Ty.

"And who's this?"

"This is Ty. My boyfriend?" I say, looking at Ty.

We're in our thirties. Is that what people still call it? I think to myself.

"Well, is he or isn't he, Matilda Bell?" my mother drawls in her Georgian accent, not quite glaring at me but not exactly looking at me with kindness either.

"Yes, ma'am," Ty answers for me, extending out his hand to my mother. "Ty Waters. Very nice to meet you."

"Ty," she says to him, then looks at me. "What kind of name is Ty?"

"Short for Tiberius, ma'am," Ty answers for me again, and my mother looks back at him, this time with what looks to be respect. "Tiberius Waters."

"Well, that's a mouthful, but much better than Ty," she says, accepting his hand and then taking my father's. "Come, Henry. We'll catch up later. This here's a party. Eleanor and Mark out back, I suppose?" my mother asks me.

"Ah, yes… She's out back," I say, unsure I want our interaction cut so short.

I watch as my parents make their way toward the back of the house, wondering when Mark—if Mark—is going to come home for his daughters' birthday party.

Speak of the devil.

Well, not really the devil. I look out through the open front door and watch Mark as he hoists both his daughters up high in the air. Having not seen their daddy in two weeks, they're all giggles and hugs.

Mark walks in, hand in hand with Allysa and Allysn, and my breath catches at who I'm about to finally meet.

"Allysa. Allysn. Say hello to your Auntie Matty," Mark says, and I bend down in awe of my two beautiful nieces.

Fraternal twins, Allysa has long, bouncy brunette hair, much like Eleanor's when we were kids. As for Allysn, her long hair is blonde like mine.

"Hello, girls. I'm so, so happy to finally meet you," I say.

Before I can speak another word or shed another tear, the girls embrace me in such a hug we all three end up on the floor of the foyer, laughing.

As we get up, I hear Mark and Ty say hello to each other. Watch as Allysa and Allysn see the party going on out back.

"Surprise!" Mark says, but his voice is not solo.

"Mommy!" the girls cry and run up to El, obviously in love. I put a hand to my heart and smile at their reunion.

"Happy birthday, girls. How was your trip?"

Chattered responses from the two echo in the foyer and through the house and out to the back patio as El leads her daughters out to the party. Mark follows, joining his family as if nothing were amiss.

"They look happy," Ty says by my side.

"'Look.' That's the key word here." When he gives me a quizzical look, I add, "Long story. Some other time," before I lean up and plant a kiss on his lips. "Want to go out back?"

More people show up, and the party starts to bustle with activity and lively chatter, which is a welcoming distraction from the nervous chatter my heart is making inside my chest at seeing my parents for the first time in ten years. Although our reunion was brief, it was warm. Not as estranged as I imagined it would feel. My mother, her normal self. My father, his.

Although she didn't hug me at first sight, throughout the party, my mother finds me off and on and gives me half, sideway hugs while introducing me to the people she knows.

My daughter. Matilda Bell.

My father is much more forward, giving me full-on hugs at every conversation intermission, so happy to have me back home. We enjoy small talk here, a little laughter there. With Ty ever by my side, my shakiness soon subsides, and my heart fills with joy. Although I know there are going to be questions later and answers I want to give, I'm happy to know I'm allowing myself time for each. I'm not running away this time. Not leaving tomorrow as I had planned weeks ago.

Weeks.

So much has transpired since leaving Maryland. I feel as though it's been so much more.

The backyard is full of excited children, most of whom are in the moon-bounce, the rest either waiting their turn or running laps around the inflated contraption, intermittently being yelled at by the attendant to stop.

All the while Shadow—poor Shadow—sits in his mudroom alone. Seeing his sad, droopy face, I make my way into the kitchen and grab a few pork boudins for the shaggy beast.

"Here you go, boy. Maybe in a little while, when the kids settle down, I'll let you out back."

Back in the kitchen, I watch guests as they dish out nice helpings of the appetizers and entrées Ty brought. Realizing some of the containers are being emptied quickly, I make my way through the crowd out back and find Ty.

"Not to worry," he says. "Already called for backup. Got someone from the restaurant bringing in reinforcements. More food is on the way."

"You're amazing." I breathe a sigh of relief into him, give him a squeeze. Look around the party while in his arms. "Where's El?"

"Don't know. Haven't seen her."

"Maybe she's inside," I say and search out into the living room. When I don't see her, I start to think. And worry at the image of vodka bottles dancing in my head.

I make a beeline for the spiral staircase.

Poking my head into my room, I breathe a sigh of relief when I don't find her. Walking down the hall, I see a group of people gathered in the girls' room.

"El?" I call into the room, not seeing her but seeing a lot of people in there, looking at the painted room.

"Do you know who did the painting in here?" one person asks as I'm about to leave to resume my search for my sister. "I need to hire him to do my daughter's room. Once she sees this—"

"Me, too," says another. "I'd love to know who did this. Know if she left a card?"

"Ah," I stammer, not accustomed to speaking to so many people at once. Instead of stepping up to the plate, I cower a bit and change the subject.

Guess I'll have to brave up before going into business for myself. "Have you seen El?"

"Right here," she says, walking up behind me with Allysa and Allysn. "I heard about another surprise upstairs and brought the girls." She's smiling, her eyes big and bright, although still holding onto a shred of indignation.

I ignore her with a satisfied smile. I did paint her house to get back at her in my own way, after all. I watch as everyone backs away so the twins can see their room.

"Happy Birthday, girls," I say to them.

The joy in their eyes is overwhelming, and I'm crying tears of gratitude before I can stop myself. El's crying, too—happily, thankfully. The others walk away, leaving us as a family to enjoy the moment.

Allysa bounds up to me, her little arms wrapped tightly around my neck. "I love it, Auntie Matty!" she shrieks, and I hug her tight.

"I love it, too," a gentler voice speaks up, and I look down, see Allysn.

I bend down to her.

"I'm so glad," I say and bring her in for a hug. "Happy birthday."

EPILOGUE

Dear Journal,

Hello! My name is Matty Bell. Well, Matilda Bell, but I like to be called Matty. I wish I had started this journal so long ago as so much has changed in my life. I mean, it's been three years since I found that sad note on the floor of my closet back in Baltimore.

Had I started a journal at the beginning of this journey—and a journey it's been—I'd have one heck of a collection of stories to remind me of where I've been. And how I've gotten to where I am now.

Wow. Where to begin...

Well, first off, I'm living in California now. I started my own business and, although it was a bit rough at first, I got the hang of painting for others and talking to them. I have so many clients now I can't go anywhere without someone recognizing me.

I guess it's okay. I don't mind it anymore. I just like being able to paint and be paid for it. And I'm doing quite well. Bell Designs is the name of my biz. Made a cute logo and all. Have it on the back window of my new truck.

Yep. Got a new truck. Actually, Eleanor got me a new truck. I told her no and refused her begging. But she said it was the only way she knew how to make up for everything. So I finally gave in since I needed a vehicle of my own. For crying out loud, she already lets me live at her house for free.

Well, not entirely for free. I watch Allysa and Allysn for my sister every day to help her out. I take them to school. Pick them up. Take them with Shadow to the dog beach for our daily fun walk.

The girls and I are so close now. I no longer feel as though we ever lost time. I even helped their school out with some donated painting time. Refreshed their hallways with new ocean scenes and swimming dolphins, the school's mascot.

I've been to Germany twice now to visit Claire. Once alone, once with Ty. She and her family are doing great. And Germany is breathtaking. After skiing in the Alps with Ty, I'm torn as to which is better: California or Germany? Of course, the moment we landed back in San Diego—thank God. I hate flying—it was a no brainer.

Southern California has my heart.

Linus has been out to see me here, too. He came with his new boyfriend and, after spending a few days with me, the two went on a two-week vacation, traveling up and down the coast.

But that's another story...

As for my parents, two years is a good summation of the time it's taken to mend those burned bridges. At the party, they were kind and warm. But afterward, they both showed how hurt they were by my leaving. My running away. Staying away.

We've worked on all our differences over the years. A little here. A little there. It was tough to explain to my father just why I left. Took me a few months to do it. And after I did, I had to do it all over again with my mother in the room. Listen to the two of them fight rather than my father simply giving in.

It was a first for me: seeing my parents act like that. Upset with each other over something. Anything.

Normal.

All my life they acted as though they were perfect.

With my mother sober now and my father home all the time, retired, when they disagree, they disagree right out in the open. It's not a full-on battle, but it's still startling to me: them being two normal, married, sober people. It's taking some getting used to.

My dad. The celebrity in my life. I guess I never really knew him. My mother either, I suppose. So, yeah. Time is on our side now. I'm getting to know them. And they're getting to know me.

Me.

As for me, well, a lot has happened in the last two years since I came back to California.

I found myself.

I found my family.

I found love.

Ty and I have been going strong for two years now. We see each other quite often, me not exactly spending all my nights at El's house. But we've kept it low-key as much as possible. I don't stay the night when Baz and Maia are home. Although, I don't think they'd mind. They, too, want me around all the time, and I'm happy to oblige.

I often bring Allysa and Allysn along. Or, to help Ty out and give his mother a break, I bring Maia and Baz around with me. The kids get along great and, well, I just love seeing them all happy, playing together.

Happy.

That's a word that sums things up quite nicely. I'm happy with my life again, and it feels great. Normal. I strayed so far off the path, and I'm just glad to be back. To enjoy all that life has to offer.

Speaking of all that life has to offer, are you ready for a real surprise, dear journal? I hope so, because I can't wait to tell you...

I'm getting married!

Ty asked me about six months ago, and I was so shocked I punched his arm. I sometimes ask him if the punch I answered him with still hurts.

Yeah, I freaked out, but in a good way. After I found my breath again, I said—nah, yelled—yes, yes, yes! Followed, of course, by sorry, sorry, sorry for punching his arm out of shock.

I know.

Quirky, funny me.

Okay, so I should have planned a better response. I was surprised. Am still surprised.

We're getting married. Next month.

Next month!!!

Busy with the kids and my business and not at all as talented as my sister, I'm letting El do all the wedding planning. I help her out with a yes here, a no there. But I'd like to see what my sister comes up with. She knows Ty and I are down-to-earth people. No matter what she does, it'll be a surprise. And a wonderful one, too.

Speaking of surprises . . .

Well, there's one more that I just found out about. One I'm not sure what to do about. I take that back. I know what to do about it. I just don't know how to tell anyone.

Especially Ty.

Remembering how his late wife Vanessa died, I don't know how he's going to take it. He seemed relieved when I told him I never could. So maybe I'll just keep it a secret to myself a little while longer.

I just found out today. They were wrong. My body does work.

I'm pregnant.

A Note From the Author

First and foremost, **thank you for your purchase of this book**, as it benefits the Rape, Abuse, and Incest National Network's free 24/7 sexual assault hotline (1.800.656.HOPE | www.RAINN.org).

If you were gifted this novel or would like to do more to help, please visit rainn.org to donate, knowing $0.80 of every dollar donated goes directly to RAINN's programs to help survivors, educate the public, and improve sexual assault laws and policies. Thank you for your support!

I am on a mission to raise $10,000 to help survivors of sexual assault by donating all my personal proceeds from the sales of this book to benefit RAINN.org. Visit my RAINNmaker page at www.LiaMack.com for more information.

My personal healing also benefited from a unique healing course I found online by Angela Shelton, called ***BE YOUR OWN HERO***. It was during the journaling exercises of this very healing course that I started writing this novel.

You can find more information on the healing course and Angela Shelton at www.SurvivorManual.com.(Use code **squish** for my discount.)

More Ways You Can Help

Want to do more to help trauma survivors heal?

1. **Share this Novel** – Unfortunately, we all know someone who's been effected by sexual assault. Fortunately for them, you have in your hands something that can help them in their healing journey. Please share your copy, purchase them their own or just let them know about it as a potential resource for healing.

2. **Leave a Review** – Did you know reviews are the number-one way to help others find their next favorite book? You can leave one almost anywhere you can buy a book: Goodreads.com, Amazon.com, BarnesAndNoble.com, Google.com...everywhere!.

3. **Become a Social Media Influencer** – Believe it or not, we all have platforms from which we can positively influence others. Post a photo of yourself with your copy of this book. Share your own experiences for others to be empowered by. Create a trend with a unique video… story… anything! Use your imagination. And use hashtags: *#Waiting4Paint2Dry* and *#ForwardMotionOnly.*

4. **Donate to RAINN.org** – Remember, $0.80 of every $1 donated goes to helping survivors. And even just $10 goes a long way. *Thank you for your support!*

Acknowledgements

This was a difficult book for me to write. If it wasn't for the constant support and love of so many people in my life, I'd still be dreaming… waiting for that paint to dry…

First off, I'd like to thank the team at Pen-L Publishing for believing in this book and being the first publishers of this story. I wrote it with a purpose, and they allowed every bit of that purpose to make its way into the final product. For that, I'm eternally grateful.

To my superhero, Angela Shelton, who was instrumental in the development of this novel. It was her healing course BE YOUR OWN HERO that started it all. If it wasn't for you, I don't know when I'd have figured out how to use my sword of trauma for good. Thank you, Angela, for all your beloved candidness, ceaseless love, and tireless support of survivors everywhere.

To all the women survivors I interviewed while in the research phase of this book. Thank you for your permission to not only use but also learn from your painful pasts, as well as your triumphs along your personal healing journeys. I applaud your resilience and hope all our combined stories inspire others to lead a joyful life, no matter what they've been through, as Angela says at SurvivorManual.com.

A special thank you to my parents (who are nothing like the parents in this book – this is a work of fiction, folks…)—David A. Green, Lieutenant Colonel, USAF, Ret., and Lucy Green—for giving me the most unique childhood possible: living in a loving household and growing up a military brat. It was truly a special blessing to travel the world with you. That, and thank you for always believing in me and raising me to know I could do anything I wanted to do. I just needed to put forth the effort. And dare to dream.

To Lawrence Mack, Captain, USN, Ret., for sharing the luckiest day of the year with me and his endless enthusiasm in sharing his naval expertise.

A special thank you to my all steadfast cheerleaders who keep me going: Amanda Green, Deana and Tony Cavallo, Nathan and Julia Mack, Diana Hamlin, Janet Phillips, Kacey Barnes, Daniela Allman, "Ms. Pat" Baker Lavino, Fernando Nicotera, Carolyn "Coach" Blacker, Andi Walker, Geri Wilson, John Vasqueze, Denise Corbiser, and Dharma Nicotera.

To all my writer buddies who have held my hair while I puked out all that was in me to write this book: Leslie Rhodes, Eric Nelson, Corey Ostman, Jeannette Boca, Carla Lazim, Carolyn R. Parsons, Andrea Green, Mary Doyle, Cindy Young-Turner, Gale Deitch, Yona McDonough, Ellis Shuman, Mike Green, Harrison Demchick, Ally E. Machate, and everyone at the Women's Fiction Writers Association.

To Cathy Nelson for answering all my questions about women's therapy and breathing techniques. And to Marion Anthonisen and Kathleen Murray for their help in distilling the MICA art college student experience.

I'd also like to thank Jamie Leatherman for outing me from my writing closet at my thirtieth birthday party many, many moons ago. I am truly grateful you did.

And lastly, I'd like to thank my husband, Robert Mack. Life with an artistic, creative type when you're a logical, practical engineer type is not exactly fine-tuned. Nonetheless, you believe in me and my dreams (all of them) and support me even though you don't always understand.

Thank you for loving me for being me.

About the Author

Born in Wichita, Kansas, Lia Mack has had the unique experience of growing up a military brat – *go Airforce!* – and living in many locations such as Michigan, Texas, Colorado, Latiano and San Vito dei Normanni, Italy and Maryland.

In addition to fiction, Lia's creative non-fiction has been featured in such publications as *The Washington Post*, *Nickelodeon Jr. Magazine*, *Advances in Bereavement Magazine*, and *Nesting Magazine*.

Lia currently resides in Annapolis, Maryland with her husband, two children, three American Rat Terriers, one Bearded Dragon, a Green Tree Python, a plethora of saltwater fish and one quarantine rescue cat, Meow Meow.

Waiting for Paint to Dry is her first novel.

And now...

for a

SNEAK PEEK

of the upcoming sequel to *Waiting for Paint to Dry,*

coming January 2023!

PAINT BY NUMBERS

a novel

LIA MACK

Blissfully Beguiling Books

BLISSFULLY
BEGUILING
Books

CHAPTER 1

"Why am I not fucking surprised," I mutter to myself as I pace the foyer in my gold Jimmy Choos, pausing in front of the full-length foyer mirror to recenter my diamond necklace and adjust my Spanx.

It's been an hour since I was supposed to be in downtown San Diego at my sister's engagement party. The party I planned and paid for myself. It's one of the matron-of-honor duties I insisted on doing for Matty.

Or am I her maid of honor now since Mark and I are divorced?

A thirty-five-year-old, single-mother maid of honor. Wonderful.

"Would you two please stop fidgeting with your hair." I step over to where my seven-year-old twins, Allysa and Allysn, are attempting to sit pretty, waiting for Daddy.

"Yes, Mommy," they say in unison as I fix the barrettes in their respective brunette and blonde locks.

"There," I say, admiring their sweet little heads before walking back to the front door to peer out at the long, empty drive. Then I walk toward the foyer mirror again, finding calm in the admiration of how intoxicating I look in my strappy V-neck, emerald silk dress—the one with the plunging neckline that would make anyone else question whether they should wear a cami underneath. However, all my time at the gym is showing really nicely and I want to show it off.

Running a hand over my slicked-back, shoulder-length blond bob that shows almost no brunette roots whatsoever, I decide to pull out my phone and take a selfie.

I'll post it as a story on my PhotoGram account for current and potential clients to see that, yes, I do know a thing or two about style. Naturally, I won't be adding any details about waiting for my self-centered prick of an ex-husband to pick up the girls for his weekend with them. He hasn't taken them on his past two, and I'm not allowing him to ghost the girls again.

Besides, he has to show up this time. He insisted he needs something from the house, to which he no longer has a key.

He's also insisted we need to talk. Though, seeing how we work in the same office space five days a week, I'm really not interested in what he has to say now that he couldn't have said already.

Just then, I hear the unmistakable rumble of Mark's truck pulling up the drive. His dog, Shadow, which he so graciously leaves in my care since his condo doesn't allow pets, starts barking from the backyard.

"Finally," I spit as I was stalked by the girls on my way to the garage. The twins can get to the door while I get something else.

"Hello, hello!" I hear Mark exclaim cheerfully from the front door, as he no doubt waltzes in like he's not over an hour late.

Allysn and Allysa squeal in delight now that Daddy's here, which I expected. That's why I need to open my stash.

Looking back to ensure I'm still alone in the garage, I push beach stuff out of the way and, twisting the top off quickly, take a nice swig of my beloved Tequila.

"Thought I'd find you in here," Mark states from the doorway, his broad shoulders and height making my stupid heart skip a beat despite myself and the history we share.

He never loved me. At least not in the way I wanted—needed—to be loved.

"Off the wagon already, huh?"

"Screw you," I say a little too quickly and internally kick myself for feeling guilty about something so guiltless. "Just looking for the pool noodles the girls want to take with you and… here they are," I say as I produce said items.

"Can you grab the hanging travel bag too while you're at it?" Mark asks so easily that it feels as though we're starting right back up where we left off. Right before I found him in bed with someone else.

"Travel bag?"

"Daddy, come play with us!" Allysn and Allysa pop up behind Mark, hugging his legs and jumping around, their hair falling from their barrettes.

"Girls, you're ruining your hair again," I say, instantly irritated. I'd kept them perfect for Mark, yet here they are no more than two minutes after he arrives, already a mess.

"Let them be, El. They're kids—"

"'Let them be, El. They're kids,'" I mock as I stride over to fix their hair.

Only he puts himself in my way, blocking me.

"Hey, listen girls," he says to them, bending down and reaching into his pocket. "I need to talk to Mommy for a bit. Here." He hands them each a lollipop. "Go up to your room and play."

"Mark," I warn as the girls squeal and run off, candy in hand. "I don't want their room to be a mess. You know how people are when they hear you're an interior designer. There's no telling how many are going to want a tour of my house," I say of the party guests I'm ever so late to greet.

"Girls, no!" I add, shouting for them to hear me since I no longer see them. Then back to him: "You're going to have to deal with that sugar rush, not me."

"About that..." Mark says with a pause and shrugs his shoulders.

I feel my heart thud in my chest. "Don't you dare."

"I can't take them this weekend."

"You didn't take them last time or the time before that."

"Yeah, I know, but—"

"But what? They're your daughters, too. And, if you haven't noticed, a lot more fucking excited to see you than me."

"That's not true."

"Oh, really. Just listen to them jumping around up there as though they've been caged up all day. It's like you and Matty are the only ones they like, and I'm just here to be the bitch mom—"

"Hello, hello," sings another man's voice into the front foyer.

I stop in my tracks and glare up at Mark. "Why do you always have to bring him here," I see, more a demand than a question.

"El, come on—"

Holding open my clutch to grab my keys, I take in a deep breath, trying to collect myself. "I've worked hard at making this place a home without you. I've let you go off and do your thing since, quote-unquote, coming out," I say with an eye roll. "You don't get to do this to me. You're taking them, Mark. I. Am. Late."

"You can take them with you. You know Matty and Ty wouldn't mind."

"I don't care what they wouldn't mind. You are taking them!"

Frazzled, I drop my keys twice before managing to unlock my pearl-white Mercedes. I hadn't always been so paranoid, locking my car inside a locked garage when Mark lived at home. But now I do things differently and curse life for having to do so.

Mark grabs me by the arm before I can get into the car. "I really can't take the girls this weekend. Eric and I—"

"Do NOT say his name around me," I spit out, feeling like I was punched in the gut.

"El, it's been two years—"

"Ha! It's been longer than that!" I pull my arm out of his grip.

I don't care that my husband chose a man over me. I don't care that he's gay. He could have come out to me, and I would have understood. Been supportive even. I would have been there for him.

But no. Instead of being honest, Mark was in love and sleeping with someone else the entire time I'd known him. Dated him. Been married to him. Just thinking about all I did to myself, to my life, for more than twelve years to make him love me. Want me. Give a shit about me.

It makes me sick.

"Did you talk to her yet?" Eric asks, poking his head into the garage.

"I'm getting there," Mark says.

"Well, you better hurry," Eric says with tempered enthusiasm. "Our flight leaves in three hours, and you know how I am with airports."

learn more at

www.LiaMack.com